Dl070045

THE PATTERN OF A KILLER

Maggie sipped her coffee. "Something else occurred to me, Jack. Jonie's the third person I know who has died within the last month, all of them from unnatural causes."

"Who else has died besides your brother and Jonie?"

Maggie shrugged. "I didn't know her very well. Her name was Lucy Ballatore. She was a waitress at this restaurant where I go for takeout. About three weeks ago, they found her near a railroad yard. She'd been murdered—stabbed in the throat."

"You say she was stabbed in the throat?" Jack whispered.

Maggie nodded over her coffee cup. "According to the newspapers, they found her in her bra and panties—with her hands tied behind her back. No sign of sexual assault—"

"She was in her underwear?"

Maggie nodded again. "Why? Is there any significance to that?"

Jack stared down at the tabletop. "He takes their outer clothes and uses them for something," he muttered, almost to himself.

Maggie leaned forward. "What are you talking about?"

"This waitress—Lucy—was she missing any fingers or toes?"

With a dazed look at him, Maggie slowly shook her head. "I have no idea. You mean like how my brother lost a couple of toes?"

"If there's a pattern here, that's it. He takes their clothes and some actual part of their bodies. . . ."

Books by Kevin O'Brien

ONLY SON

THE NEXT TO DIE

MAKE THEM CRY

Published by Pinnacle Books

Epilogue

Jack glanced out his window at Lake Leroy and those old, stately buildings of the campus across the way. He'd grown used to this view after so many nights staring at it from his desk. It was strange to think he wouldn't be seeing this familiar vista again after today.

St. Bartholomew Hall was almost too quiet on that Tuesday afternoon. The school year was over. All of the students had moved out during the weekend.

Jack wasn't far behind them.

He'd packed his suitcases and boxed up nearly everything, except a few items still scattered about. The new yearbook sat on his desk. Anton's photo was featured among the graduating seniors. The book had gone to print before Anton killed himself, though the powers that be at Our Lady of Sorrows weren't calling it a suicide. They maintained Anton's death was an accident.

Thanks to a busy holiday weekend in the news, coverage

of Anthony Daniel Sorenson's demise had been relegated to page six of Tuesday's *Seattle Times*.

The article speculated that stress—or possibly drugs—had caused the college senior's *"unexplainable rampage."* They described his assaults on Peter and Maggie, but didn't delve into his relationships with either of them. Peter was described as *"a freshman who was an overnight guest at his house,"* and Maggie was merely *"the sister of another seminarian, who had drowned last month."*

Three people had been in the recreational vehicle that collided with Anton's speeding Toyota on the creekside road a mile from his house. Two of them sustained minor injuries.

Jack wasn't mentioned by name in the article. His role in the events on that Sunday night was reduced to one sentence: *"A priest from the faculty of Our Lady of Sorrows tracked down Tobin at the house and phoned the police."*

What remained of Anton's hideaway home was a burnt-out shell. The fire had spread to the basement, destroying nearly everything down there. Investigators broke the locks on an old freezer in the cellar. They found twenty pounds of venison from a deer-hunting expedition Anton had taken a year ago.

Nothing was left of Anton's secret shrine, the place he'd called his "church." They found his burned corpse by a scorched, skeletal bed frame. Police and fire detectives weren't searching for any additional remains in that charred, hollowed-out sanctuary.

Jack didn't tell them about the other bones. Peter didn't say anything either. There seemed no point to it. They'd only be hurting the victims' families. As Irene McShane had pointed out, Anton's victims weren't really saints. They had secrets of their own, which best remained secret.

Maggie had said she wanted it that way, too. In their last conversation, on Memorial Day, she and Jack had decided to wait a while before getting together or talking again.

Anton Sorenson's death may have been pushed back to page six of the Seattle papers, but it was foremost on everyone's minds at Our Lady of Sorrows and the surrounding communities. If she and Jack were seen together at this time, it would only cause a lot of speculation and gossip.

Jack visited Irene McShane, bringing her the news article about Anton's death. He told her what had really happened, and the decision to remain silent about the murders. She was grateful, so grateful that she donated eighteen thousand dollars to Our Lady of Sorrows in her daughter-in-law's memory.

The money was welcome, and Tom Garcia was pleased. Jack had told him about the "martyr" killings. Of course, the college's head of administration wanted it to remain a secret. Jack pointed out a possible snag to all their secrecy. The deaths of Judge McShane and Lucy Ballatore were still considered unsolved murders. Garcia seemed to contemplate it for a moment, then nodded. "Well, if a trail of evidence leads the police to this school," he said, "we'll cooperate fully."

Garcia also suggested that it would be best for everyone, including Jack, if he and Our Lady of Sorrow parted company.

Jack had agreed with him.

He looked over the bare walls of his room, then glanced once again at Anton's photo in the yearbook. *Anthony Daniel Sorenson.* The portrait didn't look like him. He appeared too stiff and scholarly.

They'd used that same photo in the news article. If anyone had ever noticed Anton with one of his murder victims, they probably wouldn't have recognized him from that picture.

Another book sat on Jack's desk. *The Lives and Deaths of the Saints* was two days overdue at the library. Jack picked it up and flipped through the pages. Once again, he read the passage about St. Anthony Daniel.

Martyred in 1648, Anthony Daniel had been a missionary with the Society of Jesus, living among the Red Indians of Canada and teaching in their school. When the village was raided by hostile Iroquois, he refused to flee. And so, according to the book, *"Anthony Daniel was shot down by the savage invaders and thrown into his burning church."*

Anton, like Gerard Lunt, had orchestrated his own martyrdom.

Jack put down the book. Before leaving tonight, he would have to loop around to the campus library and drop it off. He would pay the late charge, too.

He'd rented a station wagon to haul away his things. Because of his foot, he was still on crutches. The doctor had said he shouldn't drive for at least a couple of more days. So Jack had asked Peter to help him load up the van and handle most of the driving.

Jack heard him coming up the hallway for another load of boxes. Pete stepped into the room. Somehow, he looked older after only a couple of weeks—not quite as innocent and gangly as before. He was wearing one of Johnny's old shirts and a pair of jeans. He still had a prominent red mark on his forehead, but the cut had healed.

"Looks like maybe three or four more trips ought to do it," he announced, staring at the boxes Jack had moved to the center of the room. From the minirefrigerator, he pulled out a bottle of water he'd been working on. He took a few gulps.

"Sorry I'm not much help," Jack said, leaning on his crutch. "This damn foot of mine."

Peter cracked a smile. "I've heard of sprained ankles and sprained toes, but how do you sprain your whole foot?"

"Saving your sorry ass, that's how," Jack replied.

Peter laughed. "Did I ever thank you for that, Father?"

"Only about a hundred times in the last two weeks. It's

my turn to thank you. I couldn't have done this today without your help.''

Peter glanced out the window. "It's weird to think neither one of us is coming back next year. I would have ended up in St. Clement Hall, maybe even on Anton's floor. You know what I heard, Father? They're converting Anton's room into a storage area next year.'' Peter let out a sad laugh. "I think he would have liked that."

Jack nodded. "Yes, he probably would have."

Peter drank some more of his bottled water, then he sat on the sofa arm. "I didn't tell you. Over the weekend, I applied to six different art schools."

"Your parents are okay with it, aren't they?"

"Yeah. But I've decided I need to discuss something else with them before I go off to a new school. I'm going to sit down with them and have a serious talk, *the* talk, if you get what I mean."

Jack leaned back against his desk. "Well, I won't guess out loud and say the wrong thing."

Peter sighed. "I'm going to tell them that I'm gay. You probably figured it out a long time ago anyway."

Jack shrugged. "It never really mattered to me, Pete."

"I know," Peter said. "That's another reason to thank you." He walked over to Jack and gave him an awkward hug. "Anyway, thanks, Father."

Jack patted him on the back. "You're a good guy," Jack said. "You'll be okay."

Peter broke away. He smiled sadly. "I miss my buddy though. It's going to be tough, starting at a new school without him."

"Johnny will be there with you, Pete," Jack said. "He'll always be with you."

Peter nodded resolutely, then wandered over to one of the boxes on the floor and hoisted it up. The box was full of keepsakes from Jack's family.

"How about you, Father?" Peter asked, resting the carton on the edge of Jack's desk. "Can I—call you once in a while? I don't know where either one of us is going. But could we still keep in touch somehow?"

"You can count on it," Jack said. "I found you a couple of Sundays ago, didn't I? I won't lose track of you, Pete."

Maggie sat at her desk in the real-estate office. She had on her favorite suit, a soft pale green number she usually wore for good luck. It must have worked, because she'd closed an important deal that morning.

It was 3:30 in the afternoon. She should have quit early and gone home to celebrate. But no one was waiting for her there. Lately, she found herself staying late at work just to avoid going back to that empty house.

Her desk was across from the office's storefront window. Maggie looked out on a quaint shopping area with a brick walkway and a little fountain. In her office, at least she could people-watch while feeling productive.

She hadn't heard from Jack since Memorial Day, two weeks before. They'd decided it was best not to talk with each other for a while. But Maggie thought the moratorium would have been lifted by now.

She still hadn't erased his message on the answering machine from that Sunday night, the one in which he'd said that he loved her and to *"hang in there."*

She was getting pretty tired of hanging in there.

Peter had told her a couple of days ago that Jack was leaving Our Lady of Sorrows. He didn't know where they were sending him. If Father Garcia had his way, they'd be shipping Jack to Siberia.

Maggie told herself it was over. Hell, it hadn't even gotten started. She'd recently commiserated to her coworker, Adele, about her disastrous luck with men: a wife-beater, a psychopath, and a totally unavailable priest. He could have at least called to say good-bye.

She was looking over some recent house listings when she heard the door open. Maggie glanced up from her computer. At first, she didn't recognize him. He wasn't wearing his clerical garb. She'd seen other priests in street clothes, and they still looked like priests. In fact, without their priestly attire, most of them seemed to lose a sense of mystery and ended up appearing rather bland. But not Jack Murphy. He wore gray trousers and a navy blue V-neck pullover that complemented his silver hair. Even though he hobbled through the doorway with the help of a crutch, he looked very sexy. He was carrying something in a plastic bag.

Dazed, Maggie stared at him. "Hi," she murmured.

He smiled. "Hi, Maggie."

"I've never seen you in regular clothes before. You look different. I mean, you look really good, just different." She let out a little laugh. "It's good to see you, Jack."

"It's been tough not calling you," he said. "A lot has happened."

She nodded. "I know. Pete told me you're being transferred from Our Lady of Sorrows."

"Well, that's not quite right," Jack replied, standing in front of her desk. "I'm no longer at Our Lady of Sorrows, because I've taken a leave of absence from the priesthood."

"What does that mean exactly?"

"It means I'll use the next six months to decide if I want to stay a priest or not," Jack explained. "I may already have a teaching job lined up at the University of Washington. I'm going in for a second interview tomorrow."

"Wow," she murmured, astonished. "Well, good luck."

"It's like a new start," Jack said. "Oh, and I brought you this." He carefully pulled a small cactus plant from the plastic bag and set it on her desk.

"What's that for?" she asked.

"I figured we could send it to your ex-husband on his next birthday." Jack gingerly touched one of the cactus stickers. "I don't know if you handle apartments or condos, but I was wondering if I could tap your expertise in finding someplace nice."

"You want me to find you a place to live?" she asked.

He nodded. "It's a start, Maggie."

She looked at the cactus plant, then gazed up at him and smiled. "I think I can help you, Jack."

Your Favorite Thriller Authors
Are Now Just A Phone Call Away

Feel the Seduction of Pinnacle Horror

__The Vampire Memoirs
  by Mara McCunniff   0-7860-1124-6 $5.99US/$7.99CAN
  & Traci Briery

__The Stake
  by Richard Laymon   0-7860-1095-9 $5.99US/$7.99CAN

__Blood of My Blood: The Vampire Legacy
  by Karen E. Taylor   0-7860-1153-X $5.99US/$7.99CAN

When Darkness Falls
Grab One of These
Pinnacle Horrors

MAKE THEM CRY

Kevin O'Brien

PINNACLE BOOKS
Kensington Publishing Corp.
http://www.kensingtonbooks.com

This book is for Cate Goethals,
who helped me become an author.

ACKNOWLEDGMENTS

A great big thank-you goes to my editor at Kensington Books—the dapper John Scognamiglio, who is also a dear friend. The sensational Doug Mendini (also with Kensington) has my undying gratitude and admiration as well. And thanks to all the other people at Kensington who got this book off the ground. I'm also grateful to my agents and friends, Mary Alice Kier and Anna Cottle.

Several people helped me with the writing, rewriting, and fact-checking for this novel. Special thanks to my buddies, Cate Goethals, Dan Stutesman, Dan Monda, David Massengill, my brother-in-law, Dennis Kinsella, and my sister Adele O'Brien Bensinger. Thanks also to David Madsen at Seattle University, for giving me a Latin translation and Bill McClure at the Seattle Medical Examiner's Office, who gave me information about coroner practices.

Thanks also to the friends and family members who really went out of their way to push my last novel to their friends or the general public, especially Beth Kinsella, Dan Annear, Paul Dwoskin, Louise Vogelwede, Doug Stutesman, Amanda Brooks, and mostly my pal, Tommy Dreiling.

Finally, all my love and gratitude to my family.

Prologue

She told herself this would be the last time. If she nipped it in the bud today, there was a good chance no one would ever find out.

Dorothy sat behind at the wheel of her BMW, studying the snaky road ahead. It was dusk, and she'd just switched on her headlights. The drive was quite pretty, taking her through a few rural towns, some farm area, then the forest. She knew the route very well by now. The two-lane highway would straighten in a few miles, and she would reach the little town of Worley. At the roadside, there would be the Worley Feed & Tackle General Store—and next to it, the motel.

Since their last rendezvous, she'd gotten her hair cut and they'd touched up the gray. She wore it short now with the bangs swept over to the side, very no-nonsense. He'd said he liked her brunet hair long and free. He would be disappointed. Too bad for him. Maybe it would make breaking up with him a little easier—or so she told herself.

In reality, she couldn't help wanting to look her best for him tonight. Dorothy wore her favorite pearl-and-gold earrings, and the rose-colored silk blouse he said made her look sexy. She was a forty-year-old mother of two, and he called her *sexy*. Small wonder she had a hard time leaving him.

But it was more than mere flattery and physical attraction. They related to each other. They'd both given up so much for their jobs, and had so many responsibilities. In their respective professions, they were under constant scrutiny and had to set good examples of moral integrity. If it was ever discovered that they were lovers, their lives would be destroyed. So far, they'd been lucky. But she couldn't afford to keep pushing her luck.

Taking another curve in the highway, Dorothy eyed the long stretch of road in front of her. She felt a twinge in her stomach. These stolen afternoons and evenings always made her nervous and a bit breathless. She would never admit it to him, but he scared her at times. Maybe that was part of the thrill.

Up ahead, she saw the yellow Co-Zee Motor Inn sign towering above two squat buildings beside the rural highway. The management still hadn't fixed the sign. Some of the letters were missing. LOW HOURLY RAT S, it said. HOT TUB & FRE ADULT MOVIES IN ROO.

The two of them had an ongoing joke about the low rats that would appear in their room every hour. They'd used the hot tub—a round, sunken Jacuzzi-for-two in the corner of the bedroom—several times.

She didn't watch the adult movies, which revolted her. He claimed that he wasn't interested in them either. Yet she'd walked in often enough and found him glued to one of those raunchy films on TV. "Just getting warmed up for you," he'd say.

Dorothy pulled into the motel's lot. The Co-Zee Motor

Inn was a tacky, late-fifties cabin-row-style lodge with about forty rooms. No question about it, the place was an adult motel. Built in the middle of nowhere, its isolation was part of the draw. There were always plenty of cars in the lot—and Do Not Disturb signs on the doors.

She parked around back—her usual spot, near their usual room. She often worried about someone seeing her BMW there, and tracing the plates back to her. It was probably silly. Still, she had to be very careful.

Dorothy had never set foot inside the Co-Zee Motor Inn's lobby for fear someone might recognize her. He always made the reservations and checked in, then waited for her in the room.

She noticed his car in the lot, a few spaces down from her.

Dorothy's stomach was still in knots. She'd tried breaking up with him before—several times. But he wouldn't let her go. Besides, it was difficult forsaking someone who loved and needed her so much. Earlier today, she'd resolved that they wouldn't make love tonight; they were only going to talk.

But now that she was here, Dorothy felt herself weakening. She wanted to be with him just one more time.

Glancing around the parking lot, she climbed out of the car. She patted her new hairstyle, then gently knocked on the door to Room 29. She waited.

No answer.

Her heart sank a little, but she didn't panic. Sometimes he'd be taking a shower, or out stretching his legs—he'd had a long drive, too. Whenever he couldn't come to the door, he left the room key on top of the door frame. Dorothy stood on tiptoe and felt around for the key. She found it, then unlocked the door.

He'd turned on the radio to some oldies station. They were playing the Beatles' "Ob-La-Di, Ob-La-Da." The shades were drawn, leaving the room rather dim despite a light coming from the bathroom and another from the nightstand lamp. The furniture was a cheesy, midsixties Mediterranean style. The turquoise-and-brown drapes matched the bedspread, and the rug was a brown shag—ideal for camouflaging cigarette burns and dirt.

Stepping into the room, Dorothy closed the door behind her. She saw an empty, large garment bag by the foot of the bed—as well as an arsenal of cleaning products crammed into a plastic bucket: Mr. Clean, Playtex gloves, a sponge and scrub brush. There was also a box of large heavy-duty trash bags.

For a moment, Dorothy wondered if she'd walked in on the maid. But she recognized his open duffle bag on the bed. "Hello?" she called nervously. "Anyone here?"

Then she spotted his reflection in the bathroom mirror. He was naked, hiding behind the half-open door. She could only see part of him in that mirror—but one of the best parts, she often liked to tell him. He had a really cute butt. He seemed to be holding something in his hand, but she couldn't make out what.

"Come out, come out, wherever you are," she chimed, sauntering toward the bathroom.

The door moved, obscuring her view of him in the bathroom mirror. "What's going on?" she said.

"You got your hair cut," he said.

"What do you think?" she asked hopefully.

"You know I liked it long."

"Listen, what's going on?" she asked. "Why is all this cleaning junk here?"

"Take off your blouse," he whispered. "Take off everything."

Dorothy hesitated. "I—I really don't like this. Would you come out from behind there, please?"

"Not until you take off your clothes and step into the hot tub. I'm naked. C'mon, play along."

Reluctantly, Dorothy set her purse down on the bed. She unbuttoned her rose silk blouse, but didn't feel at all sexy as she took it off. She stepped out of her shoes, and then her skirt. She kept staring at the cleaning products and that garment bag.

Dorothy stood near the foot of the bed in her bra, half-slip and stockings. She planted one hand on her hip. "This is as far as I go until you come out of there and talk to me," she announced.

"Get in the hot tub," he said. "Then close your eyes."

"This is crazy." With a sigh, Dorothy marched over to the sunken Jacuzzi and carefully stepped down into it. "There's no water in here. I don't understand what's going on."

"Are your eyes closed?"

Dorothy squinted toward the bathroom. If he was looking at her, he probably couldn't tell that her eyes weren't completely shut. He was opening the door now. She could make out his silhouette.

"They're closed," she lied, watching him come closer, more into focus. Indeed, he was naked. He seemed to be holding a sword. But she told herself it couldn't be. Her eyelids fluttered, and for a moment, she saw only blackness.

"Why am I standing in this stupid, empty tub?" she asked.

"So it catches all the blood," he replied.

Dorothy never had time to open her eyes—or scream.

She'd lost a button from the front of her good dark blue coat, the one she always wore to church. Irene McShane wondered if anyone at the service had noticed. They must have felt even more sorry for her—if that was possible.

Poor Irene McShane, so distraught she can barely dress herself.

But Irene didn't really care what people thought. Sitting at the wheel of the family station wagon, she watched her two grandsons scurry through the rain toward the front door. She'd given the boys her house keys and told them to go ahead. She needed a minute. There had been a crowd of reporters huddled under umbrellas, waiting at the front gate. The police kept them off the actual property—thank God—but their presence still unnerved her.

Through the rain-beaded windshield, Irene numbly stared at the Tudor-style house and allowed herself a good cry. No one could see. At the special church service for her missing daughter-in-law, neither she nor the boys had shed a tear. The McShanes weren't big on showing their emotions in public. She'd spent the last ninety minutes trying to look her stoic, matriarchal best for the congregation at St. Matthew's. How many more services would they have to attend, praying for her daughter-in-law's safe return? How many more times would she have to dress up those poor boys and parade them into St. Matthew's, when everyone knew her daughter-in-law was dead?

They'd discovered Dorothy's car today, in a cul-de-sac by an abandoned railroad yard in the small town of Gold Bar, Washington. The BMW had been stripped. All the windows were broken. Someone had stolen the tires—along with the license plates, the radio and CD player, and even one of the doors.

Almost immediately, the police began searching Gold Bar's many creeks and forests for the body of Dorothy McShane. She'd been missing now for two weeks.

Her disappearance had made the *Seattle Times* front page. Irene's daughter-in-law had the distinction of being the youngest elected judge in Washington state. That had been six years ago, when she was thirty-four. An attractive widow with two children, she was the image of respectability and honor.

Her jurisdiction and home were in the small, coastal city of Anacortes, about ninety miles north of Seattle. Dorothy had never remarried after her husband's death from cancer. Irene moved into the house to help look after the children—Michael, now eleven, and Aaron, nine. She also accompanied her daughter-in-law for several public appearances. Dorothy was smart, but lacked people skills. Irene had no such problem. At seventy, she was still a handsome woman, slim with silver-blond hair. She exuded an elegance and charm that won people over. A lot of the townsfolk said that Irene McShane had secured Dorothy the reelection.

She was also one of the last people to see Dorothy alive.

Sixteen days earlier, Dorothy had told her that she was driving down to Seattle on business and would spend the night at the Westin hotel. She always phoned home during these overnights to talk to the boys.

But this time, Dorothy didn't call. Nor did she return the next day. When Irene telephoned the Westin, they said that Dorothy McShane had never checked in. They didn't even show a reservation for her.

Irene waited another day before calling the police. She claimed not to remember where Dorothy had planned to stay in Seattle; she'd just *assumed* it was the Westin. She didn't want anyone knowing that the Honorable Dorothy McShane might have lied to her mother-in-law about her plans.

Anticipating a message from Dorothy's kidnappers, the police put a surveillance on the house and tapped the phone lines. But no one ever contacted them with a ransom demand. They combed through Dorothy's offices, both at home and in the County Court building. For all their efforts, they uncovered nothing useful to their investigation.

Irene didn't mention it to the police, but for several weeks prior to her disappearance, Dorothy's behavior had been erratic. She'd had a number of mysterious, last-minute "business" dinners and overnights. When Irene had asked if she was seeing someone, Dorothy pitched a fit and vehemently denied it. A little too vehemently, in Irene's opinion.

So, at first, Irene thought perhaps her daughter-in-law had left town with a secret lover—though it seemed out of character for Dorothy. Irene couldn't share that theory with anyone. She just kept telling herself that Dorothy was all right. She wouldn't abandon her children. She'd be back.

But Irene no longer clung to that hope. They'd found Dorothy's car today. She was dead. And all the special church services and prayers weren't going to bring her back.

So Irene cried in the idle station wagon while the rain pattered on the roof. After a couple of minutes, she wiped her eyes and took a deep breath. She glanced down at her coat and fingered the unraveled thread where the button had been.

Her daughter-in-law kept a coffee tin full of assorted buttons in her sewing room. One of them had to match. Now she had a mission—a minor one, but something to take her mind off the obvious, something she might actually fix.

When she stepped inside the house, Irene could hear the boys in the family room with the TV blaring. She shook the rain from her coat, then headed up the stairs.

Dorothy's sewing nook was at the end of the hall. Her skill with a needle and thread had become public knowledge during her election campaign. It made for a nice, homespun touch: The judicial candidate sewed her sons' school clothes, as well as some of her own dresses. Dorothy hadn't had much time for sewing lately, but the tiny room had still been her refuge. There was barely enough space for her soft easy chair, the sewing machine, a dressmaker's padded dummy, and a desk that used to belong to Jim McShane when he was a boy. But the large picture window provided a sweeping view of Puget Sound and the San Juan Islands. On this gray, rainy afternoon, the vista was wistfully beautiful. Most of Dorothy's sewing materials were stored in the small closet: yards of fabric, pattern books, boxes upon boxes of thread, and the Folger's tin full of odd buttons on the top shelf.

Irene peeled off her damp coat and draped it over the chair. She reached up for the coffee tin, but it slipped out of her hand and came crashing to the floor. Gasping, Irene reeled back. She stared down at the scores of buttons—all shapes, sizes, and colors—scattered over the floor. The coffee can rolled from side to side.

Lately, all it took to set her off was a sudden noise or a minor mishap. Irene started crying again, but she'd used up her tears. So all she could do was take deep, tortured gasps of air. She dropped to her knees, reached for the empty Folger's tin, and started gathering up the buttons. After a couple of minutes, she sighed woefully and rested. The coffee can was half full.

On the closet floor, behind a shopping full of fabric scraps, Irene noticed a stack of books in the corner. There were six books in all, bound with burgundy-colored covers and gold-embossed. She reached for the volume on top of the stack. There was a fleur-de-lis design on the cover. Irene opened the book and stared at her daughter-in-law's handwriting:

January 4, 2001—Hello to a new year & maybe a new attitude. I've been so miserable lately. Today, for example, I was having lunch at the new restaurant down the block from the courthouse. I was sitting alone & had forgotten to bring something to read, so I felt conspicuous. But there was another woman alone a few tables over. She was around my age, nicely dressed. No wedding ring. I figured she was a divorcee. After about five minutes of glancing at her & her

*glancing back, polite smiles, etc., I finally got up, went
over to her table & introduced myself. I asked if she
wanted to join me for lunch & she stared at me as if
I had two heads. She said she was waiting for someone.
Sure enough, not long after I slunk back to my table,
her boyfriend showed up, kissed her & sat down. Then
I caught them staring at me & talking. He even snickered. I wanted to run out of that place. I suppose I
was also jealous. I thought she was just like me. But
she isn't. She has someone. It was all I could do to
keep from crying. I hardly touched any of my lunch.*

*Well, it's obvious. I'm lonely. The funny thing is,
I'm lonely, yet I have no time for myself.*

*Maybe I should just count the blessings. We had a
lovely Christmas. The weather cooperated & because
I'd done my shopping early . . .*

Irene stopped reading. She sat on the floor amid the spilled
buttons, Dorothy's diary in front of her. Rain lashed against
the picture window. She could hear the boys downstairs,
arguing about something. The TV was still on.

She wondered if Dorothy's loneliness at the beginning of
the year had led to the mysterious "business" dinners and
overnights that preceded her disappearance. Who was she
seeing?

Irene didn't want to read about last Christmas. She needed
to see Dorothy's final entry in the journal. Where had her
daughter-in-law been going that day she'd vanished? Irene
flipped ahead in the book, then she stopped.

The last dozen or so pages with writing had been ripped
out. The ragged edges—some with evident curls and strokes
of a pen—still clung to the inner binding. There were a few
words at the top of the next page after the gap, but they'd
been scratched out. Irene could barely make out what it said
beneath the obliterating scribble:

can no longer go on

The rest of the page was blank.

Sighing, Irene fingered the jagged remnants of the missing pages. Were those passages so shocking that Dorothy didn't dare keep them—even in her own private journal? Irene glanced at the last remaining entry before the pages were torn out. The date was almost three months prior to her disappearance:

> *November 3, 2001—I haven't felt this way since high school. I really didn't think I'd ever have these feelings again. I'm head over heels crazy about some-one. At the same time, I know it's wrong. But I can't help myself.*
>
> *While driving back from Bellingham yesterday, I decided to loop around & check out Lake Leroy. I've never seen the seminary there, but I've heard so much about Our Lady of Sorrows. It's where I met him. He's a priest.*
>
> *It was one of those things, like out of a movie. I had parked the car & gone for a walk by the lake—*

There was nothing else. Just those words she must have written several weeks later, then scratched out:

can no longer go on

The back was a little wrinkled, but he couldn't touch it up with an iron. That would spoil it. The material from her rose silk blouse had to be preserved just as she'd last worn it.

He'd carefully measured the pattern of squares with a tailor's soap chalk. The scissors had been sharpened to near-razor quality. He didn't want any ragged edges or loose threads. He would cut a total of four square sections. He would keep the buttons, then burn the rest.

He had collected a couple of other souvenirs from Dorothy. But they were at another location.

The rose silk blouse still had faint traces of Dorothy's perfume. He started cutting into it. Focused on his task, he barely noticed the bells ringing on the hour at Our Lady of Sorrows church.

Chapter One

Father Jack Murphy trotted around the asphalt track encircling the playfield by St. Bartholomew Hall at Our Lady of Sorrows seminary. On this cold April morning, he had the track all to himself.

The run was part of Jack's daily ritual. He was spiritual advisor for the twenty-four seminarians residing on the fourth floor, north wing of the freshman dormitory. He lived with them in St. Bartholomew Hall: two dozen eighteen-year-old boys from all over the Pacific Northwest, Latin America, Vietnam, Ukraine, the Czech Republic, and China. Jack welcomed any excuse to get the hell out of there for an hour—even if the hour was an ungodly one.

So every weekday, Jack crawled out of bed at five o'clock in the morning while his freshman charges remained cozy under their covers. They still had another two hours of sleep before starting their day with a greasy breakfast in the cafeteria. But Jack was brushing his teeth and throwing on his jogging clothes.

The local TV News at Sunrise was usually just background noise. The only item that had caught Jack's attention this morning was the latest on Judge Dorothy McShane. She'd been missing for over two months now. Apparently, last night the police had been led on a wild goose chase by a renowned clairvoyant. Her psychic powers had steered investigators to a ravine in Burlington, Washington, and the grave site of someone's pet dog. They hadn't said on the news, but by all indications, the police were giving up their search for Judge McShane.

They'd given up on Dorothy McShane at Our Lady of Sorrows, too. It had been weeks since they'd included her and her family in the Prayers of the Faithful at Mass.

Jack could see his breath as he jogged around the asphalt track. Because of his daily ritual, he was still in pretty good shape. In fact, he'd found out that he made quite an impression on the visiting mothers on Parents' Day last October. He'd even acquired a nickname, "The Silver Fox," because of his thick, wavy silver-gray hair. Jack had heard a couple of the mothers whispering, "Have you ever seen eyes so blue?" and "Oh, what a waste he's a priest."

It used to bother him when people went on and on about his looks. But now, Jack liked hearing that he was still attractive. His commitment to exercising was born out of that vanity—along with a healthy need for discipline and, yes, a flight from boredom and frustration.

As he rounded a curve in the track, Jack glanced up at St. Bartholomew Hall. The wall on this side of the five-story Gothic monstrosity was covered with dead ivy that still clung to the beige brick. All the windows were still dark.

St. Bart's had been the first hall built on the Our Lady of Sorrows campus back in 1913. According to the story, they discovered it had been erected on soft ground. The building sunk nearly half an inch in the first six months.

Everyone blamed the architect, an up-and-comer named Gavin McAllister, for setting the freshman facility so close to Lake Leroy. Better soil for construction was found across the lake near the town of Leroy, where they built the rest of the college and the graduate school—using another architect's design.

Gavin McAllister's career was destroyed. On Easter Sunday, 1914, when called to dinner by his wife, the thirty-one-year-old architect stepped into his dining room with a double-barrel shotgun. He'd opened fire on his wife and six-year-old daughter, then pursed his lips around the end of those twin barrels and pulled the trigger.

Jack wasn't sure how much of the story was true, but a limerick had sprouted from the legend. Even after two world wars, most of the freshmen at Our Lady of Sorrows knew it:

> *The guy who built this here jail*
> *In doing his job did fail*
> *So Gavin slew his kid and missus*
> *Then gave the end of his shotgun kisses*
> *And off the back of his head did sail.*

The early statistics had said McAllister's building, which encompassed the freshman classrooms and a two-hundred-bedroom dormitory, would sink a little lower each year until the foundation finally crumbled.

But those statistics were wrong. The basement flooded during some of the Pacific Northwest heavy rains, but after nearly a century, St. Bartholomew Hall's foundation had settled only another inch into the earth.

Stretching the length of half a city block, St. Bart's stood alone—like an outcast child—across the lake from the rest of the campus. The turreted roof pierced the sky, dwarfing treetops from the surrounding forest. Along the top floor, staggered every six windows, the weather-worn statue of a martyred saint stood on a pedestal. Above the front doors, a slightly decrepit, cement likeness of Our Lady of Sorrows welcomed all who entered with her resigned, forlorn look and her hands folded in prayer.

An old cemetery lay between the outskirts of the forest and the playfield, where Jack now ran. It was a small grave-yard, for dearly departed priests who had taught at the fresh-man school during its first two decades. There were only a couple of dozen headstones, the most recent dated 1937.

Across the lake, the church bell rang six times. As he tallied another lap around the playfield, Jack felt the perspira-tion flying off his forehead. His gray jersey clung to his back. He noticed two students, Ernesto Rodriguez and Art Vargas, emerging from the side door of St. Bart's Hall. They were among a dozen Hispanic freshman who came from the nearby city of Ferndale. The group hung out together, dub-bing themselves the Spanish Mafia. Decked in sweatshirts and track shorts, Art and Ernesto waved at him, then started jogging toward a path that wound through the nearby forest.

The trail was known as Whopper Way, because after a half mile, it crossed over a tributary of Lake Leroy to the back lot of a Burger King. It was the quickest way by foot to town and the college campus. The seminarians would climb down to the creek, then tightrope-walk across a nar-row, cracked slab of concrete that worked as a dam. Fall one way, and the St. Bart's fugitive was up to his armpits in Lake Leroy; tumble in the other direction, and he had a five-foot drop to the rocky, shallow stream. The treacherous shortcut was dubbed Mendini's Crossing, after Frank Men-dini, a high-school junior in 1989 who'd fallen headfirst into the creek. According to the story, he spent several days in a coma, then woke up with such severe brain damage, his parents committed him to an insane asylum. Actually, Frank Mendini was unconscious for five minutes after the fall, and he took six stitches along his right temple. He stayed home that weekend, and managed to convince his parents that he didn't want to be a priest. So they took him out of Our Lady of Sorrows. Yet somehow, word swept around the school that the fall had left Frank comatose, then deranged.

Jack had used Mendini's Crossing himself—always on the sly, of course. He was supposed to set a good example for these students. But the other way to town—College Road, a two-lane drive that crossed over the creek—was a mile farther down and took twice as long. Another option was rowing across Lake Leroy in one of the boats available only to the faculty and students who had made special arrangements.

There wasn't much in the way of entertainment at St. Bartholomew Hall and on that west side of the lake—unless one was delirious about forests. There was a "social room" in the basement, open from six to ten nightly—when the cellar wasn't flooded. The room housed four archaic computers, where students—all deprived of telephone jacks in their rooms—had access to E-mail. There were two moldy pool tables, a TV with fickle reception bracketed to the wall, a couple of pinball machines which were usually out of order, four vending machines, and a bookshelf full of jigsaw puzzles and games ranging from chess to Monopoly. The torn corners of every faded box had been repeatedly taped up, and pieces were missing from each game and puzzle.

Small wonder the freshmen at St. Bart's Hall were willing to brave Mendini's Crossing for their escape. The other side of that lake offered all the splendor of a small college town: a minimall, a duplex movie theater, bowling alley, stores, pizza and burger joints—in other words, civilization and freedom.

It was no secret that some of the cooler freshmen ventured over Mendini's Crossing to party with the upperclassmen. After a few drinks, the safest way back was College Road—

or, if weather permitted, a quick swim across the narrow part of Lake Leroy. It was a nice way to sober up a bit before sneaking back into St. Bart's Hall. But not too many freshmen tried it any more, because a boy had drowned a few years back while taking one of those midnight swims. Jack didn't know the details.

He watched Ernesto and Art head down Whopper Way, then disappear into the forest. The two of them were best friends, and almost as dedicated as Jack with their morning runs.

Jack wished he had a friend here, someone he could confide in, another priest maybe. The closest person to him right now was a freshman named John Costello. At times, St. Bart's seemed like a mental institution, and John the only other sane inmate there.

During his first week at the school, Jack had had some revelations about the other teachers and resident advisers at the freshman facility. "It's sort of a proving ground for new guys like you," a priest friend had warned him. "New priests and nutcases, that's who they have running these freshman dorms, Jack. It's SOP. They don't want any of these guys managing a parish. So they stick them with these poor, vulnerable teenage boys. It's sad, really."

Of the eleven other priests at St. Bartholomew Hall, four were definitely alcoholics. Some even taught classes while drunk; and the kids weren't dumb, they knew. Most of the clergy were gay, which didn't matter to Jack. The ones who bothered him were the bullies; two priests in particular seemed to take pleasure in picking on the students. It was a weird sight, watching them hit or pinch these eighteen- and nineteen-year-old boys who probably could have taken them apart.

Jack guessed that just over half of the seminarians would actually become priests. For many students, this was a cheap college education with the archdiocese footing the bill. Still, a majority of the young men at St. Bart's had a true calling. However, a handful of them took it a bit too far, practicing self-flagellation or fasting for days at a time as a way of becoming closer to God. One student on Jack's floor woke up at dawn every morning to scrub out all the toilets and sinks in the bathroom on his floor. He said it made him happy. There were also several boys who took after those sadistic priests. They picked on their fellow students as a way of feeling powerful—or physically closer to them. All the unspoken crushes and furtive sexual activity among the boys caused one minidrama after another: fits of jealousy and contempt, friendships broken and rivalries started.

On their first day, all of Jack's residents had reported to him in St. Bartholomew Hall's basement "social room" for student orientation. It was a gorgeous, warm September day when the first of three groups were herded into that damp, musty cellar. The eight students were treated to a buffet lunch whipped up by the cafeteria staff: bologna sandwiches or peanut butter and jelly (bleeding through the bread), Fritos, Jell-O, and a choice of plain or chocolate milk. That was gourmet stuff compared to the usual fare in St. Bart's cafeteria. Jack once saw a refrigerated delivery truck unloading boxes by St. Bartholomew Hall's kitchen door. The boxes were labeled GRADE D CHICKEN — EDIBLE. The next day, he bought a minifridge and microwave oven. The cafeteria was run by a surly, chain-smoking Filipino woman named Valentina. Her staff consisted of two ancient nuns who belonged in a nursing home; Bob, a twentysomething mildly retarded man; and Valentina's creepy ex-reform-school son, a skinny, tattooed weasel named Angel who probably wasn't beyond spitting in the food when he had the chance.

None of them were in view for this desperately cheerful orientation luncheon. Jack found his first group waiting for him at their assigned table. Most of the students had arrived and unpacked the previous night. They wore their nametags, and among the eight were Peter Tobin and John Costello from Seattle. They were smart enough to forgo the cafeteria fare and split a pack of Hostess cupcakes from the vending machine.

It was hard not to single out John Costello. He was an extremely handsome kid, with straight black hair that occasionally fell over his blue eyes. Lean and tan, he looked very athletic in a white polo shirt and jeans. He didn't say much, and barely cracked a smile. The boys were supposed to introduce themselves, and talk a little about their interests and hobbies. The other newcomers were cooperating, chatting nervously about their scholastic or athletic endeavors, and how they'd spent their summer vacations.

When his turn came, John took a sip of milk, then, without looking across the table at Jack, he muttered: "I'm John Costello. I'm from Seattle, and this is my best friend, Pete."

Peter Tobin smiled and nodded at everyone around the table. Lanky and pale, with his brown hair in disarray, Pete came off as geeky beside his brooding, good-looking friend.

Jack had a list of questions he was supposed to ask—to "bring out" every freshman. It must have been drawn up in 1952, with real cornball queries such as *What's your greatest accomplishment as a Christian?* and *Tell us about your last good deed.* He consulted the list for a moment. "Um, John, do you have any hobbies or interests?"

John Costello rolled his eyes. "Not really."

"What did you do over the summer?" Jack pressed.

"I caddied at this cake-eater country club. It was pretty boring."

"How long have you known Pete here?"

"A few years."

Jack nodded. He decided to give up and turned to John's pal. "Pete, maybe you can tell us something about yourself."

"Yes, Father," Peter Tobin announced, clearing his

throat. "Well, when I was just a baby, my parents and I went down in a plane crash over the Andes. They died, and I was raised by wolves. . . ."

It took a moment for the boys at the table to realize that Peter was joking. Peter quickly went into his repartee. His sulky friend cracked a smile occasionally. In all likelihood, he'd heard the routine before.

Peter was trying a little too hard, and while the other boys were a good audience, they obviously sensed his desperation to please. Once the formal talk was over, they didn't approach him. For a few moments, Peter stood alone by the table—until Jack patted him on the shoulder. "Thanks for loosening everybody up," he said. "You really have a great sense of humor, Pete."

Most of the boys wanted to meet Peter's sullen, pouty friend, and they came up to shake John's hand. Jack figured this sullen punk was going to be a real problem.

He was scheduled for a one-on-one with him that night. Part of his job on this orientation day was to check with each boy at curfew to make sure he had settled in his room. Jack thought imposing a curfew on eighteen-year-olds was ridiculous. But he didn't make the rules.

Checking Peter Tobin's room, he found that Pete already had several of his drawings up on the walls. He was a talented artist. He let Jack see one of his sketch books, and even showed him his portable case of art supplies. It was stocked with paper, coloring pencils, and markers, and a box full of special fine-point pens from Calgary, Alberta: GOWER GRAPHIC, THE FINE POINT FOR FINE ARTISTS. He also demonstrated his juggling abilities for Jack, and admitted that he was a little homesick. So he was grateful to have his best friend, Johnny, just down the hall.

But John Costello wasn't down the hall. Jack knocked on his door, then waited—and waited. Finally, he used his pass key to let himself in. The room was empty, and the boy hadn't even unpacked yet. The sheets were still stacked and folded at the foot of his bare mattress.

Jack checked the bathroom down the hall, then glanced out the window at the end of the corridor. A full moon reflected on the lake's ripply surface, and he could see the silhouette of a young man sitting at the end of the boat dock.

Jack headed down the stairs and outside. He reached the dock, then stopped suddenly. Past the sound of water lapping against the breakers, he could hear John Costello quietly crying.

Jack stood there a moment. He cleared his throat and started down to the dock. "John?"

John Costello glanced over his shoulder. He quickly brushed his sleeve beneath his nose. "Yeah?" he replied in a raspy voice. He stood up and turned around.

In the moonlight, Jack could see tears in his eyes. "Are you okay?" he asked.

"Fine," he muttered.

"Didn't you read the list of rules they gave you at check in?" Jack asked gently. "You're not supposed to be out of your room past eleven on weeknights—unless you have permission or you're using the bathroom."

John sighed, but said nothing. He wiped his eyes.

"Didn't you know about the curfew?"

"No," he mumbled. "Guess I'm off to a bad start with you, huh?"

Jack managed to smile. "It's okay. I'll cut you a break."

"Thanks." John shoved his hands in his pockets. He caught Jack's eye for a second. "You're new here, too, aren't you? I heard a couple of the other priests talking—"

"That's right. We're in the same boat." Jack nodded toward the dorm. "Now, why don't you head inside? You ought to get your room set up."

John turned away, then gazed out at the water again. "I'm worried about my sister," he said. "She—well, she practically raised me and my other two sisters ever since my mom died. My other sisters are married now, and moved away. I'm still with Maggie. She's married, too. His name's Ray. He's a real asshole. I've seen him take off after her. He and I have tangled it up a few times, because I don't like the way he smacks her around. I'm scared what he might do to Maggie with no one there to protect her. Anyway, I don't know why I'm dumping all this on you. I'm just worried."

"There's a phone in my room," Jack said. "Would you like to call her? Make sure she's okay?"

Johnny turned to him. "Really? God, that would be great. We didn't have much time to talk yesterday. Three other guys were waiting to use the phone."

Once in his room, Jack dialed the number for Johnny. He handed him the phone, then stepped out. All was quiet as he made a couple of rounds, checking the hall. When he passed his own door, Jack heard snippets of what Johnny was saying: "... this really cool priest let me use his phone. . . . Yeah, Pete's room is just down the hall from me. . . . I'm fine, really. . . ."

Jack gave him a few more minutes, then tapped on the door and opened it. John was sitting at his desk. He glanced over his shoulder. "Hey, listen, Maggie," he said into the phone. "I should go. Talk to you again soon, okay?"

He hung up, then got to his feet. "Good news." He smiled at Jack. "My sister went apartment shopping on the sly this afternoon. She's dumping Ray's sorry ass, and putting in an application for a place—two bedrooms, one for me. Isn't that cool?"

Jack nodded. "That's great. Now, why don't you go get some sleep?"

"Sure thing. Thanks, Father." Suddenly Johnny hugged him.

For a moment, Jack stood with his arms at his sides. Then,

awkwardly, he hugged the boy back. He felt as if he was breaking some kind of guideline for the resident priests: no displays of affection with the student charges. It was all right to hit them—but not hug them.

Jack had made a friend that night. John Costello became something of a surrogate son to him. He didn't have a father, and he looked up to Jack. They sometimes ran together in the morning, though not lately. Jack figured it was just as well. He wanted John to spend more time with guys his own age. Besides, he wasn't supposed to have any favorites among the students.

Jack pressed on. Rounding the curve on the lake side of the track, he felt his lungs reach that last-lap burning point.

"Father Murphy! Oh, God, Father Murphy!"

Jack stopped, then bent forward. Hands on knees, he tried to catch his breath. He gaped at Ernesto Rodriguez, who stumbled from the forest trail. "Father Murphy, there's a body!" he cried, pointing toward the lake. "Somebody's drowned. . . . Come quick. . . ."

Jack started toward him. "Where?" He glanced down the narrow path through the trees, and saw Art Vargas urgently waving at him.

Jack patted Ernesto's shoulder. "Ernie, go inside, call 911, okay?" Then he took off down the trail toward Art.

"Over here, Father!" Art yelled. He led the way, off the trail and through the trees toward the edge of Lake Leroy. Twigs snapped underfoot, and Jack dodged rocks and shrubs as he caught up with Art. The young man pointed ahead to a pale, blue-white thing that had washed up on the rocky shore. "Ernie saw him first," he explained, out of breath. "I think it's what'shisname—Costello."

Jack told himself that he didn't hear it right. It wasn't Johnny; that lifeless creature draped over the rocks and mire couldn't be his young friend. Yet something inside him knew better, because his eyes were tearing up, and a sudden tightness grabbed him by the throat.

"Oh, God, please, no!" Jack whispered, staggering into the muddy waters. He grabbed Johnny from under his arms and pulled him out of the icy lake.

John Costello was clad only in his underwear. His blue eyes were half-open, and his face had a gray tinge. Wet leaves and bits of debris clung to his slippery, cold body. His right foot must have dragged across some rocks, because it was mangled—with a couple of toes missing.

Jack let out a strangled cry. Holding on to his young companion, he pressed his face against John's and stroked his wet, matted-down hair.

He swallowed hard, then reached down and closed John's eyes. "We—we pray for the repose of the soul of our friend, John Costello," he said, tracing a sign of the cross on John's forehead. He could hardly speak past the ache in his throat. "Come to meet him, angels of the Lord. Give him eternal rest, dear God, and may Your light shine on him forever. . . ."

Chapter Two

About fifty seminarians and several priests stood in the cold by the north door of St. Bartholomew Hall. Some of the young men had quickly thrown jackets over their pajamas. As they watched the ambulance drive away, rumors flew that classes might be canceled for the day.

Two policemen from Leroy's small force had interviewed Art and Ernesto. They'd also spoken with Jack, asking for his master key so they could check John's room for a suicide note, or perhaps a stash of drugs. They were back outside within a couple of minutes, apparently having found nothing.

Jack's colleague, Father Zeigler, announced that all freshmen would be expected to attend a special Mass for John Costello this morning at 9:15 in St. Bartholomew Hall's chapel. Before the ambulance completely pulled away, Zeigler started swatting the seminarians on the backs of their heads, telling them to get inside. He was like a drill sergeant with the eighteen-year-olds. Most of them could have flattened Father Zeigler, but his clerical collar protected him. So the boys just took his abuse in their stride.

Jack couldn't stand Harvey Zeigler. He was one of the bullies. A square-jawed, swarthy, macho runt with a pumped-up body, he lived in the other wing on Jack's floor. The little man seemed to take sadistic pride in striking fear into the hearts of his resident charges. Mostly, he picked on good-looking boys. John Costello had taken the brunt of his wrath. John was always reenacting for Jack how Father "Zeig-Heil" (his nickname among the students) had slammed him against the lockers or grabbed him by the hair. He'd recently shown Jack an ugly purple-and-yellow bruise on his arm, just above the elbow. It was a calling card from Father Zeigler, who had given him the old pinch-and-twist treatment because he'd been "dawdling" in the hallway between classes.

Jack was furious. He went to Zeigler's room and knocked on the door. Harvey answered it with his usual pious look. "Yes, Jack? Can I help you?"

"You sure can," he replied, keeping his voice low. "You can stop picking on the students. It makes me sick, Harv. In particular, if I see another mark on John Costello's body, I'll come beat the living crap out of you."

Harvey Zeigler took a step back, but he was grinning. He was good-looking in a cocky, creepy sort of way. His head seemed to duck a bit within the confines of that priestly collar—like a turtle retreating into its shell. He chuckled. "Oh, really, Jack?" he said. "Would you like to take me on?"

Jack glared at him. "You heard what I said," he whispered. Then he turned and walked down the hall.

In the three weeks since, Jack hadn't seen Father Zeigler mistreat any of the seminarians. But now John Costello was dead, and perhaps that gave Harvey a reckless sense of power over Jack. In full view of him, Harvey smacked, pinched, and shoved those young men into retreat by the side door of St. Bartholomew Hall. Most of the students were still in shock over the death of their classmate. They didn't seem to realize anyone was screaming at them until they felt the sting of Father Zeig-Heil's hand.

The ambulance turned on College Road and disappeared behind a cluster of evergreens. Jack could still hear the siren's wail. But Harvey Zeigler's barking began to compete with it.

He stared at Peter Tobin. John's best friend looked shell-shocked. His deep-set brown eyes were filled with tears, and his lip quivered. He looked so hopelessly lost. The Leroy police had spoken with Peter, too, but apparently, he had little to tell them. The interrogation had lasted five minutes.

While his classmates began to flee from Father Zeigler's tirade, Peter just stood there in his sweatpants and wind-breaker, trembling. Peter didn't seem to notice Zeigler coming at him with his hand raised.

"Harvey, that's enough," Jack said loudly.

Father Zeigler swiveled around and glared at him.

Jack stepped forward. "That's enough," he whispered.

Frowning, Zeigler backed away. He pushed the last few students toward the side door, then stepped in after them.

Gently, Jack took Peter's arm. He could feel the young man tense up. "Listen, Pete," he whispered. "You don't have to go to that Mass if you don't want—"

Wrenching away from him, Peter shook his head. "This isn't right," he said, his voice cracking. Tears streamed down his face. "He wouldn't have gone swimming. It's too cold. And even if he had, Johnny was a good swimmer, an excellent swimmer. This was no accident. . . ."

Jack grimaced. "We won't know what really happened—at least not for a day or two." He reached out to Peter again, but hesitated. "I'm here for you, Pete. But if you need to be alone, I understand. I just want you to know—"

"You're right, Father," he replied in a scratchy voice. Peter wiped his tears away. "I need to be alone."

He brushed past Jack and ducked into the side doorway.

Jack peeled off his gray jersey. It felt clammy with cold, dried sweat. He hadn't had a chance to change out of his running clothes until now. He had only a few minutes to grab a shower before rounding up students for the special Mass. No time to let anything sink in.

He had deluxe accommodations—for St. Bartholomew Hall. He and Zeigler were the only ones on the fourth floor who had their own "suites" with private baths. Jack's bedroom was tiny, with barely enough space for the dresser and nightstand. A crucifix hung on the wall over the headboard of his single bed.

The furniture in his front room was midseventies institutional. The beige couch had cigarette burns on one arm. Jack had brought in his own small TV and VCR, a stereo, a minimicrowave, and a minirefrigerator. The closet was packed with tapes and LPs. On the top shelf, he stored a couple of big Sears boxes full of old photos, finger paintings and certificates, as well as birthday, anniversary, and Father's Day cards—from years ago, when Jack had celebrated such occasions. There wasn't much room left for clothes, but priests didn't require large wardrobes.

On the walls, Jack had a school pennant and a bulletin board with announcements, cards from students, and class photos. There was also a framed movie still from *On the Waterfront,* a bloody and beaten Marlon Brando with Eva Marie Saint and a priestly Karl Malden hovering over him. It had been a gift from John Costello. They'd seen the movie together at the campus revival theater last November.

Leaning against his desk, Jack pried off his running shoes. In the distance, across the lake, he could see the ambulance threading around the streets of Leroy. It wasn't moving very fast. No need. They were probably taking John's body to the coroner's office up in Bellingham.

Jack closed his eyes and sighed, remembering the past.

He should have ridden in the ambulance with his son, Leo, but he'd decided to stay behind with his wife. He couldn't just leave Donna there. He remembered holding Leo's hand as they loaded him onto a stretcher. It seemed like a dozen police cars and medical vans had descended upon them, those red strobes flashing in the night. The crash had set off both car horns, and rescue sirens were blaring. Yet past all the noise, he'd overheard a medic say, *"The mother's dead. . . ."*

Then everything else seemed to come at Jack in fragments. Someone was setting up orange cones—and farther down the road, flares. He smelled gasoline, and something metal burning. Smoke rose from the dented hood of the blue Monte Carlo that had slammed into the side of his wife's car. All the windows were shattered. Practically nothing was left of the Monte Carlo's windshield. Jack noticed a cardboard air freshener shaped like a pine tree still swaying back and forth from the guy's rearview mirror.

They were still trying to pry Donna's body out of the car. Jack tried not to get in their way. He stayed by Leo's side as long as he could. He kept telling his fifteen-year-old son to hold on, he'd see him in a little while. "I need to stay with Mom," Jack said.

Leo's sweet face was covered with blood that glistened like water in the flashing red light. *"Dad, I'm cold,"* he whispered.

Leo died in the ambulance—on the way to the hospital.

Jack figured he should have ridden with his son. With him whispering encouragement, Leo might have lived. Or at least Jack could have been there when he slipped away.

The drunk driver's name was Lon Brodell. He'd died

instantly. Jack couldn't stay angry at a corpse. Instead, he blamed himself for the loss of his wife and son.

He missed them both so much right now. Something about the new loss triggered old grief. He longed for those mornings when he'd return from his run and see Donna asleep in their double bed. He'd grown so accustomed to that, it became routine—like breathing. When he lost them both, it was as if he had to learn how to breathe all over again.

"I don't care how long the service is—just so it gets me out of English Lit!"

Jack turned from the window and glanced toward his door. A couple of students were passing by outside. The second one shushed his friend. "Hey, dumb-ass," he whispered. "Want Father Murphy to hear you?"

Jack checked his wristwatch. He had to hurry up with his shower. He took one last look out the window across the lake. He couldn't see the ambulance anymore.

He should have asked to ride with him, even though Johnny was already dead. He should have ridden with him anyway.

Chapter Three

Except for the huge attendance, the special church service for John Costello was almost too much like a regular Mass. Jack wished a few of John's classmates would cry, but the freshmen from St. Bartholomew Hall were a stoic crowd.

They were packed into the small chapel this morning, about one hundred and eighty students, along with nine priests. At least forty of them were standing in the back and along the side aisles. Within minutes, the temperature in the little church shot up to about eighty degrees, and the place smelled like a locker room.

Jack studied the sea of faces, and wondered if any of these freshmen knew what had really happened to Johnny last night.

Peter Tobin wasn't among the mourners. John's best friend didn't attend the service. Up on the altar, Father O'Leary, the superintendent of St. Bartholomew Hall, said the Mass. He probably couldn't have picked John Costello out of a lineup, yet Father O'Leary gave a sermon about

Johnny's virtues, calling him an "inspiration," and a "soldier of Christ."

The chapel was built as an attachment to St. Bartholomew Hall in the late thirties. Here the freshmen could worship without having to boat across the lake to Our Lady of Sorrows Church. The chapel had a certain rustic, old-world charm. Its pint-size stained-glass windows, which depicted the Stations of the Cross, were works of art. And in tradition with Catholic churches of the day, the rose-marble altar had enshrined in it the bone-chip of a saint, the martyr St. Gabriel Lalemant.

The chapel was named after Gabriel, who had been canonized in 1930. Considering its troubled origin, St. Bartholomew Hall was a fitting place for Gabriel Lalemant to lend his name and a sliver of his remains. At twenty, Gabriel entered the Jesuit order and offered his services for the foreign missions. Bouts of ill health kept him in his native France for several years. Finally, he was shipped off to Quebec, and joined the Huron mission. Six months later, they were attacked by the Iroquois and Gabriel was captured. The Iroquois beat him with clubs and thorn branches, then doused him with boiling water. His tongue was cut out, and they filled his mouth with burning coals. They plucked out Gabriel's eyes, then forced fiery embers into the empty sockets. The frail, little priest continued to hang on—even after they'd hacked off his hands and seared the bloody stumps with sizzling-hot axes. He finally died from a blow to the head with a tomahawk.

The story of St. Gabriel Lalemant was drummed into the minds of arriving freshmen at St. Bartholomew Hall—lest they feel any hardships under the tyranny of their teachers and spiritual advisers. Jack remembered Johnny once joking that St. Gabriel might have preferred the Iroquois over a couple of rounds with Father Zeigler.

As Jack glanced across the aisle, he saw his colleague

poke his fist into the spine of the young man in front of him. The seminarian had committed the cardinal sin of whispering something to a classmate.

In the pulpit, Father O'Leary referred to Johnny as "young Joseph," while most of the boys looked half-asleep. Two pews ahead, Jack noticed a couple of students, Steve Goldschmidt and Greg Reimen, nudging each other and chuckling. Jack cleared his throat, and Steve glanced over his shoulder.

The young man was grinning helplessly. Jack stood up and crooked his finger at him a couple of times.

Steve followed him down the aisle and out the chapel door. The morning sun seemed so bright after the gloomy little church. It shone on Steve's blond curly hair. He seemed too skinny for his blue denim shirt and baggy gray trousers.

Jack closed the heavy wooden door. The fresh air was a relief. "Okay, Steve, get it out of your system," he said.

"Sorry, Father," he said, catching his breath. "I don't . . . mean any disrespect for Johnny. . . ."

Jack managed a smile. "I know. I've seen John Costello get the giggles in Mass often enough. He'd be the first to understand."

"It's just when O'Leary got Johnny's name wrong, Greg and I started cracking up."

"*Father* O'Leary," Jack said.

"Sorry. *Father* O'Leary. He shouldn't be up there anyway. You ought to be the one saying Mass. Johnny really looked up to you."

Jack let the remark pass.

"How did he drown exactly? I mean, do they know what happened?"

Jack shook his head. "Not yet."

"Well, Pete Tobin said it was no accident. He acts like he knows something. But if you ask me, they ought to talk to somebody over at the college. That's probably where

Johnny was coming from—a party in one of the dorms—just like with what's-his-name, Julian Doyle.''

"Who?" Jack asked.

"Julian Doyle, about three years ago. My older brother told me about it. This Doyle guy drowned swimming back from some kegger with the upperclassmen."

Jack nodded. He remembered now. The Julian Doyle "incident" was what discouraged most kids from swimming across the lake alone late at night. It had happened before Jack had come to Our Lady of Sorrows.

He couldn't imagine John partying with a bunch of upperclassmen. Yet there was no other explanation for why he had drowned—unless what Peter said was true, unless it wasn't an accident.

Frowning, Jack nudged Steve, then opened the chapel door. "C'mon, let's go back inside. . . ."

Jack knocked on Peter Tobin's door and waited.

The narrow hallway was perpetually drafty. The cold, green-tiled floor discouraged bare feet. Above every seminarian's doorway hung a small wooden crucifix. Framed sepia portraits of long-dead priests (some of them buried in the cemetery outside) lined the corridor walls. Stern, ever watchful sentries for the young men on the floor, some of the priests had a crazed, almost possessed look in their eyes. Only one appeared rather young and benign, and someone had scribbled *faggot* along the bottom of the portrait.

Jack knocked on Peter's door again. No answer.

He hadn't seen Peter since they'd taken John's body away in the ambulance this morning. All freshman classes had been canceled today—so they could "pray and meditate."

"Peter, it's Father Murphy," he called, knocking for the last time. "I just want to make sure you're okay."

No answer.

Jack finally dug out his pass key and unlocked the door.

Peter kept his small room tidy. The place had that faint, goatlike smell detectable in most of the boys' rooms. Peter's juggling pins and balls were neatly displayed on the shelf, along with his art supplies and books. Hanging on the wall was a large watercolor he'd painted of a blazing sunset. There was also an M. C. Escher poster and an illuminated Coke clock, the type delis displayed. The dorm-issue, pea green–colored drapes were closed.

An open sketchbook sat on Peter's desk. Jack glanced at a cartoon Peter had created with a family of sea monkeys, called "More Amazing Amoeba Adventures!" It was a cross between Dr. Seuss and something from *MAD* magazine. He flipped back a page to a sketch of Johnny looking like a Greek god and a self-portrait that Peter had crossed out.

Sighing, Jack headed out to the hallway. He locked the door, then started down toward the lavatory. The overhead light by Room 410 was flickering.

Room 410 had been converted from a dorm bedroom to a storage area sometime in the early sixties. They were never able to board anyone in that room, not after the "bad business" in there so many years ago.

Jack moved on into the lavatory. He didn't see any feet under the doors to the five toilet stalls. But he heard water running. He went into the shower area. All the stalls were empty, but one of the showers was going full blast. Jack drenched the arm of his suit jacket shutting off the water. He took some paper towels from the dispenser by the sinks and dabbed at his sleeve. A steady drip echoed within the tiled walls.

"Father Murphy?"

He glanced in the mirror and saw one of his students, Matt Scanlin, in the bathroom doorway. "Yes, Matt?"

"Father Zeigler's been looking for you. He said to tell

you that you should check your phone messages." Matt moved around the corner toward the urinals.

"Thanks," Jack called. "Hey, have you seen Pete Tobin?"

"Not since early this morning, Father," Matt called back.

Jack stepped out of the bathroom and started up the hallway. He paused by Room 410 and glanced up at the flickering overhead light.

"No use trying to fix that."

Jack swiveled around.

It was Duane, the janitor. Duane seemed to enjoy sneaking up on him whenever possible. Of the three custodians at St. Bartholomew Hall, he was the only one who boarded there. He had a studio apartment in the basement. Duane was about thirty-five, with a lean, wiry build, and unkempt light brown hair. He had a slick, ultracool, lady-killer manner that reminded Jack of Mickey Rourke. A lot of the freshmen looked up to him, and they swapped stories about Duane's prowess with women. Duane never discussed his legendary love life with Jack. But he clearly liked him. As a way of sparking a rapport, he often challenged Jack with criticisms of the Catholic Church: *"Did you know that there was a Pope Alexander that had an illegitimate kid? What do you think of that, Jack?"* Duane would usually sneak up on him with these obscure facts when Jack was in a hurry to get someplace.

"Oh, hi, Duane," Jack said, pausing by Room 410.

Duane held a feather duster. He wore his blue custodian shirt open, revealing a dirty T-shirt. He had an unlit cigarette behind his ear. He nodded at Jack, then gazed up at the overhead light. "Those fluorescent tube numbers are a pain in the ass to change. Besides, that light's screwy, haunted— just like the room."

Jack managed a smile, then he started walking backward down the hall. "Yeah, you're probably right. See you, Duane."

The janitor followed him. "Hey, Jack, you know, Father Zeigler was asking around for you. I guess some big shot from administration has been trying to get ahold of you."

Jack continued to back away. "Thanks. Yeah. I was just going to check my phone messages."

"Shame about the Costello kid, huh?"

"Yes, it is," Jack said quietly. He pulled out his room key and unlocked the door.

"I know you and he were buddies." Duane fingered the feather duster. "I guess I can tell you, now that he's dead and all. Your friend, John, used to sneak out a lot at night. Were you aware of that?"

Frowning, Jack shook his head. "How do you know?"

Duane shrugged. "I'd see him from my basement window, coming and going. And a few times, driving back from a hot date, I'd see him on College Road. On a couple of occasions, I even gave him a lift."

"Do you know where he was going—or coming from?" Jack asked.

"Beats the hell out of me," Duane said. "I hear he was missing a couple of his toes when you fished him out of the lake."

"Where did you hear that?" Jack murmured.

"Oh, I know pretty much everything that's going on around here." Duane leaned against the door frame. His voice dropped to a whisper. "Want to hear something pretty bizarre, Jack? Three years ago, when they fished the Doyle kid out of that same lake, he was missing a couple of fingers on one hand."

Jack just stared at him.

"Pretty bizarre," Duane repeated. He turned and sauntered down the hallway, pausing under the faulty light by Room 410. Duane casually brushed his feather duster over the glass cover, then moved on.

Chapter Four

Beep.

"Hello, Father Murphy?" The voice on his answering machine was effeminate and breathy. *"This is Deacon Robert phoning for Monsignor Fuller. It's 11:30, Thursday morning. The monsignor would like to meet with you as soon as possible. Please call me at your earliest convenience...."*

Monsignor Fuller was president of the seminary. A summons from him was a very big deal. When Jack called the office, Deacon Robert didn't explain why Fuller wanted to see him. He just said they'd expect him in forty-five minutes.

Jack had met Monsignor Fuller only once before—a brief introduction at a reception for the new priests the previous August. Fuller was a short, balding man in his midsixties, frail and liver-spotted, with huge, thick glasses that gave him a strange, buglike appearance. Jack thought he looked like E.T. And for some reason, Monsignor Fuller had let his fingernails grow. Jack remembered they were at least half an inch long.

Fuller had his office in the administration building, so Jack took one of the faculty boats and rowed across Lake Leroy to the campus. Working the oars, he gazed at the placid silver-green surface. It was hard to fathom that the lake had swallowed up John Costello last night, then spit him out on its muddy bank.

He wondered if Pete Tobin could really prove *"it was no accident."* Or was Pete simply unable to accept his best friend's death? Jack was starting to worry about him. Pete had said that he needed to be alone. He'd probably gone for a walk by himself.

Jack knew what it was like. After his wife and son had been killed, he'd shut everyone else out. At work, he barely functioned. To his students and coworkers at St. Xavier grade school, he was something of a tragic curiosity—a cross between a former mental patient and a holocaust survivor.

He leaned on Father Mike Berry, the pastor at St. Xavier's. They'd grown up together, a couple of Irish Catholic boys from Chicago. Together, they'd attended the seminary, where their education came cheap. But Jack loathed the place. With their rigid rules about when to sleep, study, pray, eat, and go to the toilet, it was like a prison. If not for Mike, he would have gone insane.

After the seminary, and during his theologate studies, Jack wrestled with the celibacy issue, and the idea of never having any children. Jack earned his Master of Divinity degree, but didn't take his vows.

Later, Mike used his clout at St. Xavier parish to recruit Jack as vice principal at the grade school. Mike presided over Jack's marriage to Donna. He baptized Leo, and taught him in confirmation classes. He also said Donna and Leo's funeral Mass.

According to Mike, after a few months as a widower,

Jack become St. Xavier's most eligible "Hunk." Scores of female parishioners were dying to fix him up—or be fixed up with him. But Jack wasn't interested in dating or starting over.

He was far more prepared for a life of sacrifice and celibacy. He found out he could use his time in the seminary and his Master of Divinity to enter the priesthood. He filled out a mountain of paperwork, sat through several interviews, and endured a year of novitiate work before his ordination. Father Jack Murphy's first assignment was teaching history and acting as resident adviser in the freshman dormitory at Our Lady of Sorrows Seminary in Leroy, Washington.

"Leroy is this tiny little burg where God lost his shoes, seventy-two miles north of Seattle," Mike told him, over pizza and beer at Sully's Inn. The tavern was Mike's favorite haunt, a real "joint," with barstools around barrel tables, and peanut shells on the floor. "This particular dorm at Our Lady of Sorrows has a bad history attached to it. . . ."

Mike told him the story of Gavin McAllister. Thirty-five years after Gavin, Abigail, and little Hazel McAllister were discovered in what became known as the Easter Sunday Massacre, St. Bartholomew Hall was host to another murder-suicide. It happened in Room 410. Two boys, Gerard Lunt and Mark Weedler, became fodder for legend, limericks, and jokes—like Gavin McAllister before them.

Mike told him the story—as much as he knew, anyway.

"That room on the fourth floor is supposed to be haunted now," Mike explained with a wry smile. "At least, that's what I hear. They've tried boarding one kid after another in there. And one kid after another has complained about the noise—things scraping against the floor and ceiling in the middle of the night, moaning, and crying. One kid said his bed shook, another claimed he felt someone grabbing at his foot while he was sleeping. The list goes on and on—"

"Well, what do you expect?" Jack countered. "I'd be

pretty shook up, too, if I had to stay in a room where something like that happened once. Small wonder these kids experienced . . . sensations—''

"None of them *ever heard* of Gerard Lunt or Mark Weedler," Mike replied, setting down his beer glass. "These were new kids. They had no idea what happened in there." He sighed. "And for that matter, neither do we."

Jack chuckled. "You've been reading too many comic books, Mike."

His friend shrugged. "Hey, I'm on the level, Jack. I'm just passing along what I heard from a friend who was there for a year. If you were moving to Sleepy Hollow, I'd want you to know about old Ichabod Crane. I mean, these freshman dorms are always a hotbed of testosterone and craziness. They all have histories with scandals and a suicide or two. But St. Bartholomew Hall is a cut above the others in that kind of history."

From the rowboat, Jack glanced back at St. Bart's, standing alone on the other side of the lake. He couldn't help thinking that now John Costello was part of its curious history.

He kept rowing toward the boat slip on the college side. Beyond that, he could see the cluster of old, ivy-covered, brick-and-mortar buildings.

Monsignor Fuller would want an explanation of how and why John Costello had drowned. Jack didn't know what to tell him.

He tied up the boat, then climbed onto the dock. Glancing at his wristwatch, he hurried toward the administration building.

Jack needn't have hurried. Deacon Robert made him wait in the tiny anteroom outside Monsignor Fuller's office for fifteen minutes. The pencil-thin, young deacon had curly black hair that he kept patting into place. He fidgeted with everything on his desk and occasionally smiled at Jack, whispering, "It won't be too much longer."

Jack nodded and smiled back. There was nothing to read except a copy of *Catholic Digest* on the end table. Finally, Deacon Robert's intercom buzzed twice, and the young man sprang to his feet. "Monsignor Fuller is ready for you now," he said, showing Jack to the door.

Jack stepped into the monsignor's office, a huge room with dark paneling, stained-glass windows, and a fireplace. The antique furniture was bulky, upholstered in elaborately patterned, faded fabric.

"Father Murphy," Deacon Robert announced.

Seated at a large mahogany desk, the diminutive, liver-spotted priest with the big glasses nodded benevolently at his assistant. "I'll have my tea in five minutes, Deacon Robert."

"Yes, Monsignor." Deacon Robert ducked out of the room.

Jack waited for Fuller to offer him a seat. But the old man started sifting through some papers on his desk. Jack noticed his fingernails were just as overgrown as they'd been last fall. Fuller seemed oblivious to Jack, who stood by the door for at least three minutes, until he finally cleared his throat. "You wanted to see me, Monsignor?"

"Have a seat, Father," he replied, not looking up from his work.

Jack sank into an armchair in front of Fuller's antique desk. The threadbare cushion had caved in, and no matter how he shifted his weight, a support beam dug painfully into his backside. Fuller continued to ignore him. He finished with the papers, and now decided to refill his stapler.

Deacon Robert knocked on the door to announce himself, then came in balancing a bulky silver service tray.

"I'll take my tea on the davenport," Fuller told him, not looking up from his busywork with the stapler.

The young deacon set the tray down on the marble-top coffee table. "Will Father Murphy be having tea?"

"No, he will not," Fuller said, getting up from his desk chair.

If the monsignor was trying to be rude, he succeeded with flying colors. Jack watched the little, bug-eyed priest pad across the worn Persian rug to the sitting area. Fuller settled back in the corner of the sofa. Then, for the first time, he actually looked at Jack. With an almost regal gesture, he pointed to an armchair at his right. "Over here, Father," he said.

Deacon Robert was still fussing over the silver service, which had to be worth about five thousand dollars. As Jack's friend, Mike, used to say about some of the more pampered priests: *"If that's what comes with a vow of poverty, bring on celibacy."*

Jack sat down across from the old priest.

"I understand you were well acquainted with the lad who drowned," Fuller said. "In fact, I'm told that you're very popular with all the students." Fuller watched Deacon Robert cut a thin slice of lemon cake, then transfer it to a gold-trimmed plate. "Among all these youngsters who hold you in such high esteem," he continued, "has anyone shared with you information regarding the circumstances behind the Costello lad's drowning?"

Jack thought of Pete Tobin for a second, but he shook his head. "No, Monsignor. They've merely speculated as to what happened."

Fuller sipped his tea. "And what did they speculate?"

Jack hesitated. Did the good monsignor know about the students' furtive trips to and from town? Was he aware of the parties and beer busts that drew some freshmen to the campus side? Fuller seemed about as in-touch with these kids as the author of that orientation questionnaire: *What's your greatest accomplishment as a Christian?*

The old priest set down his teacup. "It was a simple question, Father."

Straightening in his chair, Jack nodded. "Yes, Monsignor." He cleared his throat. "The general consensus seems to be that John must have been swimming back from a party here on the campus side."

Those bug eyes behind the huge glasses squinted at him. "Swimming?"

"Yes, Monsignor. I have a hard time believing it myself. This time of year, it's pretty cold for a dip in the lake." He shrugged. "Then again, maybe Johnny had too much to drink, and his judgment was impaired."

Fuller scowled at him. "I still don't understand about the swimming."

"Well, from this side of the lake, it's quicker to swim across to St. Bartholomew Hall than walking all the way around to the bridge on College Road."

"You sound as if these midnight swims are a regular practice among your students. And you condone these activities?"

Jack quickly shook his head. "Oh, no, Monsignor . . ."

"But you've known such practices were going on, and you did nothing about it."

"Monsignor, these late-night trips back and forth from the campus and town are nothing new. And certainly, they're not exclusive to the boys under my supervision." From the stony look on Fuller's face, Jack gathered he wasn't making much headway. "I enforce the curfew rules on my floor, Monsignor. But if a boy wants to sneak out of St, Bartholomew Hall badly enough, he can find a way. This has been going on for a long while. I understand another student was drowned three years ago—just like Johnny . . . John. His name was Julian Doyle."

Fuller had a mouthful of cake, but he may as well have had a mouthful of worms from the disgusted look on his face. He briskly set his plate on the coffee table, then wiped his lips with a cloth napkin. "So, am I to tell people that the priest supervising this unfortunate boy was aware of these late-night swims? Do I say in the school's defense that you let such dangerous practices continue under your nose—though you knew another boy had drowned a few years ago?" Fuller's face was turning red. "Perhaps if you were more concerned about supervising these youngsters— instead of winning popularity contests—the Costello boy would still be alive."

"It's not like that at all," Jack murmured, dazed by this sudden attack.

"That boy was under your care," the old priest went on, his anger now turning to feigned bewilderment and grief. "His family trusted us to look after him, keep him safe. You were responsible for him, Father Murphy, and now the poor boy's dead. How could you let that happen?"

Jack just shook his head. *"How did it happen?"* he remembered the policeman asking. The cop had to shout over the blaring car horn. It had gone off at the moment of impact, and couldn't be silenced. Jack was covered with blood from hovering over his wife and son. Yet he didn't have a bruise or cut on him. *"How did it happen?"* The question still haunted him to this day. How could a good husband and father let that happen to his family?

"You don't have an answer for me, do you?" Monsignor Fuller tried to steady his teacup with a slightly palsied hand.

"No, I don't, Monsignor," Jack replied, gazing down at the rug. "I have no excuse. You're right. John was in my care—"

Someone knocked on the door. Without waiting for a response, a tall, handsome priest with receding brown hair and an affable smile breezed into the office. He was in his late thirties, and dressed in the black suit with the turned-around collar. "Well, Monsignor, it looks like I've interrupted your teatime." He touched Fuller on the shoulder. "Forgive me for being late. Is that Nelly's famous lemon cake? Yes, it must be."

"Would you like a slice Father Garcia?" the monsignor asked.

The younger priest patted his stomach. "Oh, no thanks. I've gained five pounds just sniffing it. I came to steal away Father Murphy here. Is that all right with you, Monsignor? You're finished talking with him, aren't you?"

Within a minute, Jack found himself at the door with Father Garcia. He was grateful for the way the younger priest had just strutted in and taken over. Jack mustered up a polite farewell to Fuller and his assistant.

As soon as he stepped out to the hallway and closed the door behind them, the other priest sighed. He grabbed Jack's hand and shook it. "Jack, I'm Tom Garcia. I'm the one who wanted to talk with you."

Father Garcia led him down the hallway toward the stairwell. "I'm the school's unofficial vice president," he explained. "If you want the formal title, it's head of administration, at least, that's what they call me now. I'll be taking over for Monsignor Fuller next year. He's getting up there in age. My office is just down the hall from his, and I hear everything that goes on in there through the heating vent. He was awfully hard on you, Jack. I'm sorry I didn't come in there sooner. You didn't deserve that tongue-lashing."

"Maybe I had it coming," Jack said.

"Nonsense," Garcia said as they started down the stairs. "Considering the young man was a good friend of yours, Fuller was out of line. I heard him—trying to hold you accountable for things that have been going on at St. Bart's for decades." He let out a disgruntled laugh and turned down another set of stairs. "Here's old Clyde Fuller trying to make you believe he doesn't know anything about these moonlight swims, and you throw Julian Doyle in his face. He was running the show here when that happened three years ago. I think he'd just as soon forget about that business. But you made him remember. You and John Costello made him remember.''

Father Garcia pushed open the tall wooden door for him, and Jack stepped outside. They paused in back of the administration building, by the parking lot and Dumpsters. ''Monsignor Fuller managed to sweep the whole Julian Doyle incident under the rug. I don't think he handled it right. I wouldn't want John Costello's death to be swept under a rug, too.'' Father Garcia turned to him. ''Jack, I'd like you to help me handle this one right. Can I count on you to work with me?''

Jack nodded. ''I'll do whatever I can.''

Father Garcia patted him on the arm. ''Good.'' He squinted up at the sun, then checked his wristwatch. ''You know, it's five o'clock somewhere in the world. Time for a drink. I sure could use one. I'll take you to my favorite spot, c'mon.''

They started walking. Jack peered over his shoulder at the administrative building. In the third-floor window, he could see old Monsignor Fuller staring down at them.

Father Garcia's favorite spot was the Lakeside Inn Grill, a restaurant-tavern in Leroy's only hotel. One side of the pub had a bleakly pastoral view of Lake Leroy and the woods. Mounted fish of various sizes decorated the walls. Somehow, the restaurant always seemed dusky—even in the middle of the day. The tables were coated with layer upon layer of dark, shiny varnish. They had a muted TV on behind the bar, and schmaltzy music piped over the speakers at a low volume. Burgers and sandwiches were served in paper-lined red plastic baskets, and the drinks were strong.

Father Garcia had a scotch and water while Jack nursed a beer. From their table by the window, Jack gazed out at an elderly man shuffling down to the lake, a fishing pole slung over his shoulder.

Garcia lit up a Merit 100. "So, you knew John Costello pretty well," he said. "Did he ever mention having any upperclassman friends over at the college?"

Jack shook his head. "No. In fact, the idea that John might have been swimming back from some college party last night seems out of character to me. He wasn't much of a party boy. Still, that's the general hypothesis from most of the freshmen at St. Bart's."

"Could he have been meeting someone in town?"

Jack shrugged. "I don't know. If he had any friends on this side of the lake, he didn't tell me about them."

"But he had friends in the dorm, right?"

"Oh, yes. He was very well-liked."

"Did he have a best friend?" Tom Garcia asked.

Jack pushed away his beer stein and nodded. "Yes. His name's Peter Tobin. I haven't seen him much today. All the freshmen were excused from classes—"

"Think this Peter Tobin could know something?"

Jack hesitated. "He might. It's possible."

"Talk to him, Jack." Father Garcia stubbed out his cigarette. "Talk to as many kids as you can. Investigate every lead. If that means knocking on some dormitory doors here on the college side, fine. I'll make sure you have no interference."

Jack nodded. "All right."

"The police are letting us handle the investigation—pending autopsy results. We have their full cooperation. Everyone involved would just as soon avoid a scandal. That's why the local law enforcement is letting us handle this for now.

Any kind of bad business at Our Lady of Sorrows hurts this town.''

Father Garcia took another hit of his scotch and water, draining his glass. His voice dropped to a whisper. ''John Costello is survived by an older sister, who can cause quite a stink if she feels we're covering up any details about her brother's death. That's why I want you working on this. As John's friend and teacher, I know you'll treat this investigation with the utmost intelligence and sensitivity. I'm depending on you. If there's a scandal, this institution, this town—and your young friend's good name—will suffer.''

Jack frowned at him. ''What makes you so sure that there will be a scandal?''

''I'm prepared for the possibility,'' Tom Garcia whispered. ''You should be, too, Jack.''

Chapter Five

Dear Pete,

*Come see me as soon as possible. If I'm not in my
room when you stop by, stick around. It's important
that we talk.*

Thanks,
Father Murphy

Jack slipped the note under Peter Tobin's door. Though
Pete had been gone only a few hours, Jack was worried.
The poor kid was in a state of shock and grief. He shouldn't
have been left on his own.

Jack decided if Pete didn't show up within an hour, he'd
notify the front desk and campus security. He might just tell
Father Garcia, too—now that he had an ally among the
school's administration.

He headed down the hall to Johnny's room, then let himself in with the pass key.

The police hadn't found anything in the room earlier, but Father Garcia wanted him to take another look. One of the cops must have admired the photo of Johnny's older sister. The picture, in a cheap, drugstore frame, had been moved from its usual spot on Johnny's bookshelf to his desk. In the photo, Maggie Costello had her arm around her kid brother, and they were both laughing. A thin redhead in her early thirties, she looked like a natural beauty, who had held up well under some hard times.

Jack sat down at Johnny's desk. He flipped through two notebooks, but didn't see anything besides some class notes and doodling. No mysterious names or phone numbers. He pulled open the top drawer. It was full of junk: old letters, postcards, gum wrappers, and pens—one of them obviously borrowed from Peter's collection: *Gower Graphic—The Fine Point for Fine Artists.*

Jack glanced at one of the postcards, a photo of an obese trucker taken from behind as he sat at a diner counter. Half his buttocks was exposed. The postcard was addressed to Johnny:

Hey, Cutie,

No BUTTS about it, I really miss you. Start thinking about what color you want to paint your room, because I'm giving you a brush & putting you to work when you come home for Easter.

Hi to Pete. Keep your powder dry & phone if you need money or anything.

Love,
Mag-the-Nag

At this minute, Maggie Costello was probably on her way up to identify the body of her kid brother.

Jack pulled open the next drawer. He found a thick envelope from the Film Stop Foto Lab. About a dozen photos had been taken at a picnic, a Costello family function; Jack recognized Johnny's older sister pitching a softball in a couple of shots. The next few photos were of a young brunet, playing peekaboo from behind a semitransparent shower curtain. Jack guessed she was in her midtwenties—and a few pounds overweight. She showed off a bit of chubby thigh by curling her leg around the curtain's edge. In the last picture, she was dry—and clothed—and standing outside. Johnny had spoken many times of wanting a girlfriend when he got out of school, but he'd never mentioned actually having one.

Jack slipped the photos in his suitcoat pocket. He tried the closet shelf, and found nearly a dozen different hair products, from shampoos to styling gels. They were all the same brand, Vita Z. Johnny had never been fussy about his hair. Jack examined a pump bottle of spritz styling hold. The plastic seal around the pump cap hadn't even been broken yet.

He heard someone in the hallway outside. The doorknob rattled. Jack almost called out to ask who was there, but he hesitated. He stared at the door. A thin metal ruler worked its way through the crack. Slipping in and out like a serpent's tongue, it moved down to the lock. After a minute, there was a click, then the door slowly opened.

Peter Tobin stood at the threshold, the metal ruler in his hand. He wore a gray V-neck sweater and jeans.

"Pete, thank God," Jack murmured. "I was really worried about you."

"What are you doing in Johnny's room?"

Jack laughed. He glanced at the ruler in Peter's hand. "Huh, I could ask you the same question."

Peter said nothing.

Jack shook his head. "Never mind. How're you doing, Pete? Are you okay?"

"I'll be all right," he answered carefully. He didn't move from the doorway. "What are you doing in here?"

"I'm looking for a name or phone number, some clue as to what Johnny was doing last night." Jack picked up a notebook from the desk, then tossed it back down. "So far, I'm not having much luck. Do you know if he was meeting anyone?"

Peter shrugged. "No, I don't."

"Why did you break in here? Were you looking for something?"

"No," he murmured. "Johnny's sister is downstairs in the lobby. She wanted to see his room, only Father Zeigler won't let her. He says women aren't allowed up past the first floor. No exceptions, he says."

"Why, that stupid . . ." Jack caught himself. He shook his head. "Unbelievable, absolutely unbelievable."

"Father Zeigler just left, so I was going to smuggle Maggie up here."

Sighing, Jack brushed past Peter in the doorway. "I'll handle it, Pete. Wait for me in your room. We need to talk."

Jack took the elevator down to the lobby. He spotted her, sitting on the edge of the sofa in the visitors' lounge area by the main entrance.

Wrapped in a trenchcoat, Maggie Costello gripped a purse in her lap. Her blue eyes, still red-rimmed from crying, seemed to focus on the beige carpet. The shoulder-length red hair was combed back, away from her pale, pretty face.

Jack stepped toward her. "Maggie?"

She sprang to her feet. "Listen, I'll tell you the same thing I told that other son of a bitch," she said, glaring at him. "I'm not leaving here until you let me see my brother's room. I don't give a damn about your lousy rules. I just want to be around his things for a few minutes. That's all, then I'll leave."

Jack nodded. "It's all right. I've come to take you up there."

Maggie seemed a little dazed. Her eyes searched his for a moment. "You're Father Murphy, aren't you?"

Jack patted her arm. "Yes, c'mon." He led her toward the elevator.

"I should have recognized you," she murmured. "I'm sorry for the outburst. This other priest wouldn't let me see Johnny's room, and I—"

"It's okay," Jack said. "Don't worry about him."

The elevator arrived. Jack pulled open the accordion-style gate and they stepped inside. The cables rattled and creaked as the elevator began its ascent. Jack stole a glance at Johnny's sister. She was so lovely, he couldn't help staring. His heart broke for her.

She cleared her throat. "I just came from the police station. They had me identify the body. Didn't seem like Johnny anymore."

The elevator stopped, then hovered at the fourth floor. Jack pulled open the door for her, and they started down the narrow corridor. Among those portraits on the walls, the stern-looking priests seemed to be staring at Maggie Costello with utter disapproval.

"I—I recently found a town house for Johnny and me," she said. "But none of his things are there." A tremor crept into her voice. "I just want one more chance to feel close to him. This was his home for the past eight months. If I could only sit in his room for a few minutes . . ."

"Take as long as you want," Jack assured her. He unlocked the door and opened it for her.

Maggie stepped into her little brother's room. Jack watched her wander toward the desk and pick up the framed photo of the two of them.

He quietly closed the door. A moment later, he could hear her crying.

After fifteen minutes, Maggie emerged from the room. She managed to smile at Jack. "I hope you don't mind," she said, her voice raspy. "I'd like to take a couple of things home with me." She was holding the framed photo of her brother and herself, along with a pewter crucifix in a stand that had been on John's desk. "I can't exactly see Johnny buying this," she said. "Does it belong to the school?"

Jack nodded. "All the boys have one in their room. But you go ahead and take it home if you want."

"Thanks." She glanced down at the floor for a moment, then sighed. "Do they know why it happened?" she asked. "Between the police station and here, I stopped on the other side of the lake and talked with this old monsignor. I forget his name. He has these long fingernails—"

"Monsignor Fuller," Jack said.

"Yes. Well, he wasn't any help. I'd like to know why my brother decided to take a midnight swim when the temperature hovered around fifty degrees last night. Where was he coming from? Who was he seeing?"

"I'm trying to find out," Jack said. "As soon as I come up with anything, I'll be in touch with you."

Maggie fished a business card out of her purse and handed it to him. "Thank you, Father."

He shook her hand. "Please, call me Jack. If you need to talk, or just someone to lean on, ring me up, okay?"

Maggie studied him, then she smiled. "I can see now why Johnny liked you so much." She held on to his hand for just a moment longer. "Thank you, Jack."

Down the hall, Peter stepped out of his room.

Maggie glanced over her shoulder at him. "Pete?" Turning, she reached out her hand. "There's my guy. Honey, can you walk me to my car?"

As Peter came up to her, Maggie slid her arm around his waist. They headed toward the elevator together. They seemed to be holding each other up, comforting each other.

Jack stood alone in the hallway and watched them walk away.

He sat in a pale blue Volkswagen beetle parked in the employee lot nearby. The car blended in well with about a dozen other vehicles belonging to the maintenance and cafeteria staffs at St. Bartholomew Hall. The sun reflected off the VW's windshield. No one could see him inside the car.

But he could see them.

They stood next to her car. John Costello's sister and his friend were hugging each other. It looked like both of them were crying, but he couldn't tell for sure at this distance.

He was a bit out of breath. Less than five minutes before, he'd been inside that car of hers. The only thing he'd taken was a business card. He glanced at it now: *Maggie Costello, Realtor—John L. Scott Real Estate.* It listed her business and cell phone numbers, as well as her E-mail address. There was also a photo of her, very pretty.

He watched Maggie Costello climb inside her Saturn and drive away. Costello's friend walked toward the forest.

Slipping the business card in his pocket, he started up the VW. He glanced down at the floor on the passenger side. A Ziploc bag held John Costello's shirt, still damp with lake water from last night. He also had a small container that held two more souvenirs he'd taken off John Costello. They were packed in dry ice.

He pulled out of the lot and started to follow Maggie Costello home.

Chapter Six

"Hey, listen, why don't you just come by?"

"That's not a very good idea," Maggie told her sister over the cell phone. She was driving back from Our Lady of Sorrows, and had just passed the freeway exit for her old house, near the Northgate Shopping Center in Seattle. Her ex-husband, Ray, still lived there.

He'd volunteered to put up Maggie's younger sisters. According to Ray, there was plenty of room for his out-of-town in-laws, even sleeping bags for the kids. Maureen and Grace had quickly taken him up on his offer. Along with Johnny, they'd practically grown up in Ray's house.

"I think you're being spiteful," Maureen told her. "Ray's been a lifesaver today. And he'd like to work things out with you. He told me so. I think you owe it to the family—and Johnny—to put aside your bitterness, and try to make amends. I'm not saying it has to be permanent, though that would be nice. It's just—well, right now, we should all be together, Mag."

One hand clutching the wheel, Maggie stared at the road ahead. "I'm not going back to that house," she said into the phone. "Not ever. It took me too long to leave. I don't want to argue, Maureen. And I won't bad-mouth Ray to you, because I know he's like a second dad to you and Grace. But please, do me a favor, and respect the fact that I can't see him—especially now, when I feel so vulnerable."

Maureen didn't say anything.

"Anyway," Maggie continued. "I don't like to drive and hang on the phone at the same time. I'll be home all night tonight. Johnny's bedroom is empty, in case anyone changes their mind about staying over. We have to talk funeral arrangements. So give me a call later, okay?"

"All right," Maureen grumbled. "So long, Mag."

Maggie switched off the cellular. She surveyed the traffic around her, then sighed. Her sister didn't understand. The five-year difference in their ages had always left a giant chasm between them.

Maggie was fifteen when she'd inherited all the household duties. Her mother was dying of cancer. Maureen was ten; Grace, eight, and the baby, Johnny, hadn't even started walking yet.

Maggie's dad worked the swing shift at the Burlington Northern Repair Track in Seattle. Nearly every evening after work, Tim Costello would go to the Railroader Tavern for his midnight dinner—usually a sandwich or a burger, along with several beers. Tim's drinking buddy was Ray McDermott, a coworker and confirmed bachelor twelve years younger than he. Ray would usually drive Maggie's dad back from their drinking sessions at the Railroader.

At the funeral Mass for Maggie's mother, Ray sat in the first pew, along with the family. Tim Costello had insisted upon it.

Ray always had a present for Maggie on her birthday—along with a card containing some corny poem he'd written about how beautiful she was. Sometimes when he took her dad home, Ray would set a package by her bedroom door. Once it was a pair of earrings, and another time, bath salts.

Maggie knew he had a crush on her, and it was flattering. There weren't any guys in her life. She'd started day-hopping at Seattle Central Community College, and had strategically scheduled classes around the household chores and baby-sitting. She was forever after her younger sisters to do their part of the workload. Maureen and Grace called her "Mag the Nag." They were in high school—with social lives and dates.

Maggie enjoyed all the attention from Ray. She'd won the heart of her father's friend, a man everyone liked. So what if he was eighteen years older than her? Ray was a good-looking guy, tall with wide shoulders and a head of thick, straight blond hair. He had a certain nerdy quality that Maggie found charming and sweet. Still, Maggie used to cringe whenever she heard her father tease Ray about his secret plans to marry her.

Tim Costello wouldn't be alive to see that happen. He dropped dead of a heart attack—in a liquor store's parking lot, of all places. The insurance money he left couldn't see Maggie's younger sisters and Johnny through college. And they had to sell the house.

Meanwhile, Ray bought a place two blocks away: three bedrooms, a family room, and a big yard. He signed the papers the same week they buried Tim Costello.

The first time Ray kissed Maggie was in her father's bedroom. She was cleaning out the closet, giving Ray his pick of her dad's clothes. She started to cry, and Ray kissed her.

He asked Maggie to marry him less than a month later. He wanted her family to move in with him. Everyone thought Ray was a prince for taking care of Tim Costello's kids.

Ray lived up to his reputation as a gentleman on the wedding night. It had been his idea that they wait.

Maggie was a virgin. At the age of twenty-one, she felt backward for her lack of experience. Ray was gentle and patient with her that first night. He even laid out some towels on the hotel bed—in case she bled.

She'd heard that the first time could be painful and awkward, but with a little practice, the fun was supposed to kick in. She wanted to start enjoying it. And she wanted to please Ray.

On the second night of their honeymoon in the San Juan Islands, Maggie bought a black negligee for herself—along with over a dozen candles to place around the hotel room. She set the mood while he showered. Reclining on the bed, she waited for him.

Ray emerged from the bathroom, and he seemed startled to find her so *ready*. He grinned sheepishly at her. Despite his pale skin and bad posture, Ray looked kind of sexy in his boxer shorts. Maggie could see his manhood stirring against the flimsy cotton material.

"You like?" she asked coyly, very much the sexy siren.

In response, Ray let out a stunned laugh. Then he came to the bed. Maggie sat up and started to kiss him.

He pulled away, and shucked down his shorts, setting free his erection. Gently, he eased her back across the bed. Ray peeled down the straps of her negligee. Maggie touched his lips with her fingers, and she kissed him again.

Ray turned his head to one side. Their mouths barely met. For a moment, she thought he was purposely pulling away, but then he made a cute dog-growl sound, and she knew he was excited. Maggie laughed. She ran a hand through his damp hair. "Down, boy," she whispered.

"So sweet," he said, caressing her nipples. Ray bit at her negligee and began to tug it down with his teeth. He let out that playful dog-growl again, and Maggie chuckled. He tugged the negligee down to her waist, but her arms were slightly imprisoned by the thin straps.

Still, Maggie managed to hold his face between her hands and guide him toward her. She started to kiss him again.

"No, don't do that," he muttered.

"What?" she asked. "I was just trying to kiss you—"

He wrestled with her negligee. "Raise your hips, sweetie," he said. "I can't get this damn thing off."

Baffled, she obediently arched her pelvis a bit.

He yanked the lacy garment down past her thighs. One of the shoulder straps broke. He didn't seem to notice. He was staring at the strawberry blond triangle of pubic hair. He moved his hand between her legs.

"Ray, don't you want to kiss me?"

"I don't like kissing a girl once I've fucked her." He swung her legs toward him, then climbed on top of her.

"*What?*" Maggie squirmed beneath him.

"We fucked last night. Okay?" he said impatiently. "We've been through all the bullshit. Now, you're no longer a virgin. So just relax, sweetie. Let's have some fun. And I don't like a lot of talk either." He guided himself inside her.

Maggie winced. She didn't say anything. She didn't try to kiss him either.

It never got to be fun.

From that moment on, Maggie no longer saw any charm or sweetness in her nerdy husband. She figured financial security and the welfare of her siblings were a reasonable trade-off for the lack of passion in her marriage.

Five years after Maggie had promised "for better and for worse," the railroad cut back Ray's hours at the repair track. By that time, both of her younger sisters were away at college, and Johnny was in junior high school. Maggie had earned her real-estate license, and now she became the bread-winner.

To hear Ray tell it, her "little job" at the real-estate office kept Maggie from being bored. It was good for her to get out of the kitchen. But he was pretty darn tired of settling for TV dinners while she was out showing houses at night. And her kid brother was turning into a real wiseass punk.

The two men in Maggie's life managed to tolerate each other, but an undercurrent of tension persisted between them. Johnny was only thirteen, but close enough to his big sister to realize that she was miserable with Ray. He often wondered aloud why she didn't just leave him.

"He's always acting like we *owe* him something," Johnny pointed out one night, when Maggie was driving him home from bowling. They'd just dropped off his best friend, Peter.

"Well, we do owe him," Maggie replied, shrugging. Both hands on the wheel, she studied the road. "Ray came to our rescue after Dad died. He gave us a house to live in, and helped pay Maureen and Grace's college tuition. I wouldn't like myself very much if I suddenly dumped him just because he's down on his luck right now."

"Yeah, but he treats you like crap," Johnny replied, slouched in the passenger seat.

Maggie stole a glance at him. "He treats you okay, doesn't he? I mean, you'd tell me if he ever hit you or anything, wouldn't you?"

Johnny chuckled. "I'd like to see him try."

After a moment, he turned toward his sister. "Has Ray ever taken a swing at *you?*"

"Oh, God, no," Maggie said.

"Reason I ask is a couple of weeks back you had that puffy eye thing. I thought maybe he gave you a shiner, but I didn't want to say anything. I figured—"

"Johnny, I told you that was an eye infection."

She was lying, of course.

She blamed the black eye on Ray's drinking. More specifically, she blamed herself for getting in the way of his drinking. Ray's doctor had ordered him off the booze. That Sunday afternoon two weeks before, she'd made the mistake of mentioning to Ray that pouring himself a third scotch might be in violation of his doctor's mandate.

In response, Ray threw his chaser—a glass of amber ale—in her face. Maggie called him an asshole, or something to that effect. She wasn't quite sure what she said. She had her eyes closed. Dark beer was dripping from her face, down the front of her favorite blouse for work, a pale green, Donna Karan number. She didn't see him coming at her. She didn't see him draw back his hand. She only felt something hard smack her in the eye. The force of it knocked her down.

Ray had already started apologizing before Maggie even realized what had just happened.

"Looked more like a shiner to me," Johnny muttered, tipping his head back and propping one foot up on the dashboard.

"No, it was an eye infection," Maggie insisted.

"All the same," Johnny said. "I could get along without Ray just fine. You sell a ton of houses. Maybe you could find a place for the two of us. We'd do okay, Mag. . . ."

It would be another five years before she fully realized Johnny's plan.

Maggie parked the car and wandered up the walkway to the front door of her town house. The place really didn't have much personality yet. There was a fireplace in the living room, a large basement, and two bedrooms upstairs. Maggie managed to appropriate a few pieces of furniture that had been in the family for years: a desk, an easy chair, a sofa and coffee table. They'd seen better days. She'd been waiting for Johnny to help her pick out some new furniture.

Though she'd spent all her time there alone, the place felt particularly empty tonight. Maggie told herself not to blame her sisters for wanting to stay with Ray. They didn't understand about her and her ex-husband. Johnny was the only one who had an idea of what she'd gone through. He was the only one.

Maggie peeled off her coat and started to cry.

She cleared off a spot on the desk for Johnny's crucifix. Unlike Ray's house, her new place was deliberately void of any religious knickknacks. She'd stopped going to Mass, because practically everyone in her old parish had turned their backs on her for leaving good ol' Ray.

Yet when she'd seen that ugly, skinny crucifix on Johnny's desk this afternoon, Maggie had needed to take it home. She wasn't certain why. Maybe because it belonged to Johnny. Or perhaps right now she just needed to lean on her faith a little bit, and not feel so all alone.

Maggie wiped her eyes and blew her nose. She found a place on the side table for the picture of her and Johnny. It was a cute photo that she'd never seen before. But the frame was one of those cheap, ugly, drug store jobs with faux-gold trim.

She had several elegant frames that once held photos of her and Ray. Amid the collection, Maggie found one to complement the picture. She sat down at the desk and began to disassemble Johnny's cheap frame. As she removed the backing, Maggie gasped. She stared at what her little brother had hidden in there—behind their photograph.

Maggie had never actually handled so many one-hundred-dollar bills in her life, but now she was counting out twenty-two of them. She examined the bills to make sure they weren't fake.

Dazed, she wondered out loud, *"How on earth did Johnny get all this money?"*

It was almost ten o'clock when Jack locked up the boat-house. He'd just returned across the lake, where he'd visited one of the dorms, asking around about Johnny—if anyone knew him, if there had been any parties last night. He'd bought a green pocket-size notebook to jot down all the information, and he had the packet of photos from Johnny's desk. He must have shown Johnny's picture to a hundred students. Nothing. No leads. The little notebook was empty.

A mist hovered over Lake Leroy, and Jack could see his breath as he started toward St. Bartholomew Hall. The night clouds swept across the sky, and moonlight danced across the lone, impassive building. A few of those gargoyle-like saints along the top floor seemed to come alive for a moment as the light moved over them.

A curtain closed in one of the fourth-floor windows. It was Peter Tobin's room. Peter had managed to give him the slip after walking Maggie Costello to her car. He'd totally disappeared again.

Inside St. Bartholomew Hall, Jack trotted up the stairs to the fourth floor. A sliver of light showed beneath Peter's door. He knocked, then waited. "Pete?"

Silence.

"Pete, I know you're in there," he called.

The door swung open, and Peter frowned at him. He wore jeans and a sweatshirt. He'd taken the posters down from his wall, and on the bed was an open suitcase, half-packed.

"What's going on?" Jack asked.

"I'm leaving," Peter replied. He moved to his dresser, and started emptying out a drawer. "Johnny's the only reason I came to this stupid school. Now he's gone. So I'm taking off."

Jack stepped into the room and closed the door behind him. "What did you mean this morning when you said Johnny's drowning was 'no accident'?"

"I don't remember saying anything," Peter replied, not looking at Jack.

"You know something about John's death. Why won't

you tell me, Pete? Why have you been avoiding me all day?"

Peter dropped a stack of T-shirts in his suitcase. "My best friend is dead. I'd like to be left alone in my grief, if that's okay."

"It's not okay," Jack replied. "I'm trying to find out why Johnny died. And every time I ask you a question about it, I don't get a straight answer. You're not the only one who's grieving here. Johnny was my friend, too."

Frowning, Peter went on packing his suitcase.

"Do you know if he was meeting someone over on the campus side? Maybe a girlfriend?" Jack took the envelope from his coat pocket and found the photo of the brunet girl, the modest one taken outside. He showed it to Peter. "Do you know this girl?"

Peter glanced at the picture and frowned. "No. Who is she?"

"That's what I'm trying to find out. I think John knew her pretty well. Could she be a girlfriend he had in Seattle?"

Peter curled his lip at the photo. "I doubt it. Johnny could do a lot better. Whoever she is, she's probably a local. That purple awning in the background, it's to the arcade near the minimall across the lake."

Jack checked the picture again, then tucked it in his pocket. "Thanks. I wouldn't have known that."

Peter went back to his suitcase and shut it.

"For what it's worth, Pete, I don't think Johnny's death was an accident either. I need your help. It's one reason I want you to stay."

Peter reached for the suitcase latches to secure them, but he hesitated.

"Do you really want to leave here, not knowing why Johnny died?" Jack asked. "If you were the one who drowned, I'm guessing Johnny would bust his ass to find out why it happened. Do you think he'd up and leave school not knowing?''

Peter wandered over to his window and stared out at the lake.

''At least be practical,'' Jack continued. ''If you leave school now, you'll have to repeat the whole semester somewhere else. Why not just stick it out for the five weeks we have left?''

Peter nodded wearily. ''I hear you, Father. I—I'll think about it.'' He rubbed his eyes. ''Y'know, I really need to be alone right now.''

Jack patted him on the shoulder. ''I'm just down the hall if you want to talk. I promise, no third degree.''

He stepped out to the hallway and closed the door. As he moved toward his room, Jack could hear muffled crying. But the farther he moved away from Peter's room, the louder the tortured weeping became. It wasn't Peter he heard, but someone else toward the other end of the corridor.

Jack stopped dead. Five rooms down, the door to Room 410 was open a crack. Silently, it seemed to move by itself, opening a bit wider. The light in the hallway flickered once.

Jack felt the hairs on the back of his neck stand up. He moved toward Room 410, and the sound of a young man crying. The room was dark. He slowly pushed the door open. ''Johnny?'' he heard himself whisper.

The crying stopped.

Jack switched on the light. He gazed at the stacks of boxes, a few of them open to reveal old schoolbooks, dusty candle holders, a battered statue of St. Francis. The room was deathly cold. There wasn't anything particularly mystical about that. They'd turned off the radiator in this room years ago.

But Jack couldn't explain away the crying, or why he felt compelled to whisper Johnny's name. The door should have been locked. Besides himself, the only people who had keys to this room were the custodian, Duane, and Father Zeigler.

Jack turned toward the open door and jiggled the outside knob. It didn't move. The door was on the catch, still locked.

He gave one last look at Gerard Lunt's old quarters, then switched off the light and closed the door.

Other people had heard crying come from that room. Other people had brushes with the unexplainable when they stepped inside or merely passed Room 410. Now he had his own story to tell—only Jack didn't think he'd ever share it with anyone.

Jack heard his phone ringing as he started down the hall. By the time he unlocked and opened his door, the answering machine was picking up. Jack hurried to his desk and snatched up the receiver. "Yes, hello?" he said.

"Father Murphy?" It was a woman calling.

"Yes?"

"Jack, it's ... John's sister, Maggie Costello. I hope I didn't wake you—"

"No, not at all," Jack replied. "Did you make it home okay?"

"Yes, thanks," she said. "The reason I'm calling is ... well, I found some money Johnny had hidden behind that picture I took today. Twenty-two hundred dollars. I'm wondering how he got it."

"I have no idea," Jack murmured. "I can ask Peter about it in the morning. He might know."

"Thanks, Father," she said. "Oh, and thank you again for helping me out this afternoon."

"I didn't do much," Jack said. "I'll call you in the morning. All right?"

"That would be great. Good night."

* * *

Maggie hung up with Father Murphy. She'd already talked with both her sisters tonight. They'd been too tired to come over, and opted to discuss funeral arrangements with her tomorrow. Maureen had made another halfhearted attempt to lure her to Ray's house. He'd been outside, bundled up in his jacket, barbecuing steaks for everyone. *Good ol' Ray.*

Maggie had said she would just as soon skip it.

She hadn't eaten since breakfast. There was nothing in her refrigerator, so she jumped into her car and drove seven blocks to Parker's Pantry. They were open until midnight. The place was a bit of a dive. But they were cheap, fast, and the food came in large portions. Plus they made a great French dip. Maggie ordered it to go.

She'd come to rely on Parker's Pantry when too tired to cook—which was often. She knew most of the waitresses there. But when the new girl, Lucy, asked how she was tonight, Maggie managed a smile and said she was fine. She didn't tell her, *My baby brother drowned today.* She didn't want to start crying in this cheesy little restaurant.

Lucy handed her the carryout bag. Maggie tipped her a couple of bucks and wandered out to the car.

She didn't notice the priest who had stepped inside the restaurant a few minutes before. He'd seated himself at a table near the window.

He was now staring out at the parking lot. The headlights from Maggie's car swept across his face for a moment. It was a handsome face. Lucy certainly thought so.

A thirty-four-year-old divorcée, she had an eye for the cute guys—and vice versa. Lucy was pretty, with a shapely figure that got noticed in the restaurant, because she wore her brown waitress uniform one size too small. She had blue eyes and shoulder-length, tawny auburn hair, which she had to keep fastened in back with a barrette while at work. More than once, she'd been told she looked like Jane Fonda. She wasn't a very good waitress, but Lucy usually went home at night with more money in tips than her coworkers—plus a phone number or two.

Doreen, the older waitress on duty tonight, didn't understand her interest in this priest. "Okay, yeah, he's really cute," she whispered to Lucy. They stood near the kitchen door, staring at him from across the restaurant. "But there's the age difference thing, and more importantly, hon, he's a priest, a man of the cloth."

"I'd like to make him a man of my sheets," Lucy replied.

"You're going straight to hell, hon."

"Oh, it's fun flirting with a priest. And he's so cute. He makes me want to do something sinful. Oh, he just looked at me. To be continued . . ."

Lucy sauntered toward his table. She put her hand on the back of his chair. "What can I get for you tonight, Father?" she asked.

The way he smiled at her, the handsome priest was flirting right back. He drummed his fingertips on the cover of the closed menu. "A cheeseburger deluxe and a Miller Lite, please," he said. "And maybe you can help me with something else, too."

Lucy let out a little laugh. She touched his shoulder for a moment. "What might that be?"

"The woman who just left, the redhead. Is she a regular customer?"

Lucy frowned a little. "Yeah, she's been in here before."

"I think I might know her," the priest went on. "Her name's Maggie. She's a real estate agent. Does she ever come in here with anyone?"

Sighing, Lucy snatched his menu off the table. "No, she's usually alone. I think she's divorced. I'll be back with your beer, padre."

"Wait a second," he said, reaching out to touch her arm. Lucy turned around. "Yes?"

His eyes met hers. "I just wanted to see you smile again."

He glanced at her name tag. "You have a beautiful smile, Lucy. Is that your name, Lucy? Not Lucille?"

She laughed a little. "That's it, just plain Lucy."

"There's nothing plain about you. Did you know that there's a St. Lucy? She was a virgin martyr."

Lucy grinned at him.

She didn't know enough to take him seriously.

Chapter Seven

"No, there haven't really been any new developments," Irene McShane told the reporter over the telephone. She'd taken the call in her daughter-in-law's study so her grandsons wouldn't overhear the conversation. "You might ask the police about it," she suggested. "I can't tell you anything, except we're still praying for Dorothy's safe return."

"Even after all this time?" the reporter asked. He was with one of the Seattle papers. He'd called, saying that an article on Dorothy's disappearance might revive some interest in the case.

But Irene had serious doubts a newspaper story could bring her daughter-in-law back. The police seemed to have exhausted all avenues of their investigation. She might have helped by telling them about Dorothy's diary, and Our Lady of Sorrows. But she couldn't.

After finding the journal nine weeks ago, Irene had combed through the house in search of those mysterious missing pages. She never found them. But in the bottom drawer of that old desk in the sewing room she'd unearthed a bill from a clinic in California. It was dated three weeks before Dorothy's disappearance, at a time when Dorothy had been on a two-day business trip to Seattle—or so she'd claimed. The patient name on the form was an obvious fake. Dorothy must have been thinking of her sons, Michael and Aaron, when she'd visited the clinic.

The bill had been paid in cash by the patient, Michelle Aarons. The procedure was a TAB. Irene found out later that was the code for a therapeutic abortion.

Past the fake name and a fake California address, Irene saw the truth. Her conservative daughter-in-law, the churchgoing judge who sewed her son's school clothes, had undergone an abortion. And if the cryptic notes in Dorothy's journal were any indication, the man who had impregnated her was a priest at Our Lady of Sorrows.

One night last month, Irene had waited until the boys went to bed, then she'd made a fire in the fireplace of her daughter-in-law's study. She'd burnt all of Dorothy's journals—along with that bill from the clinic in California. It was what Dorothy would have wanted. Uncovering the circumstances of her death would also uncover Dorothy's secret shame, and Irene wasn't about to do that to her.

"Mrs. McShane?" the reporter said. "I don't mean to sound tactless, but it's been three months since her disappearance, and there are still no leads. Do you really believe Judge McShane could still be alive?"

"As I said, I'm praying for her safe return," Irene answered carefully. "Now, I'm sorry, but I have to be going, Mr. Myers. Thank you for your interest. . . ."

Once Irene hung up, she sat back in her daughter-in-law's desk chair and gazed over at the fireplace. They hadn't made a fire in there since that night she'd burned the journals last month. Nor had the maid cleaned it out. The ashes were still there.

Someone—or something—at Our Lady of Sorrows was responsible for Dorothy's death. As much as Irene tried to cover that up, it was an undeniable fact she couldn't forget. Those ashes could never be swept away.

It was 3:20 in the afternoon when Maggie's sister finally called her back. Maggie had already left two messages on her ex-husband's answering machine. She and her sisters needed to make funeral arrangements for Johnny.

"Ray's taken care of everything, Mag," Maureen told her. "The wake is at J. Tilden on Monday. And the funeral Mass will be Tuesday—at St. Joe's, of course—"

"Ray took care of everything?" Maggie murmured into the phone.

"Yes, and before you get all pissy, Mag, he's offered to foot the bill."

"But that isn't right," Maggie said. "He's no longer a part of the family. The three of us—Grace, you and I— we're responsible for the funeral. This is our little brother. Ray and Johnny weren't even talking to each other in the last eight months. Yet Ray is planning everything for Johnny's funeral? It isn't right."

"Well, Grace and I have families of our own. We can't exactly afford a big, fancy funeral for Johnny. Ray offered, and I think it's extremely generous of him—"

"Ray can't afford it either," Maggie said. "I'm the one who will have to pay for Johnny's funeral. And I wish I'd had some say in the preparations."

"Well, that's something you should discuss with Ray," Maureen said.

Maggie bit her lip. She put a hand over the mouthpiece to stifle herself.

"Anyway," Maureen went on, "the school called. They

have Johnny's stuff packed. I really don't have time to drive
up there today and—''

"I'll do it," Maggie said. "I need to do *something,* for
God's sakes."

During the drive up to Leroy, Maggie remembered what
Johnny had said when they'd moved out of Ray's house:
*"We have to stick together, Mag. We're the only family we
got."* With him gone, she felt so alone.

Father Murphy had left a message on her answering
machine this morning. Peter didn't know anything about the
twenty-two hundred dollars Johnny had tucked away. "But
I'll keep looking into it," Father Murphy had assured her.
"If I find out anything, I won't leave you in the dark. I'll
let you know right away."

She'd felt a connection to Father Murphy yesterday—an
attraction or maybe a kinship, Maggie wasn't able to put
her finger on it. She just knew she wanted to see him again.
Maybe then, she wouldn't feel so all alone and in the dark.

The blue Volkswagen was three cars behind Maggie Costello's Saturn. Its driver had been watching her town house
since seven o'clock this morning. Maggie hadn't been out
at all day—not until about an hour ago. Now she was driving
north on Interstate 5. She seemed to be heading up to the
seminary.

While following Maggie Costello, he didn't want to think
about last night. He still stank from that waitress's cheap
perfume. Getting her into bed had hardly been a challenge.
He wondered if he'd picked up any diseases from her. He
couldn't wait to get home and wash her stink off.

Maggie Costello was leading him back home. He would
put Lucy out of his mind and focus on Maggie. She probably
smelled very nice. She excited him. Maggie was the more
important kill. Blue-ribbon prey.

* * *

The resident advisers on the first two floors of St. Jude Hall had never heard of John Costello—not until the drowning yesterday. Jack focused on St. Jude Hall this afternoon, because it was considered a "party" dorm. If Johnny had been swimming back from a kegger on Wednesday night, the party had probably been at St. Jude's.

Jack trudged up to the third floor and checked his listing from the school's administration office. The resident adviser for this wing was Greg Axelrod, Room 304. Jack heard disco music as he approached the room.

He knocked on the door, and the music was tuned down. The door swung open. Greg looked startled for a moment, but then he seemed to recognize Jack. Tall and solidly built, Greg had pale skin and short curly brown hair. He wore jeans and a T-shirt that had a can of Spam pictured on the front.

"Greg, I'm Father Murphy from St. Bartholomew Hall, across the way." Jack started to pull out the photo of Johnny. "I'd like to ask you a few quick questions. Do you know if anyone in the dorm was having a party on Wednesday night?"

Warily, Greg glanced past Jack. A few doors down the hallway, another seminarian stepped out of his room. Jack peered over his shoulder and caught the other young man staring at them.

"Not here," Greg whispered.

"Can I meet you someplace?" Jack said, under his breath.

"Do you know where the St. Sebastian grotto is—in the cemetery?" he whispered.

"Yes."

"See you there in ten minutes," Greg murmured. "Be alone." He took another cautious glance at the young man loitering in the hall, then shook his head at Jack. "I'm sorry

I can't help you, Father,'' he said in a loud voice. He stepped back and closed the door on him.

The St. Sebastian grotto was one of four rock-shelter shrines in the cemetery on the college side. The dark, igloolike sanctuary housed a large statue of St. Sebastian, illuminated by a shaft of light pouring through a strategically located window. A long wooden kneeler stretched in front of the statue. There was also a stone bench by the wall. The little hut smelled muddy, but at least it provided some protection from the cold drizzle outside.

Jack gazed at the statue of the young St. Sebastian in his martyrdom. The coloring on the statue had drastically faded, so the gray loincloth seemed to blend with the ashen flesh tones. Only traces of washed-out scarlet were visible where blood oozed from his arrow wounds. A couple of arrows protruding from Sebastian had been broken off.

An officer in the imperial guard of Rome, Sebastian had been shot with arrows for being a Christian. His executioners had left him for dead, but he survived. The widow of another martyr healed Sebastian's wounds. But when the imperial guard learned of this, they tracked him down and battered him to death with clubs.

People didn't remember the last part. They just knew how St. Sebastian was depicted in so many Renaissance paintings: the near-naked young man punctured with several arrows, looking up to the heavens. People remembered the miracle of his survival, but forgot that after all his sufferings, poor Sebastian was beaten to death. Some miracle.

Jack heard somebody coming, footsteps on the gravel trail. Greg Axelrod hesitated at the archway entrance. He wore a sweatshirt and a baseball hat.

"It's okay," Jack said. "I'm alone. Just St. Sebastian and me. Thanks for coming."

The young man glanced over his shoulder, then stepped into the grotto. "Sorry I couldn't talk before. I heard you were asking around about John Costello. I figured you'd be knocking on my door soon enough."

Jack sat down on the stone bench. "This was a good suggestion. We can speak more freely here."

Greg shrugged. "I'm not sure what you expect me to tell you, Father. I didn't really know John Costello. And I don't know anything about a party on Wednesday night either."

Jack managed to smile at him. "Well, Greg, you could have told me that back at the dorm. You suggested we come here. You must have something you want to share with me."

Greg shook his head. "Not really."

"Then why are we here?"

Leaning against the rock wall by the grotto entry, Greg looked down at the ground. "Well, Mike McGoldrick was in the hallway," he muttered. "I didn't want him to think I was telling you ... stuff."

"What kind of 'stuff' are you talking about? Information about John Costello?" Jack could see he wasn't getting anywhere. He moved over and made room for him on the stone bench. "Here, take a load off."

Greg seemed embarrassed as he shuffled over to the bench and sat beside Jack. He was even blushing.

"I think you want to talk to me, otherwise we wouldn't be here."

Greg had a strange, tentative smile on his face. He shook his head.

"I'll make it easier for you," Jack said. "Repeat after me, *'Bless me, Father, for I have sinned, my last confession was ...'* " He nudged Greg. "Tell me what's on your mind, and I'll take it as a confession. I'm bound by my holy vows not to repeat it to anyone. You're protected by the sanctity of the confessional. No one will ever know we talked. C'mon, Greg. What do you want to tell me?"

Greg was trembling. "Um, I think I know who might have killed John Costello," he said.

"Who?" Jack asked.

"It's this guy I used to mess around with, a sophomore named Rick Pettinger."

"What do you mean 'used to mess around with'?"

Greg let out a nervous laugh. He took off his baseball hat, then ran his hand over his short, brown hair. "Huh, what do you think it means?"

"It sounds like you two guys were having sex."

"Are you shocked?"

"Well, I don't think you're the first seminarians to ever try it," Jack said. "I know the score, Greg. Even back in the Dark Ages when I attended the seminary, I had a pretty good idea what was going on in some of the rooms."

Greg shook his head. "Oh, you'd never catch Rick Pettinger doing the deed in his room. Too many guys coming and going in the hallways. For closet cases like Rick, the last thing they want is someone finding out they're queer. No, we'd sneak off to these remote places and do it. The creepier the spot, the safer it was. Rick's totally paranoid. He used to swear me to secrecy whenever we got together. He even threatened me a few times. Once when I kidded him about telling somebody what we were doing, he pulled a knife and put it to my throat. He was crazy." Greg glanced up at the statue, then sighed. "I must have been nuts myself—to keep meeting with him. But Rick's really handsome. Guess I must go for psychos or something."

"What does all this have to do with John Costello?" Jack asked.

"He and Rick were seeing each other."

Jack shook his head. "You must be mistaken."

Greg gave him a wry smile. "I thought you knew the score, Father."

"You're telling me that John Costello and your friend, Rick, were sexually involved?"

Greg nodded. "Rick and I broke up back in October, then he started seeing John Costello right after that. I know, because I used to follow Rick around." He rolled his eyes. "To be honest, I guess I was stalking him. But one night, I saw Rick meet John Costello by the window to the church basement."

Jack frowned. "Where?"

"There's this window to the church basement, the lock's broken. I used to meet Rick there. We'd go into the catacombs under the church. Like I said, the creepier the place, the less likely we'd be caught with our pants down."

"You had sex in the catacombs?" Jack asked, incredulous.

"Yeah. And I know he met John Costello there several nights."

Jack kept shaking his head.

"John was also working on a couple of other guys," Greg continued. "I used to watch him, too, hoping I'd find something to rub in Rick's face. Anyway, I spotted him ducking into that basement window on different occasions with those other guys."

"Who were these 'other guys'?" Jack asked.

Greg gave him a wary glance. "This is confession, right?"

Jack nodded.

"Terry Gillis and Ted Patchett. They're both sophomores on the same floor at St. Clement Hall with Rick. I don't think any of them knew they were messing around with the same freshman. That's how secretive and paranoid they are."

"Do you know if John might have been seeing anyone else besides these three sophomores?"

Greg shrugged. "I can't say for sure. One thing about the kid, he was discreet. But maybe Rick didn't think so. Maybe

Rick found out about the others. When John Costello turned up drowned yesterday, I kept remembering all those times Rick threatened me. I tell you, he's dangerous.''

Jack got to his feet and paced in front of the statue of St. Sebastian.

"You can't repeat any of this, you know," Greg said.

"I know," Jack replied. He didn't want to repeat any of it.

"You don't believe me, do you?"

"That's not it," Jack said. "I just thought I knew John Costello better."

"And now you have to adjust to the idea that he was queer, is that it?"

Jack frowned. "I wouldn't put it that way."

Greg let out a cynical laugh. "You think I'm nuts. I stalk people, so I'm not past telling these great big lies. Or maybe I'm just trying to get even with Rick for dumping me. Believe me, Father, I'm not out for revenge."

"Then what do you want?" Jack asked. "I can't pass this information along to anyone else. You must have some reason for telling me."

"I just want someone else to know," Greg replied in a shaky voice. "Maybe then, I won't feel so all alone in this, and I can stop worrying."

"Worrying about what?"

Greg gazed up at him. "That I'll be next."

Chapter Eight

The dinner crowd started trickling into the Lakeside Inn Grill. The local news ran muted on the TV behind the bar. Maggie sat alone at a table by the window. She watched darkness fall over the landscape. The lake in which her brother had drowned seemed to turn silver-black.

Maggie sipped her bourbon. One drink—just one—before heading back to Seattle, that was the plan.

She needed it. After the long drive up to Leroy, she'd found her only welcoming committee was that swaggering macho creep, Father Zeigler. She asked to take another look at Johnny's room before they packed up his things. Zeigler acted as if she were trying to sneak into a movie without paying. He claimed that Father Murphy shouldn't have taken her up there yesterday. Besides, she was too late. He'd already assigned a couple of students to pack John's things, and they were almost finished.

Maggie asked if she could talk to Peter Tobin or Father Murphy, but the snarly little priest said they were out.

A couple of students came down in the elevator with boxes full of Johnny's things. It took them three trips to load Maggie's station wagon. All the while, Father Zeigler said nothing to her. When the boys finished, Zeigler followed her outside. "I'm praying for the repose of John's soul," he told her, his tone sickeningly self-righteous.

Maggie hesitated before climbing into her car. "Pray for your own soul," she heard herself say. "What made an insensitive jerk like you think you'd be a good priest?"

Zeigler piously stared at her with half-closed eyes. "I'll attribute that comment to the fact that you're grieving."

"No," Maggie said. "Attribute it to the fact that you're an insensitive jerk."

Those were her parting words to Father Zeigler. She drove off feeling triumphant—for about fifteen seconds. Then she started crying. She pulled over to the side of the road, leaned on the wheel, and sobbed. After a few minutes, she sat back and wiped her tears.

That was when she'd decided she needed a drink before heading back to Seattle.

"How are you doing here?" the waitress asked.

Maggie turned from the window and looked up at the stocky middle-aged woman with brassy red hair. "I'm okay for now," she said with a pale smile.

"Are you visiting a cousin or a brother at the college?" the waitress asked.

Maggie hesitated.

"The reason I ask is, I haven't seen you around. Hardly anyone comes here unless it's to see one of the boys at seminary. You look way too young to have a son in college."

"My brother's a freshman here," Maggie said.

"Then he's at St. Bartholomew Hall. Did you hear what happened? One of the boys drowned in the lake night before last. They managed to keep it off the news. Just like that other kid three years ago."

"Another boy drowned?" Maggie asked.

"Yeah, and they hushed that up, too. I tell you, I've been working here practically since the Stone Age, and every year or two, something happens at St. Bart's—a suicide, or an accident, or some tragedy. It's weird. They say the place is cursed. And you know what? I believe it."

Maggie glanced out the window at that silver-black lake.

"Oh, but listen to me go on," she heard the waitress say. "It's no way for me to talk when you have a brother staying there. I'm sure he'll be fine."

Maggie nodded absently, then she slid her empty glass toward the edge of the table. "Can I have another, please?"

"No, I've ever seen him before," Terry Gillis said, studying the photo of John Costello. The young man had an olive complexion and close-cropped black hair. He was husky, with a slight beer gut. Jack figured Terry was a party animal. One wall of his dorm room was lined with makeshift shelf after shelf of empty beer bottles, all various brands. Standing at the threshold of the room, Jack could smell stale cigarettes.

"He doesn't even look familiar?" Jack asked. "Why don't you take another gander at the picture?"

Terry gave the snapshot back to him. "Sorry, I can't help you, Father."

Terry Gillis was one of the three sophomores who'd allegedly had sex with Johnny. Jack couldn't repeat any of Greg's "confession" in the grotto. The only way he could act on the information was to visit St. Clement Hall's third floor, and go from room to room, asking each resident if he knew John Costello.

He still didn't want to believe Greg's story. So far, none of the sophomores he'd interviewed on this floor had heard of John Costello until news of the drowning yesterday. Like Terry, they didn't recognize his photograph either.

Jack put the photo back in his pocket. "Listen, Terry, do you know anyone else who might have hung around with him?"

"Who? Costello?" He shrugged. "No, like I say, I've never even seen him before."

Jack nodded at the beer bottle collection against the wall. "I see you've accrued a lot of dead soldiers there. You must know where all the parties are. Did you hear if there was something going on around here on Wednesday night? Anything at all on campus?"

Terry shook his head. "Sorry, Father. I was working on a term paper in the library on Wednesday night. I save my partying for the weekends." He glanced past Jack, at someone else in the hallway.

Jack turned and saw a strapping, Nordic-blond man approaching them. He was good-looking with deep-set blue eyes, and an impressive physique. Obviously, he'd just been working out. He wore track shorts and a torn, sleeveless sweatshirt, stained with perspiration. "Hi, Father," he said, extending his hand. "I'm Anton Sorenson, the R.A. for this floor. Is Terry in trouble? Has he been stealing wine from the sacristy again?"

He had a sweaty, bone-crunching handshake. Jack smiled at his joke. "No, he's okay." He turned to Terry. "If you hear anything or suddenly remember something that might help me out, could you give me a call at St. Bartholomew Hall?"

"Sure thing, Father." Terry gave his R.A. a narrow-eyed grin. "Wiseass," he muttered. He stepped back into his room and shut the door.

"You're from St. Bart's?" Anton asked.

Jack nodded. "I'm Father Murphy. I was hoping one of your residents could shed some light on what happened with that drowning yesterday."

Anton Sorenson wiped his shiny forehead. "Oh, boy, I'm

such an ass. I'm sorry. I'm making with the jokes, and you're here on serious business. The kid's name was John Costello, right?"

"That's right." Jack pulled out the photo of Johnny. "Seems he might have been returning from a party or visiting a friend here on this side of the campus. I'm trying to track down who might have seen him last."

Anton glanced at the picture. "Oh, yeah, I know him. He used to hang around here. But I didn't see him Wednesday night. I wasn't here. Hey, you know who we should ask? Rick Pettinger. He and this Costello guy used to pal around together." Anton cocked his head to one side. "Rick's room is just down the hall. I'm pretty sure he's in. C'mon."

Anton started up the hallway and knocked on the door to Room 311. "Hey, Rick?" he called.

The door opened. Despite a slightly pockmarked complexion, Rick Pettinger was a tall, good-looking kid with green eyes and wavy black hair. He wore a pressed yellow oxford shirt and jeans. Wide-eyed, he gazed at Anton, then at Jack. "What's going on?"

"Hey, Rick-o, this is Father Murphy from St. Bart's," Anton started in. "He just wants to ask you some questions about your buddy who drowned, John Costello."

"What?" Rick stepped back. "John Costello? I—I hardly knew him at all."

Anton stepped into the room. "Oh, come on, I've seen you two guys hanging around together."

"Well, you're mistaken," Rick replied, an edge to his voice. "I didn't know him."

Anton laughed. "Oh, you lie like a rug! What are you trying to pull here? You are so full of it. What's going on? What are you hiding?"

"Anton, I'd like to talk with Rick alone," Jack said. "Thanks for your help. You can go now."

Anton shrugged, then he started for the door. "Okay,

Father. But don't believe a word he says.'' He turned in the doorway and glared at Rick Pettinger. ''You're lying to a priest, y'know. Talk about morally bankrupt. You better come clean, mister.''

''Okay, Anton, bye,'' Jack said, closing the door on him. He turned to Rick Pettinger. ''*'Morally bankrupt.'* I've never heard that one before. Have you?''

Rick regarded him with visible wariness.

Jack glanced around the room for a moment. There was a print of Salvador Dalí's *The Sacrament of the Last Supper* over the bed, and he spotted a couple of books about Marilyn Monroe on the shelf. On the desk was a half-full ashtray and a pack of Winston Lights.

Jack turned and gave the young man a reassuring smile. ''Anton was way out of line. This is no formal investigation. I'm just trying to find out what John Costello was doing on Wednesday night. They think he might have been with a friend here—or at a party. They're simply looking for an explanation, that's all.''

Rick sat on the edge of his bed. ''Well, I hardly knew him. In fact, when I heard about the drowning yesterday, I didn't connect him to the guy who hung around the hallway from time to time. I certainly didn't see him here on Wednesday night.'' He shrugged. ''I don't know what else I can tell you, Father.''

''If he hung around here, as you say, who do you think he was seeing?''

''I have no idea,'' Rick answered. ''I mean, I didn't even know Johnny Costello.''

Jack stared at him for a moment. ''But you knew him well enough to call him Johnny.''

''Johnny, John, what's the difference?''

''It's the difference between a friend and someone you might notice in the corridor from time to time. Why would Anton be so insistent that you and John were buddies?''

"I don't know," Rick grunted. "He's crazy."

"Did you ever hear any rumors about John Costello meeting with certain guys on this floor to have sex?"

Rick took a deep breath and quickly shook his head. "I don't associate with queers. And as for John Costello—or Johnny—or whatever you want to call him, I barely knew the kid. How many times do I have to tell you?"

With a sigh, Jack grabbed a pen from the desk. "Okay, listen," he said. "I'm giving you my phone number at St. Bartholomew Hall." He jotted it down on Rick's memo pad. "If you suddenly remember something, or if you need to change your story, you know where to reach me."

"I'm not changing my story," Rick said. "Why would I do that?"

"Because what you've been telling me so far is a lie," Jack said. He started toward the door. "You know it, Rick. I know it, and so does your R.A., Anton. When you're ready to start telling me the truth, I'll do everything I can to cut you a break and keep it confidential. Call me."

Jack stepped out to the hallway and closed Rick's door.

Anton Sorenson was waiting for him. He'd taken off his sweatshirt, and now had a towel draped over his shoulder. He seemed to like showing off his physique. "Did he tell you anything, Father?" Anton asked, hands on hips.

"No," Jack said, figuring it was none of his business.

"I was trying the good-cop-bad-cop routine. Didn't it help any?"

Jack managed to smile. "Oh, that's what you were doing. Sorry, it didn't take."

Anton shrugged. "Well, for what it's worth, I know he's lying. I wish I knew the reason. Did he say where he was on Wednesday night?"

"I didn't ask him."

"Well, pardon me for being a big buttinski, but if I were

you, Father, I'd be asking every guy on this floor where he was on Wednesday night.''

Jack considered it for a moment. "All right. You mentioned that you weren't here. Where were you? Why weren't you on R.A. duty?"

Anton chuckled. "This isn't St. Bart's, Father. They don't have you on such a tight leash at these upperclassman dorms. I signed out for the night, borrowed a friend's car, and drove down to Seattle."

"What was going on in Seattle?"

"You know the Cinerama Theater, Father? The place has this huge, seventy-foot screen. They had a special ten-o'clock showing of *The Great Escape*. Have you ever seen it?"

Smiling, Jack nodded. "Only about five or six times."

"It was awesome, and the place was packed. Anyway, I was gone from about eight until three-thirty in the morning. I blew off a philosophy class and slept all the next day. In fact, I didn't hear about that drowning until late afternoon." Anton nudged him. "How's that for an alibi?"

"Well, I didn't really ask for one," Jack said. "I was just wondering where you were night before last. But you're right. I'd like to talk with the other residents here. And if it's okay with you, I'm better off interviewing them one-on-one."

"You sure?" Anton asked. "We could try the good-cop-bad-cop routine. It almost worked with Pettinger."

"Thanks anyway."

"If you don't mind my asking," Anton said, leaning against the wall, "how many guys on this floor have you talked with so far?"

"Six, including Rick," Jack said. "Seven, if I include you."

"How many admitted they've seen John Costello hanging around?"

"Just you and Rick. The rest didn't know him at all."

Anton frowned. "John Costello was here often enough. More people should have recognized his picture. Doesn't that seem odd? A kid's been drowned, and all these guys suddenly don't know him. What do you think they're hiding?"

"That's what I'm trying to find out," Jack said. Then he started down the hallway to knock on some more doors.

Anton was right. None of the sophomores admitted to knowing John Costello. Of the sixteen boys Jack questioned, only two students recognized John's photograph. But they weren't much help beyond that.

Jack spoke to John's other alleged sex partner, Ted Patchett. He could tell Ted was lying during the questioning. He was as nervous and agitated as Rick Pettinger. A couple of times, Jack caught him contradicting himself.

He wondered if Johnny's trio of "boyfriends" weren't all somehow involved in the drowning. Had the three of them been in on it together? Was it some kind of sexual hazing that had gone wrong?

Jack was about to duck out of St. Clement Hall when Anton caught him in the stairwell. Anton volunteered to "keep digging" with the investigation. Jack thanked him, but said he could handle the inquiries himself. He left the dorm at a quarter past ten.

Anton was a bit too helpful, too eager, and too quick with his alibi. His strange enthusiasm was almost as suspicious as the denials from John's alleged boyfriends. Jack swung by the college library and browsed the current newspapers and periodicals. He looked up the lifestyle section in Wednesday's *Seattle Times*. There was a ten-o'clock screening of *The Great Escape* at the Cinerama Theater.

Anton hadn't been lying about the movie. But three sophomores on Anton's floor had indeed lied to him. They were the ones with something to hide.

Jack wandered out of the library into the damp night air. He turned up the collar of his jacket as he wandered through the maze of old, ivy-covered buildings toward the faculty boat dock. At the edge of campus, he walked by Our Lady of Sorrows Church. Jack hesitated, then he glanced up at the tall, Gothic edifice.

"There's this window to the church basement, the lock's broken. . . . We'd go into the catacombs under the church. . . . I know he met John Costello there several nights."

Jack turned, then slowly circled around the church. Looking past the bushes and flower beds, he studied the basement windows for one with a broken latch. He found the window on the lake side. A few old cigarette butts scattered on the ground gave it away. He picked up one of the butts: a Winston Light, Rick Pettinger's brand.

Jack glanced around to make sure he was alone. The muddy ground felt soft beneath his feet as he moved closer to the side of the building. Bending down, he pushed at the window. With only slight resistance, it swung open. He dug a miniflashlight from his coat pocket. It was on his second key ring, along with a spare set of keys for St. Bartholomew Hall.

He shined the light into the darkened basement. A squat cabinet had been shoved against the cellar wall beneath the window. Jack could see shoe prints on top of the cabinet. It was obvious how the boys had climbed down into the basement. He wondered if John's shoe prints were amid the many left there.

Jack crawled through the small window. He almost tipped over the cabinet as he climbed down into the dark, dank cellar.

A dim light filtered from the stairwell, and Jack could

make out an array of old, broken-down altar fixtures, standing crucifixes, and even a couple of receptacles for holy water. After a moment, his eyes adjusted to the darkness. Jack gazed at all the abandoned artifacts, then he saw something that made his heart stop.

He pointed the miniflashlight at the tall, thin shadowy figure. "Oh, shit." He laughed. It was a life-size statue of St. Joseph. The paint was flaking off his face, and he had a haunting, pious gaze that seemed almost demonic. Sitting through Mass and staring at that thing must have given churchgoers nightmares.

He'd been in this cellar once before, when another priest had given him a tour his first week at the school. Jack remembered the catacombs were on the other side of the large, dull metal door, which looked like the entry for a bomb shelter. The door wasn't far from where St. Joseph stood glaring at him.

Jack pulled at the elongated handle. Locked. He searched around for the key. He thought about switching on the light, but didn't want anyone to know he was down here. After a couple of minutes, he finally found the key under an old pulpit.

The metal door was heavy, but swung open easily. A button fixed to the door frame triggered the catacomb lights—a series of bare, low-watt bulbs that hung several feet apart from a cable down the center of the tunnel-like cavern. A few of the bulbs had burnt out. Jack directed his flashlight at the dusty cement floor. More shoe prints.

He couldn't believe that anyone in their right mind would want to have sex in such a god-awful, creepy place. Then again, these were horny teenage boys. They entered this place with a friend, a sex partner, and it was an adventure.

Jack figured that he must be the crazy one, sneaking down here alone at night. He trained his flashlight toward an alcove on his right. Floating dust caught in the beam of light like tiny moths. In the alcove, a cement crucifix served as the grave marker for a priest who had lived from 1872 until 1921.

Jack moved deeper into the recesses of the catacombs, all the while aiming his light on the trail of shoe prints. They bypassed a number of alcoves on either side of him. With a glance over his shoulder, Jack checked the door in the distance behind him, but he could barely see it anymore.

He followed the shoe prints as they diverted from the dimly lit center pathway. A niche on his left seemed to be the lure. Jack pointed the miniflashlight on a long slab of marble, two feet high. The marker for the final resting place of Monsignor Thayer Swann (1859–1931) almost looked like a bed. A couple of burnt-out votive candles had been left at the foot of the slab. Jack picked up one of the votives. The candle was pine scented.

Out of the corner of his eye, he caught a glimpse of something shiny behind the head of the stone. Jack trained the light on it. Bursting at the seams, a black plastic trash bag had been crammed between the catacomb wall and the head of that grave marker.

Jack nudged the trash bag with his toe. It felt soft. He unfastened the twist-tie. Inside the bag were two pillows and an old, pale blue comforter. The boys weren't exactly roughing it down here, with their scented candles and soft bedding. And Monsignor Swann wasn't complaining.

Jack started to shove the bedding back into the plastic bag, then he heard something. It sounded like a door shutting. But it couldn't have been the door to the catacombs; the lights would have gone out.

Quickly, Jack tied up the bag. He started to pull out the tiny flashlight again, but he heard another noise—louder this time. He dropped his light on the dusty floor. It illuminated the side of the marble slab and a series of rust red specks. Something had splashed on the side of the grave marker, something that looked like blood.

Jack remained very still for a moment. He waited for another sound, but didn't hear anything.

He took one last look at the dried crimson stains, then ducked out of the alcove. In the dim light, he couldn't see the door at the far end of the cavern. On either side of him were the shadowy grave sites, one after another. "Is anyone there?" Jack called. He heard a tiny scraping sound; it could have been a rat or something upstairs. The acoustics in the place were crazy.

Jack started walking faster toward the open doorway ahead. But he stopped in his tracks as a large shadow swept across the wall. "Who's there?" he called.

No answer, not a sound.

He moved toward the open door. The shadow continued to dance across that wall in a rhythmic pattern. Then Jack saw it was one of the hanging lights, the second from the doorway, swaying back and forth. He wondered why none of the other lights were moving. Why just that one?

"I know someone's here," he announced, stepping toward the door. The shadows and light kept rippling against that wall. "Talk to me," he said.

Again, no response.

Jack emerged from the catacombs. He was almost relieved to see old, demonic-looking St. Joseph again. He pulled at the door. "I'm locking up," he said out loud. "If anyone's in the catacombs, you're screwed. This is your last chance. . . ."

Jack closed the old metal door and locked it. He pocketed the key and glanced around the darkened storage area. He told himself he was alone down here. Yet as he climbed out the basement window, he couldn't shake the feeling that someone was watching him.

* * *

"Do you have any idea what time it is?"

Father Tom Garcia sounded groggy over the phone. Jack knew he'd woken him. The digital clock on his desk read 11:11.

"Sorry if I woke you," Jack said. He sat at his desk. "It's about John Costello's drowning. I followed a lead, and snuck into the church basement. I just came back. There's something in the catacombs I think you should take a look at."

"What did you find?" Garcia asked.

"A few of the boys have been using one of the grave sites for a meeting place. I found something that looks like blood on one of the stones."

"Was the blood still wet?"

"No, it was dry."

"Well, we can't do anything about it now," Garcia said, yawning. "Let's wait until morning, Jack. I'll meet you in front of the church at six. If this . . . um, blood is already dry, it's not about to evaporate before then."

"All right. I'll see you tomorrow, Father."

"Call me Tom. Oh, and Jack, you haven't told anyone about this . . . new discovery, have you?"

"No, nobody."

"Let's keep it that way for now. Okay? See you in the A.M."

Jack hung up the phone. He started to pull off his dirty trousers. The phone rang. He thought Tom Garcia was calling back, and he grabbed the receiver. "Hello?"

"Father Murphy?" It was a woman, her voice raspy. In the background, Jack could hear music, and people chattering. "It's Maggie Costello, Father. Did I wake you up? Were you sleeping?"

"No, it's okay. How are you?"

"Well, I'm not so hot," she said. "I missed you this afternoon. I drove up to collect Johnny's things."

"Oh, I wish I'd known you were coming by."

"Listen, are you busy right now?" she asked. "I'd really like to talk with you. I don't have anyone else I can talk with. I—I'm here across the lake from you at the Lakeside Inn. Will you come have a drink with me?"

"With all the people I talked to yesterday, why didn't anyone tell me about this other boy who drowned in Lake Leroy?" Maggie asked him. She took a sip of her drink. "The waitress said they hushed it up. So tell me what's going on. Are they trying to hush up Johnny's death, too?"

Jack shrugged uneasily. People were staring at them: a priest and a pretty woman sitting at the window table, wrapped up in quiet conversation. He shouldn't have worn his clerical collar here tonight.

Maggie looked beautiful, her red hair and pale skin illuminated by an amber neon light in the window. She wore a black, scooped-neck pullover. She'd clearly had a few drinks; her speech was slightly muddled.

"I don't think they're trying to 'hush up' John's death," Jack said carefully. "Until they find out exactly what happened, they'd like to avoid a lot of bad press and gossip."

"Did you know about this other boy who drowned?" she asked pointedly.

"Not much, but it sounds similar to Johnny's situation. He was a freshman, swimming back from a party one night." Jack glanced down at the varnished tabletop. He didn't think he should tell her about Julian Doyle's missing fingers. He wasn't even sure if Maggie knew that a couple of Johnny's toes had been severed. What was to be gained by citing those grisly similarities?

He sighed. "Anyway, this other drowning happened three years ago, before I came here."

Maggie studied him. "I think the school is keeping certain things from me, Jack. Tell me the truth. Was Johnny involved in something shady? Is that why he was killed? I keep wondering about that money he had hidden."

Jack shrugged. "I don't know how he got that money." He couldn't say anything more. He thought about the evidence down in the catacombs—and the string of so-called lovers Johnny was supposed to have. This was her baby brother. She didn't need to hear these things now—especially when he wasn't even certain they were true.

He sipped his beer. "I'm still interviewing and investigating," he said. "As soon as I find out something definite, I'll let you know, Maggie. I promise."

She reached over the table and placed her hand over his. "I'm counting on you," she whispered.

"Can I get you folks another round?"

It was the waitress.

Maggie pulled her hand away. "Nothing more for me," she said.

"We're fine, thank you," Jack said.

Maggie watched the waitress amble back toward the bar. She sighed and looked down at her near-empty glass. "I've had too much to drink."

"You better not drive," Jack said. "Why don't you get a room here at the inn tonight?"

She nodded. "Good idea."

"Is there someone you need to call?" he asked. "Someone who should know where you are?"

"No," Maggie said. "There's nobody."

Maggie Costello seemed to glow under the amber neon light in the tavern's window. She looked quite pretty tonight.

He could tell, even at this distance. He stood behind the shack where the Lakeside Inn rented fishing and boating equipment for its guests. He knew she couldn't see him amid the shadows outside.

He turned up his jacket collar from the damp cold near the lake. He'd been watching Maggie in that window for almost two hours. She'd had three drinks, and one little crying jag. He knew the reason behind her tears, and he had to smile. He liked to make them cry.

Father Murphy had arrived about twenty-five minutes ago. Even at this distance, he could tell the good father wanted her. It was so obvious. The people in the bar probably saw it, too. Poor love-starved, love-struck Father Murphy.

He watched Murphy pay for the drinks, then help Maggie to her feet. They started to move away from the table—and out of his line of vision.

Nothing would ever happen between those two. Murphy didn't have a chance.

He would see to it. He would make Maggie Costello his. And once he was through with her, he would keep a lock of her beautiful red hair—along with the usual souvenirs.

The middle-aged woman at the registration desk kept glancing at Jack, then at his priest's collar, then at Maggie. Her stare—from behind a pair of cat-eye glasses—graduated from curious to disapproving; so by the time she handed Maggie the room key, the woman was almost scowling at them.

"They'll be gossiping about us tomorrow," Maggie said, as Jack walked with her down the inn's second-floor corridor. She was weaving a tiny bit.

He kept his hand poised by her arm, ready to catch her if she stumbled. "Let them talk," he said.

She shrugged. "I'm used to it anyway. When I left my

husband, I was the bad guy, the talk of the parish. Everyone loved him. No one knew what an asshole he was to me.'' Maggie stopped by the door to the room. ''Can I tell you something kind of crude?''

''Sure,'' Jack said.

''I'm going to send Ray a cactus plant on his birthday every year—just to remind him of what a prick he is.''

Jack laughed.

''Only I'm not sending him any cacti until I'm in a relationship myself. That's a must. I don't want it to be like I'm bitter. I want to do it when I'm happy. In fact, I won't even tell Ray it's because he's a prick. That'll be a private joke between me and my significant other. When I can laugh about it, that's when I'll send him a cactus plant on his birthday.''

Jack managed to smile. ''Good idea.''

''He and Johnny didn't get along,'' Maggie said. She handed Jack the room key. ''I don't really believe it was an accident. Johnny was a good swimmer. I taught him to swim. Did you know that?''

''No, I didn't,'' Jack murmured. He opened the door, then handed the key back to her.

''I taught him to swim when he was five,'' she continued. ''You should should have seen him at the beach. They had the wading area roped off for the kids. And every time Johnny went beyond those ropes, the lifeguards would call to him on the bullhorn, and make him take a swim test. He'd always pass, then race out to the raft. I can still see him, the smallest kid out there, so skinny in his big purple trunks. . . .''

Tears began to fill her eyes. ''Oh, damn it,'' she whispered. ''I didn't want to do this in front of you.'' She retreated into the room, then found the bathroom, where she switched on the light. She plucked a few tissues from the dispenser on the sink counter. ''I'm sorry,'' she said into a wad of Kleenex. "There's nothing worse than someone who's drunk and weepy."

"It's all right," Jack said, standing at her threshold.

Maggie leaned against the door frame. "I used to live my life for my family," she said, her voice quivering. "Now, I feel like an outsider with my sisters. And Johnny's gone. How do you keep going when you've lost everyone dear to you?"

Jack didn't know how to answer her, beyond the usual priestly jargon about time and faith.

"How did *you* do it?" she asked. "Johnny told me how you lost your wife and son. How did you go on?"

"I almost didn't," Jack admitted. "But I hung in there. Different people helped me out, one old friend in particular."

She gave him a wary sidelong glance and let out a sad little laugh. "You mean God?"

He managed to smile. "Well, being a priest, I guess that should have been my standard answer."

"Thank you, Jack," she said. "For not giving me the standard answer. If you cannot be a priest for just one more minute, I want to ask you something." Her voice started to shake. "Do you hurt as much as I do? Do you miss Johnny, too?"

"Yes, Maggie," he whispered. "I miss him very much."

Maggie wrapped her arms around him. Jack felt her warm, wet tears along the side of his neck. He wanted to hold her and stroke her hair. But he couldn't. He couldn't even let himself step inside that room with her.

Maggie kissed his cheek. Then her moist lips slid over to his mouth. Her body trembled against his.

He started to pull back. But she held on to him tighter, until Jack had to wrest away from her. "I'm sorry," he said.

She started crying again. "Can't you just hold me for a little while? Even if you don't like me? I feel so alone, please—"

He shook his head. "No, Maggie," he muttered, aching with regret.

She let out a bitter laugh, and wiped her tears away. "That's fine, don't worry, *Father.*" Maggie staggered toward the bed and sat down. "I'm drunk," she announced, prying off her shoes. "I'm drunk. It's the prize excuse for everything. Forgive me, Father, for I have drunk. Do you forgive me?"

"Yes, of course," he muttered.

"Good. You've done you're priestly duty. Now, why don't you get the hell out of here?"

"Good night," Jack said. Stepping back, he gently closed the door. He could hear her crying on the other side.

Maggie suddenly woke up, not knowing where she was. She couldn't see a thing, except for a crack of moonlight peeking between a set of closed curtains. Everything else was pitch-black. She had no idea of the time either. For a moment, the only thing she felt sure about was the presence of someone else in the dark room.

Lying still beneath the covers, Maggie was afraid to move. She didn't want the intruder to know she was awake and onto him. Her head throbbed, and her mouth was so dry she couldn't swallow. She had to go to the bathroom, too. Yet she didn't budge.

She remembered drinking an awful lot, and embarrassing herself with Jack Murphy. He'd taken her to this room at the Lakeside Inn. She hadn't locked up after he'd left. She'd passed out on the bed. Anyone could have slipped in.

Maggie tried to adjust her eyes to the darkness. If there was a clock on the nightstand, she didn't see it. Still, she felt someone hovering over her.

Blindly, she reached for a lamp at her bedside. Her hand fanned at the air for a moment. She kept expecting the intruder to grab her by the wrist. She felt so vulnerable and helpless. At last, she found the lamp and fumbled for the switch.

She squinted in the light. The rest of the room was still shrouded in darkness. But at least she could see that no one was standing near the bed. And she could find her way to the bathroom. Maggie threw back the covers and hurried into the john. She peed, flushed the toilet, then gulped down a glass of water. Before wandering back to bed, she checked the door to her room. It wasn't locked. She pressed the button in the center of the doorknob and fixed the chain lock.

Climbing back into bed, she switched off the light. As she drifted off, Maggie thought about checking the closet or behind the drapes. Just a few minutes before, she'd been so sure someone was in the room with her.

If that was true, she'd just locked him inside. As far as she was concerned, he could go ahead and kill her. She didn't care. Her brother was dead. She'd made an ass out of herself with this sexy priest. She was miffed at her sisters and ex-husband. And tomorrow, she'd have one hell of a hangover. If someone killed her in her sleep, he'd be doing her a big favor.

When Maggie woke up again, it was morning. She crawled out of bed and staggered toward the bathroom. But she saw something that made her stop dead. She squinted at the room door. She didn't understand. Hadn't she set the chain lock a couple of hours ago?

She couldn't have dreamed it. Yet now the chain lock was off. It didn't make sense.

The only way someone could have unlatched that chain was if they'd already been in the room with her when she'd woken up last night.

Chapter Nine

The church basement seemed quite different with the overhead fluorescent on and birds chirping outside. Morning light filtered through the small windows. The statue of St. Joseph looked benign now. For this return trip to the catacombs, Jack wasn't alone, and he didn't have to climb though a window. He and Father Garcia had come down the basement stairs.

Jack was tired and blurry-eyed. He'd left Maggie Costello at the Lakeside Inn at 1:30 this morning. He couldn't have caught more than four hours of sleep. Tom Garcia, on the other hand, was full of energy. He smelled of Old Spice and cigarettes.

Walking amid the dusty, discarded altar decorations, they reached the crypt door. "Last night on the phone," Garcia said, "you mentioned you'd checked out this place 'following a lead'?"

"That's right," Jack replied, pulling the key from his pocket. "But I can't really talk about it." He nodded ahead at the tunnel-like cavern. "I'll show you what I found here and let you draw your own conclusions."

Garcia frowned. "I don't understand."

"You'll see what I mean," Jack assured him.

They started down the center of the catacombs together. Garcia kept looking left and right as they passed the shadowy nooks. "Jack Murphy, you must have more balls than a Christmas tree to come down here alone in the dead of night."

Jack directed his miniflashlight on the floor so Garcia could see all the shoe prints. "Looks like the boys who come down here are usually in pairs. If I remember right, the tracks veer to the left pretty soon."

They found the final resting place for Monsignor Thayer Swann, but the votive candles weren't there anymore. Jack trained the flashlight around the base of the marble slab. "Someone's been down here," he said. "Everything's gone. There were scented candles and a bag full of bedding, pillows, and a comforter."

Garcia frowned at him. "Last night on the phone, you told me that the boys were using the catacombs for a 'meeting place.' Now you're talking about scented candles and bedsheets. What's going on here, Jack?"

"I was hoping I could show you, and let you figure it out from there."

"Figure what out?" He shook his head. "I can't play these guessing games with you, Jack. You'll have to help me out. Now, first, who told you about this place?"

"Sorry if I seem evasive," Jack replied. "I had an anonymous tip, that's all I can say. Last night, when I was down here, I found a bag full of bedding behind this grave marker—along with scented candles. Now they're gone."

"Bedding and scented candles? Secret meetings between seminarians?" Garcia raised his eyebrows. "Huh, I see. Were these private, one-on-one meetings?"

"I think so," Jack said. He aimed his flashlight on the marker. "All the comforts of home were right here, but not anymore."

"Maybe we're in the wrong alcove."

"No, it's Thayer Swann's grave," Jack said. "You don't forget a name like that. You know, I thought someone else was here last night. They must have their own key." Jack directed the flashlight toward the slab once more. "The stains are still there," he murmured.

Garcia crouched down by the rust-colored specks on the marble marker. "Sure looks like blood." With a groan, he straightened up. "Tell you what. I'll have Father Stutesman from the science department make an analysis. He's no forensics expert, but maybe he can come up with the blood type for us. We'll see if it matches John Costello's."

Garcia took out a tiny pocketknife and a handkerchief, then he squatted down by the bloodstain again. Jack watched him start to scrape at the dried crimson specks and catch the residue in his handkerchief. "Shouldn't we leave that for the police?" he said. "It's evidence."

"The police investigation is closed, Jack. The autopsy results came in yesterday afternoon. Death by drowning." He stood up, carefully folded the handkerchief, then slipped it in his pocket. "This is for our own in-house investigation. I don't want it getting out that some of our seminarians are sneaking into the catacombs beneath the church at night to have sex." He shook his head. "Huh, incredible. I can't believe it."

"Neither can I," Jack admitted.

Garcia patted him on the shoulder. "Well, you've done a bang-up job of looking into this for us, Jack. I want to thank you."

"Hey, don't thank me yet. I'm not finished."

"Well, yes, you are," Garcia said. "For now, you better not dig into this any deeper."

"But John's death wasn't an accident. I saw his body, and it was battered. A couple of his toes were sliced off."

"He got knocked around in the water for several hours, Jack. There are a lot of sharp rocks and debris in that lake. It's mentioned in the coroner's report. I'll make a copy for you if you want."

"What about his clothes? He was in his underwear, no room key, no wallet—"

"He probably had them in a taped-up plastic bag," Garcia said. "Isn't that what some of these guys do when they swim across the lake? My guess is he had the bag in the water with him when he got a cramp or whatever. Considering all the tributaries off this lake, his stuff could be washed up on some riverbank in Alberta, Canada, by now. It'll turn up—eventually."

He patted Jack's shoulder again. "Now, c'mon, let's get out of here. It's as cold as a polar bear's you-know-what in this place."

"Tom, listen." Jack took hold of his arm. "My source indicated that John used to meet other boys here in secret. I think something happened in these catacombs Wednesday night, and one of Johnny's 'friends' is covering it up."

"Covering up what?" Garcia asked. "Evidence of a homicide?"

"Maybe," he said.

Garcia pried away from his hold. He smiled patiently. "Or maybe a kid was scared someone would find out where he and a buddy were messing around. You're best off leaving this investigation alone for now, Jack."

He touched the handkerchief in his breast pocket. "I'll see if Father Stutesman can analyze this blood. It shouldn't take too long. I'll let you know the results. Now, c'mon, let's get out of here."

Walking with Father Garcia up the center aisle of the catacombs, Jack wondered if the school's head of administration was protecting the college, someone else, or maybe even himself.

He remembered Maggie asking him last night if they were trying to "hush up" Johnny's death. He'd promised her that he would keep investigating. *"I'm counting on you,"* she'd said.

As they reached the catacomb door, Garcia paused. "I'll lock up, Jack," he said. Then he held out his hand. "I'd like to hold on to the key, too."

Jack surrendered the key to him. "Of course," he murmured. "Whatever you say."

"That color looks good on you, Pete," Maggie said.

Peter held one of Johnny's shirts in front of him. He and Maggie stood by her car in the parking lot near St. Bartholomew Hall. She'd treated Peter to breakfast at the Lakeside Inn, and now invited him to rummage through the boxes of Johnny's personal effects for anything he wanted.

Three aspirin and two cups of coffee had helped chase away her hangover—along with some of her concerns. Maggie reasoned that in her blind, drunken stupor last night, she probably hadn't fixed the chain lock on the hotel room door.

The idea that someone had been in the room with her—watching her sleep—was just too frightening to consider. She hadn't been harmed. She wasn't missing any money or jewelry. Too much drink had impaired her judgment about the chain lock. That was all.

Amazingly, she and Peter had made it through breakfast without crying.

But now as she watched him handling Johnny's clothes, Maggie noticed Peter's brown eyes filling up with tears. Yet he seemed determined not to cry. He was a good-looking kid with wavy brown hair, endearingly gawky and thin. He'd worshiped Johnny, and always had a bit of a crush on her, too; Maggie could tell.

"Pete, what do you think really happened to Johnny?"

He set down the shirt. "I don't know."

"Half the clothes in there he bought over the summer with money he'd made caddying. It doesn't make sense he'd still have twenty-two hundred dollars left over. Hell, he couldn't have even earned that much all summer. But when Father Murphy asked you about the money he had hidden, you told him Johnny must have saved it from caddying."

Peter shrugged. "God, Maggie, I was just guessing. I don't know."

She rested a hand on his shoulder. "Listen, Pete, if Johnny was involved in something secret or shady, I need to know. I don't want you trying to spare my feelings. I know Johnny was no saint. That money had something to do with his death, I'm sure of it. Was Johnny dealing drugs?"

"God, no," Peter said, frowning.

"Then what?" Maggie's eyes searched his. "You're holding something back, Pete. I can tell."

"I'm not," he said, exasperated. "I swear."

Across the lake, the church bell rang ten times. "Listen, I'll be late for the prayer service," he said, then he started to turn away.

"Well, wait a minute," Maggie said. "Don't leave without some of these things. Johnny would want you to have them."

Peter collected two of the boxes. "I'm sorry I'm not more of a help to you, Maggie," he murmured.

She gave him a quick kiss on the cheek. "Do me a favor, and sit beside me at the funeral Mass, okay?"

Peter nodded sheepishly. Then he retreated into the dorm with the boxes of clothes he'd inherited from his dead friend.

* * *

There was no prayer service on Saturday morning. Peter had lied to Maggie about that. He'd lied about the money too.

As he rode up in the elevator to the fourth floor, Peter fought the tightness in his throat. He prayed no one would get on from another floor, because they'd see his eyes full of tears.

Loaded down with the two boxes, he managed to make it to his room and shut the door before he burst out crying. The boxes fell to the floor. He pulled out a blue shirt Johnny had been wearing on Tuesday. He could still smell him on it.

Peter buried his face in the shirt, then he curled up on his bed and sobbed. *"You know, I really hate it when you act like a girl,"* he could almost hear his best friend saying.

Johnny had actually said that to him once, during high school freshman year. Peter didn't remember exactly what he was doing that seemed girlish. But he was so humiliated when Johnny had made that comment.

He'd met John Costello his first week in high school. Peter was always a loner. He'd spent so much time by himself, drawing, that he hardly knew anyone who wasn't from his Catholic grade school. He didn't even know Johnny, who lived only four blocks away. Johnny was the last stop on the high-school bus route. Peter was the next to last. One Friday afternoon, Johnny simply got off the bus with him. They played video games at Peter's house, and Johnny stayed for dinner. After that, they were inseparable.

Johnny became a semipermanent member of the Tobin household. Apparently, things were pretty tense at his brother-in-law's house. Peter rarely went over there, but often enough to develop a little platonic crush on Maggie Costello.

Peter didn't want to acknowledge, not even to himself, that he had a different kind of crush on his best friend. Johnny unwittingly became his hero, and he very much looked the part. He had a great build: muscular arms and a lean, smoothly chiseled frame. With his "black Irish" looks, he was one of the handsomest guys in his class.

During the summers, they caddied at the same country club. In the evenings they'd go to the beach, the movies, gorge on pizza, or browse the mall. Johnny had always been short of money. But in the summer after their junior year, he started picking up the tab at the pizza parlor, and he didn't hesitate to buy anything that caught his fancy—a sweater or a skateboard or tickets to a Mariners game.

"How did you become Mr. Got-Bucks all of the sudden?" Peter asked him one night as they left a music store. Johnny had just splurged on three CDs. "I'm practically broke trying to keep up with you. We make the same kind of money at the country club. I don't get it. Where's all the dough coming from?"

Johnny shrugged. "I must make better tips than you."

"From those tightwads?"

"Guess I'm just a better caddie than you," Johnny replied. "Now, c'mon, let's get move it. We'll be late for the movie. My treat."

Ironically, lack of money was one of the reasons Johnny decided to attend college at the seminary. He had no intention of becoming a priest. But at Our Lady of Sorrows, room, board, and education came cheap, and he wouldn't be too far away from his sister.

Peter thought he was nuts at first. Johnny studying for the priesthood? He couldn't picture his friend going to Mass every day, poring over the Bible, and totally relinquishing girls.

Peter also couldn't picture himself making it through the next four years without Johnny. He applied to Our Lady of Sorrows the same day as his best friend.

There was a lot to hate about the school. But on the plus side, it wasn't a big sports college, so Peter didn't feel ostracized for his athletic shortcomings. Besides, Johnny was there.

But after a few weeks, Johnny and Father Murphy became fast friends. Peter felt abandoned. He pulled back from Johnny, giving him some distance and hoping Johnny would notice. This tactic only left Peter more isolated and alone. Johnny started hanging out with the upperclassmen on the other side of the lake. He wasn't lonely.

Peter tried to accept the fact that things were different. By Christmas break, he thought about leaving Our Lady of Sorrows and starting at another college. But he stayed.

Late one night in February, Peter had just switched off his reading light and slid under the covers when somebody tapped on his door. "Hey, Pete," he heard Johnny whisper from the hallway. "You still awake? Pete?"

He climbed out of bed and opened the door. Johnny wore a white T-shirt, jeans, and black tennis shoes. His face and arms were so pink, he almost looked sunburned. He was shivering. The guys weren't supposed to be in each others' rooms after the eleven o'clock curfew on week nights, and it was almost one in the morning. Pete grabbed Johnny's arm to pull him inside. His skin was like ice. "Jesus, you're freezing," Peter said, closing the door behind him. "What's going on?"

Johnny hurried to the closet, took out Peter's winter jacket, and threw it on. "I left my coat at St. Clement's, and my keys were in the pocket. I'm locked out of my room."

"You walked all the way from the other side of the lake without a jacket or anything?" Peter asked. Even if Johnny had taken the Whopper Way shortcut, it was still a fifteen minute trek. They were predicting snow for that night.

Johnny nodded. Still shivering, he sat down on the edge of Peter's bed.

"Are you nuts? Why didn't you just turn around and pick up your coat while you were still there?"

"I had a fight with this guy, and I didn't want to go back."

"A fight-fight with fists?" Peter asked.

"It almost got that way," Johnny muttered. "I'm hoping he cools off by morning. Then I can go back and pick up my coat—if you let me borrow a sweater or something."

Peter nodded. "Sure, no problem."

"Can I crash here tonight?"

"Well, yeah, sure, no problem," Peter said again, shrugging.

Immediately, Johnny threw off the jacket, then he stripped down to his white briefs. "Which pillow can I use?"

"The blue striped," Peter said. He reached back to lock the door, but hesitated. "Don't you need to pee or anything?"

"I peed outside, before I came in." Johnny jumped under the covers. "This okay? Am I taking up too much room?"

Peter just shook his head. For a moment, he stood at the foot of the bed. He felt a bit overdressed in his T-shirt and flannel pajama bottoms—considering his friend wore so little.

Johnny squinted at him. "So—are you coming to bed or what?"

Peter nodded a few more times than necessary. "Oh, yeah, sure."

A minute after he settled under the covers and rolled away from Johnny, he sensed some movement at the tail of his T-shirt. Suddenly, a chilly hand glided up the center of his back. His whole body automatically flinched. "Feel how cold I still am," Johnny whispered, laughing.

"Yeah, no shit, Sherlock," Peter said. "Cut it out."

This only encouraged Johnny to rub his cold feet against his. And that icy hand continued to work beneath his T-shirt, roaming up and down his back, cold skin on warm skin. Peter started to get an erection. He didn't want Johnny to know. "Hey, I said you could bunk in with me. I didn't say you could molest me."

Laughing, Johnny pulled away. Peter tugged at the covers and shifted a bit. He still had his back to him. "Who'd you have the fight with?" he asked.

"A sophomore, Rick Pettinger. You don't know him."

"What did you guys fight about?"

"Oh, it's stupid. I'd rather not go into it."

"How come you never talk about these guys?" Peter asked. "This bunch of sophomores, they're like your secret friends or something."

Johnny didn't say anything.

"You awake?" Peter rolled over on his back and glanced at him.

Staring up at the ceiling, Johnny sighed. "Do you really want to have this conversation?"

"Sure, why not?"

"Because some of what I have to say might gross you out. Huh, I'm getting pretty sick of it myself."

"Sick of what?"

"I've been screwing around with these three guys from St. Clement Hall. They don't know about each other. I think if they did, I'd be a dead duck. I was taking money from them—at least that's how it started. Now I don't know how to stop it."

Peter half sat up. "You were having sex with *guys?* For money?"

Johnny frowned. "You just don't understand. Your folks

have money coming out of their ears. They send you a check every month. With my sister and I, things are different. It's tough on Maggie, trying to make ends meet. I feel shitty taking money from her.''

''But you seemed to have enough money the last couple of summers.''

''That's because I had something going on at the country club,'' Johnny whispered. ''How do you think I got all that dough? Not on the golf course, that's for sure. Remember how I was doing yard work for the Chantlers on Monday afternoons two summers ago?''

Peter nodded. He'd caddied for Mr. Chantler—not a great tipper, but a nice enough guy. An ex-jock gone to seed, he was about fifty—with a little potbelly and a deep tan. Johnny was always going on about his wife, a slim brunet in her midthirties with beautiful legs and a big smile. She was always flirting with him.

''The first time I went over there, Mr. Chantler wanted me to help him clean out their garage,'' Johnny explained. ''I wasn't even working ten minutes, and I found a stash of porn magazines in this box. Now that I think back, I bet he planted them there. He told me I could take some of them home, because he was only going to throw them out. Anyway, we started looking at the magazines together. Most of them were of guys and girls together, a few of them were gay. I think it was a setup, y'know? Because for the next couple of hours, while we were working, he was telling me about all these sexual adventures he had before he got married—guys, girls, twosomes, threesomes, orgies, sex clubs, you name it. And he went into details. I'm telling you, Pete, it was like one of those letters to *Penthouse*. The weird part is, I was really creeped out, but kind of turned on at the same time. Anyway, it was hot that day. So he said, before I go, why didn't I cool off with a dip in the pool? He said, 'We're very informal here. No need for any swimsuits. The neighbors can't see. . . .' "

Reclining on one elbow, Peter listened intently.

"Anyway," Johnny continued, "I knew he was coming on to me, so I told him, 'Thanks all the same, but I'll just take my twenty dollars and hit the road.' That's when Mr. Chantler said to me, 'How would you like to leave here with *one hundred* and twenty dollars? Mrs. Chantler and I would like you to stay.' "

"Holy shit," Pete murmured.

"Yeah, *Mrs. Chantler,* too. Well, he took me around to the pool, and I could hear someone splashing in the water. He called her, and she swam over to the shallow end, where the steps were. And she came out of that pool, all wet and naked, smiling at me. I mean, I instantly got hard. She had these perfect little white breasts against her tan, and her nipples were erect. And her legs, God . . ." He let out a little laugh. "Anyway, she undressed me, and we messed around in the pool."

"What was Mr. Chantler doing?" Peter asked.

"Mostly, he was just watching us and playing with himself." Johnny shrugged. "Anyway, they must have had a good time, because I went home with a hundred and twenty bucks that afternoon. And Mr. Chantler asked me back for the next week—and the week after, and so on."

"Jesus," Peter whispered.

Johnny made a sour face. "The third time, Mrs. Chantler wasn't there. It was just Mr. Chantler and me. That's the way it was from then on, a hundred and twenty bucks every week. Mr. Chantler had me meet him at this hotel near the Space Needle."

Propped up on one elbow, Peter stared at him. "So—do you think you're bisexual?" he asked.

"Hell, I don't know," Johnny said. "Maybe. I like girls. I always have. But I got pretty heavily involved with this guy here. I can't talk about it. He'd kill me if I ever blabbed to anyone about us. Anyway, it's pretty much over now. Doesn't matter.''

"Is he one of the guys at St. Clement Hall you were talking about?" Peter asked.

Johnny smiled a bit. "No, he's not one of them."

"How did you meet these guys?"

"I got to drinking with a guy over there from the third floor one night, and I mentioned how I made that extra money last summer. And he said he'd pay, too. So we went somewhere and messed around. He gave me thirty. He said he knew two other guys on his floor who would probably pay, too, both of them closet cases. Isn't that crazy? Practically half of the guys at this school are gay, humping away in their rooms with their buddies. But there are still guys here who don't want anyone to know. They'd rather go to some secret, isolated place to have sex. And they'll pay for it—gladly. It's like they want to suffer or feel guilty.''

Peter knew exactly what Johnny was talking about. If there was someone like Johnny, and he could go to a secret place with him, where they could get naked and touch each other, he'd pay for that. Even with Johnny lying beside him, baring his soul—and most of his body—Peter couldn't admit to his friend what he really wanted.

Johnny stared at the ceiling, a tormented look on his face. "So I started working on these guys, Rick and Ted. Right off, I could tell they were gay. I don't know who they were trying to fool. Their classmate, Terry, had them pegged. They're from rich families, on the same floor as him in St. Clement's. Anyway, I've always been safe. But you'd be surprised at all the weird places off and on campus that I've had sex with these guys.''

"You mean like an orgy?" Peter asked.

"God, no, it's always one on one, very secretive. Anyway, I'm fed up. It's not very fun. I don't think it ever was. At this point, I'd pay to have them leave me alone. That's what the fight with this other guy was about tonight. It's a real mess."

"Why not just tell them you don't want to see them any more?"

"I've tried," Johnny answered. "But I might as well be breaking up with some nutcase girlfriend. *Fatal Attraction* times three."

"Does Father Murphy know?"

"What? About me whoring around? Are you nuts? I'm not telling Father Murphy, no way. You're the only person I can tell this to, Pete. Nobody else."

"Why is that?" he asked. He wondered if Johnny knew how much he was like these closeted gay sophomores who were in love with him. Peter felt his whole body tense up, and he shifted slightly to put some distance between Johnny and himself. "Why tell me and nobody else?" he pressed.

"Because you're my best friend, stupid."

Peter let out a stunned little laugh. "Well, you're my best friend too."

Johnny gazed at him sheepishly. "Still? Even with what you know about me now?"

"Doesn't change anything," Peter reassured him.

He lifted his head from the pillow, and before Peter knew what was happening, Johnny kissed him on the lips. "Thanks, Pete," he whispered.

Stunned, Peter said nothing.

Johnny mussed his hair. Then he settled back, gave his pillow a punch, and tugged the covers up around his neck. He rolled over on his side, his back to Peter.

"You going to sleep now?" Peter asked quietly.

"Yeah, I'm tired." He reached back and patted Peter's hip. "G'night, Pete."

"Good night, Johnny," he replied. Peter slid under the covers. He knew he wouldn't sleep a wink.

In the weeks to come, he'd occasionally ask Johnny about the sophomores across the lake. Johnny would just shake his head, and say, "It's still a mess." Clearly Johnny didn't want to talk about it. As for the good-night kiss, neither one of them ever mentioned it. But that was all it took for Peter to become even more infatuated with his best friend.

He didn't wash that blue-striped pillowcase for several days, because he could still smell Johnny on it. He'd hold that pillow through the night—as he wished he could have held Johnny.

That same familiar scent now lingered on Johnny's blue shirt. Peter clung to it, knowing the smell would soon fade.

He climbed off the bed and went to the window, Johnny's shirt balled up in his hands. He stared out across the lake, at the buildings on campus. He could just make out the rooftop of St. Clement Hall.

Those sophomores Johnny had been seeing all lived on the third floor. Peter knew their names. He also knew one of them was a murderer.

Chapter Ten

Rick Pettinger wasn't answering his door. Peter kept knocking anyway; he even rattled the doorknob. He wanted to confront this Pettinger creep right now. Even if Rick hadn't actually murdered Johnny, he was somehow mixed up in his death.

Peter put his ear to the door. Nothing. He slumped against the wall, then glanced at the other names and room numbers he'd jotted down while in St. Clement Hall's lobby.

Two more sophomores on this floor were involved with Johnny. *Ted* was one of the names Johnny had mentioned. According to the lobby's mailboxes, there was a Ted Patchett in Room 309. Peter headed down the hallway and knocked on the door.

No answer.

He tried again, harder this time.

"What are you trying to do? Break the damn door down?"

Peter swiveled around. Coming up the hallway toward him was a skinny young man with short, wiry brown hair.

He was trying to grow a mustache, and obviously not having much luck with it. A large strawberry mark covered his right cheek, past the jawline to his neck. He wore a long-sleeve black T-shirt and jeans. He must have been coming from the bathroom at the end of the hall. "What's going on? Who are you?" he demanded.

"Are you Ted Patchett?" Peter asked.

"Yeah." He stopped in front of him, hands on hips. "Who are you?"

"I'm Peter Tobin," he said, looking him in the eye. "John Costello was my friend."

Ted sneered at him. "Yeah, so?" He pulled his room key out his pocket.

"Johnny told me all about you," Peter said evenly.

"Well, big whoop. I don't know what you're talking about." Ted unlocked his door.

"You paid him to have sex with you," Peter whispered.

Ted glared at him, then he suddenly pushed Peter against the wall. "Get the hell out of here," he growled.

Peter couldn't breathe for a moment. He felt this sick, dreadful sensation rush through him. He was about to get the crap beaten out of him, and he knew it.

"Did Father Murphy send you here?" Patchett asked hotly. He lodged his forearm under Peter's chin, against his neck. "Are you Father Murphy's little errand boy?"

"What are you two jokers doing in my hallway? Dancing?"

Still wedged between Ted Patchett and the wall, Peter glanced down the corridor. A good-looking blond man came toward them. He wore sweatpants and a tight T-shirt that showed off his powerful physique. "Hey, may I cut in?" he joked.

Ted released Peter, then backed off a bit. "This doesn't concern you, Anton," he said to the blond man.

"Au contraire," he replied with a grin. "A fight in my

hallway concerns me a lot, Patchett. Now, what's this about?''

Peter caught his breath. He stood between the two of them.

Ted Patchett stepped back toward his door. ''It's nothing,'' he said. ''Just a little misunderstanding.''

''That's no way for a future priest to act, is it?'' Anton asked, his tone patronizing.

''Well, it's over with anyway,'' Ted replied. He glared at Peter. ''This kid was just leaving.''

''Then I'll walk him out,'' Anton said. He slapped his hand down on Peter's shoulder and let it rest there. ''C'mon, sport.'' He led him toward the stairwell.

Peter glanced back and saw Ted Patchett lingering in his doorway, watching them.

''What's your name, bud?'' the blond man asked.

''Peter Tobin,'' he murmured. ''I'm a friend of Johnny Costello's.'' He was still trembling a bit from the brush with Ted Patchett.

''I'm Anton, the R.A. on this floor. What did you do to make Ted lose his cool?''

''Nothing,'' Peter said. ''I just had a few questions for him, that's all. No big deal.''

''Ted didn't seem to think so. What were you asking him? Did it have anything to do with your buddy, John Costello?''

''Something like that,'' Peter admitted.

''I came in for the tail end of that exchange. I thought I heard someone mention Father Murphy. Did Murphy send you here?''

Peter shook his head. ''No, I'm here on my own.''

''Thought so,'' Anton said. He gave Peter's shoulder a squeeze. They paused at the top of the stairs. Anton sighed. ''Father Murphy knows about these guys. He talked to them yesterday.''

''Really?'' Peter asked.

Anton nodded. "And if you ask me, he's going too easy on these bozos. One of them, Rick Pettinger—have you heard the name?"

Peter nodded.

"He's already left school. They let him get away. Isn't that crazy? The way they're handling this stinks. You can tell that to Father Murphy for me, too." Anton let out a little laugh. "On second thought, you better not admit you were here. They probably don't want you snooping around, kiddo."

"Did you know Johnny?" Peter asked.

"I saw him hanging around on occasion, but never talked with him. He looked like a nice enough kid. So do you." Anton frowned. "You came here looking for trouble, and you found it. Now trouble just might come looking for you. Watch your back. I can't help thinking about your buddy, and what happened to him." Anton gave him a pat on the shoulder. "Now, you better scram, Pete."

Once Peter stepped outside, he glanced back up at St. Clement Hall. He saw a curtain move in one of the windows along the third floor. Peter turned and walked on. All the while, he felt trouble was looking.

"I know you only have a minute till showtime, but I'd like a word with you, Jack."

Father Garcia stood in the doorway to the sacristy of St. Gabriel Lalemant Chapel. An altar boy was going through the ritual of helping Jack don his vestments in preparation for the Saturday morning eleven-o'clock Mass. There was hardly enough space for the three of them in the little room behind the church. A glorified walk-in closet, it held vestments, altar cloths, candles, cruets, and other artifacts. The wine, hosts, and chalices were all kept under lock and key in a special cabinet.

Jack was tying the sash to the white robe that covered his street clothes. He caught the sober look on Garcia's face, then turned to the altar boy. "Bill, can you step outside for a minute?"

"Yes, Father." The young man brushed by Father Garcia in the doorway.

Jack waited until Bill had left. "Was it Johnny's blood?" he asked.

Garcia shook his head. "Type AB. Johnny was type O, according to the coroner's report. We're dropping the investigation, Jack. John Costello's death was an accident."

"I don't believe that," Jack replied.

"Doesn't matter," Garcia said. "This inquiry of yours has already cost the school dearly. I'm not blaming you, Jack. I instigated it. And now I'm dropping it."

"But why? Even if Johnny's death was accidental, the circumstances—"

"You talked to some sophomores at St. Clement Hall yesterday, didn't you?"

Jack nodded.

"Well, one of them didn't appreciate being interrogated, and he left school this morning. Not a good thing. This particular student is Rick Pettinger—as in Pettinger Intermodal? His father's corporation donated fifty-five thousand dollars to the archdiocese last year. I don't think we can expect the same kind of generosity from them next year. Mr. Pettinger didn't take kindly to the intimidation tactics you used on his son."

"Oh, please, give me a break," Jack protested, rolling his eyes. "Trust me, I went easy on the kid. Can't you see? He's hiding something. He was involved with John Costello, and he lied to me about that—"

"It doesn't matter. The investigation's over, Jack."

"Well, I promised John's sister I'd keep searching for an explanation. We owe her that much."

"The official explanation is accidental death by drowning. That's what we've told her. We don't owe her anything else except our prayers and sympathies."

Jack glared at him. "You're right," he said. "I suppose she's not as important as Pettinger Intermodal."

"You're skating on thin ice, Jack," Garcia whispered. "As for John Costello's sister, you're not to see her anymore. This is a small town. People are already talking about the two of you at the Lakeside Inn last night. You were seen drinking together, and checking into a room—"

"Nothing happened," Jack said. "I walked her to her door. That's all—"

"I don't care what actually happened. I'm concerned about how it looks—for you and the school." He glanced at his wristwatch. "You're late for your Mass. So here it is in a nutshell: The investigation into John Costello's death is officially closed. If you want to avoid disgracing this school and John Costello's memory, you'll put on the brakes, Jack. And you're not to see the sister again. Am I making myself clear?"

Jack nodded. "I understand," he said coolly. Indeed, he did understand. But he had no intention of actually obeying the son of a bitch.

The congregation trickled out the chapel door, a few of them pausing to shake Jack's hand. But Maggie lingered in the back of the church. Jack kept glancing at her out of the corner of his eye. He shouldn't have given a damn, but a couple of parishioners—both older women—had been a bit icy toward him with their greetings. Had they already heard the gossip about Father Murphy and the dead boy's sister in a tête-à-tête at the Lakeside Inn?

Maggie finally emerged from the church. Jack couldn't help glancing around to make sure they didn't have an audience. Unsmiling, Maggie shook his hand. "I owe you an apology," she said coolly. "I wish I had no recollection of last night. Unfortunately, I remember the whole humiliating mess."

"No need to apologize, none at all."

"Well, thanks, Father," she muttered.

He smiled. "Under the circumstances, you can call me Jack."

"I think we better stick with the formalities," she replied.

Jack just nodded. Johnny's sister didn't do much to conceal her resentment. And why not? In her grief, she'd reached out to him, and he'd rejected her. Maggie Costello had no idea how much he'd wanted to step across that threshold last night.

Her eyes met his for a moment, then she looked away. "They're telling me Johnny must have been coming back from a party at one of the dorms across the lake. Has anyone bothered to ask around at the dorms?"

"Yes, I've done that," Jack replied. "I—I've gone as far as I can go with it for now. I hit a roadblock. I've talked with a few seminarians who knew Johnny. But no one can tell me where he was Wednesday night."

"Do you think he might have been seeing a girl, someone in town?"

Jack hesitated. "It's possible. I found some pictures in his desk. They were of a girl. I showed them to Pete. He thinks she's a local, but he didn't recognize her—"

"What?" She scowled at him. "Why didn't you tell me about this earlier? I can't believe you went through my brother's desk and took certain things without telling me."

"These were 'cheesecake' photos of some girl taking a shower. I didn't think letting you know about it would do any good."

"My God, who do you think you are, determining what's

good and not good for me?'' she said. ''I really resent that. What else are you keeping from me, Father Murphy?''

''Maggie, I . . .'' He hesitated, then shook his head. ''I apologize.''

''Well, we have to find this girl,'' Maggie said. ''Whoever she is, she could have been the last person to see Johnny alive. Where are these *scandalous* photos?''

''In my room.''

''May I see them, please?''

''Of course,'' Jack said. He glanced down at his church vestment. ''Let me change out of this thing. I'll only be a minute.''

While she waited by her car for him, Maggie had the eerie sensation that someone was studying her every move. As much as she tried to push the thought from her mind, she kept remembering last night. Had someone really been in the room with her, watching her sleep? Was he—looking at her now?

Maybe it was just St. Bartholomew Hall, with all its dark windows, and those statues of the martyrs piously gazing down from their pedestals near the roof. A wind swept in from the lake, and Maggie shuddered. She caught her reflection in the car window. She looked pale and tired.

She could also see the boxes full of Johnny's personal effects. According to Peter, a sweater and a picture book on twentieth-century American history actually belonged to Father Murphy. Johnny had borrowed them.

Maggie opened the back door and started rummaging through one of the boxes. She felt someone coming up behind her. She swiveled around.

It was Jack. He'd changed out of the church vestment and wore his regular priest clothes. ''I'll get those pictures now,'' he said, heading toward the dorm. ''Be right back.''

"Well, hold on a minute." She went back to digging though one of the boxes. "As long as you're going up to your room, I have a book and a sweater somewhere in here that belong to you." Maggie rummaged through a second box. "What did this girl in the cheesecake photos look like anyway?"

"Midtwenties, no raving beauty, but sweet-looking."

Maggie collected three bottles of men's hair care products. "Do you want any of these?" She showed the Vita Z bottles to Jack. "I can't use them. They haven't even been opened."

Jack shook his head. "Thanks anyway. But I don't put any of that stuff in my hair."

"Well, neither did Johnny—if I remember right."

"I can always put them on the shelf outside the shower room," Jack offered. "They'll get used."

Giving him a strained smile, Maggie unloaded the hair products into his cradled hands. "Someone must have given all this junk to Johnny. I can't see him buying any of it. They must have raided a hair salon."

"Maggie?"

She'd started to duck back into the car, but turned to look at him.

Jack glanced down at the hair salon products in his hands. "I suddenly have a pretty good idea where we might find this girl."

They didn't have any luck at the first hair salon, in a minimall by the campus. It was called the Mane Event, and they carried Vita Z hair products, but none of the employees recognized photos of Johnny or the girl.

While Maggie drove to the next spot, she barely said a word to Jack. He'd brought along his Yellow Pages, which included Mt. Vernon–Burlington and neighboring communities like Leroy. Still, it was a thin volume, with only four hair salons listed in the town of Leroy.

The second place, Verna's Beauty Boutique, was for the older generation: pink hair rollers, blue rinses, and a row of huge helmet dryers. No one on the all-female staff was under the age of fifty. Jack and Maggie went through the motions anyway, showing everyone pictures of the girl and Johnny. But it was pointless.

In the car, on their way to the third salon, Maggie's attitude toward him continued to be icy and formal. She seemed barely able to tolerate his presence in the passenger seat. Jack wanted so much to set things right with her. He liked her. In fact, he liked her far more than he was supposed to. Maybe they were both better off with her resenting him.

He had the photos of Johnny's mystery girl in his hand. But he could have been totally off base about this girl and her job. He'd heard those stories about Johnny. Maybe a man working in a salon had showered Johnny with all the free hair supplies.

There hadn't been any men working in the first two beauty parlors, just women.

"We have to take into account that she might not look like she does in those pictures anymore," Maggie announced, watching the road ahead. "The girls and guys who work at my hair place are constantly changing their looks—hair color, style, you name it."

"We might not find her at all," Jack said. "I was merely guessing that she works at a salon."

"Well, obviously *somebody* who knows Johnny works in one," Maggie pointed out.

Jack saw a bit of Johnny in her expression, a vulnerable quality. The wind whipped through the half-open car window, and Maggie's red hair fluttered in the breeze. Jack had to push away the memory of her kiss last night.

"Is this Prescott Street up here?" she asked.

"Yes, um, turn right at the stop sign."

Prescott Street was Leroy's little bohemian section, a block of quaint stores in the middle of a residential area by the lake. The hair salon, called Curl Up and Dye, was sandwiched between a coffee shop and a natural food store. Maggie and Jack parked in front of the salon.

Inside, the place looked like a cellar. It was dark, with track lighting aimed at the three salon chairs, two sinks, and a shelf full of Vita Z hair care products. Pictures of film stars and models had been ripped out of magazines and taped to the burgundy walls. The smell of chemicals and perfumes was overpowering. A radio provided the background music: alternative rock. Jack didn't recognize the song or the group.

And he didn't recognize John's girlfriend among the three women working at their stations. He pulled out the photos again. He and Maggie studied them once more.

"Someone will be with you in a minute," the blonde at the first station called to them, her tone apathetic.

"Thanks," Jack called back, glancing up at her. She wore dark cranberry lipstick and too much mascara. Her platinum hair had black roots.

"I really shouldn't have come into work today," she was telling her customer. She put the finishing touches on a young woman's magenta hair. "I'm still in shock, y'know? I mean, Johnny and I were in love. It's been devastating, it really has."

Now Maggie was looking at the blond girl, too.

"The last person who was in here," the girl went on, "her brother was killed in an automobile accident, which is, like, almost as bad. And she practically had a nervous breakdown, she said."

She'd lost a little weight, and changed her hair. But it was the same girl in the photo. Maggie and Jack watched as she unclipped the customer's smock and led her to the register counter. She gave Jack and his clerical collar a fleeting, curious look.

"Hey, I'm going for a smoke!" she called to someone in the back room. She grabbed her cigarettes from under the counter and started for the door. "We got people up front!"

"Actually, we want to talk with you," Jack said, stepping toward her.

"Who are you guys?" Her heavily made-up eyes shifted from Jack to Maggie.

"This is John Costello's sister," Jack said. "And I'm Father Murphy. I was Johnny's adviser at school."

She nodded. "Oh, yeah, you're his priest friend."

Jack smiled. "I'm sorry, we don't know your name."

"Jonie," she said. "Jonie Sorretto. Actually, it's Joan. But I prefer Joanie, only I changed it, so it spells different: J-O-N-I-E."

Maggie worked up a smile. "That's very unusual."

"How did you guys find me?"

"Just a lucky hunch," Jack said.

"Do you have a few minutes?" Maggie asked. "We need to ask you some questions about Johnny."

"Well, I'm not sure I should be talking with you," she said warily.

"Why not?" Maggie asked. "I mean, well, I couldn't help overhearing. Weren't you just talking to that customer about Johnny?"

Jonie glanced down at the pack of cigarettes in her hand. "I guess it's okay. I really need a smoke. Can we talk outside?"

Jonie's makeup looked harsher in the daylight. She leaned against the salon window and lit up a cigarette. "I only have a few minutes till my next client," she said. "It's Saturday, y'know."

"We'll try to make it quick," Jack said. "How long did you know Johnny?"

"Four, maybe five months. He came in here for a haircut one afternoon. He was my last client of the day. So—we went out for coffee and a walk after. We ended up at my place."

"So—was this a one-time thing?" Jack asked. "Or did you two keep seeing each other?"

Jonie nervously puffed on her cigarette. "I don't think I should be telling you any of this."

"Why do you keep saying that?" Maggie asked.

"What I mean is . . . yeah, I was Johnny's girlfriend. But he wanted me to keep it secret, y'know, the seminary and all that."

Jack smiled at her. "Jonie, I don't think John would mind you confiding in us—especially now. Did you see a lot of each other?"

She nodded. "Yeah. Johnny and I got together maybe once or twice a week—regular."

"When did you last see him?" Jack asked.

"Friday, after work. I cooked him dinner, Kraft macaroni and cheese. He said he couldn't stay long, because he had to go do something his friend—um, what's his name, the queer . . ."

Jack just shook his head and glanced at Maggie.

"Peter?" she offered.

"That's right," Jonie said, nodding. She took another drag off her cigarette. "The way Johnny talked about him, I'm pretty sure he's gay. I even asked Johnny once. He said he didn't know, and it really didn't matter to him. He wasn't into judging people, y'know?" She tossed away her cigarette, then exhaled a last stream of smoke.

"Did Johnny mention any other friends he had?" Jack asked. "Anyone on this side of the lake?"

She hesitated, then shook her head. "Nope."

"Do you know what he was doing on Wednesday night?"

"I don't have a clue. In fact, I really can't stay out here talking to you." She moved toward the salon entrance. "My break's over, and I have another client coming in."

"Jonie?" Maggie said.

She stopped and turned in the doorway.

"I know he wanted to keep it a secret," Maggie said. "But Johnny told me about you. He really, really cared about you, Jonie. I know how much you must be hurting right now, and how difficult it is to talk about it." She dug a card out of her purse. "If you think of anything that might help us figure out what happened Wednesday night, call me. Or if you just want to talk, give me a ring. Okay?"

"Okay," Jonie said, tucking Maggie's business card into her pack of cigarettes.

"I'm sure Johnny would have wanted us to be friends."

"Okay," Jonie said again. She gave them both a slightly uneasy look, then retreated into the salon.

Jack and Maggie started toward the car. "Bless me, Father, for I have sinned," she said. "I just lied to that girl."

"You pulled it off with finesse."

"Really? I kept thinking she could see my disapproval. I know it sounds rotten. But I always pictured my little brother finding some sweet, junior-league Gwyneth Paltrow for a girlfriend. Instead, I find out he was messing around with . . ." She trailed off. "Well, I'm sure Jonie's very nice."

They climbed inside her car. Maggie settled behind the wheel, but she didn't start up the engine. She stared ahead through the windshield. "Did you get the impression that someone told her not to talk with us?"

"Definitely," Jack nodded. "She only said it about three times."

"Yet she was chatting that customer's ear off about Johnny when we first came in."

"Like you said. She must have been told not to talk to *us*."

"Then somebody knew we'd be coming to talk to her," Maggie said. "You know, for the last three days, I've had this feeling that I'm being watched—especially during my visits up here. I know it sounds crazy. But it's just a sensation I have."

Jack frowned. "Actually, Maggie, people have been watching us. There's been some backlash from last night. We were seen together at the Lakeside Inn tavern, and checking into a room." He sighed. "This is a lousy time to bring it up. But we have to be careful. The decree from above is that I'm not to see you anymore."

Maggie started up the car, then she pulled away from the curb. "I'm sorry, Jack," she said finally. "I shouldn't have called you last night—"

"No. I'm glad you did." Jack sighed. "I'm just sorry for the way it turned out. I understand why you're upset with me—"

"Yes, well, let's drop it, okay?" she cut in.

"All right," Jack muttered, embarrassed. "But according to the police and the school administration, Johnny's death was an accident. That's the official word."

Maggie gave him a wary sidelong glance. "And you're not to rock the boat, is that it?"

"Those are my orders," Jack said. "Only I'm not giving up until we have an explanation for what happened to Johnny."

"Thank you, Jack," she said, keeping her eyes on the road.

They approached the College Road bridge, which crossed over Lake Leroy to St. Bart's. "It might be best if you drop me off here, rather than in front of the dorm,'' Jack announced. ''We shouldn't push our luck.''

Maggie veered over to the side of the road and slowed to a stop. ''You feel it, too, don't you?'' she said.

He hesitated before climbing out of the car. ''Feel what?''

''That we're being watched.''

''Yes, Maggie,'' he whispered. ''I feel it, too. Take care, okay?''

Jack climbed out and closed the door. He stepped aside as the car pulled away. It disappeared around a curve in the road.

Peter shouldn't have come to the Ham & Egger. The old greasy spoon was on the edge of campus, a dingy place with tiled floors, orange Formica booths, and a jukebox that played mostly country-and-western music. It was a wonder the little restaurant stayed in business, because it was never crowded, and the waitresses were impersonal to the point of rudeness. Still, the Ham & Egger had great, cheap, all-day breakfasts with huge helpings. Peter and Johnny had discovered the place during their second week at Our Lady of Sorrows. They'd gone there for a dinner-breakfast every Thursday night. The reprieve from St. Bartholomew Hall's cafeteria had become a tradition.

But Peter hadn't realized how depressing and seedy the Ham & Egger was until now, sitting alone in there for the first time. He stared at the sun-faded Pepsi clock, the cigarette burns on the Formica tabletop, and the grimy, smoke-stained walls. He did his best to avoid looking at the only other customer in the joint: an old man with a toupee and a bad case of the shakes, seated by the window.

Peter picked at his pigs-in-blankets. He really wasn't very hungry. He'd already had a big breakfast with Maggie, and it was a bit too early for dinner.

He'd spent the better part of his afternoon wandering from one campus locale to another—all of the places he used to go with Johnny: the lakeside park where they'd often thrown around a frisbee, the arcade, the video store, and the Triplex movie theater. But he didn't pay much attention to the film.

He kept thinking about how he should have stood up to Ted Patchett. He could have taken on that skinny weasel. One good adrenaline rush, and he'd have beaten the crap out of him.

After the movie got out, Peter had roamed around the campus in a daze. He'd thought about Father Murphy letting those sophomores from St. Clement Hall get away with murder—literally. Peter didn't trust him anymore. He didn't trust anyone. His one true friend was gone. He had no one looking out for him. He had to watch his back, like Anton had said.

A loud crash startled him, and he turned to see the waitress standing over a broken plate and a mess of food on the floor. "Son of a bitch!" she growled.

Peter suddenly had to get out of there. He left some money on the table and hurried outside. As he walked past the front window, the old man with palsy gaped at him.

Peter ducked into an alley beside the Ham & Egger, then started crying. He'd never lost anyone close to him before. He didn't realize how grief could sometimes overtake him with sneak attacks. This one lasted only a couple of minutes.

It wasn't until he blew his nose and wiped his eyes that Peter noticed the dark, ominous clouds sweeping across the sky. The wind blew a few pieces of trash by him. A storm was coming up. Yet it was still very quiet. Peter suddenly didn't feel safe in that alley. He'd been trying to ignore the twinge in his gut all afternoon, the notion that someone was following him.

He wandered back to the sidewalk. A blue Volkswagen bug pulled out of a spot across the street. Earlier this afternoon, Peter had seen a car just like that one, parked outside the arcade. A man had been sitting behind the wheel. He'd worn a stocking cap and sunglasses. Peter had thought the man was staring at him.

If this was the same VW, it wasn't following him. The car turned down the street a couple of blocks ahead. Peter told himself that he was being paranoid. He moved on.

A couple of raindrops hit him. If he wanted to beat the oncoming storm, he had to take the Whopper Way shortcut to the dorm. The Burger King was only four blocks away. He could see St. Bart's on the other side of the lake. One by one, lights went on in the dorm.

As he started toward the Burger King, Peter decided to pack up and leave school tonight. He didn't feel safe here. There was no reason to stay with Johnny gone. He shouldn't have let Father Murphy talk him into staying.

A flash of lightning appeared over the treetops across the lake. Peter picked up his pace as he approached the Burger King. He started to cut through the parking lot to the back, but suddenly stopped in his tracks.

He saw the blue VW bug parked behind the squat building. The car was empty. Peter backed up and peeked into the restaurant. He didn't see anyone in there with a stocking cap or sunglasses—no one with the general look of that anonymous man.

He hurried to the opening in the fence, then started down the slope toward Mendini's Crossing. Weaving around bushes and rocks, he watched the sky grow even darker. He felt an occasional raindrop. In a few minutes, the old slab of concrete that parted the stream would be too slippery for him.

Even now, as he started across the narrow barricade, Peter had to watch his footing. He held his arms out to balance himself.

Another flash lit up the sky, and Peter hesitated for a

moment. The woods on the other side of Mendini's Crossing were dark and still. Yet the flicker of light seemed to illuminate a figure standing amid the shadowy trees.

Peter didn't move. Frozen on the concrete slab, he couldn't take his eyes off that spot in the forest across the way. In the distance, he heard the rumble of thunder.

Another blink of lightning, and Peter saw him again. It was the man with the stocking cap, only now he had the cap pulled down over his face. He wore an old lumber jacket. Peter thought he saw something shiny in his hand. The lumberjack man darted from one tree to another, then suddenly came out from the shadows.

Peter tried to back away, and almost lost his footing. He wanted to scream out, but he couldn't get a breath. The faceless lumberjack scurried down the slope toward him. He held a knife in his hand.

Peter tried to turn around and run, but his feet slipped out from under him. Suddenly he was falling. Flailing his arms, he could only grab at the air. In that instant, he felt so helpless and stupid. And doomed.

All at once, he plunged into the cold, murky water. He hit his head against something hard. Peter barely felt any of it. The last image in his mind was of that faceless man coming toward him.

Then blackness.

"Are you still cold, buddy? You're trembling."

Peter sat in the tub. Anton Sorenson was bent over him, dabbing his upper forehead with a cold washcloth. "Is the water warm enough?" he asked.

"It's fine," Peter said.

They were in Anton's bathroom. Anton had undressed down to his jeans. Peter couldn't help admiring his strong physique, that rippling torso and the broad chest, still glistening with sweat and rainwater. His blond hair was in damp, dark ringlets.

Anton took the washcloth away. "You'll probably have a goose-egg on your noggin by tonight."

Peter didn't recall Anton diving into that tributary of Lake Leroy to rescue him. But through a fog he'd heard someone urging him to hold on. The next thing he knew, Anton was pulling him out of the cold water. "Did you get a look at the guy who attacked you?" he asked, catching his breath. "I only saw him from behind—running into the woods. He was dressed like a lumberjack. . . ."

Peter remembered leaning on Anton while they made their way up the slope to the Burger King parking lot. Anton waved a hand in front of his face. "How many fingers am I holding up?"

He must have answered correctly, because Anton chuckled and said, "You'll be okay, Pete."

By the time they reached St. Clement Hall, the rain pelted them, and they were both shivering. Peter felt a bit woozy as they climbed the stairs to the third floor. Anton practically carried him into his room, then he started up the bath and helped him undress. At the time, Peter had been too dazed to feel embarrassed.

But now that he'd had a few minutes to soak and recuperate in the warm tub, he was indeed very self-conscious. He'd taken showers with other guys in the locker room after gym class, and on a couple of memorable overnights, he'd seen Johnny naked—briefly. But he'd never felt this intimately naked with another guy—and a guy like Anton, too, older and so good-looking. Peter tried not to gawk at him.

"Boy, listen to it thunder," Anton said. He lowered the toilet seat lid and sat down. "Isn't it cool? I spent a couple of years living in Virginia, and we had some great thunderstorms out there. I miss them. We don't get them out here." He reached down and fanned the bathwater with his hand, accidentally brushing his fingertips against Peter's knee. "Still warm enough?"

"Yeah, thanks," Peter said. "Thanks for saving me, too."

Anton flicked water into Peter's face. "Hey, no sweat."

For a moment, neither of them said anything. Peter listened to the rain outside; it sounded tinny coming through the bathroom vent.

Anton stood up and unzipped his jeans. Peter quickly looked away. He heard Anton's belt buckle clink against the tile floor. When he peeked up, Anton was once again sitting on the toilet seat lid—this time in his underwear. The damp white briefs had become transparent in spots. He went through the pockets of his wet jeans.

"Did you want to get in?" Peter asked nervously. "I mean, I can get out of the tub, if you want to get in. I mean, you must be pretty cold—"

"Relax," Anton said. "I'm not in any hurry." He stood up, then draped his jeans over the towel rack. Peter watched him out of the corner of his eye. The way Anton's briefs clung to him, he might as well have been naked. Peter tried not to stare.

He shifted in the tub, bringing his knees up closer to his chest. When he glanced up at Anton again, the handsome senior was running his thumbs around the elastic banding of his briefs. He started to peel them off, but turned and walked out of the bathroom.

"I saw the jacket he was wearing," Anton called from the bedroom. "If the creep who attacked you is one of the guys on my floor, I'll find him, Pete. Believe you me. I'll do a room-to-room search, and track down who has that lumber jacket."

Peter caught Anton's reflection in the mirror on the bathroom door. The bedroom was dark, but Peter could see Anton naked, stepping into a pair of sweatpants. "It looked like he was wearing a ski mask," Anton continued. "You didn't see his face, did you?"

"Um, not really, but I know his car." Peter touched the bump on his forehead. "A pale blue Volkswagen bug was following me around this afternoon. I saw it in the Burger King parking lot, too. He must have known where I was headed."

Tying up the front of his sweatpants, Anton returned to the bathroom. "Did you get a license-plate number or anything?"

"No, sorry." Peter hugged his knees to his chest.

"Between the jacket and the car, we're going to find this guy," Anton said. "I have a feeling this phantom lumberjack is one of the guys you spoke with here earlier today—or maybe someone who's afraid you'll eventually get to him. He's obviously somehow involved in your buddy's death. For my money, it's one of the guys on this floor."

Peter sighed. "Well, I don't think it's that asshole I was talking with earlier."

"Ted Patchett?"

"Yeah, he's too skinny. The lumberjack guy was bigger, taller."

"Rick Pettinger is tall," Anton said. "He left school this morning, but he could have come back. He's the one I told you about, the one Murphy let get away. And he'd have access to a car—maybe a blue VW bug."

"But he doesn't even know me," Peter said.

Anton sat on the edge of the tub. "He could have heard about you from John Costello. Take my word, Rick Pettinger's as guilty as sin. I saw him with your friend, John, on several occasions, but he lied to Murphy about it—said he barely even knew John Costello."

"Well, then, you're right. He's a liar," Peter said. He remembered Rick was the one who'd had a fight with Johnny that night a couple of months ago.

"So Rick Pettinger is our main suspect. Listen, do you want to work together on this, Pete?"

Peter hesitated.

Anton shrugged and absently scratched his bare chest. "Unless you want to go to the police, tell them you were attacked today. But I don't know what they'd do about it—except make a report and let the school look into it."

Peter sighed. "You're probably right."

Anton put a hand on his knee. "You know it, bud. Starting tonight, I'll check room to room for that lumber jacket. Tomorrow, we'll call Rick Pettinger, and let him know he's not getting away with anything. In the meantime, no one should know we're working together. It would really screw things up if Father Murphy or anyone else found out. Dig?"

Peter nodded. "Okay."

At that point, he'd have agreed to anything Anton asked of him.

Chapter Eleven

SORRETTO, J was printed on the buzzer. According to the phone book, the neglected, dark wood-frame duplex was Jonie's current address. Jack stood on the front stoop, where someone had left a large open bag of kitty litter. Old bed-sheets hung in the first-floor window in lieu of curtains.

In his hand, Jack held his green, pocket-size notebook. The first ten pages were now full of names and ideas. The name he'd written down most was Rick Pettinger, the semi-narian who had denied knowing Johnny, then suddenly left school. Rick's former lover had called him "dangerous."

Did Jonie know about Johnny's other relationships? Had she ever heard of Rick Pettinger? Jack had wanted to ask her yesterday, but couldn't bring it up in front of Maggie.

He hadn't phoned Jonie in advance. It was 11:30 on Sunday morning. She was probably pulling herself out of bed just about now.

Jack put the notebook in his pocket and pressed the buzzer. He waited a minute, then pressed it again.

"Whozit?" was the response over the intercom.

"It's Father Murphy, Jonie. Can I come up?"

Silence.

"Jonie?"

"Be right down," she replied.

Jack waited. And waited. At least three or four minutes passed. He thought about walking around the house to see if she'd ducked out a back way. He was about to buzz again when the door flung open.

"Yeah, what do you want?" Jonie asked, half hiding behind the door. She was dressed in black jeans and a ratty black pullover. Her dyed platinum hair was pinned up in back. She smoked a cigarette. Her black cherry lipstick left a mark on the filter.

"I'd like to ask you a couple more questions," Jack said.

She rolled her raccoon-painted eyes. "I really don't have time right now."

"It won't take long," Jack assured her.

She sighed and blew out a stream of smoke. "Okay, what?"

"Did Johnny ever mention a friend named Rick Pettinger?"

She quickly shook her head. "Nope. I told you yesterday, he never talked about any of his friends except for what's-his-name—Peter. And I already told you yesterday everything I know about him." She took a drag from her cigarette. "Now, is that it? Because I'm meeting a friend to go up to Vancouver, and I'm late."

"Please, just one more minute, okay?" Jack said. "Has anyone else come to you about Johnny? The police or anyone from the faculty of Our Lady of Sorrows?"

"No. You and his sister are the only ones."

"Then why did you keep saying yesterday that you weren't supposed to talk to us?"

"I don't get what you mean," Jonie replied, frowning.

"You said it two or three times, *'I don't think I should be talking to you.'* Did someone tell you not to talk with us?"

"Yeah, Johnny," she said, impatiently. "Shit, I already explained that to you. He wanted to keep it a secret about us." She glanced at her wristwatch. "Hey, look. I gotta go."

She turned and ran up the stairs to her apartment. But she'd left the door open. Jack stepped in and listened to her stomping around. It sounded like she was alone up there. In less than a minute, she scurried back down the stairs, carrying a black leather jacket and her purse.

"Jesus, I thought we were through," Jonie grumbled. She closed the door this time and locked it. "Listen, I've already told you everything I know."

Jack followed her to her car, parked on the street in front of the duplex. "Jonie, you know what really happened to Johnny, don't you? Did somebody kill him?"

Jonie fumbled with her keys, then unlocked the car door. "I gotta go," she muttered. She ducked into her car, then started up the engine.

Jack stepped aside as she pulled away from the curb. Its tires screeching, the car picked up speed.

Frowning, he watched the blue Volkswagen bug peel down the road.

Peter sat at one of the white plastic café tables by the side entrance to the Stop 'n' Fuel-Up Mart. It was a combination gas station, convenience store, and snack bar on the edge of town. The hot food they served was limited to items from the microwave or burgers and hot dogs that had been under heater-lights for about six hours. Peter bought a Super-Sip twenty-four-ounce Coke, which tasted a little funny, like they'd used too much soap to clean the machine, but he sipped it anyway.

Though the sun had come out, Peter still felt cold, so he kept his jacket on. He watched cars pull up to the self-serve pumps, but none of the customers looked like anyone from the college. Nobody recognized him, and nobody was following him.

"Hey, partner."

Peter turned and smiled at him. He never seemed to see Anton coming. This time, Anton had appeared from around the back of the squat building. He wore a thin sweatshirt and track shorts. A V-shaped stain of perspiration seeped through the front of his pullover, and he was a little out of breath. He flopped down in the other plastic chair. "I jogged over," he announced. "How are you doin'? That bump on your forehead doesn't look so bad. Can I have a gulp?"

Peter started to nod when Anton grabbed the twenty-four-ounce container and drew from the straw. "Tastes soapy," Anton commented. "So, hey, did you tell anybody about meeting me here today?"

Peter shook his head. "You told me not to."

"Cool," he said, glancing around. "Did anything happen since yesterday? Anything I should know about?"

Peter shrugged. "Nothing. Zip."

"Well, I've been busier than a mosquito in a nudist colony," Anton said. "I checked five rooms in my wing last night and two more this morning. No sign of that lumber jacket. Maybe it's stashed someplace else. As for the car, a junior over in St. Matthew Hall owns a silver-gray VW bug. His name's Larry Blades, and I've seen him hanging around with some of the guys from my floor. He's one of the few guys who has a car—"

"No," Peter cut in, shaking his head. "The car I saw was light blue."

"You sure? Light blue and gray are pretty close—"

"No. This was light blue. I'm positive."

Anton sighed, then took another swig of Coke. "Well, I'll keep looking," he said. "Maybe one of the locals has a light blue Volkswagen." He pulled up his sweatshirt to reveal a money belt. He unzipped the side pouch and fished out a fistful of quarters. "Ready to make a few long-distance calls?" he asked, spilling the coins across the tabletop. He reached back into his pouch and drew out a piece of paper with a phone number written on it. "Do you remember what you're supposed to tell him?"

Grimacing, Peter nodded. "I'm a little nervous."

"Then c'mon," Anton replied, getting to his feet. "Let's get it over with. Sooner the better. Grab that change, will ya?"

Anton picked up the Super-Sip, and they walked around the corner to the pay phone. The call had to be made from a pay phone so it couldn't be traced to them. "You know, I'd make the call myself," Anton said. "But he might recognize my voice. Just hang up if he's not home or you get an answering machine."

Peter grabbed the receiver. Anton read him the number, and he punched it in.

Anton sipped his Coke and leaned closer to him.

Peter counted three ring tones, then someone picked up. "Hello?"

"Rick Pettinger?" Peter asked, trying to make his voice gravelly.

"Who's calling?"

"Rick, I need to ask you something," Peter said. "After you drowned him, what did you do with John Costello's clothes?"

Rounding a curve in the track, Jack glanced over at the old cemetery. The little plot of land looked particularly eerie at night with those decrepit statues and headstones, and the dark forest looming beyond it.

Jack usually didn't run in the evenings, but he hadn't had any real exercise in a while. He needed to work off the tension. All day, he'd felt frustrated and irritable. And he hadn't accomplished a damn thing.

Going to see Jonie Sorretto had been a waste of time. He thought about consulting Father Garcia, telling him about Jonie. But he didn't trust Garcia anymore. The school's head of administration had originally been so keen on digging for the truth. Now he seemed bent on covering up everything connected with John's death.

Jack wasn't even sure Garcia had actually checked that blood sample from the grave marker down in the crypt. Was it really someone else's blood type? Garcia could have lied to him about it.

Jack spent the afternoon hunting down Father Stutesman in the science department. When he finally got a hold of Stutesman on the phone the science professor confirmed Garcia's story. He'd examined the blood scrapings. And yes, it was a bit peculiar that Father Garcia had brought him the sample in a handkerchief. But the tests showed the blood type as AB, no mistake about it. And didn't the seminarian who drowned have type O blood?

Jack thanked Father Stutesman and hung up.

He also talked to Maggie. She'd phoned, asking if there were any new developments in the investigation. He felt so lame, admitting to her that he had nothing.

"Nothing at all?" she'd asked. "No leads about the twenty-two hundred dollars or anything?"

"I'm sorry. I've been running in circles today. It's been very defeating."

"Well, Johnny's funeral Mass is on Tuesday. It's going to be here in Seattle, Jack. I was wondering if you could deliver the eulogy. I know Johnny would have wanted you to. And I want you to."

She took him by surprise. "I'd be honored, Maggie," he managed to say. "Of course I will."

But later, as he tried to write the eulogy, Jack drew a blank. All he could think of was that he'd been responsible for Johnny, and he'd let him die.

So Jack had put on his sweats and his running shoes, then taken to the track. He poured it on as he tallied up his seventh lap around the playfield. Perspiration covered his face and neck. Jack was so focused on pushing and punishing himself that he didn't see anything except the asphalt track in front of him.

He didn't notice that someone else was out there.

"Father Murphy?"

Jack almost stumbled when he caught sight of a man, silhouetted by the lights of St. Bartholomew Hall. He slowed down and tried to get his breath back. He approached the shadowy figure. "Yeah?" he said. "Who's over there?"

As he came closer, Jack recognized Tom Garcia. The priest stood with his hands in the pockets of his overcoat. He was frowning. "Get cleaned up and dressed, Jack," he said. "I'll meet you in front of St. Bart's in five minutes."

"What's this about?" Jack asked.

Garcia turned and started walking away from him. "Five minutes," he called over his shoulder. "Wear your clerical clothes."

Jack took a thirty-second shower, then quickly donned his black suit and his clerical shirt and collar. He wondered what Garcia wanted. Had Father Stutesman given him away? Jack was sweating again by the time he stepped out of St. Bartholomew Hall's front entrance.

Smoking a cigarette, Tom Garcia leaned against a shiny, black Lexus parked in the driveway. When he saw Jack, Garcia tossed aside his cigarette, then he nodded toward the car's passenger door. "Get in," he said. "We have at least an hour's drive ahead of us. There's a social call we need to make down in Everett."

Jack ducked into the passenger side and noticed the leather seats. The car still smelled new. It didn't make sense that they couldn't get computers for certain freshman classes, but the school's head of administration had to drive around in a forty-thousand-dollar automobile.

Jack waited until Garcia had situated himself behind the wheel and fastened his seat belt. "Would it be out of line for me to ask what all this is about?" he said finally.

Garcia started up the ignition. "We're going to see Rick Pettinger in the hospital. He asked for you."

"What's he doing in the hospital? Is he sick?"

His eyes on the road, Garcia shifted gears. "Rick Pettinger's in the hospital because he tried to commit suicide this afternoon."

With the Pettinger dollars at work, Rick had been given a private room at Everett General Hospital, with a beautiful view of Everett Bay. For the Pettingers, the hospital staff also bent visiting hours a little, especially since the visitors were a couple of priests.

Jack and Father Garcia arrived at 9:35. Mr. Pettinger had been waiting for them and obviously had been giving all the nurses a hard time. He was a cold, tightly wound gray-haired man in his midfifties. Pouring on the charm, Father Garcia took Pettinger down the hall for coffee while Jack went in to see Rick.

He looked pale and emaciated in that hospital bed. His black hair was unwashed. It appeared as if he'd been deprived of sleep and nourishment in the two days since Jack had last seen him. They had Rick on an IV for dehydration, and there were bandages on his wrists.

He'd made the cuts with a paint-scraping razor that he'd smuggled from his father's basement workroom to his own bathroom on the second floor. Rick's sister had heard a thud upstairs. She'd discovered him, passed out in a pool of blood on the bathroom floor.

"You want to hear something funny?" Rick asked. His hospital bed had been adjusted so he was sitting up a little. He didn't move his head from the pillow, but he gave Jack a weary smile.

"Sure," Jack said quietly. "I could use a laugh right about now." He pulled a chair beside Rick's bed and sat down.

"They had to give me a transfusion when they first brought me here. And I guess my father made a big stink about the blood supply. He wanted to make sure no 'queers' were donating blood, because of AIDS and all. Isn't that funny?"

Jack shrugged. "Maybe you'll be able to educate him—in time."

"I doubt it." Rick sighed.

"You never know," Jack replied, patting his shoulder. "People can change. For example, only two days ago, you were telling me that you didn't associate with 'queers'."

"Yeah, that was a pretty shitty thing to say, I guess."

"The point is, I know it took a lot of guts for you to confide in me just now. I appreciate your honesty, Rick."

Rick tugged at the bedsheets, rearranging them. "When you almost die, it makes you reevaluate things. Putting up a front isn't so important anymore."

"So, are you ready to tell me about John?" Jack asked gently. "Is that why you asked for me?"

"First things first," Rick said with a wary glance. "You didn't have anything to do with those phone calls this afternoon, did you?"

Jack shook his head. "What are you talking about?"

"I figured you wouldn't know," Rick replied. "You're a decent guy. As much as I resented you the other night at St. Clement's, I could tell you were a real decent guy, Father Murphy."

"What about these phone calls?" Jack asked.

"Some creep kept phoning me this afternoon—three different calls in an hour's time. I tried to do a last-call return, but the number wasn't listed. This guy kept saying these awful things about Johnny and me, things like how long did it take to drown him, and what did I do with his clothes, and did I have sex with him first."

Rick gazed down at the bedsheets and slowly shook his head. "Do you know what it's like to hear that about someone close to you?"

"So—you did know Johnny?" he asked.

Rick nodded. "I was with him on Wednesday night. We met down in the catacombs beneath the church. We had an argument. I found out he was seeing a couple of other guys on my floor. I kind of suspected as much, but I didn't want to believe it. I knew Johnny and his sister weren't very well-off financially. So every time we got together, I gave him some money. Well, he told me he'd been taking money from these other guys, too."

"Did he say how much money he was getting?" Jack asked.

"I don't know about the others, but I usually gave him between twenty and forty bucks whenever we met."

Dumbfounded, Jack nodded. Now he knew how Johnny had saved up that twenty-two hundred dollars. As he did the math, Jack realized that John must have been very busy.

Rick tugged at his bedding again. "Anyway, it was humiliating to hear about the other guys—and the money. I was devastated."

"Of course you were," Jack said. He was devastated,

too—for different reasons. Johnny wasn't the golden boy he'd thought him to be.

"Maybe I should have seen it coming. Johnny had been pulling away from me the last few weeks. But it all came to a boil on Wednesday night. I—I slapped him. And he punched me in the face. Gave me a bloody nose. Right away, Johnny started apologizing. But I was so mad. I mean, I was bleeding all over the place."

"Are you type AB blood?" Jack asked.

"Yeah, why do you ask?"

"Nothing," Jack muttered. "Go on."

"I know he felt bad, but I wanted him to feel even worse," Rick admitted. "So I called him a whore, and every hateful thing I could think of, whatever I figured would hurt him. Johnny got dressed and left. I remember wishing he were dead." Rick wiped his eyes again, then let out a sad laugh. "And wouldn't you know? I got my goddamn wish."

"It doesn't work that way," Jack said. "It's not your fault."

"If only I really believed that," Rick replied, his voice broken with emotion. "It was the last I saw of him. During lunch the next day, I heard that he'd drowned. I couldn't believe it. I kept thinking about all the horrible things I said to him that night. I didn't mean any of it. Do you suppose Johnny knew that?"

"Friends quarrel and they say harsh words to each other," Jack pointed out. "That's just a part of friendship sometimes."

"Well, Johnny and I were more than 'friends'." Rick frowned. "I couldn't admit that to you the other night. When you came to talk to me, I was so confused and scared. All I could think of was protecting myself. And Anton, he was so . . . obnoxious, I got all defensive." He squirmed beneath the bedsheets. "I wouldn't be surprised if Anton was somehow behind those calls today."

"I'll look into it," Jack said. "Listen, the other night, did you follow me to the church basement?"

"Yeah," Rick whispered. "I have my own key. I was afraid you'd eventually find some stuff I had hidden down there by one of the graves."

"Monsignor Thayer Swann's grave?" Jack asked.

Rick nodded. "Then you found them. I was praying you hadn't. After you left, I gathered up everything and tossed it in a Dumpster behind St. Matthew Hall. I hardly slept a wink that night. That's when I decided to get out. I just couldn't stay at Our Lady of Sorrows any longer. I had to leave."

"Why?" Jack asked quietly. "Because you didn't want anyone finding out about you and Johnny?"

"That's a big part of it, yes," Rick admitted. "But it's the school, too. There's something wrong with the place. Don't you feel it at times? Johnny's death, the other kid who drowned three years ago, and the one who committed suicide—"

"What suicide?"

"Don't you know about the guy who hung himself?" Rick asked.

Jack shook his head.

"It happened the same year as that drowning. I remember, because that's all they talked about my freshman year—what went on the year before. Julian Doyle drowned, and this other guy, Oliver Theron, killed himself. He was a senior. I heard he left school all of a sudden. Then a couple of days later, while his parents were gone, he went up on the roof of his house. He tied one end of a rope around the chimney and the other end around his neck, then he jumped off the edge of the roof. I guess his parents found him there."

"I never heard that story," Jack murmured.

"Huh, I just had a weird thought," Rick said. "Maybe

one had to do with the other. The drowning, then the suicide, it happened in that order." He let out a sad laugh. "Y'know, if I'd gotten it right this afternoon, history would have repeated itself. Another drowning followed by another suicide. That would have been a real weird coincidence."

"That's no way to talk, Rick. What you tried this afternoon was really foolish. You might be in a hospital bed and feeling pretty shitty, but you're so much better off right now than you were when we last talked. You're going to be okay."

" 'Suicide is a permanent solution to a temporary problem,' " Rick said, shifting under the covers. "That's what the hospital social worker told me this afternoon. I think she got it out of some teen suicide prevention handbook."

"Nevertheless, it's true," Jack said, patting his shoulder. "Quit being ashamed and beating yourself up over who you are."

His head tipped back on the pillow, Rick gave him a cynical smile. "Is that the Catholic Church's official stance on the subject of who I am?"

"Well, make it *your* official stance," Jack replied. "And stop blaming yourself over what happened. John's death was an accident."

Rick gazed at him. "You don't really believe Johnny's death was accidental, do you?"

Jack frowned, then shook his head. "No, I don't."

There was an abrupt knock on the door, then Rick's father poked his head in. Jack stood up.

Mr. Pettinger gazed narrowly at his son. "Well, are you finished with whatever it is you needed to get off your chest?"

Rick stared at Jack, and gave him a faint smile. "Yes, we're finished here, Father."

* * *

"Then it's finished," Father Garcia said.

Having assigned chauffeur duty to Jack, he sat on the passenger side of the Lexus. The headlights from oncoming cars cast harsh shadows across Garcia's unsmiling face. They were headed back to Our Lady of Sorrows. Jack had told him about his discussion with Rick. He didn't share with him the revelation that Johnny had been taking money for sex.

Apparently, Garcia had managed to placate Rick's father, who didn't really blame Our Lady of Sorrows for his son's bizarre behavior. The Pettinger dollars would still be working for the archdiocese. They'd even discussed the possibility of Rick taking his final exams during the summer—so he could return to the seminary next semester.

"We have things under control now, Jack," Garcia continued. "So that's that, okay? End of story, case closed. We're all going to put John Costello's death behind us. If his sister should call you up, refer her to me. I don't want you to have anything more to do with her—or this case."

"That won't be easy," Jack said, his eyes on the highway. "Maggie Costello asked me to give the eulogy at Johnny's funeral Mass on Tuesday."

"I'll call her tomorrow morning and convey your regrets."

"Actually, I'd like to give the talk. It's very important to me. John was my friend."

"I'm sorry, Jack. But the more you distance yourself from this case, the better. And I repeat, the same thing goes for the sister." He sighed. "I met her briefly that afternoon you and I first talked. She came to talk with Monsignor Fuller. She's a very attractive woman."

"What does that have to do with anything?" Jack asked.

"Do you have feelings for her?"

"I'm sorry, Tom, but I don't think that's any of your business."

"It certainly is my business when you put the school's reputation at risk. You have feelings for this girl, don't you?"

"Yes," Jack muttered.

"Then don't see her again."

"But the funeral—"

"You're not delivering John Costello's eulogy. You're not even attending the funeral. Those are my orders. End of discussion."

Jack was silent for a moment. He stared at the road ahead. "I guess I missed something," he finally said, tightening his grip on the steering wheel. "A few days ago, I thought you didn't want to sweep John Costello's death under the rug. I thought you were a real nice guy, Tom. When did you suddenly become such a son of a bitch?"

Garcia glanced out his window. "I'll pretend I didn't hear that, Jack."

For the next hour, all the way back to the seminary, they didn't say a word to each other.

Chapter Twelve

Phillip Koehler's room was extremely tidy, with two big Edward Hopper prints on the wall. Though unlit, the orange spice votive on his desk still gave off a pleasant scent. Peter had sneaked into four sophomores' rooms this afternoon, and Phillip Koehler's was the nicest so far.

Phillip was in a group with other seminarians on the third floor of St. Clement Hall volunteering at a nursing home every other Monday afternoon. They'd gone off to Bellingham in a van, and wouldn't be back until six.

Anton figured it was a perfect time for Peter and him to conduct room checks in search of the lumber jacket. It was the key to finding Peter's attacker, who was most likely also John Costello's killer.

For the past couple of days, Anton had been conducting the room-to-room investigation on his own. In his search, he'd unearthed a stash of marijuana in one of the rooms. He'd stolen enough for a joint they could share some time later. He'd also found various assortments of nudie magazines. He'd told Peter which seminarians were into gay, straight, or kinky porn. But Anton had made Peter swear he wouldn't tell anyone. "Everything I've told you about these guys is in confidence," Anton maintained. "We're partners in an investigation. It's all about keeping secrets. Besides, we don't anyone to know we're in cahoots, right?"

Peter thought the room checks were more productive than those phone calls he'd made to Rick Pettinger the previous day. The tactic hadn't seemed to do any good. By the third call, he'd felt as if he were just being cruel, and he'd asked Anton if they could stop.

Sneaking into all these rooms was a lot more interesting— if not a bit dangerous. With Anton working next door or across the hall, they inspected eleven rooms in a little over an hour. In the corner of one seminarian's closet, hidden in a shoe box, Peter had found a half dozen *Playboys*. But he hadn't uncovered anything else very significant.

So far, there were no hidden treasures in Phillip Koehler's quarters. It was close to six o'clock, and they wouldn't have time to check any more rooms after this. Just as well. The novelty of going through other peoples' things had worn off a while ago.

Next door, Anton knocked twice on the wall, indicating that he was finishing up. Peter heard him open and close the door to the next room. He checked Phillip's closet, and did a double take. Among the clothes on their hangers, he saw something with the same blackwatch plaid pattern as the mackinaw, but it was a flannel shirt—not a lumber jacket.

Anton started to whistle in the hallway. It was their signal that someone was out there. Peter had to stay inside the room until he got the all clear, which would be Anton whistling the theme to *Green Acres*.

Peter quietly closed the closet door. He glanced around the room to make sure he'd left everything in its place. Anton stopped whistling.

Peter kept waiting for him to start up with a rendition of the TV show he knew from Nick at Night. He thought he heard Anton talking to someone. He crept to the door. Suddenly, Anton's voice got louder: "So, Phillip, are you back from the nursing home already?"

Peter froze by the door.

"Yeah, I got a ride with Father Swanson. The rest are taking the van."

"Hey, Phillip, you know—"

"What are you talking so loud for? Cut me a break. I get enough of that from all those poor, old deaf patients at the home. Would you mind stepping aside?"

Peter heard the key in the door lock. He couldn't move.

"Did you see that note about you in the bathroom?" Anton asked.

"What note?"

"It said, *Phil Koehler gives good head,* and had your phone number underneath."

"What? Where did you see this?"

"In the bathroom down the hall, the far stall on the right. Someone wrote it in laundry marker. I saw it this morning. You should take a look, Phil. Maybe you'll recognize the handwriting."

"Oh, shit. Why would anybody write that? Of all the stupid. . . ."

The doorknob rattled some more. Peter realized Phillip Koehler was removing the key.

He remained perfectly still, and listened to Phillip's voice grow fainter as he moved farther down the hallway. Peter waited another few moments, then he heard Anton whistling again. He recognized the tune: *"Green Acres is the place to be. . . ."*

Peter swung open the door. Halfway down the hallway, Anton urgently waved at him to hurry. With the other hand, he held a finger to his lips. Peter ran toward him. "Get your ass in my room, fast!" Anton whispered.

He scurried down the hall and found Anton's door open. He ducked inside, then hid behind the door, leaving it ajar. His heart was racing and he could hardly catch his breath.

"Hey, Anton, I didn't see anything," he heard Phillip say. He was just passing by the door. "I looked in every stall. What are you talking about?"

"I swear," Anton said. "It was there this morning: *Phil Koehler gives good head.* I guess some Good Samaritan must have washed it off. I'm glad. By the way, Phil, is it true?"

"Is what true?"

"That you give good head?"

Peter heard Phillip Koehler laugh. "Blow it out your ass, Anton."

"Have a good night, Phil!" Anton called.

"You too."

Peter heard a door shut down the hall. A moment later, Anton staggered into the room.

"Oh, my God," he whispered. "I thought we were cooked, I thought we were toast." He closed the door behind him. "I kid you not, Phil was a gnat's eyelash away from walking in on you, Pete. My God, I thought I was gonna have a goddamn heart attack."

Peter felt giddy with relief. "I heard you talking to him. You were great!"

"Oh, it weren't nothing," Anton said. "I hear he really does give good head."

Peter laughed out loud, but Anton quickly shushed him. He pointed toward the door. They heard footsteps.

Someone knocked.

Peter let out a gasp, then he covered his mouth. He knew he had to be quiet. Anton was trying to compose himself, too. He pushed Peter into the corner of the room, then he went to the door and opened it.

"Hey, Father Murphy," Peter heard him say.

"Hi, Anton, how are you?"

"Fine as frog's hair, Father." Anton stepped out to the hallway and closed the door behind him. "What can I do for you?"

Peter crept toward the door. But they moved farther down the hallway, and he couldn't hear what they were saying.

Anton seemed to lead the way as they headed toward the stairwell. Jack glanced back at Anton's door.

"My room's a mess," Anton said. "Otherwise, I'd ask you in. I was just about to step out. Want to get some air?"

"Sure," Jack said.

They started down the stairs.

"How's your investigation going?" Anton asked.

"Actually, I had a long talk with Rick Pettinger," Jack said. "He had to go home for a while, due to health reasons."

Anton laughed. "I could have sworn he was avoiding you, me, and the truth." He stopped on the second-floor landing. "Rick was lying to us the other day, Father. I know you think I was being too pushy. But if someone on my floor is in any way responsible for the death of John Costello, I feel responsible, too."

"That's very admirable," Jack said, continuing down the steps. "I want to set your mind at ease about Rick Pettinger. I talked to him last night, and he answered all my questions. He was very helpful."

"Was he able to tell you anything?"

"As I said, he was very helpful," Jack replied. "The point is, someone—possibly someone from St. Clement Hall—called Rick's home several times yesterday, harassing him."

"Really?"

"Really and truly," Jack said, as they headed through the lobby. "Anyway, Anton, I'm not interested in who was behind the phone calls. But I know you have your finger on the pulse of this place. If you have any idea who it is, I'd appreciate it if you discreetly took them aside and told them to stop."

They stepped outside. A cool breeze came with dusk. The windows of the tall old buildings on campus reflected the orange and amber streaks of sunset. Anton wandered toward the bike racks by the dorm's front doors. "Heck, Father Murphy," he said, shrugging. "I don't know about any phone calls."

"Well, you're a resourceful guy," Jack said. "If you happen to hear anything about it, could you—in your own quiet way—get the perpetrator to cease and desist?"

Anton nodded. "I'll do what I can, Father."

"I appreciate it."

"So—where do you stand with the investigation?" Anton asked.

"Well, the school agrees with the police findings that John Costello's death was an accident."

"But you don't really believe that, do you, Father?"

"It's what the school says."

"So there's no more investigation?"

Jack nodded. "It's what the school says," he repeated.

"I don't know how Rick Pettinger figured out it was us," Anton said, shutting his bedroom door. "But he told Murphy about the phone calls, and blew the whistle on me."

"How?" Peter asked.

Anton shrugged. "Like I say, I don't know. He must have guessed. For a minute there, I thought my ass was grass and Murphy was a Lawn-Boy. But he was cool about it. And don't worry, your name never came up. The real pisser is that they're dropping the investigation. They're calling your buddy's death an accident."

"You're kidding!" Peter said.

Anton shushed him, then glanced at the door. "I don't want anybody to know you're in here."

"They're calling it an accident," Peter whispered. "Yeah, forget the fact that it's April, and nobody in their right mind would go swimming right now. And if Johnny accidentally fell in the water, then what the hell happened to his clothes? How could they just ignore stuff like that?"

"Obviously, because they're covering up something," Anton said, sitting on the edge of his desk. "Maybe a priest was involved. Maybe what happened to John Costello goes beyond a few kids on this floor." He shot Peter a narrow look. "When you were asking around about Johnny, what made you come to this floor anyway? What do you know about Rick and Ted and maybe a couple of others that you're not sharing with me?"

Peter felt his face flush. "Johnny told me in confidence. I don't want to repeat it."

"He had something going on with a few of the guys on this floor, didn't he? Rick and Ted and somebody else? Was he supplying them drugs?"

Peter shook his head.

"Sex?"

"I can't say." Peter frowned.

"That's cool. I respect that. But tell me this, did Johnny let on that he was involved with anyone else? Like a priest maybe?"

"He mentioned someone a while back, didn't tell me the name. But he said it was over. That's all I know."

Anton moved from the desk and sat down beside Peter. "Do you think it was Murphy?"

"No, they were friends. Johnny didn't feel that way about him."

"Yeah, but we don't know how Father Murphy really felt about Johnny."

Peter shook his head. "I don't think Murphy's that way. Before he came here, he had a wife and son who died."

"Are you kidding? That doesn't mean anything." Anton got to his feet, and started to pace in front of Peter. "I think we've made a mistake," he said. "We've been assuming that the person who killed John Costello and attacked you is someone from this floor. But it could be anybody—a priest, or maybe even someone from outside the school. He must have been worried that Johnny told you something, and that's why he went after you on Saturday."

He turned to Peter. "That was dumb, searching through the guys' rooms. All we did was waste time. My mistake. We've checked every room now, and there's no lumber jacket. You know why?"

Peter shook his head.

"Think about it, Pete. If a jacket was part of your disguise when you went to kill somebody, and they survived, would you hold on to that evidence? Would you leave it hanging in your closet?"

"No way," Peter said. "I'd burn it, or throw it in a Dumpster someplace."

"Exactly," Anton agreed. "I forget what day they collect the garbage around here—"

"Wednesday mornings."

"That means the lumber jacket might still be in a Dumpster somewhere on campus. Are you up for a digging expedition?"

"Through garbage?"

Anton nodded. "Who knows, Pete? Maybe when we find that jacket, we'll also find Johnny Costello's missing clothes."

* * *

Jack sat at his desk with a pile of test papers that should have been graded the previous week. Fortified with a beer and a bag of pretzels, he worked his way through the pile. Every once in a while, he stared out at the lights from the campus across the lake, and he thought of Maggie. She hadn't called, and the funeral was tomorrow. Garcia or someone else from administration must have already phoned her to cancel for him. Jack imagined the impersonal message from some stranger: *"Father Murphy won't be available to deliver the eulogy at your brother's funeral Mass. He conveys his regrets."*

The only worthwhile thing he'd accomplished today was getting Anton to lay off poor Rick Pettinger. He was pretty certain Anton had been the one behind those calls. He hoped he'd gotten through to him.

Jack didn't know where to go from here. John Costello had been his surrogate son. He still didn't want to believe Johnny had made a practice of taking money for sex.

Perhaps Garcia was right. So far, Jack didn't like anything he'd uncovered in this investigation. He couldn't do any good with it. He'd only found things that could hurt people. Why did he want to keep digging?

Jack sipped his beer and started in on another test paper.

The phone rang. He glanced at the clock: 10:25. He put down his red pen, then grabbed the receiver. "Hello?"

"Hi, it's—it's Maggie calling, Jack."

"How are you?" he asked.

"Well, confused. I got a call this morning from some other priest telling me that you won't be giving the eulogy at Johnny's funeral tomorrow."

"I'm very sorry, Maggie," he said. "I wanted to call you

myself, but—well, I can't even make it to the funeral. There's a conflict, and I—I can't get away.''

"What conflict? Why are you being this way?''

Jack sighed.

"Is someone else there with you?'' she asked. "Can't you talk now?''

"Maggie, we can't talk at all,'' he said finally. "I'm sorry. Please know that I'll be thinking of Johnny and praying for him.''

"What am I supposed to do with that, Jack?'' she replied. "It doesn't help me at all. It's just a 'priest' thing to say.''

"But that's what I am,'' he said quietly. "And I have to do what they tell me.''

"So you're not going to see me or talk to me. And Johnny's death was just an unfortunate accident. Is that what you're saying?''

"Maggie, I'm so sorry,'' he whispered.

"You're always sorry, Jack,'' she muttered. "You're one of the sorriest individuals I know. I'll say a prayer for you tomorrow when they bury my brother.''

Then she hung up.

Peter rolled up the sleeves of his good white shirt. He probably should have changed his clothes before digging into the Dumpster behind St. Bart's, but he was pressed for time. Only a couple of hours of daylight were left, and he wanted to go through two more Dumpsters on the other side of the lake after this one. The garbagemen were coming tomorrow morning.

Anton and he had checked the Dumpster behind St. Clement's last night. But after a few minutes, it had grown too dark to see anything. Anton had carried on the work today. Just minutes ago, Peter had found a note slipped under his door:

Dude,

    Checked St. Matthew's, St. Jude's & the library this afternoon. Nothing. Will try behind the student union later. Come by side door—11 tonight.

                                      Dude

Peter had just returned from Johnny's funeral. About thirty students had gone down to Seattle in carpools, Peter among them. While the others sat in back of the church, Peter shared a front pew with Maggie Costello. She'd insisted. It made him feel important, necessary.

Peter was surprised that Father Murphy hadn't shown up. When he asked Maggie about it, she'd frowned and muttered, "He couldn't make it. He has a conflict."

That was all she would say.

Father Murphy's no-show seemed awfully strange, right up there with Rick Pettinger's sudden departure from school. Three other priests had taken the day off from classes to attend the funeral. Why couldn't Murphy?

Peter hadn't seen Murphy around when he'd returned from the funeral. He hadn't wasted any time after finding Anton's note. Throwing off his navy blue blazer and tie, he'd hurried down the stairs, then outside to the Dumpster around back.

He started digging through the garbage, and tried not to gag. It smelled like sour milk and vomit. He held his breath half the time and turned his head away to gasp for air. He and Anton had discovered yesterday that among the trash were razor blades, shattered glass, and broken lightbulbs. They also had to pick through used Kleenex, cigarette butts, moldy food, unidentifiable sticky substances, and, as Anton put it, "things you can't flush."

Peter had already thought up a cover story in case someone

came along and asked what the hell he was doing. He'd tell them that he had accidentally thrown away some class notes.

He hadn't even dug through the second layer of garbage when he'd dirtied his shirtsleeve and gotten his hand wet with God only knew what. He wasn't about to guess by smelling his hand either. He kept sorting through the debris.

Peter couldn't quite see what was under a heavy trash bag, but he touched the edge of something made of a rough, woven fabric. It sure felt like a lumber jacket. Anxiously he tugged at the material until it slid out from under the weighty bag. "Oh, shit," he grumbled, peeking down at the old bathroom rug. Bent over the side of the Dumpster, he shoved the smelly thing aside, then dug deeper. "Shit, shit, shit, shit," he muttered to himself. "This is ridiculous, I'm never going to find . . ."

He found something. He saw the blackwatch plaid pattern on an article of clothing rolled up under some Burger King bags and a pizza delivery box. Peter kept telling himself that it was another false alarm. But he pulled the garment out from the rubbish, and saw it was the lumber jacket, the first real clue in solving his friend's murder.

Jack had noticed the empty chairs in his classroom that morning. Several students had been excused so they could attend the funeral service down in Seattle. Father Zeigler had been assigned to arrange carpools for the special excursion. Jack had been left out of the loop completely.

They were burying his young friend, and Jack had to go about business as usual. It killed him not to be there. He wanted so much to call Maggie.

That afternoon, he'd overheard a student referring to the spot where they'd found Johnny's body as Costello Bay. Already Johnny was becoming part of St. Bartholomew Hall's morbid folklore. Jack thought about the others: Gerard

Lunt and Mark Weedler, the two boys who had died in that murder-suicide down the hall in Room 410; the other drowning victim, Julian Doyle; and the one he'd just learned about, Oliver Theron, who had hanged himself.

He added those names to his green pocket-size notebook.

After curfew, Jack went down to the dark, deserted first floor. He used his pass key to get into St. Bart's small library. A study haven with its good light and several comfortable chairs, the library closed its doors at ten o'clock weeknights. They had only about four thousand titles on hand, most of them reference books and encyclopedias. The entire fiction section took up two small shelves below a window looking out at Lake Leroy. It wasn't much of a library, but they had every yearbook from Our Lady of Sorrows since 1945.

Jack switched on the overhead and walked over to the yearbook shelf. It was so quiet, every noise he made seemed exaggerated: his footsteps, a yearbook falling on its side on the shelf, the chair squeaking as he sat down. He thought he heard someone outside. But in the darkened windows, he could only see his reflection.

The annual was from three years ago. In the index, he looked up *Doyle, Julian* and found only one picture—on page 39. It was a group shot of the Latin Club, seventeen seminarians posing in bright sunshine in front of the church. *Doyle, J.* was the far right, second row, the short young man with a mop of blond hair. He was slightly out of focus. Squinting and smiling, he wore a cardigan sweater. The gawky freshman didn't look much like a party boy. But he'd supposedly drowned while swimming back from a kegger with the older seminarians. Had anyone actually seen him at a party? Or maybe people just assumed that, the way they'd made assumptions about the circumstances of Johnny's death. Jack wondered what month Julian had drowned. Had it been a warm night? Or was it another case of someone taking an unseasonable swim?

In the same yearbook, *Theron, Oliver* was on page 22, a
mere dot among the dozens of seniors posing for a group
shot of the Honor Society. His photo with the Big Brother
Volunteers was more clear, one of thirteen young men posed
near the dock. Squatting in the foreground of the picture,
Oliver was handsome with wavy hair, glasses, and an appeal-
ingly goofy smile. It was hard to imagine him hanging
himself.

The annual didn't include Oliver's senior portrait, and
there was no mention of him or Julian Doyle in memoriam.

Jack returned the yearbook to the shelf. He found the
annual from 1949. In the index, he looked up *Lunt, Gerard*
and *Weedler, Mark*. They were listed on pages 54 and 55.
Jack flipped through the yearbook and came to a stop. He
frowned. The book went from page 52 to page 57. The pages
in between had been torn out.

Toting the lumber jacket in a plastic bag, Peter navigated
across the narrow concrete boulder. He couldn't help feeling
nervous every time he used Mendini's Crossing now. He
kept remembering that man with the ski mask who had
attacked him on this very spot. Peter's heart was still beating
hard from the near sprint he'd made through the darkened
forest along Whopper Way.

Passing over Mendini's Crossing, he had the lights from
Burger King to help guide him. He made it up to the parking
lot and caught his breath. With the cars, the lights, and a
handful of people in the restaurant, Peter felt as if he'd
reached safety. Civilization at last.

The plastic bag in tow, he hurried toward the campus and
St. Clement Hall. He found Anton waiting for him by the
side the building. Despite the evening chill, Anton wore
only a white T-shirt and jeans. His blond hair shining in the
moonlight, he leaned against the east door with his arms

folded. "Hey, Pete," he called softly. "How was the funeral?"

"It was okay," Peter replied, shrugging.

"Well, I've been up to my ass and elbows in garbage all day," Anton said, yawning. "Didn't find a damn thing. What's in the bag?"

"Just this." Smiling proudly, Peter pulled the smelly lumber jacket from the plastic bag.

"Holy shit," Anton murmured. "That's it, isn't it? I— I'd given up. Where the hell did you find it?"

"The Dumpster in back of St. Bart's."

Anton kept shaking his head. "I can't believe it." He started to reach out for the jacket, but stopped suddenly.

Peter heard footsteps, and a couple of guys talking.

Anton quickly pulled out his keys and opened the side door. "C'mon," he whispered.

Peter followed him inside, then through a back hallway. Anton unlocked another door, and pulled Peter into a storage room. He flicked on the light switch. The cold, tiny room was crammed with folding chairs and tables, all collapsed and stacked against each other. Anton and Peter didn't have much space to move around. Anton had to stoop a bit to avoid hitting his head on the low ceiling.

"Let's see it," he whispered. "I can't believe you found the damn thing."

Peter laid the jacket across a row of folding chairs. It was strange to think a few days ago, a man wearing this jacket had tried to kill him. "I've already gone through the pockets," he said. "There isn't much."

"Sure stinks." Anton grimaced as he handled the jacket. From the right pocket, he pulled an empty, crushed Marlboro cigarette pack, a book of matches, and some used Kleenex. "Was this junk originally in this pocket?"

Peter nodded. "I'm pretty sure."

"Well, you should be positive," Anton said. "See, the

left pocket is empty. If this crap was all in the right pocket, it means he's probably right-handed. That's a clue.''

"I hadn't even thought of that," Peter muttered.

"That's why we're a good team," Anton said. "This guy also smokes Marlboros." Anton glanced at the matchbook and opened it up. "Plus he's been to the Lakeside Inn Grill. They're notorious for carding seminarians. You need to be twenty-one to get in there. Only a couple of the matches have been used. He probably didn't get these matches secondhand."

"So what does that mean?"

"If you go by these matches, this guy is twenty-one or older. You can forget all your freshman classmates, and all the guys on my floor. We're looking for someone older, right-handed, and he smokes Marlboros. You know, the Lakeside Inn is real popular with the faculty and administration."

"Do you think it might be a priest?"

Still inspecting the jacket, Anton nodded. "That's a real possibility. Check out the label here, too. Marshall Fields."

"What's that?" Peter asked.

"It's a department store in Chicago."

"Jesus," Peter whispered. "Father Murphy's from Chicago. You know, he didn't show up to Johnny's funeral today. I thought it was awfully suspicious."

"Well, now, take it easy," Anton said. "This jacket looks old. Someone could have bought it at a used-clothing store or consignment shop. There are a ton of those stores around here, and the stuff they have is from all over. I'm not crazy about Murphy, but let's not convict him just yet. Does he even smoke?"

"No, he's a real health nut. But I've seen him pick up trash on the sidewalk and other places. Murphy hates litterbugs. He could have picked up that empty cigarette pack. How tall would you say he is? About six feet?"

Anton nodded. "I guess."

"He's shorter than you, Anton. Try on the jacket."

"What are you, high?" Anton asked. "It's filthy. You try it on."

"I already did. It's too big on me. C'mon, please, try it on."

Frowning, Anton started to put on the jacket. He moved awkwardly within the confines of the claustrophobic storage room, and Peter had to step out of his way.

"Hope you're happy," Anton grumbled. "I'll have to take another shower now." The sleeves were a couple of inches too high, and Anton's shoulders seemed squeezed into the jacket.

"I'm six-two. So this guy's around six feet—and skinnier than me." Anton took off the jacket and tossed it across the row of folding chairs. "He probably lives in St. Bart's and he's *not* a student there. He knew John Costello. He must know you, too. Otherwise, he wouldn't have been able to pick you out and follow you around."

"Do you think it's Murphy?" Peter asked.

"It's possible. But there are eleven other priests in St. Bart's. You need to look at each one of them, and remember all the clues, kiddo. In the meantime, you hold on to that jacket, hide it well, and watch your ass, Pete. You're probably living under the same roof as the guy who murdered your friend. He's already tried to kill you once. I don't think he'll give up until you're dead."

By the time Peter reached St. Bartholomew Hall, he was gasping for air. He'd run practically all the way back from St. Clement's. He let himself in the same side door that Johnny must have used when sneaking back from his own late-night excursions. Apparently, unbeknownst to the priests on the premises, any room key from St. Bart's worked the lock on that side door.

Once inside, Peter raced up the back stairwell, four flights. All the while, he was lugging the lumber jacket inside the plastic bag. Keys clutched in his hand, he staggered toward his room. He tried not to make any noise in the dim, quiet hallway. He started to unlock his door.

"Pete?"

He swiveled around.

Father Murphy stood outside his door. Dressed in a T-shirt and sweatpants, he ran a hand through his silver-gray hair. He looked tired. "Hey, good morning," he whispered.

Peter gaped at him. "You scared the hell out of me."

"Sorry," Father Murphy said in a hushed voice. "Listen, I need to talk with you, Pete. Let's go into the stairwell, so we don't wake the others."

Peter hesitated, then he set the bag down beside his door.

"What's in there?" Jack asked, nodding at the bag.

"Nothing," he muttered, wide-eyed. "Just . . . an old blanket I bought at a junk store earlier today."

"Well, come on," Father Murphy said. He held open the hallway door.

Peter reluctantly followed him into the cold, gloomy stairwell. Father Murphy sat on the window ledge. Behind him, there was a view of the moonlit lake, and the campus beyond that.

Shuffling down a few stairs, Peter sat on the second step from the bottom. "I'm really tired, Father," he said.

"So am I, Pete," he replied. "Where were you tonight?"

He shrugged. "I just went for a walk in the woods and lost track of the time, that's all."

"You went for a walk by yourself in those dark woods? At one in the morning? Are you certifiable?"

"I was *near* the woods—more by the lake. I didn't mean

to break curfew, I'm sorry." He reached for the banister and started to pull himself up. "Can I go to bed now, please?"

Jack shook his head. "Not yet."

Swallowing hard, Peter sat down on the stairs again.

"Were you with anyone tonight?" Jack asked.

"I told you, I was alone," Peter answered steadily. "I needed to be by myself so I could think about Johnny. Maybe you can't understand that."

"No, I understand completely," Jack said. "I miss him, too."

"Really? Then why didn't you come to the funeral today?"

A sad look passed across Father Murphy's face. He shrugged. "I couldn't. I wanted to, but I had other commitments."

Peter just frowned at him, then he glanced down at the stairs.

"How's his sister doing?" Father Murphy asked. "How's Maggie holding up? Is she all right?"

"As good as to be expected, I guess," Peter muttered. "I sat with her in the front pew during the service."

Father Murphy gave him a strange smile. "Good. You know, John was lucky to have you for a best friend, Pete. You've been very loyal to him. As much as your silence has driven me nuts the last few days, I understand why you couldn't tell me about John's ... affiliation with some of the sophomores over at St. Clement Hall. I know how John made all that money. I don't want to spread that secret around any more than you do."

Peter eyed him warily. "How did you find out?"

"It doesn't matter," he replied. "But if you know something else about John or what happened on the night he died, I wish you'd tell me."

Peter slowly shook his head. "I don't know anything else, Father," he said. "I really don't. I swear."

Father Murphy stared at him for a moment, then he sighed. "All right. You can go to bed now."

He got to his feet, then started up the stairs.

"Pete?"

He turned and glanced down at Father Murphy.

"If I catch you out after curfew again, I'll have to bust you. I'm not saying this to be a hard-ass. I'm thinking of Johnny, sneaking out on the night he was killed. I don't want anything like that happening to you. Okay?"

"Okay," Peter said numbly.

"Good night, Pete."

Chapter Thirteen

Maggie figured it out. The worst waitress at Parker's Pantry was the one named Lucy. Maggie stood by the pie counter, where she had a view of the kitchen. Her chicken stir-fry had been sitting in the carryout container under the hot lights for five minutes now.

But Lucy was oblivious. Hugging an empty tray to her chest, she leaned against the salad station and gossiped with another waitress. Apparently, some male customer thought she looked liked Jane Fonda. A very big deal.

"I get that all the time," Lucy explained.

Maggie didn't see much of a resemblance—except maybe from *The China Syndrome,* when Jane had the long auburn hair and a certain high-strung, vulnerable quality that this waitress also possessed. Maggie glanced back at her carryout box under those heater lights.

"The guy who was telling me this, he was kind of a hunk," Lucy continued. "I think he was interested, too."

"Why should you care?" her waitress friend retorted,

laughing. "You already have your secret lover boy, giving all his secret lover boy love. He's married, isn't he? That's why you can't talk about him. Either that or he's in the Mafia."

Lucy giggled.

"Or maybe he's a priest. Like that cutie-pie who was in here a couple of weeks ago."

Grinning, Lucy shook her head. "I'll never tell."

Maggie coughed loudly to get Lucy's attention. It didn't work. Someone was clanking dishes in the kitchen. The waitresses went right on talking. Maggie couldn't hear what they were saying.

Just as well, she told herself. Right now, she didn't need to hear about someone's love affair with a priest—even if they were kidding.

It had been a week since she'd last talked to Jack Murphy. She felt betrayed by him. She'd counted on him, and he let her down.

At the funeral, she felt isolated. Her only ally was Peter Tobin, who sat in the front pew with her. They both managed to hold back their tears. Across from them sat Ray and her sisters. Maggie's old parish priest gave the eulogy, and he spent half the time praising the virtues of her ex-husband, "who became like a father to this orphaned boy, and gave him a home."

After the burial, they had a brunch at Ray's house, but Maggie didn't attend.

Her sisters had gone back to their respective homes in Yakima and Portland. Maggie had visited Johnny's grave twice so far. They still hadn't put up the headstone yet. She tried not to obsess over all the unanswered questions surrounding his death. And she tried not to think about Jack Murphy.

She pored all her energy into her work. There was a lot of catching up to do. Besides, staying late at the office, she didn't have to go home and face her loneliness and depression.

She'd been at the real-estate office until 9:15 tonight; hence the Parker's Pantry carryout dinner.

Maggie was now glaring at the stupid waitress, who had been neglecting her order for nearly ten minutes. "Excuse me?" she finally called to her. "Excuse me, miss?"

Lucy turned and gave her one of those "who-are-you?" looks.

Maggie nodded toward the kitchen. "I think my order has been ready for quite a while now."

"Oh, God, I'm so sorry!" Lucy said. She hurried into the kitchen, then, a minute later, she was back, carrying a bag. "I'm such a space case," she announced. She tossed some napkins and a plastic fork in the bag. "I put another container in here for you. It's a piece of chocolate layer cake, the best thing they got in this place. That's on me tonight." She handed the bag to Maggie. "You've been very nice. Thanks for putting up with me."

Maggie took the bag. She managed a smile. "Well, that's okay. It's no big deal. Thank you."

"Enjoy the cake!" the waitress called to her as she stepped out of Parker's Pantry.

A couple of outside lights weren't working, and their parking lot was dark. The night wind kicked up. Clutching her coat collar with one hand, Maggie balanced the bag upright. She started toward her car, but suddenly stopped dead.

If not for the headlights of a passing car, Maggie might not have seen him. He sat alone at the wheel of a blue VW bug, parked three spaces away from her. She couldn't make out his face. It was swallowed up in shadow, and illuminated all too briefly. But somehow, she knew he was watching her.

Maggie hurried toward her car. She set her carryout bag

on the roof, and frantically searched for the keys in her purse. With a shaky hand, she unlocked her car door, opened it, and ducked inside. She started the ignition, but remembered her bag on the car roof.

Quickly, Maggie climbed out of her car, retrieved the bag, and jumped behind the wheel again. She shut her door and locked it. Only then did she dare to glance over at the Volkswagen. The man was turned toward her. Just then, another car passed, and its headlights swept across his face.

Maggie gasped. He seemed hideously deformed. His features looked so unreal. It took a moment for her to realize that he was wearing a cheap, opaque mask. A grinning clown stared back at her. Grinding the gears, Maggie jerked back out of her space. The car made a screeching noise as she turned and sped out of the lot.

In the Volkswagen's rearview mirror, he watched her car peel away down the road. They'd just had their first meeting. He'd scared her. It was like flirting, and he felt a little giddy. Maggie Costello excited him.

The little brush with her a minute ago made him all the more anxious to finish up with the waitress tonight. He pulled off the clown mask and gazed toward the restaurant.

"G'night, hon," Doreen called. "Don't take any candy from strangers on the way home."

"See ya tomorrow, Doreen," Lucy replied, waving at her coworker. She started off in the other direction.

It was 12:20. They'd had the closing shift tonight, and just locked up the place. Lucy glanced back over her shoulder at the darkened restaurant.

She saw Doreen turn the corner. Then from the other side of the restaurant came a man. He was tall and thin, with the hood pulled up on his dark blue windbreaker. His face was shrouded in shadow, and his hands were shoved into the pockets of the jacket. He moved at a strange, brisk clip that seemed almost animated. He was heading toward her.

A car passed by. Lucy glanced around for any other pedestrians in the area, but she was alone with him. The next couple of blocks were fairly well-lit. Still, the tall man with the hood gave her the creeps. She veered from the sidewalk to the center of the street. At least she was in the open there. He couldn't grab her and drag her into the bushes.

She casually glanced back at him again. He was on the sidewalk, not far behind her. He had his head down. She still couldn't see his face.

Lucy moved a little slower and let him pass. She watched him out of the corner of her eye. He really did walk like a nut. He kept going and didn't even look her way.

Lucy lived seven blocks from the restaurant. She was used to walking home alone this late at night. Only on a few occasions had she ever been scared. She had a pocket-size pepper-spray dispenser in her purse. It was about two years old, and probably didn't work. But it made her feel a little safer.

A car was coming up the street, so Lucy went back onto the sidewalk. At the end of the block, she turned down a residential road with more trees and fewer streetlights.

Her feet were sore. She promised herself some ice cream tonight. She'd also taped her soaps. She would dip into the Ben & Jerry's while watching *Days of Our Lives*. It was a nice consolation prize for having to spend the evening alone. He was busy tonight, he'd said.

She turned down another block and almost stopped dead. The tall man with the hooded windbreaker emerged from the shadows across the street. He paused under a blinking streetlight. She still couldn't see his face.

Lucy felt her heart skip. She hurried toward the middle

of the street and glanced back at him. With that rapid walk of his, he darted across the way to where she'd just been on the sidewalk. His hands were still in the pockets of his windbreaker.

Lucy picked up her pace, not quite breaking into a trot. She had only another block until she'd reach her town house. Already, she started digging into her purse for the keys. She glanced up at a small apartment building on her left. Only one light was on. Would they hear her if she screamed?

She found her keys, then felt around for the pepper spray. Her town house loomed just ahead. Lucy gave up on the spray. She had her keys out and ready. Making a beeline for the front door, she shot a look over her shoulder.

The man hurried from the sidewalk toward the curb. He was coming at her.

Frantic, Lucy unlocked the door, then the dead bolt. "God, please," she whispered, under her breath. Flinging open the door, she glanced back at him one last time.

He'd moved on. He was walking down the center of the street, that same strange brisk gait of his.

Lucy let out a weak laugh and slumped against the door frame. Her heart was still racing. She reached for the hall light and flicked the switch.

Nothing. The bulb must have burnt out. She didn't need this now. "Shit," she muttered, warily stepping inside.

Suddenly, someone sneaked up behind her. He'd been waiting in the front hall. His hand clasped over her mouth before she had a chance to scream. He snapped her head back.

Lucy started to struggle. He grabbed her by the wrist and pulled her arm behind her. She tried to yell out, but couldn't even breathe. He covered her mouth and nose. He drew her hand down, and she felt his stomach. Bare skin. It took her a moment to realize he was naked. He guided her hand to his erection.

"Hey, babe," he whispered in her ear.

She couldn't help laughing a little. "Jesus, you scared me!" she gasped. "You told me you were busy tonight, you rat."

His hand slid down from her mouth to her breast. He caressed her, then ran his tongue along the side of her face and neck.

Lucy wanted him to stop for a moment, so she could catch her breath at least. But he seemed so immersed in his sexual-assault fantasy, and she didn't want to disappoint him. She surrendered to it, and grew weak in his arms. Her whole body tingled.

He tugged at the zipper to her waitress uniform and rubbed himself against her buttocks. She stroked his hard manhood, gliding her fingers over the silky head.

She stepped out of her uniform. All the while, he stood behind her. She felt his warm breath on the back of her neck. In the darkness, what they were doing seemed like an anonymous encounter. Every time she tried to turn and kiss him, he twisted her around again. It was almost a struggle, and she let him overpower her.

Kissing the back of her neck, he took the barrette from her hair. Lucy felt him rolling down her pantyhose, and she helped him along. His hand came between her legs and he fondled her. She let out a grateful moan.

Lucy almost tripped as she kicked off the loose hosiery, and they both laughed. Her head was swimming. She felt giddy as his hands and mouth feverishly explored her body.

She wanted her mouth on his, and tried to turn toward him again. But he grabbed her by the shoulders and spun her around. It was a little rough, but a moment later, he playfully nibbled at the back her neck. "I want to kiss you, stupid," she said, laughing.

She felt him squatting down behind her. He caressed and kissed the back of her legs. It tickled. He pulled at her hands, and she felt something against her wrist. It was her hosiery. He started tying her hands together. Squirming, she chuckled. "Oh, c'mon, don't," she said weakly. "Really, don't . . ."

The hose were so tight, they cut off the circulation in her hands. "That's hurting, honey. Stop it. . . ."

Suddenly he yanked her bound hands up behind her. Lucy shrieked at the pain. She thought he was going to break both her arms. She screamed out again. But all at once, he stuffed something in her mouth. All at once, he was leading her toward the bedroom.

She was scared and trembling. This was no game. She tried to resist, but he was too strong for her. He picked her up from behind and carried her through the darkened bedroom. Her legs flailed and kicked. He passed by the bed and hoisted her over the bathroom threshold. He paused to switch on the light.

In horror and confusion, Lucy gazed at the plastic tarp he'd laid across her bathroom floor to the edge of the tub. The toilet seat lid was down. A sword rested on top of it.

She tried to scream, but couldn't. As he hauled her toward the tub, Lucy glimpsed his face in the medicine chest mirror. It was her first look at him since she'd stepped into the house. He was flushed, and grinning.

She told herself this wasn't happening.

With a kick of his foot, he shut the bathroom door.

A man in a clown mask, sitting alone in a parked car— Maggie told herself there were several different, harmless explanations. He was surprising someone, or playing a joke; he was bored while waiting for a friend; or maybe he was just nuts.

One thing, he wasn't after her. She thought about calling the police, but talked herself out of it. She was being silly.

Okay, if she heard on the evening news that the restaurant was held up, she'd contact the police.

By the time Maggie returned home, ate her stir-fry, and had a couple of bites of the chocolate layer cake, she'd already forgotten about the clown incident. She didn't even remember to check the evening news.

Lately, she'd let the stupidest little things scare her. Someone had called her house three times the other night. They hadn't said anything, but hadn't hung up when she'd answered either. They'd just stayed on the line and listened to her. Caller ID couldn't trace the call. Then yesterday, somebody had been through her garbage outside.

Simple explanation: a transient had been poking around in there for something salvageable. As for the phone calls, they were probably just a crank. She could explain away everything.

But a few nights after that Parker's Pantry dinner, she had good reason to be afraid. She had a seven-o'clock appointment with a new prospective buyer from out of town. He hadn't been referred to her by anyone. He just liked her ad in the *Seattle Weekly,* or so he said.

It was one of the hazards of the real estate business. Her photo and business phone number were in all her ads, which left her susceptible to every nutcase who simply liked the way she looked on a flyer or in the newspaper. As a rule, Maggie researched all her cold callers, and she never met them at an unfamiliar or isolated location.

But she hadn't had a chance to check on this Steve Dettermann, who was moving down from Juno, Alaska. As for the beach-view, two-bedroom house he wanted to see, it was at the end of a cul-de-sac in West Seattle. Maggie drove out there with her cellular and a small canister of mace in her purse. She also brought along a newspaper to read in case he was late.

The house stood alone on a plateau, halfway downhill

from the poorly lit cul-de-sac. Ordinarily, Maggie would have waited in her car for him. But he could have been down at the house already.

With a sigh, she grabbed her purse and the newspaper, then started toward the little lamppost with the house address on a shingle, along with the FOR SALE sign. A stone-step pathway led to the front door, then farther down to the beach. Dwarfed and shadowed by trees, the little brown-shingle rambler seemed to be hiding from humanity. It was also a dump—or a *real fixer-upper,* as they called them in the business. Someone had already tinkered with the place, adding a second floor that clashed architecturally with the original seaside cottage style. There weren't any lights on inside the house.

Making her way to the front stoop, Maggie warily glanced around. She didn't see anyone. All she could hear were the waves from Puget Sound. The real-estate agent's lockbox was on the door handle. Maggie worked the combination, took out the key, and unlocked the front door. But she hesitated before stepping inside.

She pulled out her cellular and speed-dialed the office. Her friend, Adele, was working late. "John L. Scott Real Estate," she answered.

"Hi, Adele. It's Maggie. I'm at this West Seattle place for that new client, Steve Dettermann. Did he call or anything?"

"No, Maggie."

"Well, listen. I don't like the setup here. It's a little too remote. Do you have the address of this place?"

"Sure do."

With the phone to her ear, Maggie stepped over the threshold into the darkened house. She found a double light switch and flicked them both on. Overhead track lights illuminated the living room. Outside, she noticed a row of ground lights around the steps, along with a lamp by the front door.

"Can you stick around the office a little longer?" Maggie asked.

"I'm not going anywhere," Adele replied. "Call me every five or ten minutes, okay? That way, I'll know you're all right."

"Will do," Maggie said. "You read my mind. Thanks, Adele."

After Maggie clicked off, she ventured into the tiny kitchen and switched on the overhead. The upstairs light wasn't working, so she didn't go up there. The living room had a built-in window seat, with a view of Puget Sound through the trees. All the other furniture had been moved out already. The place was slightly dilapidated, in need of a carpenter and a paint job.

She glanced at her wristwatch: 7:05. Steve Dettermann was only a few minutes late.

Settling at the window seat, Maggie opened up her newspaper. She heard a faint rustling upstairs. She told herself it was just the house creaking. Or maybe in a place like this, so close to the water, they had rats. Whatever it was, it went away. Maggie listened for another moment, then she returned to her newspaper.

She noticed the headline on page three: POLICE BAFFLED BY SLAYING OF NORTH SEATTLE WOMAN.

The victim's picture ran alongside the article—probably a driver's-license photo: *Lucy Ballatore, 34, had been missing two days before her body was discovered.*

The dark-haired woman in the photo was smiling. She looked a tiny bit like Jane Fonda.

"Oh, my God," Maggie whispered. The newspaper crinkled in her grasp. She could see the waitress from Parker's Pantry smiling at her. *"It's a piece of chocolate layer cake, the best thing they got in this place. That's on me tonight."*

"It can't be her," Maggie murmured. She anxiously read the article:

> *The body of a northside Seattle woman was discovered Thursday morning in a ravine near the Burlington Northern switchyard in Auburn, Washington. The victim, identified as Lucy Dee Ballatore, 34, had been stabbed in the throat.*
>
> *Railroad yardman Ricardo Hernandez, 49, found the underwear-clad body in a ditch, several yards from the train tracks. Ballatore's hands had been tied behind her back with a pair of panty hose. Early police reports indicate that the victim had been dead approximately two days. There was no sign of sexual assault.*
>
> *Ms. Ballatore worked as a waitress at Parker's Pantry, a northside restaurant. She was last seen there on Monday evening, after the restaurant closed at midnight. Ms. Ballatore and a coworker, Doreen Helm, 54, talked briefly in the establishment's parking lot. "I watched Lucy start to walk down the street," Helm said. "Then I got inside my car. We waved to each other. That's the last I saw her. She didn't show up for work the next day."*
>
> *King County Sheriff's Department issued a statement, urging anyone who might have information—*

A knock on the front door startled her. Maggie jumped to her feet. Quickly, she set aside the newspaper. In her mind, she kept seeing that man with the opaque clown mask, sitting alone at the wheel of his car. Had he been waiting for Lucy Ballatore?

For a crazy moment, she imagined that same man in his harlequin disguise, now on the front stoop, waiting for her. She dug the little canister of mace from her purse.

There was another knock on the door.

"Coming!" she called out nervously. The small canister

buried in her fist, Maggie hurried to the door. She glanced out the peephole.

He was handsome, with auburn hair and glasses that lent a sensitivity to the strapping, tall man who wore them. Maggie was surprised at how young he looked. She guessed he was around twenty-five. He wore a denim shirt and sports jacket.

"Steve Dettermann?" Maggie called.

"Yes, sorry I'm a little late," he called back.

Maggie opened the door. She managed a smile at him. "Um, something's come up, and I can't show the house right now," she explained. She retreated toward the window seat. "I'm sorry you had to come all this way out here for nothing."

"Actually, I've seen enough here," Steve Dettermann said, glancing about. He stepped across the threshold and stood by the door. "This place looks like it needs more TLC than I'm willing to give it. That's TLC, as in Time, Labor, and Cash."

Maggie nodded distractedly. She glanced at Lucy Ballatore's photo before folding up the newspaper. She stepped into the kitchen to turn off the light. When she emerged, she saw him holding the door open for her. He seemed perfectly nice, but he was a stranger, and she couldn't carry on with business as usual right now. She turned off the lights, and brushed past him out the doorway.

Once outside, Maggie struggled in the dark with the lockbox. She felt him hovering behind her. "Need a flashlight?" he asked. "I have one in my car."

"No, I'm fine." She snapped the lock shut, then started up the unlit stone steps toward the cul-de-sac. "I'm sorry to be in such a rush," she said, with a glance over her shoulder at him.

"That's all right," he replied, catching up alongside Maggie as she headed toward her car. "Like I say, I'm not crazy about the place. Can I call you tomorrow?"

"That would be great," she said, ducking into the car. She reached over to shut the door, but he held it open.

Maggie gave him a wary look. He grinned, then extended his hand. "We'll talk tomorrow, then."

She briskly shook his hand. "Right," she replied.

"I thought you were pretty in your picture," he said. "But in person, you're beautiful. I'll call you tomorrow. Drive safely, Maggie Costello."

Then he closed her door. Maggie started up the engine and turned the car around. She glanced at him in the rearview mirror as she pulled away. He stood at the end of the cul-de-sac, with his hands in his pockets, watching her.

She was driving across the West Seattle Bridge when her cellular rang. It was Adele, checking up on her. Maggie said she was all right, and on her way home.

Once she set foot in the door, Maggie called the police. There was a hot-line number for anyone with information regarding Lucy Ballatore's murder. Maggie thought the woman on the other end of the line seemed unimpressed with her story about the man in the restaurant parking lot on Monday evening. Maggie described the clown mask he wore, but couldn't quite remember the color of the Volkswagen—only that it was a light shade, possibly white, silver, or pale blue. She didn't get a license plate number. The woman asked for Maggie's home and work phone numbers, then said the police department appreciated the information.

After Maggie hung up, she figured hers was probably one of dozens of calls they'd received today. They probably had every nutcase who ever ate in Parker's Pantry calling with "inside information." And here she was describing a "killer clown'' in a VW. What made her think they'd take her seriously?

No one from the police department ever called back.

She didn't hear back from Steve Dettermann either. Talk about somebody who probably thought she was nuts. Maggie didn't count on seeing him again.

That Sunday, three days after meeting him at the West Seattle cottage, Maggie had to facilitate at an open house. It was a $240,000 one-bedroom condominium in Capitol Hill, near downtown Seattle. The area attracted everyone from old-money millionaires to street kids with drug problems. For the first two and a half hours, Maggie showed the place to several of those old-money people, a lot of gay singles and couples, some yuppies, and the occasional browser who had no intention of buying.

Maggie had set up her station—a card table and folding chair—by the front door. With a fireplace, tons of old-world charm, a view of Puget Sound, the Olympic Mountains, and downtown, the condo seemed to sell itself.

She had fifteen more minutes before she could take down the open house sign. That was when the street urchins wandered in.

"Is this your place?" the tall, skinny, twentysomething man asked. He was dressed in faded black jeans, a silver-studded black belt, black T-shirt, and a torn denim jacket. He had piercings in his lip, nose, and eyebrow. His hair was so filthy and messy, Maggie wasn't certain of the color. He stank of cigarettes and B.O. He nudged his friend. "Would you fucking look at this place?"

His companion was a slightly plump, dishwater blonde who was about thirty. She wore the same faded black clothes, but added to the ensemble was a blood-soaked Band-Aid on her greasy forehead. She seemed in a daze, smiling but saying nothing.

"I'm just about to wrap it up here, folks," Maggie said.

"You got a cigarette?" the young man asked.

Maggie shrugged. "Sorry, I don't smoke. And there's no smoking in here anyway."

He wandered past her, through the dining room to the kitchen. The woman huddled close to him. They whispered to each other, then she giggled. He opened the refrigerator, found it empty, then moved to the sink, where he helped himself to some water from the faucet. He gargled, then spit some water at his girlfriend.

"Fucking cut it out!" she screeched.

He did it again, most of the water landing on the floor this time. "You're pissing me off," his girlfriend warned.

He went back to the sink and tested the garbage disposal, switching it on and off repeatedly.

Maggie came to the kitchen doorway. "Hey, I'm sorry," she said during a break in the grinding noise. "I have to ask you to leave. Okay?"

"I gotta take a piss," the young man replied. "Where's the bathroom?"

Maggie shook her head. "It's not a public bathroom. Sorry."

Smirking, he flicked the garbage disposal on and off again.

"You have to leave!" Maggie yelled over the noise.

Ignoring her, the young man kept playing with the switch until something he saw made him stop. He was looking just past Maggie's right shoulder.

Maggie turned around. With all the disposal noise, the tall, handsome man had come in undetected. He wore jeans and a white oxford shirt. It took Maggie a moment to recognize Steve Dettermann without his glasses. He was glaring at the street urchin.

The punk sneered at him. "Who are you, man? Her fucking butler?"

"No, I'm the guy who's kicking you out," Steve Dettermann growled. "Only first, you're going to apologize to this lady for being such an obnoxious pest."

With half-closed eyes, the young man glared back at him for a moment. "Shit, man," he muttered. "Sorry. You don't have to bite my fucking head off." Then he sighed and wandered past them toward the door. Behind him, his girl-friend still had a dazed smile on her face. They left the door open behind them.

Steve went to shut it.

"Better leave it open," Maggie suggested. "Air out the place."

He chuckled. "Yeah, they were pretty ripe, weren't they?"

She nodded. "Thanks for coming to my rescue." She retreated to the kitchen, took some paper towels, and started wiping the water off the floor. "Are you looking at condos today? I thought you were more interested in a house."

He leaned against the kitchen doorway. "Actually, I decided renting is the best way to go right now—so I guess I won't be needing an agent."

Maggie tossed the soggy paper towel in the trash under the sink. "Then you were just out browsing?"

He gave her a shy smile. "Well, the truth is, I saw your ad for an open house in the paper, and I figured it was a chance to see you again."

Maggie leaned back against the kitchen counter. "I thought you said you won't be needing an agent."

"That's right. I was wondering if we could get together for dinner sometime. Y'know, like a date?"

Maggie let out a nervous little laugh. He was very hand-some, with an endearingly cute smile. "Well, I'm flattered, Steve," she said. "I really am. But I . . . um, I'm quite a few years older than you."

"I'm twenty-eight," he replied.

"I repeat," Maggie said. "I'm quite a few years older than you."

"You don't have a boyfriend or anything like that, do you?"

"No, but—"

"Then what's to stop us from having a friendly dinner together?" he asked. "I'm new in town, and don't know many people. You'd be doing a good deed. And besides, you owe me. I just rescued you."

Maggie smiled wryly. "Is that how it works?"

He nodded. "Better work that way. Otherwise, I'm going to chase that punk down and get my twenty bucks back. I didn't set this up for nothing, y'know."

Maggie stared at him.

He broke into a grin. "Maggie, I'm kidding."

"Of course you are." She laughed, then shook her head. "I'm sorry, Steve, it's just that I really don't know you. . . ."

"What do you think dinner's for?" he countered. "Getting to know each other, talking, eating." He reached in his back pocket, pulled out his wallet, then gave her his business card. "Here. The phone number's temporary. I'm staying at a friend's basement apartment up in Everett. The number should be good for about a month. So, if within the next four weeks you want to be treated to a nice dinner out with a guy who thinks you're pretty damn special, then call that number. Okay, Maggie?"

Tucking his card in the pocket of her blouse, she smiled at him. "Okay, Steve."

She'd had an "Annette Bening" afternoon. That was what Maggie called open-house sittings which were a total waste of time. It was the scene right out of *American Beauty* when

Annette tries to spiff up a dump and every potential buyer looks at her as if she were crazy for praising the virtues of the place. Maggie watched her Saturday afternoon go down the toilet with her own Annette Bening open house.

As if she weren't miserable enough, she looped around to the cemetery on her way home and visited Johnny's and her parents' graves. She'd been thinking of Johnny—and of Jack Murphy—all afternoon.

She took another side trip to the video store. But after forty-five minutes, she still couldn't decide on a movie that might make her Saturday night alone bearable. She wanted to treat herself to carryout, but Parker's Pantry wasn't an option. The place had become something of a morbid tourist attraction, and it was always mobbed now.

Maggie poured herself a glass of wine when she got home. Then she sat by the phone, debating whether or not to call Jack Murphy. She thought about driving up there and getting drunk at that little tavern again. Then she could call him, and he'd have to come rescue her—like last time.

He's a priest, you idiot, she told herself. And he'd let her down. She couldn't count on him.

Still, she dug through her purse for his number at the seminary. In her search, she came across a business card:

STEVE DETTERMANN
360-555-4772

Maggie stared at it for a moment. She remembered his shy smile. "*. . . a nice dinner out with a guy who thinks you're pretty damn special . . .*"

She dialed the number. It rang twice before he picked up. "Hello?"

"Is this Steve?" she asked.

"Yes."

"Hi, Steve. It's Maggie Costello calling."

"Oh, my God, it only took you a week. So, are we going to do that dinner thing?"

She let out an awkward laugh. "Yes, if your offer still stands."

"You bet it does. What about tonight?"

"Well, I kind of had Tuesday night in mind," Maggie said. She figured it would give her something to look forward to.

"Tuesday it is, Maggie," he said. "Maggie, is that short for Margaret?"

"Actually, it's Agnes Marie, but I hate the name Agnes."

"Are you Catholic?"

She laughed again. "Yeah. Why?"

"So am I. My old Catholic grade-school education suddenly came back to me. Agnes is a real Catholic name. Can I ask you something else?"

"Sure, I guess," she replied. "Go ahead."

"Do you have an ex-husband or ex-boyfriend?"

"I have an ex-husband," Maggie said, her guard suddenly up. "Why?"

"Is he following you around?"

"What do you mean?"

"Well, I have a confession," Steve said. "I've driven by your office a couple of times since I first met you. I hope that doesn't creep you out or anything. But I think you should know, on both occasions, there's been this guy in a Volkswagen parked outside the place. And last week, he was parked near that condominium where you had the open house. He was down the block, just sitting in his car. I figured he must be acquainted with you. Does that sound like your ex?"

"No, it doesn't," Maggie murmured. "It doesn't sound like anyone I know."

"Huh. If I ever spot him again, I'll chase him away for you," Steve said lightly.

When Maggie hung up with him five minutes later, she went into the living room and peered out the front window. She didn't see anyone parked outside.

Then again, maybe he was hiding.

Chapter Fourteen

Peter hid the lumber jacket on the top shelf of his closet. Having conducted those secret room-to-room checks with Anton made him paranoid about one of the priests at St. Bart's invading his privacy the same way. They all had pass keys to the dorm rooms. Any one of them could break into his room if he wanted.

As a precaution, Peter kept the jacket in the plastic bag, then covered it with a blanket. Whenever he was in his room, he dead-bolted the door. He hadn't been so careful in the past, but now, every night before going to sleep, he checked the dead bolt.

Anton didn't think it was smart for him to go back and forth to the upperclassman side—especially by way of Mendini's Crossing, where he'd been attacked before. He suggested they lay low for a while, and not see each other so much.

Tonight they were getting together for the first time since Peter had found the jacket nearly two weeks ago. Peter would bring Anton the list he'd been working on. For the past ten days, he'd made a study of all the priests at St. Bartholomew Hall, sizing them up as suspects:

Priest	Smokes?	L/R Handed?	Height?	Knew John/Me?	Comment
Murphy	*No*	*Right*	*6 ft*	*Yes/Yes*	*Suspect*
Zeigler	*All Brands*	*Right*	*5'6"*	*Yes/Yes*	*Suspect*
Reynolds	*Only Camels*	*Left*	*6'3"*	*?/Yes*	*Too Tall*
Bourm	*No*	*Right*	*6'2"*	*Yes/Yes*	*Too Nice*

From his list of twelve priests, Peter had fully discounted two: Father Konradt was in his seventies, and Father Weiss wore a leg brace and walked with a cane.

With all his research, he still didn't have a main suspect among them. Father Zeig Heil seemed like the strongest candidate. He'd always had it out for Johnny. He wasn't particular about cigarette brands, and though he seemed too short, he had broad shoulders and could have rolled up the sleeves to the lumber jacket.

Peter couldn't quite eliminate Murphy as a suspect yet either. For the past couple of weeks, he hadn't seen much of him, except in class. At nights, Murphy usually shut himself off in his room. He seemed to be withdrawing from the world.

Without Murphy on the lookout, it was fairly easy for Peter to sneak out after curfew.

He met Anton at the side door of St. Clement Hall, then they snuck up to the roof. They sat near the ledge, looking over most of the campus and St. Bartholomew Hall across the lake. It was a warm, starry night.

Anton had a paper bag with him. It looked like a schoolboy's sack lunch. When Peter asked what was in the bag, Anton gave him a sly smile. "A treat for later," he said. "Let's see that list of suspects first."

Peter showed him the roster he'd been working on.

Anton studied it for a couple of minutes. The paper fluttered from the breeze up on the rooftop. "You're right, Pete," he said finally. "Any one of these guys could be our man—or maybe none of them. We've got to shake things up a little."

"How are we going to do that?"

"I'm not sure. But we have to come up with something that will bring him out, give him a scare."

"Like what?" Peter asked.

"I'm thinking," Anton said. With a grin, he reached into his bag. "And you know, I do some of my best thinking with a good buzz on. Remember what I found a couple of weeks ago?"

He pulled out a Baggie that contained about enough marijuana for two joints. He also had rolling papers and matches. "Hold your hands around here, so the wind doesn't blow any of it away," Anton said, shaking some grass onto the paper.

Peter had tried pot only a couple of times before—with Johnny. It had never done anything for him. But while smoking a joint with Anton under the stars, something kicked in.

For the first time since Johnny's death, he actually felt happy. He and Anton talked and laughed about the dumbest things. At one point, Anton put his arm around him, and Peter just melted inside.

He'd never known a guy so handsome and sexy. But more than that, Anton made him feel important. He was the only person—besides his parents and Johnny—who really seemed to care about him. Anton had come to his rescue at a time when he felt there was nothing to live for.

There on the roof, he talked Anton's ear off about Johnny. He kept apologizing for babbling on about the best friend he'd lost. But Anton insisted that he wanted to know about Johnny, since he'd never actually met him. Peter even admitted that he used to have "kind of a crush" on Johnny, and Anton acted as if it were no big deal.

Of course, he couldn't admit to Anton his true feelings for him. He didn't want to ruin what they had. He couldn't risk Anton pulling away. He'd be lost without him. Besides, who else could he count on to help him find Johnny's killer?

"So, I think I figured out how we're going to get this guy," Anton announced, nudging Peter. "We'll smoke him out."

"Smoke him out?" Peter repeated, laughing. He had a sore throat and a case of cottonmouth from talking so much—or maybe it was from the pot. But his head was clear now. "How are we going to get him?"

Anton glanced once again at the list of priests. "It should only take a couple of nights," he said. "Then we'll know. If it's one of these guys, we'll catch this killer."

Peter could see the faculty boathouse from his bedroom window. It was where he'd made an appointment with his attacker—and Johnny's murderer.

He'd set Anton's plan into motion today, slipping a note under the door of each priest in residence at St. Bartholomew Hall—except for the two he'd already dismissed from the list of suspects. He'd written the notes himself, all capital block letters on plain notebook paper:

FATHER:

I HAVE YOUR LUMBER JACKET. I KNOW SOME-ONE WHO IS LOOKING FOR IT. IF YOU WANT IT BACK, MEET ME BY THE FACULTY BOATHOUSE AT 8:30 TONIGHT.

A FRIEND

The meeting time varied on each note, forty-five-minute intervals for five different priests. He had rendezvous times set for the five remaining priests tomorrow, starting again at 8:30.

It was a nearly risk-free venture. With the lights off in his room, no one would see him watching from his bedroom window. Peter had the meeting times logged for each priest. Whoever showed up at the boathouse at his assigned time would be there to barter for his jacket.

Anton didn't want Peter taking any chances. "Let's not try to trap this killer or anything," he'd said. "Let's just find out who it is first." Peter was supposed to phone him once he'd spotted their man at the boathouse.

Peter sat in the dark, staring out the window—for nearly four hours. None of the five priests on tonight's docket had taken the bait. Not even a false alarm.

Adding to Peter's frustration was what Father Murphy had done the next morning. Murphy posted the "blackmail" note on his own door—along with a Post-it, on which he'd written: *HAS ANYONE LOST A JACKET?*

That night was a repeat of the previous evening's disappointment. No one came to the boathouse.

"No one? Nothing?" Anton asked.

"Zip, zilch, zero," Peter replied, disgusted. "I sat at that window tonight for four and a half boring hours."

Anton had met him at the side door of St. Clement Hall again, and they'd gone up to his room. Wearing his usual T-shirt and sweatpants, Anton took a beer out of his minirefrigerator and handed it to Peter.

"Thanks," Peter mumbled.

Anton slowly shook his head. "You'd think at least one of them would have been curious enough to go down to that stupid boathouse to see what the note was about."

"Guess not." Peter sat on the bed. "Seemed like such a good idea, too."

"That's what we get for coming up with a great scheme while stoned out of our minds."

Peter sipped his beer. "You know, I heard some guys talking the other day at lunch. They were saying St. Bartholomew Hall is cursed. They said it started with the guy who built the place, then carried on to all the other guys who died there or committed suicide."

Anton let out a skeptical laugh. "What are you saying? That your pal, Johnny, died because of some curse on St. Bart's?"

"I don't know," Peter muttered, shrugging. "What? Don't you believe in curses?"

"I believe people create their own curses," Anton replied, pulling a second beer out of the minifridge. "They jinx themselves. Take Johnny, I didn't know him, and I don't mean to judge. But I saw him over here often enough to know that he was up to something with a few of the guys on my floor. You've been pretty tight-lipped about it, Pete. But I respect that. Friends should keep secrets for each other. Like you and me."

Anton sat on the floor. He leaned back against the bed and sipped his beer. "Anyway, I think Johnny was jinxing himself, living on the edge a little too much." He sighed. "Anyway, I don't think there's a curse on St. Bart's. But I do know for a fact that the place is haunted."

"Haunted?" Peter slid down beside him on the floor. "You mean that room down the hall from me?"

Anton nodded. "Gerard Lunt in 410. I've heard him in that room. My freshman year when I lived in St. Bart's, I snuck in there after curfew a few times. I'd sit in that room for a couple of hours with the door closed."

"By yourself?" Peter asked, his eyes widening.

"Yeah, but I wasn't really alone," Anton said. "I heard him laughing and crying. I could even hear him talking to his friend—but I couldn't make out the words."

Peter laughed. "Bullshit. You're just trying to freak me out."

Anton shushed him. "Not so loud," he whispered. "Why would I try to yank your chain, Pete? I'm telling you this because I trust you." Anton nudged Peter's foot with his own. "Y'know, one of the times I was in there, it was a warm night in May. The windows were closed, but that room got so fucking cold I could see my breath.

"After that, I found out everything I could about the murder-suicide back in 1949. I probably know more about what happened in there that night with Gerry and Mark than any living soul."

He stood up and went to his desk drawer. "Take a look at this. I've never shown this to anyone else." He removed an old, yellowed newspaper from a plastic sleeve and handed it to Peter. It was a *True Crimes Gazette* from 1949.

Anton sat down next to him, shoulder to shoulder. "I found this at a local antiques store last year," Anton explained. "The dealer had a stack of them. Said they used to have these type of newspapers in barbershops."

Peter stared at the headline on the front page: SCREAMS IN THE NIGHT SHOCK QUIET SEMINARY. They carried a photo of Gerard Lunt's room from that evening, a blurry black-and-white shot—with captioned arrows for people who couldn't quite comprehend what they were seeing. The body of Gerard's friend, Mark Weedler, had been blacked out. But it was easy to discern his form, lying on the bed, a headless thing sprawled across some rumpled, bloodstained sheets. An arrow pointed to the wastebasket, where Mark's head was found, wrapped in a pillowcase. The broken window, from which Gerard dove, appeared retouched in the old photo.

Another photograph—showing the south side of St. Bartholomew Hall—included a crude dotted line with an arrow, indicating the trajectory Gerard's body took from that fourth-floor window to the pavement below.

Peter shook his head. It was eerie to think that this blood-bath had occurred just down the hall from him. "So—what exactly happened?" he murmured.

Anton took a sip of beer, then told him the story of Gerard Lunt.

A quiet, short, blond-haired boy, he was called Gerry by his friends. The first sign of something wrong came when he complained to his neighbor in 408 about all the noise. But the young man in 408 claimed he was usually asleep by the time the disturbances supposedly started. Gerry insisted that he could hear people talking in foreign languages on the other side of the wall. It was like gibberish.

Gerry also swore somebody was breaking into his room at night and playing tricks on him. How else could he explain a picture flying off the wall—or a chair tipping over—in the middle of the night?

He began having nightmares. His shrieks echoed down the fourth-floor corridor of St. Bartholomew Hall, waking up several of the other boys. They said Gerry spewed out foreign words and phrases.

That was all Gerry's resident adviser, Father Gallagher, needed to hear. He figured the boy for a phony, trying to get attention. Still, Gallagher had a hard time explaining away the flickering lights in Gerard's room whenever he woke up screaming from a nightmare.

Then there was the "stigmata incident," when Gerry woke up Father Gallagher, pounding on his door at three in the morning. He yelled that he was bleeding.

When Gallagher came to his door, Gerry was in a panic. He showed him the bloody punctures in the palms of his hands. He had similar wounds in his feet—one small, blood-seeping hole in each foot. There were red smudges all over the front of his light blue pajama top, where he'd wiped his hands. Gerry claimed the bleeding had happened all of the sudden; he didn't know how or why.

Gallagher eventually calmed him down. Then he followed the bloody footprints back to Room 410, right up to Gerry's desk. The study lamp was still on. In a pool of blood on the desktop, he saw the tracing compass Gerry must have used to puncture himself.

The news about Gerard Lunt's "stigmata" swept through St. Bartholomew Hall. Gerry's parents were called. The Lunts indicated that they would take the boy out of school so he could be examined by a specialist in Seattle. That was Thursday, November 10, 1949—three days after Gerald's "stigmata."

Gerry didn't go to classes that day. He spent the afternoon in his room, packing. During dinner in the cafeteria, he showed up to say good-bye to several classmates, but didn't eat anything. One of those classmates was Mark Weedler, probably his closest friend at St. Bartholomew Hall. He lived down the corridor in 401.

Gerry's appearance in the cafeteria was the last time anyone saw him alive. When they heard the scream at approximately 11:45 that night, most of the seminarians on the fourth floor assumed Gerry was having another nightmare. But then the shattering of glass woke up half the dorm. Several young men on the east side of St. Bartholomew Hall claimed they saw the body fall. It made a wide arc from the dorm window as it plummeted down to the cement below. They said it was almost as if Gerry were trying to reach the lake when he jumped.

Everyone on the fourth floor came out of their rooms to see what the commotion was about—everyone except Mark Weedler.

Father Gallagher entered Room 410 with his pass key. The lights flickered on and off. Gerry's window had been smashed, and the curtains billowed in the November breeze.

Lying across his bed was the underwear-clad, headless body of Mark Weedler.

They discovered the bloodied Japanese saber on Gerard Lunt's radiator cover by the window. The sword had belonged to Mark, a souvenir gift from his father, who had fought in the Pacific. One of Mark's other friends claimed to have seen the saber, displayed in its usual spot on Mark's bookshelf, that Thursday afternoon before dinner.

Mark had to have brought the sword to Gerry's room that evening. People speculated as to whether or not they'd had a suicide pact. Several students were pulled out of Our Lady of Sorrows that year. Enrollment dropped, and for a brief time, there was talk of closing the freshman facility. But St. Bartholomew Hall persevered. The deaths of Gerard Lunt and Mark Weedler became fodder for legend, limericks, and jokes—like Galvin McAllister thirty-five years earlier.

"Do you know any of the jokes?" Peter asked.

"I probably know them all," Anton said. "But none of them are very funny. And I can't really laugh about it." He shook his empty beer can to see if any was left. "Anyway, now you're better acquainted with your neighbor down the hall, the one who's never moving out."

"How do you know all this stuff?" Peter asked.

"Newspaper articles and research," Anton said. "Father Gallagher died in 1972, but I interviewed someone who became his confidant in his final years. Plus I did some investigating around here. I have a special understanding about this case. I know a couple of things that no one else knows—secrets Gerard Lunt thought he'd taken to his grave."

"Like what?" Peter asked.

Anton glanced at his wristwatch, then smiled. "It's getting late, Pete," he said. "I'll walk you to Mendini's Crossing."

The Burger King was closed. Without the lights from their parking lot, Peter could barely navigate the rocky trail to the boulder crossing. But Anton was at his side in case he stumbled.

They reached the narrow concrete slab that cut through the tributary of Lake Leroy. Anton reached over and gave Peter a hug. His lips brushed against Peter's ear. "I'll tell you about Gerard Lunt's secret—very soon," he whispered. Then he pulled away. "We'll be the only ones who know, Pete. Just you, me, and Gerry."

Anton's warm breath was still swirling in his ear as Peter made his way over Mendini's Crossing. Once he reached the other side, he turned to glance back at Anton. But he was gone.

"That's my place right over there," Maggie said, pointing to her town house.

"I know," Steve said, at the wheel of his Toyota. "I picked you up here. Remember?"

"Of course," she murmured.

Maggie liked him. He certainly was a great-looking young man. She'd noticed a few women sizing him up at the restaurant. He was tall, with a very solid build. He wore a white shirt and khakis. With his tan, and a touch of gel in his short brown hair, he looked so sleek, all brown and white. He has such a sexy, confident smile, too. And when he'd slipped on his glasses to check the menu, he looked damn cute.

He'd taken her to the Palisades, where they had a gorgeous view of the city and Elliott Bay. Her salmon entrée was as savory as it was sumptuous. Over dinner, he said she looked beautiful in her little black sleeveless dress. "Like Audrey Hepburn," he said. Talk about scoring points with her. He asked her about her work, and just enough about her divorce to show interest without spoiling the mood.

For the past eighteen months, he'd been a reporter, working the police beat in Juno, Alaska. His father had died recently, leaving him a good deal of money. So he'd quit his job and moved to Seattle. "... And you're the first woman I've gone out with here. How am I doing so far?"

He'd been doing great—until coffee and dessert, when he smiled, reached across the table, and took hold of her hand. Maggie felt so nervous. She kept smiling back at him, but all the while, she just wanted to be home by herself again, comfortable and safe.

They drove to a lookout point in Queen Anne, where the Space Needle dominated a sweeping view of the city lights and Puget Sound. They stepped out of his car and strolled around the park. He held her hand again as they watched the ferries moving back and forth on the water. After a few minutes, Maggie announced that she'd better go home.

Steve became quiet in the car. He pulled over to the curb in front of her house.

"Well, Steve, thanks very much," Maggie said, opening her door. "I had a really nice time."

He hopped out of the car, then hurried around to her side, where he closed the car door behind her.

"Thanks," she murmured.

Steve walked with her to the front door. "Are you going to invite me in for coffee?" he asked.

"Didn't we already have coffee at the restaurant?" she replied. Then she realized how awful that sounded.

"You've had a lousy time tonight, haven't you?" Steve asked, leaning against the door frame.

She dug the keys out of her purse. "No, actually, I think you're terrific guy—"

"But?" he said, with a cynical smile.

"In the past thirteen years, I've been on two dates." She

unlocked the door and opened it, then she turned to Steve. "There was this abysmal fix-up with a boring guy who sweated a lot and chewed with his mouth open. That was a couple of months ago. Then there was you, and you're perfect. I keep wondering what's really wrong with you."

He shrugged. "Well, nothing."

She laughed. Indeed, he was perfect, and he obviously liked her. Why was she pushing him away? She thought of Jack Murphy, who was totally unavailable to her.

"What is it?" Steve asked. "During dinner, I kept thinking you were—well, distracted. Is there another guy?"

"It's real screwed-up," Maggie admitted. "I'll probably never see him again. There isn't a snowball's chance in hell we'll ever get together."

"Is he married?"

Maggie hesitated before answering. "Yeah, he's taken. I must be crazy, because we didn't even spend much time together, and nothing ever happened. But he's still on my mind. Anyway, it's not fair to you, Steve."

"Let me worry whether or not I'm getting a fair deal here," he said. "Did you have an okay time tonight?"

Maggie managed to smile. "Actually, I had a lovely time."

"Then can we go out again?"

She nodded. "Sure. I'd like that."

"Can I come in for a glass of water?"

She gave him a wary look, then opened the door wider. "A glass of water, huh?"

"And maybe a good-night kiss," he said shyly.

Maggie switched on the lamp in the living room. "I'll get you that water," she said, retreating to the kitchen.

She really didn't want him to stay. She couldn't relax with him right now. Her stomach was in knots. She just wanted to be by herself and unwind. They had another date planned. She would stretch her comfort zone then.

"I have an early appointment tomorrow," she called, pulling the Brita pitcher out of the refrigerator. She poured a glass of water, then started to bring it out to him. "I'll need to kick you out in a couple of minutes. . . ."

Maggie stopped when she saw him in the living room. He was standing at her desk, holding the framed photo of her with Johnny. Steve turned and smiled at her. He put the photo down, then picked up the thin, pewter crucifix. "I see you weren't beating around the bush when you said you were Catholic."

He started to set the crucifix down on the desk again, but the metal base slipped off. "God, I'm sorry—"

"No, it's okay," Maggie said. She handed him his water, then retrieved the base. She slid the crucifix back in the receptacle, then returned it to the desk. Steve was standing very close.

"I'm Catholic, too," he said.

"Yeah, you told me."

"Who's the guy in the picture?"

"That's my brother."

Steve sipped his water. "Good-looking kid. Runs in the family. You mentioned your folks passed away. Does he live with you?"

"No," she said, with a shrug. "He—well, he's with them, actually. I have to remind myself of that, he's with our mom and dad now. See, he . . . um, drowned four weeks ago."

"Oh, Maggie," he whispered. "I'm so sorry." He put down his water and reached out to her.

She shook her head. "No, I'm fine. I didn't mean to make you uncomfortable." She started to back away, then stopped when she noticed the tears in his eyes.

"Are you crying?" she whispered.

"No, I'm not."

"Yes, you are." Maggie took hold of his hand. "My God, you're so sweet," she heard herself say. She was tearing up, too.

He reached under his glasses and wiped his eyes. "Well, I should probably be going, huh?" he muttered, his voice a little raspy.

"You can stay a little while, can't you?" Maggie asked.

He stayed until 1:30 in the morning. They sat on the living-room sofa and talked. Maggie found herself opening up to him. Still, all the while, she kept wondering when he was going to make a move. He didn't until she showed him to the door.

Steve said he'd call her. Then he wrapped his strong arms around her and tenderly kissed her on the lips, a long, slow, wet kiss. His body pressed against hers for a moment, then he stepped back. "Good night, Maggie," he whispered.

"That was nice," she admitted, standing by the open door.

"Sure was." He kissed her again, a fleeting brush against her lips with his open mouth. Then he stepped outside.

He left her wanting more.

He was so sexy and sweet, almost too good to be true. She really liked Steve, yet she couldn't help feeling blocked somehow. Part of her still thought of Jack Murphy. She was mad at herself for nearly letting him jinx her first date with this terrific guy.

From her front door, she waved at Steve as his car pulled away. Smiling, Maggie watched the Toyota cruise down the street.

She heard the telephone ring and hurried back into the house. She grabbed the cordless in the kitchen before the machine came on. "Hello?" she said, a little out of breath.

No response.

"Hello?" she repeated.

"Maggie?" she heard someone whisper in a raspy voice.

"Yes, who's calling?"

"You're alone now, aren't you?"

"Who is this?" she asked.

"I want to watch you sleep again, like I did that night at the inn. It was nice, Maggie. It was the closest thing to seeing you dead."

The phone rang again twenty-five minutes later. Maggie snatched up the receiver. "Hello?"

"Hi, it's Steve. Are you okay?"

"Yeah, thanks for getting back to me."

She'd called him. She'd tried *69 on the anonymous caller, and a recorded voice had told her that the number was blocked.

She'd thought about phoning the police. But how could she explain to them about her experience at the Lakeside Inn? The only person who might understand was Jack Murphy, and she couldn't call him.

Maggie had found Steve's business card in her purse. She'd dialed the number and gotten his machine. "Hi, Steve," she'd said after the beep. "Um, I know you're just getting in. But I'm wondering if you could grab some things and come back. I just got a really creepy call, and I'm a little nervous about being alone. If you could crash here in my brother's room for the night, I'd really appreciate it. Call me, okay?"

She'd spent the last twenty minutes nervously peering out the front window and talking herself out of phoning Jack Murphy.

Steve's call back was a godsend. "You sure you're all right?" he asked.

"Yeah, I'm fine. You really don't have to come here—"

"No, I'm on my way," Steve said. "In the meantime,

you should call the police about this crank. They might not be able to do anything about it. But you should report it."

"Okay, I'll do that," Maggie said.

"See you in a little bit."

"Thanks, Steve," she said. Maggie felt better already.

Chapter Fifteen

From the highway, Jack could see the Clark Federal Penitentiary. It was a sprawling, squat building isolated on a pastoral plain in a rural area about fifty miles south of Leroy.

Jack was driving one of the two station wagons available to the faculty at St. Bartholomew Hall. He'd lied on the sign-out sheet, saying he was using the car to minister at a rest home outside Seattle.

After pulling off the highway, he took the winding, narrow road that led to the prison. A couple of weeks ago, his old friend, Mike Berry, had warned him that he might end up at a place like this.

"You called Father Tom Garcia a son of a bitch—to his face?" Mike had said over the phone, long-distance. "You know how much clout he has, Jack? He's the archbishop's golden boy. You don't want to be on his bad side. I know you're grieving and frustrated over what happened to that kid, but locking horns with Tom Garcia could really cost you. At the snap of his fingers, he can have your ass transferred God-knows-where. You're lucky to still be at Our Lady of Sorrows. Hell, he could make you the chaplain-in-residence at some state prison. How does that sound to you?''

Apparently, Tom Garcia hadn't exercised his enormous clout, at least not yet. But Jack felt as if he were on borrowed time at Our Lady of Sorrows.

For a while, he withdrew from everyone, as he had during that guilt-ridden, grieving period after Donna and Leo's deaths. He merely went through the motions during classes and his other obligations. At night, he stayed in his room and drank more than he should have. He couldn't help feeling that he'd let everyone down, especially Maggie.

In his retreat from the world around him, Jack became preoccupied with Julian Doyle's drowning in Lake Leroy three years ago. There were too many similarities to Johnny's death. Both cases seemed to have been quickly and quietly dismissed as sad accidents.

Exactly three weeks after John's funeral, Jack had stopped by the administration building and checked the college's Office of Records. He wanted to find out more about Julian Doyle: who his teachers were, what room number he had in St. Bartholomew Hall, and exactly when he'd died.

The seminarian at the desk must have been from the theologate school. He was about twenty-five and slightly overweight, with short brown hair and thick glasses. He wore his clerical collar with a short-sleeve black shirt.

As Jack walked into the office, he caught the theologate student checking him up and down. Jack managed to smile back at him. "Hi. I'm wondering if you can help me," he said. "I'm Father Murphy. I need to look at the records for one of our students from three years ago, a freshman named Julian Doyle.''

"Oh, gosh, Father," he said. "I'm sorry, but I need authorization before I can pull a student's file.''

"Do you know how I can get authorization?"

"You'd have to go through Father Garcia or someone in the Administration Office. Sorry."

Jack glanced at his wristwatch. "They close up shop at five, don't they?"

Wincing, the seminarian nodded. "I'm afraid you've missed them."

"Well, isn't that just my dumb luck?" Jack said. He put on a smile. "You're probably trying to wrap it up here yourself—um, I didn't get your name."

"Charles," he said. "You're not holding me up, really. I'm stuck here for another fifteen minutes."

Jack leaned against the counter. "Listen, Charles, I know you have rules to follow, and I don't want to get anyone in trouble. But is there some way you can give me a break? I really need to look up this student's record."

Charles stared at him for a moment, then he moved to the computer terminal at the end of the counter. "What's the name again?"

"Doyle, Julian."

Jack got a two-page printout on Julian Doyle. Julian had lived in Room 330 at St. Bartholomew Hall. Four of the priests currently at St. Bart's had been his teachers. His grades had been good. And as the file said: *Subject deceased: 4/4/99.*

Unless there was a heat wave that April, Julian Doyle's swim—like Johnny's—had been as unseasonable as it was fatal.

Jack was late for confessions that afternoon, and he'd had to tutor a couple of students in the evening. He decided to wait until the next day to check the old newspapers at the college library. Then he'd look up the weather for that April fourth.

But the following day, Father Garcia showed up twenty

minutes into Jack's history class. Slouched in their chairs, the students stared at them with a modicum of curiosity.

"We need to talk, Jack," he whispered, patting his arm. "Dismiss the class."

Jack stepped away from the blackboard. He turned toward his twenty-two seminarians. "Something has come up, so I'm letting you out early. Don't forget, those essays are due on Friday. So get cracking."

As the students started to file out, Garcia leaned closer to Jack. "I'd like to talk with you up in your room."

Garcia didn't say a word as they rode up in the elevator together. He remained silent until they'd stepped into Jack's room. He closed the door. "Something has come to my attention," he said, pulling his cigarettes out of his suit coat pocket. "Yesterday afternoon, a student record was pulled without any authorization. Our computers picked it up. I talked to the seminarian in our Office of Records, and he said that you requested information."

"That's right," Jack said, moving toward his desk. "I wanted to look at what we had on the other student who drowned, Julian Doyle. You mentioned the other day that the case had been . . . *'swept under the rug.'* I just wanted to see what we had on him."

"Didn't we have a talk about three weeks ago?" Garcia asked, lighting his cigarette. "I thought we had an understanding, Jack. You were supposed to drop this investigation." He looked around for someplace to toss his match.

From his desk drawer, Jack took an ashtray that he used as a coaster and handed it to him. "I did drop that investigation, Tom," he explained. "This is someone else. This is Julian Doyle."

Glaring at him, Garcia took a long drag from his cigarette.

Jack sighed. "Listen, Tom, I didn't go to the funeral last month, like you told me. I haven't seen Maggie Costello either. I was just curious about the Julian Doyle case, because there were some similarities to John Costello's death." From under a pile of test papers he pulled the computer printout. "For example, look at this. Julian Doyle took his swim in early April. No one in their right mind would go for a midnight dip that time of year—"

"Jack, we've been through all this before. I'm not denying there are similarities. I'm not denying there are some unanswered questions. What I'm denying is your access to any more student records." He took the printout, then folded it up. "This is unauthorized information, Jack," he muttered, tucking the paper into his suit coat pocket. "That young man at our Office of Records never should have given this to you."

"Well, it's my fault," Jack admitted. "I don't want him getting into any trouble over this."

"I understand you were late for confessions yesterday, too. Father Zeigler said you showed up only for the last ten minutes."

"Yes, I know, I'm sorry."

Garcia took another long drag from his cigarette. "I'm thinking maybe you need some time away, Jack," he said. "A retreat for a couple of weeks, then a transfer. Of course, we'll have to find someone to take over your classes for the next two weeks until the end of the school year."

"Please, Tom. I don't want to leave here," Jack whispered.

"And I don't want to lose a good priest at this school, Jack," Garcia replied, with a pained look. "Don't make me send you away, okay?"

Jack nodded.

Garcia stubbed out his cigarette. "No more investigations, and no more unauthorized access to student records." He gave his suit coat pocket a little pat and started for the door. "And no more warnings, Jack. We understand each other, don't we?"

"Yes," Jack said, opening the door for him.

"I'll see myself out downstairs." Garcia started down the hallway.

Biting his lip, Jack closed the door. He walked over to his desk and pulled out his pocket-size notebook from the side drawer. He flipped through a few pages until he reached the most recent entry. Jack stared at the notes he'd written:

Julian Doyle—died: 4/4/99—weather? day of week?
Rm. 330
Teachers: Zeigler, Bourm, Von Borstel, Weiss, Konradt, Reynolds
chk against J's teachers?
Latin Club
What side of Lake Leroy was he found? Witnesses?

Jack did his laundry that night. The custodian, Duane, had his quarters next door to the faculty laundry room in the basement. Jack rarely got through the first spin cycle without Duane dropping by to spark a debate in religious social studies.

That Wednesday evening was no different, except Jack managed to steer the conversation his way. "You said something to me the morning we found John Costello's body." He stood at the dryer, folding T-shirts. "You said it was a strange coincidence that John was missing a couple of toes, because the other boy who drowned had lost some fingers from his hand."

Duane leaned back in the battered old kitchen chair they kept down in the laundry room. He wore an old T-shirt that hugged his chest and said, PARTY ANIMAL. His crudely handsome face pinched up for a moment, then he nodded. "Julian Doyle, three years ago. Just like your buddy."

"In what way was he like John?"

"The way they both died, man," Duane said, fingering

the cigarette behind his ear. "Y'know, both drowning and missing digits."

"What side of the lake did they find Julian's body?"

"This side, except about half a mile further north from where you found your pal. Some fishermen spotted him. I hear he was naked."

"Did they ever find his clothes?" Jack asked.

Duane shrugged. "Beats me."

"Did you know him well?" Jack asked.

"Who, Doyle?" Duane shook his head. "Oh, man, no. He was kind of a twerpy kid, kept to himself."

"You told me John often used to sneak out at night. Did you ever notice Julian Doyle out past curfew?"

Duane gave him a wry smile. "Naw. I'm telling you, Jack, the kid was a bookworm, a real yo-yo."

"Yet he was supposed to be swimming back from a party the night he drowned," Jack said.

"Yeah." Duane chuckled. "Go figure."

"Was there any explanation for the missing fingers?"

Duane let out another snort. "What was the explanation for John Costello's missing toes? Piranha in Lake Leroy? I don't think so."

"The way I heard it, a lot of junk has been thrown in that lake, and some sharp objects are under the surface."

Duane leaned forward in the chair. "Well, just mull that one over, Jack. With all the people who have swum in that lake, has anyone else lost a toe or a finger? How come it's just the dead guys that happened to, huh?"

Jack stopped folding his clothes. "How much do you know about a student named Oliver Theron from around the same time Julian Doyle drowned? He hanged himself from the roof of his parents' house."

Rubbing his chin, Duane nodded grimly. "He was a senior, but spent a lot of time here. I think he was a teacher's assistant or something."

"Do you remember when these deaths occurred? What time of year?"

"Well, let me think," Duane said. "It was a couple of weeks before Easter break when the Doyle kid drowned. I remember, because I was dating this ditzy flight attendant at the time. The other guy, Theron, hanged himself a little while after that. I think it was in May."

Jack returned to his room long enough to set his clean laundry on the sofa. The place still stunk from Garcia's cigarette smoke this afternoon. Jack cracked a window, then threw on his jacket and headed outside. He took the Mendini's Crossing shortcut over to the college library.

He stayed past midnight, looking up microfiche files of old local newspapers from May, three years before. He sat at a desk in front of the microfiche screen. There was no monthly index for the news stories, and Jack didn't have the exact date of Oliver Theron's suicide. He got blurry-eyed scanning each article in the news section and all the obituaries—for every day, starting with May first. But he finally found a headline on page four of the *Everett Herald*'s front section, dated May 26th: Grief and Shock over "Rooftop" suicide.

Jack read the article, which was a disappointment. Rick Pettinger had given him more details about the actual suicide than were described in the news story. There was nothing connecting Oliver Theron with Julian Doyle or Johnny. It was just the story of a young man who wanted to be a priest, who ended up leaving the seminary and killing himself within two weeks of graduation. *"Oliver wanted to be a teacher,"* according to his best friend, a fellow seminarian named Bernard McKenna. He was quoted throughout the article. *"Everyone liked Oliver. He was one of the kindest and most considerate people I'll ever know. He would have made a great priest."*

The next afternoon, Jack got Bernard McKenna's current

address from Charles at the college Office of Records. At least, he was pretty certain he recognized Charles's voice on the other end of the line. Jack put on a friendly, business-like tone and explained that he was Mitch Berrenger from the Student Alumni Association. "We're trying to track down a current address for Bernard McKenna, Class of Ninety-nine," Jack told him. "Do you have anything in your records that might help?"

"Um, I'm bringing it up here now," Charles said. "It shows Father McKenna can be reached care of the Clark Federal Penitentiary in South Skagit County. Huh, how about that?"

Jack had called the penitentiary and set up an appointment to meet Bernard McKenna there at four o'clock the following afternoon.

According to the dashboard clock, Jack was five minutes early. He glanced in his rearview mirror and watched the guard flick a switch that closed the tall chain-link gate behind him. Jack had been given a visitor's badge to wear and a placard for the dashboard of his car. The guard had told him to follow the signs for visitors' parking.

Once he parked the car, another guard at another guard-house pointed him to an annex off the main, three-story concrete compound. On his way into the visitors' waiting area, Jack passed through a metal detector and the scrutiniz-ing gaze of two more armed guards before they buzzed him in.

He sat down in one of the orange plastic bucket-style chairs bolted to the linoleum floor. On the walls, posters reminded everyone that there was NO SMOKING, and this was a DRUG-FREE ZONE. The place was crowded and smelly, a human zoo. Babies screamed, and mothers screamed even louder at their kids. Other mothers blithely ignored their children and let them run wild.

Jack sat there, trying not to make eye contact with anyone.

His priest's collar was an open invitation for strangers to unload their troubles on him and talk his ear off. And these people looked like they had a lot of troubles.

With his eyes riveted to the floor, Jack spotted Father McKenna's shoes before he saw Father McKenna.

The younger priest wore black high-tops with his casual priestly attire: a black short-sleeve shirt and the clerical collar. He looked a little like a beatnik with his pale complexion, a goatee, and his light brown hair trimmed short and spiked up. He also had a black eye. "Jack Murphy?" he asked, smiling. "I'm Bernie McKenna."

Jack stood up and shook his hand. "Thanks for seeing me," he said. He couldn't help staring at the discolored, puffy eye.

Bernie laughed and touched the side of his face. "Just got this yesterday, a hazard of being the chaplain here. I thought one of the new guys was ready for some spiritual guidance, and he disagreed with me." Bernie glanced around the crowded waiting room. "Want to talk outside? It's too nice an afternoon to stay cooped up in here."

Bernie led the way, first working a combination lock on one door, then passing through a hallway, where a guard in a glass booth buzzed him through a second door. They stepped outside. Three stories of concrete obstructed most of the view—except for a glimpse of the visitors' parking lot. They strolled through a maze of chain-link fencing. As they talked, Jack noticed the razor coils running along the top of the fence. They ended up in what must have been the recreation area. There were park benches, cement picnic tables, and, beyond another tall fence, a basketball court with bleachers. Despite the blue sky above, the area still seemed confined by concrete, chain link, and barbed wire. No one else was around this time of the afternoon.

"I read about that drowning last month," Bernie said. He settled down at a picnic table. "Now that I know you were friends with John Costello, I understand your frustration. After Oliver's death, I spent weeks beating my head against the wall, wondering why it happened. I must have gone off in dozens of different directions searching for an explanation.''

"Did you ever find one?" Jack asked, sitting down across from him.

Bernie frowned. "Nothing definite. Just a half-baked theory."

"However it's cooked, I'd like to hear it."

Bernie pulled a pack of cigarettes from his shirt pocket and lit one up. "Well, in the last few weeks of his life, Oliver spent a lot of time over at St. Bartholomew Hall. He was a teacher's assistant there. But I noticed he'd go back across the lake later in the evening too. He was very mysterious about these trips. I remember once I asked him about it, and he said he liked going for walks alone in the woods. He used to tramp mud and pine needles back into the dorm. So I believed him about the walks in the woods. I just didn't believe he was alone."

Bernie puffed his cigarette, and squinted over the fence top at the sky. "I think Oliver had a thing for one of the priests at St. Bart's—or maybe a student. I'd always suspected he was gay, but we never discussed it. He thought homosexuality was immoral. He was very serious about the celibacy issue. Anyway, I think Oliver fell for some guy—and he fell hard."

"Do you have any idea who it might have been?" Jack asked.

Bernie shook his head. "Not a clue. This is all just speculation, Jack, a half-baked theory, like I said."

"Do you think he might have been seeing the boy who drowned, Julian Doyle?"

"That thought crossed my mind, too," Bernie said. "But I was with Oliver when we heard about Julian Doyle drowning. He seemed sorry for the kid, and said he knew him remotely. But he wasn't particularly traumatized by the news. So if Oliver was seeing somebody, I don't think it was Julian Doyle.''

"Who was this teacher Oliver worked with?"

"Father Dominkus. He died of cancer two years ago. He was battling it all through that last semester. That's why he took Oliver on as an assistant.'' Bernie dropped his cigarette on the ground, stepped on it, then picked up the stub and set it on the picnic table. "Anyway, Jack," he said, "I'm not sure I'm any help to you. I can't imagine what this has to do with your friend, John Costello.''

"Nothing, I suppose," Jack muttered. "I'm just looking for an explanation, a pattern. I only recently found out about Oliver's suicide.''

"I still miss him," Bernie admitted. "Imagine what it must have been like for his poor parents. They were returning from some charity benefit when they found Oliver in his underpants, swinging by the neck from a rope tied to the chimney.''

"In his underpants?'' Jack said.

"Yeah.'' Bernie nodded.

"You know, when we found Johnny, all he had on were his underpants. And I hear Julian Doyle was naked when they discovered his body.''

Bernie gave him a strained, sympathetic smile. "You might be grabbing at straws, Jack. I mean, if a guy's going for a swim, he's likely to shed some of his clothes.''

"But why would someone strip down to his underwear to go out on a rooftop and hang himself?''

Bernie scratched his goatee. "No one knows what Oliver was thinking that night.''

"Was he missing any digits when they found his body?''

"What?''

"A couple of fingers were missing from Julian Doyle's

hand when they found him. Two of Johnny's toes were gone. Were all of Oliver's fingers and toes intact?''

Bernie stared at Jack for a moment. ''Nothing was missing when they found him,'' he said. ''But I can't say for sure about later.''

''What do you mean, *about later?''*

Bernie sighed. ''It's kind of a secret. Oliver's family didn't want this ever getting out. . . .''

''What?'' Jack asked. ''Listen, Bernie, whatever it is, I won't repeat it. All this is strictly between us.''

Bernie's eyes wrestled with his for a moment, then he glanced down at the tabletop. ''There's always been a rumor that Oliver's corpse was stolen from his grave.''

''They don't know for sure?'' Jack asked.

''No, they don't. Two days after Oliver's funeral, a caretaker at the cemetery reported that someone had dug down past all the new topsoil and grass seedling on Oliver's grave. They didn't know exactly how far down the digging had gone, and they wanted permission from Oliver's family to exhume the coffin and check it to see if anything was missing. But his folks had been through enough. They had the cemetery people restore the topsoil and reseed—that's all. They didn't want to know.''

''How did you find out about this?'' Jack murmured.

''Oliver's mom told me a couple of months after his suicide. I remember her saying that, for all we knew, there was just an empty casket buried in the Theron family plot.''

Shrugging, Bernie picked at his cigarette butt. His eyes were tearing up. ''So, to answer your question, Jack,'' he said in a shaky voice, ''I'm not sure whether or not my buddy, Oliver, was missing any digits. Whoever tampered with his grave, they could have dug all the way down to the casket, then opened it up and cut off a finger or a toe. They could have stolen poor Oliver's body, too. We'll never know for sure.''

"Why not?" Jack asked quietly. "Can't they investigate it?"

"They'd have to exhume Oliver's corpse," Bernie said, wiping his eyes. "I don't think Oliver's parents want to relive all that pain. I understand how they feel. There are some things you're better off not knowing. They've closed the book on it, Jack. I've even stopped questioning what really happened with Oliver. And I was just like you are now with your friend. At one time, it totally consumed me. But not anymore."

Shaking his head, he gave Jack a sad smile. "No one will be digging into that grave again."

Chapter Sixteen

The camping trip was her parents' idea. *Family fun,* they said. A weekend of misery and boredom was more like it. Kerry Ostrander was missing out on a big party. Most of the in crowd from her high-school sophomore class would be there. She felt like the Invisible Girl half the time at school. Attending that party would have been her big chance to get noticed.

But no, *family fun* came first. She'd spent three hours riding in the back of the minivan with her obnoxious kid brother and listening to her parents' eighties greatest hits tapes, one after another. They ended up by some stream off Lake Wenatchee, where her father insisted on fishing for their lunch. Why didn't he just shoot her and get it over with? They weren't even at a regular campsite. No one else was around. They had to park the car on some dirt road and weave around all these trees and bushes to the stream.

Her father and little brother actually caught some fish,

and her mother was going to cook them over an open fire. Real rustic crap. Kerry hated fish.

Kerry's mother told her to stop complaining, then gave her a bucket and sent her on a rock-gathering expedition. She said something about how medium-size rocks around the campfire would keep the flame hotter and contained. Kerry really wasn't listening. She was just glad for an excuse to wander off by herself.

She strolled along the riverbank. In some areas the water came right up to the shrubs, and Kerry had to walk in the river. She got her sandals wet and muddy. But she didn't care. The sun was hot, and the water felt refreshing.

While lamenting over the party she would miss tonight, Kerry gathered up stones—each one about the size of her fist. She noticed a small rock pile in the shade by a section of a fallen tree. Foliage brushed against her toes and ankles as she stepped toward the rock pile. Kerry made a mental note to kill her parents if she wound up with poison ivy.

It was dry and cool in the shaded area. Kerry sat down on the tree and stared down at the rocks. Then she noticed a pearl-and-gold earring amid the rubble. But it took her another moment to realize that the long, brownish tuft of grass was actually human hair. And that dried-up, raisinlike thing was a woman's ear.

Kerry suddenly couldn't breathe. She reeled back, knocking over the bucket of rocks.

She was gaping at a half-buried skull—not quite picked to the bone. One hollow eye socket stared back at her, and a few exposed teeth revealed the corner of a skeletal grin. A spider crawled out of the mouth, then moved up the cheekbone and over that beautiful pearl-and-gold earring.

Kerry's screams reverberated down the river's current to where her parents and kid brother had set up camp.

Whether she liked it or not, by Monday morning, Kerry Ostrander, the Invisible Girl, would be the talk of the school.

* * *

The phone rang at ten o'clock on Friday night. Irene McShane's grandson, Michael, had gone out to a fellow sixth-grader's birthday party, and the eight-year-old, Aaron, was watching TV with her in the family room.

Irene grabbed the cordless on the third ring. "Hello?"

"Mrs. McShane?"

"Yes?"

"This is Detective Dreiling with the Wenatchee police."

"Yes?" Somehow, she knew what it was about before he even said anything. Irene took the cordless phone into her daughter-in-law's study—out of earshot from Aaron. As he told her, Irene felt her legs start to teeter. She sank down in Dorothy's easy chair.

All she heard was, *"We've found some remains . . ."* The rest was lost to her.

"Are they sure it's Dorothy?" she asked after a moment.

"Positive identification, ma'am. The dental records match. I'm very sorry, Mrs. McShane. Right now, we're searching the area for the rest of her body—"

"What do you mean? Where's the rest of her body?" Irene asked numbly.

"I'm sorry, Mrs. McShane," the detective said, sounding a bit flustered. "I didn't make myself clear. All we found this afternoon was the skull. We're still looking for her body."

"Oh, my God," she murmured. "He—he cut off her head? Why? What kind of monster would do something like that?"

The detective kept apologizing, but she barely heard him. All the while, Irene wondered how she would tell her grandsons that their mother was dead. She couldn't hope to shield them from the truth—and all the gruesome details. They were bound to find out at school or read it in the newspapers.

The police had found Judge Dorothy McShane's head, but not her body.

Jack had smuggled an early edition of the newspaper into the confessional. The 4:00 to 4:45 confessional duty on Saturday afternoon was pretty much a waste of time. It was tough enough persuading people to atone for their sins, but expecting them to do so in the middle of a warm Saturday afternoon bordered on ludicrous. Confessions offered at St. Gabriel Chapel on Monday and Wednesday were better attended.

The newspaper helped take his mind off the fact that he'd been sitting in this hot little box for the past forty minutes. So far, he'd had only two people in confession—both old women "regulars."

The headline at the bottom of page one caught his eye: MISSING V.I.P., JUDGE MCSHANE, CONFIRMED DEAD.

Like everyone else, Jack had been following accounts of Dorothy McShane's disappearance since February. There had been little reported since the discovery of her abandoned car a couple of months ago. But yesterday, a teenage girl had found a skull near a creek about seventy miles southeast of Our Lady of Sorrows.

Apparently, the police weren't any closer to finding Judge McShane's killer than they'd been when she'd first disappeared.

Jack knew how they must have felt, fumbling around for any clue that could help their investigation. Since talking with Father McKenna yesterday, he'd been running into one dead end after another.

He'd spent several hours at the college library's periodical room. Hidden away in a stuffy cubicle, Jack had gone through more old newspaper microfiche files for follow-up stories on Oliver Theron's "suicide" and Julian Doyle's drowning. But he hadn't come up with anything. He couldn't link them to Johnny either. The only common denominator was St. Bartholomew Hall. Yet for some reason, he couldn't get past the idea that all of their deaths had to be somehow connected.

Jack glanced at his wristwatch: 4:45, quitting time. Folding up the newspaper, he got to his feet and switched off the little confessional light.

Just then, he heard someone walk into the chapel. Footsteps. They came toward the confessionals, but stopped. Jack couldn't tell if they were coming in or not. He waited a minute, then finally opened the door.

Jonie Sorretto gasped. Reeling back, she bumped into a pew. Without her raccoonlike eye makeup and blackberry lipstick, she looked rather pretty—in a mousy sort of way. She wore black jeans and a ratty maroon pullover. The black roots to her platinum hair needed touching up. "Jesus, you scared the shit out of me," she said, a hand over her heart.

"Are you okay? Can I help you?"

"Yeah, I guess so." She took a deep breath. "I need to talk to you about Johnny."

He nodded. "All right."

"I—well, I haven't been very honest with you. I keep thinking about Johnny's sister—and you. You haven't gotten the whole story." She nervously glanced at the altar for a moment, then at the church doors. "I gotta admit, I don't feel so good about coming here. The last thing I need right now is to be seen talking with you."

He pointed toward the confessionals. "Would you rather talk in there? We'll have total privacy."

Frowning, she shook her head. "No I'm sorry. Y'know, this was a really dumb idea. I shouldn't have come. I think someone's following me. I'm sorry. I—I gotta get out of here."

"No, wait." Jack grabbed her arm. "Jonie. I'm trying to

find out why John Costello is dead. You know something. If you cared about Johnny at all, you'd tell me.''

Jonie wrenched free of him. ''I can't talk with you here—''

''Then we'll go someplace else.''

She backed away from him. ''Okay, okay. Come to my place in an hour or so. We'll talk there. Make sure no one's following you.''

He nodded. ''All right, but—''

''See you in an hour.'' Jonie turned, then hurried out of St. Gabriel Chapel.

Jonie parked in front of her duplex. She fiddled with the seat and the rearview mirror of her sky blue VW bug. Every time she let him borrow her car, he readjusted the seat and the rearview mirror. She'd been looking out for him in that slightly cockeyed rearview mirror all the way back from St. Bartholomew Hall's chapel. Jonie kept having to remind herself that she had the car. How could he be following her?

On the front stoop, someone had knocked over the old bag of kitty litter. Jonie stepped over the mess. She pulled out her key and started to insert it in the lock, but the front door inched open on its own.

Jonie stepped back from the threshold. Had she left the door like that? She couldn't remember now. She gazed at the stairs beyond the half-open door. Something was wrong.

Reaching into her purse again, she pulled out her cigarettes and lit one up. She hesitated for another moment, then told herself that she was being silly. Jonie walked inside and started up a couple of steps. They creaked, and in her nervousness, the noise seemed so loud. She couldn't hear anyone upstairs. But if someone was there, they certainly could hear her coming. She knew it was silly, but couldn't help feeling uneasy.

Jonie took another puff of her cigarette and climbed the rest of the stairs. She peered past the railing at her living room and kitchen area. The usual disaster area, only someone had opened a couple of windows. "Hey, is anybody here?" she called skittishly.

"Just me," she heard him answer.

"Where are you?" she asked, clutching the railing. "What's going on?"

"I never see you without a cigarette, Jonie."

She couldn't tell where his voice was coming from.

"That smoking is going to kill you one of these days," he said.

"Why are you hiding?" she asked. She took another puff of her cigarette. "C'mon, cut out this bullshit. Let me see you."

"Take off your clothes first," she heard him reply. "C'mon, Jonie. Play along."

Three blocks from Jonie's duplex, Jack could smell the smoke.

He'd walked over from St. Bartholomew Hall. He must have picked up some of Jonie's paranoia, because he'd kept glancing back over his shoulder most of the way. No one had been following him.

But something else was wrong. That sharp, sooty, burning odor filled his nostrils. Jack picked up the pace, and by the time he turned down Jonie's block, he was running. He saw the ambulance, police cars, and fire trucks. Dozens of onlookers crowded the sidewalk across the street from Jonie's duplex. They stood behind a line of yellow tape and a patrolman on guard.

"Oh, God, no," Jack whispered, slowing down.

Except for the broken-down front door, the first floor appeared untouched by the fire. But all the windows on the second floor had been smashed. Remnants of smoke continued to waft out, blackening the duplex's dirty beige exterior.

Jack started toward the ambulance, but a policeman stopped him. The cop didn't say anything, he just shook his head and braced a hand against Jack's shoulder.

"Let him through!" one of the firemen yelled. He was built like a football player, and his face was covered with soot. He stood by the ambulance's open rear door. "She was asking for a priest. Let him pass!"

"Sorry, Father. Go on through," the cop said.

Dazed, Jack moved into the chaos of patrol cars, cops, and flashing red lights. Then he saw the fireman waving him on. "She was asking for a priest earlier," he explained. He opened the door wider, so Jack could see her.

Lying on a stretcher, Jonie was clad in only her black bra and panties. Her pale body had been singed crimson. Her face was turned away from him. But from the side, he could tell she was already blistered, and nearly all of her platinum-dyed hair had been burnt off.

"She was dead by the time we got her out here," Jack heard the fireman say. "We couldn't resuscitate her. In the house, she muttered something about needing to see a priest. I guess she must have known she wouldn't make it."

Jack crawled into the back of the ambulance with Jonie's corpse. He almost choked on the smell of burnt flesh. He wanted to cry out with anger, frustration, and grief.

He never should have let her go this afternoon.

"Looks like she was smoking in bed and fell asleep," the fireman explained.

Jack knew it hadn't happened that way at all.

He took a deep breath and made the sign of the cross. He reached toward her forehead, the skin pink and raw. Jonie's face slowly turned toward him. Her mouth was open. Her lips had been singed off, and three of her front upper teeth were missing.

"Holy Jesus," he murmured.

"You looking at the teeth?" he heard the fireman ask. "We noticed it, too. I think she must have woken up, then tripped or something."

Hovering over the corpse, he studied Jonie's blistered, blackened hands—and her stubby feet. Every finger and toe was intact. Then he stared at the traces of blood in and around her mouth.

"We were looking for her teeth on the floor—around where she fell," the fireman explained. "We haven't found them yet."

"I don't think you ever will," Jack said.

He traced a sign of the cross on Jonie's burnt-raw forehead. Just an hour ago, she'd been so scared.

"We pray," he said, his voice quivering. "We pray for the repose of the soul of Your daughter, Jonie. Please, give her eternal peace and rest, Dear God. . . ."

He stood with the others crowding behind the police tape, gawking at the fire. These people had nothing better to do with their time. They were the same kind of idiots who caused traffic jams because they had to slow down and gape at accidents on the side of the road. He couldn't stand to be among them much longer.

But Jack Murphy had walked by him just a few minutes ago, and he needed to make sure the good father had a chance to see Jonie. Murphy was with her in the ambulance now. Did he notice that some of her teeth were missing?

Extracting them hadn't been easy. She'd passed out. He'd gotten her saliva all over his hands, trying to prop open that slippery little mouth of hers. Pressing his knee on her chest, he'd pulled and twisted at her teeth with the pliers. He'd kept thinking he might snap her neck. The last thing he wanted was to break her stupid neck. That wouldn't have been any good. He needed her to die in the fire.

From across the street, he'd seen them bring her out on the stretcher. One of the paramedics had been working over her, but they'd finally covered her up before loading her into the ambulance.

His work was done. He had his souvenirs. They were in his pocket right now, three teeth wrapped in a handkerchief. He smiled a little. He was the only one smiling in the crowd.

Chapter Seventeen

"Maggie?"

She recognized Jack's voice immediately.

With Steve out of town, Maggie had tried to make the best of her Saturday night alone. She'd rented a two-tape video to occupy her whole night, then ordered a pizza. Half the pizza had wound up in the refrigerator.

When the phone rang, she put *The English Patient* on pause. On her TV, Ralph Fiennes and Kristin Scott Thomas were frozen in a passionate embrace.

Maggie didn't want Jack Murphy knowing that she recognized his voice after almost a month. In fact, she was annoyed that he'd called. She'd just started dating Steve, a rich, handsome, sensitive guy who was clearly interested in her. He'd been a perfect gentleman on that first date. He'd come to her rescue, and spent the night in Johnny's room. He'd come through for her. She wasn't supposed to care anymore about some totally unavailable priest.

"Yes, this is Maggie," she said. "Who's calling?"

"It's Jack Murphy," he said. "How are you?"

"All right, I guess," she said, sitting on the edge of her couch, the cordless phone in her hand. "I didn't think I'd hear from you again. You made that pretty clear to me the last time we talked."

"I'm sorry about that conversation, Maggie," he said. "I had no choice. The head of administration here is a guy named Father Garcia, and he laid down the law. He forbade me to see you under any circumstances. That included attending John's funeral. I couldn't go against him and expect to stay on here. He has a lot of clout."

Maggie didn't say anything for a moment. She stared at the TV screen, with Ralph and Kristin locked in their embrace. Jack hadn't said anything about missing her, or that he'd thought of her at all these past few weeks. She felt like such an idiot that it should matter, but it did.

She grabbed the remote and switched off the TV. "So . . . what's going on?" she asked finally. "To what do I owe this call?"

"Something happened," he said. "You know Jonie? The girl we spoke with at the hair salon—"

"Yes . . ."

"Well, her apartment caught on fire this afternoon. She's dead."

"My God," Maggie murmured.

"She came to me in the chapel earlier today, wanting to talk about Johnny. She admitted that she hadn't been very honest with us. That's all I got out of her before she seemed to lose her nerve. We were supposed to meet at her apartment. Only when I arrived there, she was already dead. I'm sorry to be telling you this over the phone, Maggie."

"No, I'm glad you called," she heard herself say. "Thank you."

"By any chance, did Jonie ever contact you?"

"I never heard from her at all," Maggie said numbly.

"She didn't even come to the funeral. My God, Jack. What's going on?"

"I don't know. I phoned the hair salon where she worked, and they were closed. They're open from noon until five tomorrow. I'm going there to see if Jonie told a coworker what she couldn't tell us."

"I'd like to come along," Maggie said.

"I don't think we should be seen together, Maggie—"

"The girls at the salon might not want to talk to you. It'll help if you have a woman with you."

"Well, don't come to the school," he said. "Let's meet in front of the beauty parlor. Is noon okay?"

"Noon's fine," she said.

"Actually, I'm glad you're coming up," he said. "It'll be good to see you again, Maggie."

She smiled. "Thank you, Jack."

"G'night," he said. Then he hung up.

Jack held the receiver in its cradle for a moment, then he picked it up and dialed a number he'd written down in his pocket-size notebook. It rang twice before someone answered. "Hello?"

"Hello, is this Aaron Del Toro?" Jack asked. Aaron was the fireman who had talked with him in the ambulance.

"Yes, this is Aaron."

"Hello, this is Father Murphy—from earlier today?"

"Oh, sure. Hi, Father."

"Listen, I want to thank you for your help today. Also I was wondering. Did they . . . ever find any of her teeth?"

"No, you sure called that one, Father. They couldn't locate them anywhere in the apartment. The coroner didn't find any teeth lodged in her throat either. I talked with him tonight. He said those teeth weren't knocked out, they were yanked out. Even a couple of the roots were gone. Apparently, she'd had a lot to drink and snort—a regular little party for herself. It's bizarre. I've heard of people doing some pretty weird shit—um, excuse me, Father—*stuff* when they're high. But I tell ya, I'd have to be pretty far gone to tear out my own teeth.''

''Someone must have done it to her,'' Jack said. ''Then they probably set fire to her apartment.''

''Well, so far, our fire detective is ninety-nine percent sure it was an accident,'' Aaron said. ''The girl smoked like a chimney, I guess. Today wasn't the first time we responded to a fire at that address. She had us there on two previous occasions. Minor stuff, but enough to tell us that she was pretty damn careless. Her downstairs neighbor confirmed it. This old, half-blind, half-deaf lady with about eight cats, she said Jonie Soretto was always setting off the smoke detector with one little fire after another—tossing live cigarettes in the trash, and one time, accidentally torching a sofa pillow, things like that.''

''I suppose this neighbor couldn't tell us whether or not Jonie had any visitors when this fire started,'' Jack said glumly.

''No, she wasn't home at the time. And I wouldn't count on her for too much beyond what she told us today. On top of her sight and hearing problems, she's pretty much on the loopy side.''

''Isn't it possible—likely, even—that someone was with Jonie when the fire started?''

''Well, it'll be difficult to determine with all the damage done to the place. But we'll look into it. And if those missing teeth turn up, I'll definitely let you know.''

''Well, thank you, Aaron,'' Jack said. ''You're never going to find them. But thank you anyway.''

* * *

"Is this thing much further?" Peter asked.

"About another five minutes," Anton said, leading the way. "Don't be such a pussy, Pete."

"Well, when you said you wanted to show me something in the woods, I didn't think we had a five-mile hike ahead of us. It's getting really dark."

Peter had really been looking forward to seeing Anton tonight. It had been over a week since they'd last gotten together. Anton was going to borrow a car from a friend. They'd planned to drive all over Leroy in search of that pale blue Volkswagen bug. If they didn't find it by nine o'clock, they planned to go for pizza as a consolation prize.

Instead, Anton had met Peter at the Stop 'n' Fuel-Up, explaining that his friend had flaked out on him, so no car. Then he had a brilliant idea about going into the forest so they could revisit a site somehow connected with the Gerard Lunt murder-suicide case in 1949.

Peter had been a bit wary at first. Seven-fifteen at night wasn't exactly the best time to go exploring in that thick forest on the west side of Lake Leroy. The sun had already been setting.

But Anton had mentioned that the site wasn't far from a secluded hot spring. "It's just going to be you and me, so we can go naked," he'd said. "It'll be an adventure. C'mon, what do you say?"

That had been nearly two hours ago. They'd wandered off a main trail, and Anton followed markings he'd once made on the trees along the way. He used a flashlight he'd picked up at the last minute from the Stop 'n' Fuel-Up. It had grown so dark in the woods that Peter doubted he'd even cop a decent look at Anton naked.

He trailed behind Anton, blindly navigating the rocks and tree roots in his path. Patches of moonlight peeked through the treetops. He could hear rustling in the bushes, and he wondered out loud if there were bears in these woods.

"Just possums and raccoons, Pete," Anton told him. "We're almost there. Aren't you having fun?"

"Yeah, sure, a great time," he lied. "I hope the batteries in that flashlight last, otherwise we're screwed. Are the hot springs very far from this place we're going?"

"Not far at all," Anton said. "In fact, our destination is just up ahead." He aimed the flashlight through the trees.

Peter could only see branches illuminated by the beam. "Is this going to creep me out?" he asked. "I keep expecting to see something out of *The Blair Witch Project*."

"C'mon," Anton said, quickening his pace.

Peter tried to keep up without stumbling in the dark. He saw a small clearing, and over to the side, an old, dilapidated shack, no bigger than a dorm room at St. Bart's. Anton trained the light across the screened windows, which were falling apart.

"We're not going in there, are we?" Peter asked.

"Don't be such a wimp." Anton led the way. He stepped inside first, and held open the rickety screen door for Peter.

At the threshold, Peter hesitated. Anton swept the flashlight beam across three old trash bags on the floor, one of them torn open with garbage spilling out: paper plates, food wrappers, and rusty Coke cans. There was a broken hardback chair, tipped on its side, and a couple of picnic table benches. A battered dresser stood against one wall, most of the drawers pulled out or broken.

Anton moved toward the dresser. Then the flashlight went out.

"What happened?" Peter asked, panic-stricken.

"Relax," Anton said. He lit a match, then held it to the wick of an old oil lamp. The flickering lamp illuminated the screened-in little room. "Light at last!" Anton announced, grinning.

Peter glanced around. "Now that I can see this dump, I think I liked it better in the dark." He also got his first good look at Anton in over an hour. The handsome senior was sweating and dirty. But he was grinning at him.

"Come take a look at something." He nodded at the hollow opening where someone had removed the dresser's bottom drawer. "Reach down in there."

"Yeah, screw that." Peter laughed. "You reach in there."

"For God's sakes," he muttered. He stooped down and stuck his hand in the dresser opening. "It's still here. Nobody's found it yet." Anton pulled out a small tin box. He straightened up and showed the container to Peter. Barely legible under a layer of rust and dirt, OWENS COUGH DROPS was printed in swirly script on the lid.

"What is that?" Peter asked.

Anton handed the container to him. "Open it," he whispered.

The little box felt empty. It hardly weighed anything. Peter pried off the lid. There was some wax paper, brittle, yellowing, and folded up like a tiny packet. Inside, Peter could see a lock of hair. Someone had written on the wax paper in red crayon.

"Take a look," Anton said. "Just be careful. There's another one underneath that. See the initials?"

"Initials?" The second packet was just like the first, with a lock of hair preserved in folded-up wax paper. Peter squinted at the faded writing: G. L. was marked on one packet; M. W. on the other.

"Gerard Lunt and Mark Weedler," Anton said. "That's their hair you're holding."

Peter could tell—just by looking at the two keepsakes and the old cough-drop tin—that Anton was telling the truth. He felt his skin prickle. "Where did you get these?" he asked numbly.

"Just where I showed you," Anton replied. "They've been there in that cough-drop box since 1949, when Gerard

Lunt hid it underneath the dresser. You and me are the only living people who know about it, Pete.''

Peter felt so strange, examining souvenirs from those two long-dead boys, St. Bartholomew Hall's notorious murder-suicide victims. With a shaky hand, he carefully set the packets back inside the tin, then gave it to Anton. ''How did you know where to find it?'' he asked.

''Promise you won't think I'm crazy. And I'm *not* bull-shitting you,'' Anton said. ''Remember, I told you that when I was a freshman, I used to spend hours at a time alone in Room 410?''

''Yeah,'' Peter nodded.

''I heard them sometimes.''

''Heard who?''

''Gerard and Mark. I'd hear them talking. I picked up different things. They used to come to this place.'' Leaning against the bureau, Anton glanced around the shack. ''Even back in '49, it was abandoned and neglected. Gerard and Mark used to practice saying Mass here. This old dresser was their altar.''

Shaking his head, Peter squinted at him. ''How do you know all this?''

''I just told you, Pete. I heard them talking. Don't you sometimes still feel that Johnny's around—in a room with you or by your side? It was kind of like that for me and Gerry. The day after I heard him talking with Mark, I came out here. In the daylight, it's not such a long hike. I knew I'd find something if I kept looking.'' Anton held up the cough-drop tin. ''And I found this, Pete. We have to keep this secret. We're the only ones who can know.''

Dazed, Peter watched Anton set the little container back in the hollowed-out bottom of that ancient dresser. There was a certain reverence in the way he did it. He seemed to have a true connection to the spirit world.

''There's something else about Mark and Gerry you don't

know,'' Anton announced. ''But you're not ready to hear it yet.''

''What is it?'' Peter asked.

''I'll tell you sometime, soon.''

He snuffed out the oil lamp, and the little cabin was cloaked in darkness once more. Switching on his flashlight, Anton trained the beam toward the screen door and led the way for Peter.

''So, Pete,'' he said, stepping outside. ''Want to take a dip in the hot springs before we head back?''

''Sure.'' Peter shrugged with feigned nonchalance. ''Sounds cool.''

He felt a pang in his stomach, butterflies, nervous anticipation. His eyes had adjusted to the light, and he could see Anton pretty clearly. He still thought about that time they'd been in Anton's bathroom together, and he'd glimpsed him naked. Anton probably had no idea how sexy he was.

''I'm glad we came out here,'' Peter announced. ''I'm sorry if I was whining earlier. I thought maybe—''

''Shhhh,'' Anton cut in. He stopped dead. ''Did you hear that?''

''What?'' Peter froze. He glanced around the darkened woods and listened carefully for the sound that had stopped Anton in his tracks. There was a rustling noise, but it could have been the wind.

''I just heard someone,'' Anton said under his breath.

''Stop it.'' Peter let out a skittish laugh and nudged Anton. ''You're creeping me out.''

''I'm pretty creeped out myself. I don't like this at all.'' With the flashlight, he swept a beam across the cluster of trees and bushes. Shadows seemed to dance in every nook. ''All right, who's there?'' Anton called. ''Cut the bullshit.''

No response, just the rustling sound.

''I don't think there's anyone—''

''Oh, Jesus,'' Anton murmured. The beacon of light

seemed to catch something past the first row of trees. Peter thought he saw it, too, or maybe his eyes were playing tricks on him.

"Stay here," Anton said.

"Wait! No!"

But Anton took off.

Peter stood paralyzed for a moment. His heart was racing. He watched Anton dart past some trees, then disappear in the thicket. The flashlight went out. Peter could hear the twigs snapping beneath Anton's feet. He seemed to be slowing down. Or was he just getting farther and farther away?

"Anton?" he called at last.

No answer.

Peter glanced down at the ground and spotted a thick, broken section of a tree branch. He swiped it off the forest floor. It was bulky and awkward to carry, but nearly the size of a baseball bat. Peter figured he could defend himself with it.

"Anton? Where are you?" he called again, a slight tremor in his voice. He listened for another minute, but there was nothing. Then it suddenly occurred to him: *It's a prank.* He hadn't actually seen or heard anything. Anton was pulling his leg, having a little fun.

But it wasn't funny.

"Hey, Anton, I get the joke," he announced loudly. "I know you can hear me. Why don't you answer?"

Again, no response. Peter tightened his grip on the makeshift club. All at once, Anton's voice broke the stillness.

"Oh, Jesus, *no, don't*—"

Then there was a heavy thud. Peter's whole body stiffened. He wanted to run, but couldn't move. He couldn't even breathe. He listened to the twigs snapping underfoot.

"Anton, quit kidding around!" he cried. "It's not funny!"

The footsteps seemed to be coming closer. Peter wasn't

sure which way to run. His eyes brimmed with tears. He was certain he would die in these lonely, dark woods.

Then he heard the laughter, a low snickering. It was Anton. He emerged from the shadows, holding the flashlight up, directly under his face. It gave him a demonic look. "Sucker!" He grinned. "You fell for it!"

Peter quickly wiped his tears away. "Fuck you," he said. "You're not funny."

"Oh, c'mon, lighten up."

Peter shook his head. "No, that was a shitty thing to do."

"God, can't you take a joke? I thought after all that seriousness, we could use a laugh." Anton tried to put his arm around him, but Peter pulled away. "Hey, c'mon, sport. I know what you need. The hot springs will help you mellow out."

"No," Peter heard himself saying. "I don't want to go there. I can't trust you now. I just want to get out of these fucking woods and go home."

Anton stared at him in the darkness for a moment, then he sighed. "Suit yourself, Pete." He brushed past him, then shined his flashlight on the trees, looking for markings to the trail back.

Peter let Anton lead the way. Neither of them uttered a word for the next ninety minutes. The moon reflecting off Lake Leroy made it easier to navigate as they came closer to the end of the trail.

"Those locks of hair in the cough-drop box," Peter said, finally. "Were those a joke, too?"

Anton didn't answer him right away. He kept walking, the flashlight beam aimed straight ahead. "No, they weren't a joke," Anton said at last. He stopped and turned to Peter. "You're the only person I've ever shown that to. Listen, are you still pissed off?"

Peter frowned. "Well, what do you think? You scared the crap out of me."

"I'm sorry, Pete. I figured we'd both get a laugh out of it." Anton nudged him, then held out his arms. "C'mon, what do you say? Are we friends again?"

Peter hesitated, then he hugged Anton. "I thought you'd been killed," he said quietly. "Someone is out there killing people. He drowned Johnny. I thought he'd murdered you."

"Jesus, Pete. I'm really sorry," Anton muttered. "I wasn't thinking."

They continued down the trail. Peter walked alongside him. He still couldn't quite let go of his anger—and his fear.

"I was going to wait until I had more information, but maybe I should tell you now," Anton said. "Then you won't be so mad at me anymore."

"Tell me what?" Peter asked, not sure he was really interested.

"I think I have a good lead toward our killer, Pete. I think he must have borrowed that VW bug from someone else when he went after you, because this guy has his own car."

"Who?"

"Let me tell you tomorrow when I'll know more," Anton said. "I've been waiting for an E-mail to confirm something. In the morning, I'll have to do a little fancy footwork, maybe even some breaking and entering. You shouldn't be involved. I don't want to get you in trouble."

"Can't you give me a hint who it is?" Peter asked.

"I'll tell you tomorrow. Meet me up on the roof of St. Clement's around noon. You remember, I showed you how to get up there."

Peter gave him a skeptical look. "If you really have a suspect in mind, you should at least give me one tiny little hint about him."

"All right," Anton said soberly. "Take it as advice, too. He can get at you very easily, Pete. Don't wander around alone unless it's to come see me. While you're in your room, keep the door bolted. If you need to use the can late at night, make a lot of noise in the hall. Wake people up. Make sure someone else is always around—and knows where you are. You don't want to be caught alone anywhere in that building.''

"I'm doing that already," Peter admitted. But Anton's warning still frightened him.

The two of them continued to walk in silence. They passed by the area some of the guys now called Costello Bay. Peter could see the lights of St. Bartholomew Hall in the distance.

Jack rowed across the lake in one of the faculty dinghies. It was an overcast Sunday morning. The surface of Lake Leroy rippled with the slight breeze. Once docked on the upperclassman side, he'd have about a fifteen-minute walk to the hair salon.

He secured the boat to the pier. He had a few moments, so he leaned against a pole and took out his little green notebook. He flipped through a few pages, then stopped and stared at something he'd scribbled down while in the library this week:

ST. BART'S HALL????

JULIAN (freshman)—3 fingers missing—drown/accident?—April/99
OLIVER (senior)—corpse stolen?—hung himself/murder?—May/99
JOHNNY (freshman)—2 toes missing—drown/murder? manslaughter?—April/2002

He wondered if he could add Jonie Soretto to that list: *three teeth missing—burned in a fire/accident?* Or was he looking for a connection that didn't exist? Three freak accidents and a suicide, is that all they were?

Jack kept staring at those names—and how these young people had died. He heard the dock's floorboards creak and he turned.

"Hello, Jack." It was Father Garcia. He wore his clerical garb and—despite the overcast skies—a pair of designer sunglasses. He took a drag from his cigarette. "I was just about to paddle over and pay you a visit."

Jack quickly shoved the little notebook back into his pants pocket.

Garcia gave him one of his charm-boy smiles. "Looks like you saved me a trip. What makes you a refugee from St. Bart's this morning?"

Jack shrugged. "Just shopping for some supplies."

"I understand you said a prayer over a girl who burned to death in her apartment yesterday. It was on this side of the lake."

"That's right," Jack said.

"Did you just happen to be passing by the scene, or were you acquainted with her?"

Jack hesitated. "I knew her. She'd been seeing John Costello."

"I was afraid it would be something like that."

Garcia let out a long sigh. "Your young friend certainly got around, didn't he? How long have you known about this girl?"

"I found out about her a couple of days after John was killed. She came to me yesterday, very frightened. She wanted to tell me something about Johnny, and asked me to meet her at her apartment. She was already dead when I got there."

Garcia seemed to be glaring at him from behind the sunglasses. "Why didn't you report any of this to me yesterday?"

"Because you would have told me to let it go," Jack answered steadily. "No disrespect, Tom, but every time I uncover an unpleasant truth about this case, you want to bury it. I think someone killed John Costello. This girl knew about it, and she was killed, too." Jack shook his head. "I can't just ignore that. But you're going to tell me to leave it be. In fact, you're going to *order* me to leave it be. Am I right?"

Garcia flicked his cigarette into the lake. "You can count on it, Jack. Think of the big picture here, and the cost of your truth. How would you like to tell the Costello woman that her sweet baby brother was having sex with a group of older seminarians? Are you prepared to shatter her memories of him? That's all she has left of the boy. And would you like to see the reputation of this school go down the toilet? Because that's what's going to happen when it gets out about John Costello's sexual proclivities. And there's his association with you, Jack. Wholesome as it was, there's room for speculation and innuendo. If that isn't bad enough, half this town has you shacked up with his sister at the Lakeside Inn."

"I told you before that nothing happened—"

"I don't care. You're still a public relations nightmare for the school. Now there's this business with the girl. In addition to John Costello's homosexual activities, he was also involved with this woman, who was older than him and a drug user."

"How do you know she took drugs?" Jack asked quietly.

"The police told me. They told me about you praying over the body, too. As for your crazy theory that she was murdered, the police said that the fire appears to have been caused by her—and her alone. And I know about the teeth, Jack. They think she tripped and knocked them loose, then pulled them out herself. She was all doped up at the time. She probably didn't know what she was doing."

Jack frowned. "I don't believe that."

"It doesn't matter what you believe. You didn't see the inside of the apartment, and you didn't examine her corpse. But the police did. And they're calling it an accident. So are we."

Garcia took off his sunglasses and gave him an ominous look. "I told you last time, no more warnings. Leave it be, Jack. That's an order. Leave it be—and go with God."

Even with Father Garcia holding him up, Jack would be early meeting Maggie. He strolled along a narrow road by the lake and stared at the backs of the squat houses along the way.

Jack wondered where they would send him after booting him out of Our Lady of Sorrows. And indeed they would boot him out.

He couldn't abide by Garcia's orders and just *leave it be*. Besides, he didn't trust Garcia. In fact, so far, Tom Garcia was the closest thing he had to a suspect in these murders. If nothing else, his deliberate cover-up of certain facts surrounding these deaths bordered on criminal.

But Father Garcia was right regarding one thing. Jack couldn't keep Maggie forever in the dark about her little brother's varied sexual activities. That was one reason he'd gone along with Garcia's mandate to cease all contact with Maggie. He couldn't keep lying to her. Besides that, he was starting to fall for her. One sad look on that beautiful face of hers, or a hug at Johnny's funeral, and he'd have thrown away his priest's collar. He needed some distance from her.

Yet here he was now, on his way to meet her. As he started up the block, Jack recognized Maggie's car, parked across from the Curl Up and Dye hair salon. She'd arrived early, too.

The car was empty. Jack glanced over at the darkened

beauty-shop window. They hadn't opened yet. But next door, the Coffee Buzz was doing business. He spotted Maggie at a table by the window.

Through the glass, she stared back at him and slowly set down her coffee mug.

Jack gave her a hesitant wave.

She smiled, then waved him inside.

"Guess we're both early," Jack said, stepping up to her table. She wore jeans and a lavender pullover that complemented her red hair and creamy pale skin. The hair was swept back in a ponytail. He'd forgotten how beautiful she was.

Awkwardly, he reached out to shake her hand. "It's good to see you again, Maggie."

She held on to his hand a moment longer than necessary. "You, too, Jack."

He sat down across from her. "You look really nice," he heard himself say. He sounded so lame.

"Well, thanks," she said with a little shrug. "You're here early."

"I figured I might catch them before they open the shop."

"*If* they open the shop today. You never know. They might stay closed, because of Jonie. That thought hit me on the way up here." She sipped her coffee. "Something else occurred to me. Jonie's the third person I know who has died within the last month, all of them from unnatural causes. Maybe losing Johnny so suddenly has me aware of things like that, but it's definitely strange."

"Who else has died besides Johnny and Jonie?"

Maggie shrugged. "I didn't know her very well. Her name was Lucy Ballatore. She was a waitress at this restaurant where I go for takeout. About three weeks ago, they found her near a railroad yard. She'd been murdered, stabbed in the throat. She handled my order at the restaurant the last night she was seen alive. I'll never forget, as I was leaving,

I noticed this guy wearing a clown mask, sitting alone in his car in the parking lot. Sounds kind of funny now, but at the time, it scared the hell out of me. I told the police about him, but they must not have thought it was very important, because they never called me back.''

"You say she was stabbed in the throat?" Jack whispered.

Maggie nodded over her coffee cup. "According to the newspapers. They found her in her bra and panties—with her hands tied behind her back. No sign of sexual assault—"

"She was in her underwear?"

Maggie nodded again. "Why? Is there any significance to that?"

Jack stared down at the tabletop. "He takes their outer clothes and uses them for something," he muttered, almost to himself.

Maggie leaned forward. "What are you talking about?"

"This waitress—Lucy—was she missing any fingers or toes?"

With a dazed look at him, Maggie slowly shook her head. "I have no idea. You mean like how Johnny lost a couple of toes?"

Jack nodded. "I was with Jonie in the ambulance. Three of her teeth were missing. All she had on were her bra and panties. It's the same way with the others. Johnny was in his underpants, two toes missing. That other student who drowned three years ago, Julian Doyle, he was found naked, two fingers missing. There was also a suicide three years ago; a senior named Oliver Theron hanged himself in his underwear. They think his body was stolen from his grave. If there's a pattern here, that's it. He takes their clothes and some actual part of their bodies."

Wincing, Maggie shook her head. "But why?"

"I wish I knew," Jack replied glumly. "Listen, Maggie, could you help me track down the Seattle newspaper that carried the story about this waitress's murder?"

"Of course," Maggie answered. Something outside suddenly seemed to catch her eye. "Jack, look," she said, nodding at the window.

He glanced back over his shoulder. A woman approached the hair salon. She was about twenty-five, Hispanic, and pretty in an exotic way, with her pierced nose and the magenta streak in her black, shoulder-length hair. She had a large piece of cardboard tucked under her arm and a roll of tape in her hand.

When Jack and Maggie emerged from the coffee shop next door, the young woman was already inside Curl Up and Dye. She'd left the door open while she posted the homemade sign in the shop's window:

> *CLOSED TODAY*
> *due to death in our family*
> *we'll miss you, jonie*

Jack poked his head into the salon. "Excuse me?"

"I'm sorry, we're closed," the young woman said with a slightly annoyed look.

"I know," Jack said. "Jonie came to me yesterday. We were supposed to get together. I wonder if you could help me out by answering a couple of questions. . . ."

"Yeah, Jonie was really crazy for him," the young woman said, sipping her cafe mocha out of a tall paper cup. "Johnny was so handsome and sweet. But it was almost like a maternal thing, because he was only eighteen, just a kid really."

Jack and Maggie stood talking to the manager, Tina, at the same spot they'd first spoken with Jonie, outside Curl Up and Dye. The CLOSED TODAY sign was posted in the window.

"I met him once—at the store," Tina went on. "Such a

cutie. It was supposed to be this big secret that he was seeing Jonie. But she let that cat out of the bag early on.'' Leaning against the building, Tina uttered a sad, wistful laugh. ''You know, it's weird, both of them dying within weeks of each other. I still can't believe Jonie's gone.''

''When Jonie came to me yesterday, she was very scared,'' Jack said. ''I think she was keeping some other kind of secret—maybe about Johnny or the way he died. Did she say anything to you about that?''

''No, not about Johnny,'' Tina said. ''To tell you the truth, it's not like they had this great, big, passionate sexual thing going on. She was getting that from another guy.''

''She was seeing someone else?'' Jack asked. ''Are you sure?''

Stirring her café mocha, she nodded. ''Oh, yeah. I remember this one time, Jonie let it slip. We were talking about Johnny being like a typical teenager and all that, and Jonie said it was okay, because she had herself a real man.''

''Do you have any idea who this other man might have been?'' Jack asked. ''Even a guess might help us.''

''Well, it would have to be somebody older,'' Tina replied. ''And he'd have to be a pretty 'take-charge' guy to get Jonie to keep quiet about them. I'm thinking it was a priest.''

''Why do you say that?'' Maggie asked.

''Well, for one, this place is lousy with them. And two, a few months back, Jonie mentioned that she'd met this priest—a real hot number. I remember thinking at the time, *What is she getting herself into?* Talk about a dead end. Falling in love with a priest, it doesn't get more pointless than that.''

Frowning a little, Maggie cleared her throat. ''So—you think she had something going on with a priest at the same time she was seeing Johnny?''

Sipping her café mocha, Tina shrugged. ''Well, who— other than a married guy or a priest—would be so on-her-ass to keep their relationship a secret? I mean, he must have had a lot of power over her."

"Enough power that she was scared of him?" Jack asked.

Tina stirred her coffee drink some more. "Yeah," she said finally. "And whoever he is, I don't think we'll see him at Jonie's funeral."

Tina had several calls to make—including one to Jonie's long-estranged mother in Idaho. Jack and Maggie thanked her for her time. From the front stoop of the hair salon, they watched her duck into her car and drive away.

Maggie finally broke the silence. "You know how I told you about being in the restaurant that night the waitress was last seen alive?"

Jack nodded. "You said she handled your food order."

"I overheard her talking to a coworker." Maggie stared off in the direction in which Tina had driven. "Lucy had a secret boyfriend, too. Her waitress friend was teasing her about it. She said her 'mystery man' was probably this handsome priest who had been in the restaurant a couple of weeks before."

"What did she say to that?" Jack asked.

"Nothing," Maggie replied. "As far as I know, she took that secret to her grave—just like Jonie."

Chapter Eighteen

Maggie was driving Jack to the library. They avoided the main campus roads. She knew how to look up the date of the newspaper story on Lucy Ballatore's murder. It was the same day she'd first met Steve at that run-down beach house in West Seattle. She kept a notebook in her car, logging the automobile mileage for all work-related driving. The entry was at the top of a new page:

Date	Destination/Client Name	Start	Finish	Miles
5/9	*West Seattle/Steve Detterman*	*78,591*	*78,618*	*27*

She hadn't told Jack that she was seeing someone. It just didn't seem relevant. It really wasn't any of his business anyway. Besides, Father Murphy was more concerned about tracking down a *Seattle Times* or *Post-Intelligencer* from May 9th.

Maggie pulled over on a back road near the edge of campus. The library was only four blocks away. Jack said she needn't bother to stick around. He would call her later. For now, they shouldn't be seen together.

"You want to keep our relationship a secret, Father Murphy?" Maggie asked pointedly.

He hesitated before opening the car door. "What?"

"All this secrecy and sneaking around," Maggie said. "Isn't that what this killer-priest does with his victims? If I didn't know better, I'd say you're a perfect suspect, Jack."

He squinted at her. "Maggie, I already explained to you why we can't be seen together—"

"I know," she said. "You made it very clear. Father Garcia laid down the law. Well, you might be required to follow his orders, but not me. Do you still have my cell phone number?"

He continued to eye her warily. "Yes, it's in my wallet."

"I'm sticking around, Jack. Call me when you're done at the library. I'll be close by."

"Fine," he muttered in resignation. Then he climbed out of the car and shut the door.

Maggie watched him head toward the campus. The Our Lady of Sorrows church tower loomed above the other buildings.

She parked her car, stuck the cell phone in her purse, and walked to the college library. Jack had entered through the same door just five minutes before her. She'd told him that she would be close by.

There was a seminarian on duty at the front desk. Maggie asked where they kept the old college yearbooks. He led her to a bookcase in the Grand Room. Grabbing the four most recent volumes, Maggie thanked him, then she sat down at one of the long study tables.

The head of administration, Father Tom Garcia, was listed in the index of last year's yearbook, but not in any of the others before that. He wasn't at Our Lady of Sorrows three years ago when that one boy had hanged himself and the other one had drowned.

Maggie had met Garcia a month ago, just after Johnny's death. He'd certainly fit their killer-priest's profile: full of charisma and a somewhat manipulative charm. Most suspicious of all was his determination to suppress any further inquiries into Johnny's drowning. Besides, Garcia was the one who had forbidden Jack to see her, and that was another reason not to like him.

Maggie was almost disappointed that the yearbook listings exonerated him. Maybe he wasn't a murderer, but Garcia had initiated a cover-up just the same. Why? What was he afraid they'd find?

As Maggie returned the yearbooks to the shelf, she caught a glimpse of Jack across the room. He was sifting through a stack of newspapers in a bookcase. He pulled two editions of the *Seattle Times* off the shelf, then carried them toward an arch-shaped alcove. He ducked inside the little nook, out of sight.

Maggie wandered past several study tables until she could see him again. He sat alone with his newspapers at a small desk. Bent forward, he read intently. Behind him, a saint depicted in the stained-glass window seemed to be peering over his shoulder. With a sword lifted toward the heavens, the saint wore a coat of armor and a bright yellow halo.

Jack glanced up from the newspaper. He locked eyes with Maggie and gave her a sour frown.

Maggie stepped into his semiprivate study area. "Relax," she whispered. "No one has seen us together. I'm keeping an eye out. I just came in to look up Father Garcia in some old yearbooks. I figured if anyone's a likely suspect, it's him. But he wasn't at Our Lady of Sorrows three years ago when those other boys died."

"He was in the archdiocese," Jack whispered. "He could have taken a few day trips up here. I wish there were a way of looking that up, but he's a tough one to investigate. He must have ears and eyes all over this place. He seems to know my every move.''

''So, Garcia could have come up here before he started on last year?''

Jack nodded. ''Officially or unofficially. He's in with the bishop. He probably asked to be sent here. If that's true, he'd have scouted the place out first.'' Jack shook his head. ''No, we shouldn't eliminate good old Tom as a suspect just yet.''

She nodded at the newspapers. ''Have you found anything helpful in there? Anything at all?''

Leaning back in his chair, Jack sighed and shook his head. ''Not much beyond what you already told me. The one detail that keeps gnawing at me is the way this woman died. She was stabbed in the throat. The newspapers didn't say her throat had been slashed or cut. They said 'stabbed.' It's a little unusual.''

''No kidding,'' Maggie said, sitting on the edge of the desk.

''In Roman times—two or three hundred years A.D.— that was a common form of execution: a sword-thrust in the throat.''

''Sweet,'' Maggie muttered.

''A lot of the saints were martyred that way,'' Jack added.

Maggie sighed. She glanced up at the stained-glass window. ''Speaking of saints, who is that?''

Jack peeked back over his shoulder. ''Joan of Arc. Don't you recognize her in the armor?''

''With the short hair, I thought it was a man. Now, if they'd shown her being burned at the stake, I'd have figured out who she was.''

Jack stared at the window for another moment, then he slowly turned toward her. ''Jonie was burned,'' he whispered.

"What?"

"Jonie Sorretto was burned—like Joan of Arc." The chair made a scraping noise against the tiled floor as Jack got to his feet. "My God, I think I know what's happening. They're all martyrs."

"I don't understand," Maggie murmured.

"Wait here. I'll be right back."

Baffled, Maggie watched Jack hurry toward the front desk. He spoke briefly with the seminarian on duty, who pointed him toward a room on his right. Jack took off in that direction, disappearing around the corner.

At that same moment, Father Garcia strolled into the library. Wide-eyed, Maggie held her breath and watched him. Garcia nodded at the seminarian behind the front desk, then he started into the Grand Room.

Maggie stepped back farther into the niche, hiding in the shadows of the alcove. After a few seconds, she craned her neck and saw Father Garcia heading down the center of the room—between the two rows of long study tables. He glanced in her direction.

Maggie braced herself against the wall. She told herself that Garcia had no authority over her. She shouldn't be hiding from him. Yet she didn't want to ruin things for Jack. The two of them couldn't be seen together.

She spied on Garcia as he walked up to a younger priest, who was immersed in a textbook at one of the tables. The younger man stood and shook Garcia's hand. They talked quietly. Maggie couldn't hear what they were saying.

Out of the corner of her eye, she spotted Jack returning to the Grand Room. At a brisk clip, he headed toward the alcove, waving a book at her. Maggie gave her head a little shake, then ducked deeper into the alcove.

Jack stopped abruptly. All at once, he seemed to notice that Garcia was there, only a few table rows away. He quickly sat down at one of the desks and opened the book.

By now, Garcia was watching him. Jack hunched over the study table, his nose in the reading material.

Maggie stayed pressed against the alcove wall.

Garcia and his friend strolled toward Jack, who looked up from his book very nonchalantly. He gave Garcia a reserved smile, and the head of administration acknowledged him with a nod. Then Garcia and his friend kept walking toward the library exit.

Jack waited another minute. He glanced back over his shoulder, then looked toward her. Maggie emerged from the shadows. Jack gave her one of those smiles that comes after a close call. He got to his feet and brought the book with him to their secluded alcove. He set it down on the table in front of her. The smile had left his face.

The book was titled *The Lives and Deaths of the Saints.* Jack opened it and started flipping through the pages. "They're all in here," he said. "Let me find you the section about St. Lucy. . . ."

After a moment, Jack handed her the book, opened to a particular page. Maggie stared at a detailed etching with the caption: *The death of St. Lucy (c.304), virgin martyr.* The stilted, old-fashioned graphic was of a young woman on her knees, in prayer. A Roman soldier stood above her, his sword poised at the base of her throat.

"Remember the other boy who drowned?" Jack said. "His name was Julian Doyle. Turn to the synopsis on St. Julian of Antioch."

Maggie flipped back a couple of pages until she found it:

JULIAN OF ANTIOCH (feast day: March 16) The dates for this Christian martyr from Cilicia are unknown. What is known, however, is that after enduring many sufferings from his persecutors, Julian was tied in a sack and drowned in the sea. . . .

A chill passed through Maggie. She stared at the page and shook her head.

"St. Oliver," she heard Jack say.

Automatically, she turned several pages until she found the listing:

OLIVER PLUNKET (feast day: July 1) b. 1625; d. in London 1681. Archbishop of Armagh and primate of all Ireland, Oliver Plunket was arrested under false charges of subversion in 1678. Convicted and sentenced to death, St. Oliver was hanged, then his body was disemboweled and quartered. . . .

"Can you see what's happening?" Jack whispered.

Dumbfounded, Maggie just nodded.

"After he supposedly hanged himself from his parents' roof, Oliver Theron was buried in the family plot. But someone stole the body two days later."

"To disembowel and quarter it?" Maggie murmured.

"Maybe," Jack said.

She set the book down on the table. Her hand trembled as she pushed it away. She didn't want to read any more. "And Johnny?"

Jack picked up the book again. Maggie sat down at the desk. She could hear him in back of her, turning the pages. "There are several St. Johns listed. Here's the one. *'St. John of Nepomuk,'*" Jack read soberly. "*'Feast day, June twelve. Born 1345, died—'*"

"Please, don't read it to me," she cut in. "Just tell me."

"He was a priest from Prague. He fell out of favor with the king. So he was thrown—bound and gagged—into the River Vltava."

"Where he drowned," Maggie said, closing her eyes.

Jack set the book back down on the desk. "I'm sorry," he whispered.

Her eyes brimmed with tears. "Can we get out of here, please?" she murmured.

"I don't think you'll get very tan," Peter said. "Looks like it's going to rain." He gazed up at the gray clouds drifting across the sky. The wind had a kick to it this morning, especially six stories high on the roof of St. Clement Hall.

"You can really burn when it's overcast," Anton said. He was lying faceup on his beach towel. He wore sunglasses and his black Speedos. He'd come prepared—with a backpack, boom box and Evian water. He pulled a bottle of suntan lotion from the backpack, then tossed it at Peter. "Take off your shirt and put some of this on," he said. "When I turn over in a few minutes, could you do my back?"

"Sure, yeah, no sweat," Peter said nervously. He was admiring Anton's powerful physique. The hair on his muscular arms and chest was matted down with the suntan oil. Peter felt so white and skinny as he removed his shirt. He kicked off his sneakers and set them on top of the shirt so it wouldn't blow away.

"Anybody see you coming up here?" Anton asked.

"No, the dorm is dead," Peter answered, sitting next to Anton's blanket. "It's the same way over at St. Bart's. I think most everyone went home for Memorial Day weekend."

"So, are you still sore at me about last night? That prank in the forest?"

Peter forced a smile. "Naw, it's okay," he said. He really couldn't stay mad at him. Anton was the only friend he had.

"Last night, you said you couldn't trust me anymore."

"Did I?" Peter asked. "I don't remember. I was pretty pissed off. But I'm okay now. So, who's this suspect you were telling me about?"

"Well, I'm not sure we should even discuss it," Anton

said. "Are you going to believe me? I mean, if you don't trust me—"

Peter let out an awkward laugh. "No, I—I trust you, Anton."

He sat up. "Prove it."

"How? You want me to open a vein and write it in blood?"

"No, I want you to take a trust test." Anton removed his sunglasses. "Stand up."

Peter grimaced. "Geez, Anton, can't you just tell me about this guy? Do I really have to go through some stupid test?"

Anton got to his feet. With the sky behind him, he stared down at Peter and shook his head. "I was right. You've lost your faith in me. Y'know, Pete, friendship is about trust. If that's gone, you might as well pull the plug—"

"Okay, okay," Peter interrupted, springing to his feet. "I'm standing up. What do you want me to do?"

Anton grabbed his hand and led him farther away from the ledge—toward the center of the roof. "Close your eyes," he said.

"I don't like this already," Peter muttered. He pretended to shut his eyes, but he was merely squinting. He could see Anton—slightly out of focus—through narrow slits and past his own eyelashes. "Okay, they're closed. How come I have the feeling I'm going to end up pizza on the pavement six stories below here?"

"Because you don't fucking trust me, that's why," Anton grumbled. "Do you want to quit? Is that it?"

Peter sighed. "I'm just not in the mood for a big scare right now, y'know? Maybe you'll get a kick out of it, but I won't."

"If you'd really put your trust in me, you shouldn't be scared." Anton started to twirl Peter around in a circle. "Now, keep your eyes closed and keep spinning."

Peter went along with it, yet he felt sick to his stomach with dread. He had a hard time seeing anything with his eyes half-shut. It was all just a blur. "Hey, go easy, okay?" he said. "Want me to barf?"

Suddenly, Anton stopped and came up behind him. Peter flinched as Anton's hand covered his eyes. Now, he truly couldn't see. He felt Anton's hairy chest—slick with suntan lotion—rubbing against his back. Anton's other hand came around and held his stomach. He began walking in circles, and Peter had to follow along. It felt like some sort of strange, deadly dance.

Peter squirmed a bit. He was dizzy with vertigo. The wind pelted him, while Anton's warm, oiled body still pressed against his back. He knew Anton was leading him toward the roof's ledge.

"You trust me?" Anton whispered in his ear.

"Yes, I trust you," he whispered, trembling. There was something about it that felt exciting, dangerous and sexual. But he wanted Anton to stop.

"I've got you, Pete," he heard him say. Blindly, he followed along a few more steps. "You're shaking. You shouldn't be scared. Keep the old peepers shut."

Anton took his hand away. Peter could sense the light against his closed eyelids. He felt the breeze on his face. Anton slowly pushed at him from behind until he was bent forward.

"Okay, Pete. I'm not going to let you fall. You can look now."

He swallowed hard, then opened his eyes. He was staring down at Anton's towel.

Laughing, Anton gave him a little push, and Peter fell down on the towel. A moment later, Anton was on top of him, tickling him. "I bet you thought I'd take you to the ledge." He chuckled. "I wouldn't do that to you. . . ."

Giddy with relief, Peter writhed beneath him. His head

was spinning. Anton pinned his hands down and leaned over him. He suddenly stopped laughing and became very still. His face hovered directly over Peter's. They were both breathing hard. "Guess what?" he whispered.

"What?" Peter asked.

The handsome senior rolled off him. "You were right earlier," he said. "It's beginning to rain. I just felt a couple of drops on my back. We can't stay up here much longer or we'll get soaked."

Anton suddenly looked very serious as he reached for his backpack. "We better get down to business," he said. "I've had a tense morning. It was good, blowing off a little steam just now."

Still catching his breath, Peter sat up and wrapped his arms around his legs. "So . . . um, what's going on?"

"It hit me a few days ago," Anton explained. "I was thinking back to when we couldn't get any of the padres at St. Bart's to take our bait. Not one of them really fit all the criteria on that list you made. Besides, none of them owns a car. All they have are those two old station wagons they share. So, where did the blue VW come from?"

"You said last night that whoever attacked me must have borrowed the car from someone."

"Right." Anton nodded. "I remembered something during my freshman year. This bimbo from the town used to come around once in a while. She drove a pale blue Volkswagen beetle. She used to park it and wait in the employee lot."

"Who was she waiting for?"

"For her on-again-off-again boyfriend," Anton said, reaching into his backpack. He glanced up at the rain clouds for a second, then pulled out a document and handed it to Peter. "Recognize him? He's been living in St. Bartholomew Hall for six years now."

Peter stared at the slightly blurred mug shots on an arrest

record for twenty-three-year-old Duane Ryker. St. Bart's resident custodian appeared much younger in the police photos, taken twelve years ago, when he'd been arrested for armed robbery. "Where did you get this?" Peter asked.

"A friend of mine from the King County Hall of Records owed me a favor. An E-mail with this attachment was waiting for me when I got back from the woods last night." Anton nodded toward the paper in Peter's hand. "I printed that up. Besides a five-year stint at Clark Penitentiary for armed robbery, good old Duane also served time for passing a bad check. And he was arrested for statutory rape, assault, and indecent exposure, but none of the charges stuck. He has two strikes against him. I often wondered why someone who seemed so slick with the chicks and so full of smarts would let himself get stuck in this nowhere janitor job—at a seminary no less, here in Boring Town, Dullsville, U.S.A. Now it makes sense."

Peter studied the document. "With a record like this, why would they have hired him on here?"

"Some do-gooder in administration probably thought he deserved another chance. What I'm wondering is how well Johnny knew him. Did he ever talk about Duane with you?"

Peter shook his head. "We never discussed him, at least not in any significant way. He knew Duane pretty much the same way I do."

"I was thinking last night—Johnny could have seen Duane doing something that would have given him three strikes. You said Johnny used to sneak out at night. Unless Duane has changed his ways, he always has one late-night date after another. Johnny could have witnessed something."

"Like what?" Peter asked.

"Well, I figured, with Duane's history of assault and rape, Johnny could have seen him attack one of his girlfriends— or worse. Another possibility I considered has to do with Duane's five years in prison. He's probably been with guys.

Maybe he's a switch-hitter. He could have gone after Johnny, or maybe even had a secret thing with him." Anton sighed. "But that's all theory, speculation. Until this morning, I couldn't really connect Johnny with Duane. I had no evidence."

"What happened this morning?"

"I broke into Duane's room."

"My God," Peter murmured.

"I remembered Duane always used to go to the Ham and Egger for Sunday breakfast. So this morning, I waited around and watched him walk down Whopper Way. I picked the lock to his room and went through the place inch by inch. The bad news is I didn't find a damn thing connecting him to Johnny."

Peter frowned. He felt raindrops hitting his shoulders and back.

"What I discovered," Anton continued, "connects him with you, Pete. How tall was that guy who attacked you?"

"Around six feet."

"Look at the height in that description of our janitor friend."

"Five-eleven," Peter read out loud.

"Duane's right-handed, too. I was watching him this morning. He fits the physical description. That's strike one." Anton reached into his backpack and pulled out something wrapped in tin foil. "I got this from the ashtray on his desk."

He carefully peeled back the foil. Peter stared at the used book of matches from the Lakeside Inn Grill. He picked up one of the three cigarette butts and read the brand name printed by the filter: *Marlboro*.

"That's strike two," Anton said. He dug deeper into the backpack. "And here's strike three, Pete. I found it in his closet. Look familiar?"

Anton showed him a black ski mask.

"Jesus," Peter whispered.

Anton squinted up at the rain, then he started loading the evidence back into his bag. "You mentioned the guy had a knife," he said. "Duane had some knives, but I wasn't sure what to look for. Was it a switchblade?"

"I think that's what it was," Peter said, reaching for his shirt.

"Well, I didn't see one in his place. So I decided to try that ugly van of his, the one always parked in the employee lot. I figured maybe I'd even find Johnny's missing clothes or something. But I can't identify Johnny's clothes. I barely knew him."

"Well, I could do that," Peter said.

"Really? I didn't even have a chance to try. I'd just gotten the van's side door unlocked when I saw Duane coming back from breakfast. So I got the hell out of there. I've been sitting here, trying to figure out if I should go back or not. I think the van is still unlocked."

"I could search through it," Peter whispered eagerly.

Getting to his feet, Anton stepped into his cutoffs. "Not a good idea," he said. "Too dangerous. Duane's sure to know something's up. I tried to cover my tracks when I went through his room, but he might have figured out someone was in there. It's only a matter of time before he discovers his ski mask is missing. He'll be on his guard today."

"Then we'll create a diversion," Peter suggested. "Duane has a phone in his room, doesn't he?"

Anton stopped dressing. "Yeah."

"You can make an anonymous call to him, saying that you have the jacket. Tell him if he wants it back, he'll have to come meet you on the other side of the lake. Tell him to walk over, otherwise no deal. While he's gone, I'll go through the van."

"Pete, it's dangerous. You make the phone call. I'll search the van."

"You just said you couldn't identify Johnny's clothes. I'm the only one who could do that. It has to be me."

The rain started to come down heavier. "Okay," Anton said, nodding. His shirt fluttered in the wind as he put it on. "We have to move fast. C'mon, shake a leg before we get completely soaked."

It started raining as they walked back to Maggie's car. "We shouldn't stay here," she said in a shaky voice. "Garcia might still be around. Could you drive, Jack? It doesn't matter where, anyplace we don't have to worry about someone seeing us."

Jack got behind the wheel and drove just outside town. He pulled into a dead-end road he'd discovered during one of his runs. It was on a bluff overlooking the lake. The rain had become heavier during their brief drive. They didn't say anything to each other. Most of the time, Maggie just leaned toward the window, her face turned away from him.

He parked the car, then switched off the wipers. Directly ahead of them was a low guardrail, and beyond that, the lake. Rain pattered its silver-green surface. Jack listened to the tapping on the car roof. He could also hear Maggie, sobbing quietly.

He reached over and put his arm around her. Maggie let out a grateful little cry, then buried her face in his shoulder. He gently stroked her hair—and even dared to kiss her forehead.

After a while, Maggie pulled back, then she dug a Kleenex from her purse. "Sorry about the tears," she said, wiping her eyes and nose. "It's like finding out all over again that he's dead. I just can't accept it."

Her red-rimmed eyes wrestled with his. "Jack, I know I haven't gotten the whole story about Johnny. If you're holding back on something, you might as well tell me. Dump it on me now, one big load.''

''What do you want to know?'' he asked.

''I keep thinking about that money Johnny had hidden away. Did you ever find out about that?''

He nodded. ''Yes. I know how he got the money.''

''Does it have anything to do with Father Garcia's cover-up?'' Maggie pressed. ''Did Johnny do something—pretty bad?''

Jack glanced out the rain-beaded windshield at the lake. ''John was a good-looking young man, and a very sweet kid, but I don't have to tell you that.'' He sighed. ''John's good looks weren't lost on some of the guys at Our Lady of Sorrows. A few of them even offered to pay him for sex, and John went along with it. That's how he got the money.''

Maggie squirmed, then took a deep breath. ''So these people who . . . um, paid my brother for sex,'' she said, an edginess in her voice. ''Were they priests?''

''No,'' Jack said. ''They were sophomores at the college, three very closeted seminarians. I think they were paying Johnny for his secrecy as much as they were paying to be with him. And he kept their secret. I didn't find out about it until a few weeks ago.''

Maggie rolled down her window. The cool, wet spring air wafted into the car. She wouldn't look at Jack. She rested one elbow on the car door and rubbed her forehead. ''You and Johnny were supposed to be close. You had no idea any of this was going on?''

''Not a clue,'' Jack answered. ''I'm sorry.''

''It wasn't your fault.''

''Yes, it was. Johnny was my responsibility.''

''Well, I'm not holding you accountable.'' Maggie stared out the window. ''Maybe if I'd been a better provider, Johnny wouldn't have had to resort to such measures for money.''

"Now who's trying to take the blame?" Jack said quietly. "I've struggled with it, too. It all boils down to this: Johnny probably did what he did out of some sort of need—money, affection, or validation, or whatever. I don't think he meant to hurt anybody. My feelings for Johnny haven't changed. I still love him like he was my own son."

Maggie continued to stare out the window. She wiped her eyes, then bit down on her fist. "Listen, do you think any of these seminarians were involved in his death?"

"No, I looked into that already," Jack answered. "Whoever killed John, his territory goes beyond this seminary. Lucy is the key to proving that. It sounds gruesome, but we need to see if her death was like the others—down to the last detail. There must be some way we can find out if any of her teeth were gone, or if she was missing any fingers or toes."

Maggie grimaced. "Well, I know someone who could look into that for us," she said. "He's a journalist. He used to work the police beat in Juno, Alaska. His name's Steve. We've gone out a couple of times. I know he likes me. He might have some connections with the Seattle police. I'm sure he'll do whatever he can for me."

Jack nodded soberly. He was surprised that she'd started seeing someone. Then again, why shouldn't she? He had no claim on her. He had no right to question what she did with her love life.

Maggie was quiet for a moment. "The rain didn't last long," she remarked finally. "I should stretch my legs before the drive back."

She opened her door and climbed out of the car.

Jack stayed behind the wheel. He watched her through the rain-beaded windshield. Maggie's back was to him as she looked out at the lake.

After a couple of minutes, he stepped out of the car and came up beside her. "Are you going to be okay?" he asked.

"Jack, how do you feel about me seeing this guy?" she asked, her eyes searching his. "He's interested in me, and very good-looking. And he's young—almost too young. Does me telling you this affect you in any way?"

"Maggie, I don't know how to answer that."

She turned and gazed out at the lake again. The wind whipped at her red hair. "I care about you, Jack," she said. "I guess that's no secret. I've humiliated myself with you a couple of times now. I know you have feelings for me, too. Tell me I'm wrong."

"You're not wrong, Maggie," he admitted. "But I'm a priest. It's way out of line for me to say how I feel about you."

She gave a sad little laugh. "If you want my opinion, you're not a very good priest. You're not exactly sticking to that vow of obedience. And I don't think you're cut out for the celibacy bit either." Maggie shyly took hold of his arm. "I'll bet you were much better at being a husband and father."

"Not me," he muttered. "A good husband and father doesn't let his family get killed."

"Johnny told me they died in an automobile accident. It's a tragedy, but it isn't your fault—"

"Let's not talk about this anymore," Jack cut in. He handed her the keys, then walked back to the car. "Would you mind dropping me near the library? I want to check out that book on the saints."

With Maggie at the wheel, they rode in silence toward the edge of campus. The sun was peeking through the clouds, making the wet pavement shiny. Maggie took her eyes off the road every now and then to glance at Jack, who seemed deep in thought.

"I'm sorry, Jack," she said finally. "I know what you

went through is much worse than my experience, and it doesn't compare to the time I spent with a stupid husband who treated me like crap.''

Jack smiled sadly. ''The one who'll get a cactus plant on his birthday?''

''I told you about that, huh?''

He nodded. ''That night at the Lakeside Inn.''

''I meant it. Once I'm with someone else, I'll send Ray a cactus plant for his birthday. It'll be an acknowledgment of my moving on and letting go of all the pain. Can't you do that, too?''

''I don't understand,'' Jack said.

''Can't you move on?'' she asked. ''I know it's none of my business, and not the same as my situation. But I don't understand why you're blaming yourself for what happened to your wife and son three years ago. Why can't you let it go? A drunk driver ran into your car.''

''He didn't run into my car. He smashed into my *wife's* car.''

''Your car, your wife's car, what's the difference?''

''The difference is I was in my own car, driving ahead of my wife and my son. We were returning home from a party. We'd come in separate cars. This oncoming car veered into my lane, and I swerved over to avoid him. As soon as I did, I realized what I'd done.''

''Oh, Jesus,'' Maggie whispered.

Jack stared straight ahead. He sighed. ''You know, there was a moment before I heard the crash—I thought they were all right. And I wondered how I could have forgotten—even for just a second—that they were behind me.

''People who heard about the accident, they just assumed I was in the car with them. The ones who knew we'd taken two cars that night, they figured I was riding behind. After all, what good husband and father would let that happen to his family?''

Maggie pulled the car over to the curb, then shifted into park. She grabbed hold of his hand. "God, Jack, it wasn't your fault. Why would you choose to take on all that guilt? Isn't it bad enough that they're dead and you miss them? Why do you want to punish yourself?"

"Because I screwed up," he muttered. "You know, with your brother—our friendship, and the way he was like a son to me—I felt as if God were giving me a second chance. Johnny was my opportunity to make things right. But I screwed up on that, too."

Maggie started crying. "No, you didn't," she said, hugging him. "Stop blaming yourself. Johnny loved your friendship. . . ."

She began to kiss his face, but Jack pulled away.

"I—I better go," he said, wiping his eyes. He opened the car door.

She reached across and grabbed his arm.

"Maggie, I'm sorry—"

"Listen to me, Jack," she said steadily. "You can't just retreat from life and join the priesthood because you had a real bad break. You can't keep blaming yourself either—or you'll be no good to anyone. A minute ago, you said Johnny was your second chance. Well, did you ever stop to think that maybe *I'm* your second chance?"

With a tortured look, he shook his head. "Then that's a lousy deal for you, Maggie."

He turned and walked away.

As he stepped into the library, Jack felt derailed somehow. Maggie was forcing him to look at himself, and he didn't want to do that—not now. They needed to find Johnny's killer. There was no time to think about anything else, except stopping this self-proclaimed executioner before he "martyred" another person.

Jack found the book on the saints where they'd left it: on the study desk in the alcove. Joan of Arc stood guard over it.

He started back toward the check-out desk. He noticed a section of the newspaper that had fallen from one of the study tables onto the floor. Jack picked it up and set it back on the table, then he started to move on.

He'd seen the headline, but it didn't register for a moment. He had to turn back and glance at the newspaper again. The story was on the front page of the regional news section, not so much newsworthy as it was a sad acknowledgment. The headline ran across the bottom of the page: POLICE CONFIRM DISCOVERY OF JUDGE MCSHANE'S REMAINS.

They'd found Dorothy McShane's headless body four miles downstream from where her skull had been discovered.

Jack sank down in the desk chair. He stared at the cover of his book on the saints. Finally, he opened it and paged through to the Ds.

DOROTHY (feast day: February 6) c.303. A maiden of Caesarea in Cappadacia, she was arrested for being a Christian, and sentenced to death. St. Dorothy was beheaded, and her relics were stored in a church in Rome . . .

Chapter Nineteen

"I know most of the officers you work with are prison guards," Jack said over the phone to Father McKenna at the Clark Federal Penitentiary. "But you're the only person I know who might have some connection to local law enforcement."

"What can I do for you, Jack?" Bernie McKenna asked.

"I need to find out where they're holding the remains of Judge Dorothy McShane."

Jack arrived at the Enright Funeral Home dressed in his clerical clothes and carrying a little black bag.

It had taken Bernie McKenna only twenty minutes to get back to him with the location of Judge McShane's corpse. They had performed the autopsy at the funeral home the previous night, and as far as Bernie knew, the body was still there.

Jack had secured one of the faculty cars for the afternoon.

The drive took about an hour. He had to watch his time. He was scheduled to say 5:30 Mass at St. Gabriel Chapel. If he didn't show up, it would certainly get back to Father Garcia.

Enright Funeral Home was at the edge of downtown Burlington. A redbrick building with white shutters, it looked like an old-money estate. The parking lot beside it was nearly empty. Jack had expected reporters and police. He wondered if Bernie had sent him to the wrong place. Or perhaps they'd already moved the body.

Jack stepped into the vestibule, but found the inner door locked. A brass plate beneath the doorbell read, RING FOR ASSISTANCE. Jack pressed the doorbell and waited.

The inner door had a window, allowing him a peek into the funeral home's lobby: very elegant, with dark paneling, a fireplace, a couple of richly upholstered sofas, mahogany tables, and two large, potted palms.

After a minute, a man came into view, buttoning his navy blue blazer. He was about thirty, with glasses and neatly trimmed brown hair. He gave Jack a courteous smile before opening the door. "Good afternoon. Can I help you?" he asked.

"I'm Father Murphy from Our Lady of Sorrows," Jack said. "I'm here at the request of the McShane family. They asked me to bless Judge McShane's remains."

The man's pleasant smile seemed to freeze. "Bless her remains? That's a bit unusual."

"Well, this is an unusual case," Jack said. "The judge's body is still here, isn't it?"

"Yes, it's here," he replied. He opened the door wider. "Please, come in. Um, I didn't see anything listed on the docket today for a visit. Did you make an appointment, Father?"

Stepping inside, Jack set down his black bag and pulled out a prayer stole. He kissed it, then set it over his shoulders.

The little ritual wasn't lost on the gentleman. "The archbishop's office arranged it for me yesterday," Jack said, at last. "They usually don't make mistakes."

"Well, it was pretty hectic here last night—what with the police and reporters. I'll try to straighten this out, Father—"

"Murphy, Jack Murphy," he said.

"I'm Gregory Fleischel, the assistant manager here, Father." He shook Jack's hand. "May I ask for some identification, please? It's police procedure in cases like this one."

"Certainly," Jack said, giving him his driver's license.

"Please, have a seat," he said, motioning toward one of the sofas. "I'll be right back." He retreated with Jack's license to a side door.

Jack sat on the sofa and nervously tapped his foot. He didn't think he could pull this off. It was such a crazy long shot. He wondered if perhaps Gregory Fleischel was right now phoning the archbishop's office. Perhaps he had the county sheriff on the line, or maybe even the McShanes' attorney. Somehow, this was bound to get back to the school and Father Garcia. Still, he had to take a chance.

Three or four minutes passed. Jack heard a police siren in the distance. It seemed to be coming closer. He got to his feet and moved to the window.

"Father Murphy?"

He turned and saw Gregory emerging from the side door. He had a clipboard tucked under his arm. The siren got louder. "This mother's a felony raid," he heard the assistant manager say over the deafening noise.

"What?" Jack murmured. The siren was right in front of the building. Jack glanced back out the window in time to see the squad car speed past them down the block.

"I said, 'There's another formality, I'm afraid,' " Gregory repeated loudly, still competing with the siren's wail. He gave Jack his license, then showed him a form on the clipboard and handed him a pen. "I'll need you to sign in for the visit, Father."

Managing to smile, Jack took the pen and clipboard from him. "Thanks very much."

Gregory led him to a back hallway and a door that had an EMPLOYEES ONLY placard on it. He unlocked the door, and Jack followed him down a short corridor to a dark, cinderblock stairway. "Did you have to call anyone?" Jack asked, his voice echoing as they started down the stairwell.

"I just needed confirmation," Gregory said. "Sorry for the delay, Father." He reached for his keys again and took Jack down another hallway to a door with COUNTY MEDICAL EXAMINER stenciled across it.

Gregory opened the door and switched on the overhead, which was almost too bright. The polished metal cabinets, equipment, and tables sparkled under the harsh light. The compact, windowless room had a green tiled floor and anatomy posters on the walls. It smelled of disinfectant, but there was also an underlying odor that reminded Jack of rotten food.

"I should warn you, Father," Gregory said. "The corpse is badly deteriorated." He fiddled with his keys once again and unlocked a large metal door. "If you wait here, I'll bring the deceased out to you."

Jack set his black bag on the long metal cabinet—beside a butcher's meat cutter. He opened up the bag, then took out a prayer book and a vial of holy water.

With that big, metal door open, the fetid smell wafted from the cold storage locker. Jack could hear what sounded like squeaky wheels on a shopping cart. He turned and saw Gregory pushing a metal table on wheels. The plastic body bag on top of the gurney was opaque with a zipper down the front. Jack could make out the shape of an emaciated human being. They'd rested her skull where it belonged— above her withered frame. The coloring was a murky gray with dark maroon lines—stitches from the autopsy, he gathered. Jack could see the spindly legs and arms. But he couldn't see her fingers and toes.

It became hard to breathe without gagging, and Gregory hadn't even unzipped the bag yet. Perhaps he didn't expect to, because he stepped away from the portable table.

Jack steadily gazed at the funeral home's assistant manager. "I'll need to anoint her hands and feet," he said.

"You made it home okay. I'm glad."

"Yes, Jack, I'm fine," Maggie replied coolly.

He stood in a phone booth by a Texaco station in downtown Burlington. "Listen, Maggie," he said into the phone. "I'm sorry about earlier."

"You're always sorry," she replied. "I think if you apologize to me one more time, I'll scream."

"All right, I won't," he said. "Have you talked with your reporter friend yet?"

"I've left him a couple of messages, but he hasn't called back."

"Well, this thing is definitely beyond the seminary. I just came from a funeral home here in Burlington. We can add Judge Dorothy McShane to the list of 'martyrs.' St. Dorothy was beheaded—just like the missing judge. I had a look at her remains. He got greedy with the souvenirs this time. Three fingers and four toes were missing. The man at the funeral home said, in all likelihood, the digits had been gnawed off by coyotes or some other wild animals. It's possible, I guess."

"You and I know better," Maggie said.

Jack sighed. "There has to be a reason he's taking their fingers, toes, and teeth."

"He takes their clothes, too, you said."

"Maybe he uses them in some sort of ritual."

"If Lucy's like the others," Maggie said. "If she's missing a finger or toe, how many 'martyrs' does that make so far?"

"Six that we know of, including Johnny. Listen, do you have any friends you can stay with tonight? I'd feel better if I knew you weren't alone."

"I'll have Steve spend the night," Maggie replied.

Jack rubbed his forehead. He didn't say anything into the phone.

"It's not what you think," she explained. "I've had him spend the night before. He'll sleep in Johnny's room."

"Are you sure—"

"He's okay. In fact, I think he just beeped in. I'll be fine, Jack. Call you later."

He heard a click on the other end of the line.

"Hey, sweetheart, how are you?"

"I'm okay," Maggie said. But she wasn't quite comfortable with Steve calling her "sweetheart" this soon in the game. "Did you get my messages?"

"No, I haven't been home all day. What's going on?"

"I need to ask you a big favor," Maggie said.

"Shoot, babe."

"I know you worked the police beat in Juno. Do you have any connection with the police around here?"

"I know a couple of guys," Steve replied. "Why?"

"Remember I told you about that waitress who was murdered?"

"Yeah, sure, Lucy Something."

"Lucy Ballatore. Could you use your police connections to find out about the condition of her corpse when they found it? I think she might have been missing some fingers or toes or teeth. I want you to check for me."

"Jesus, honey, what for?" he murmured.

"For my peace of mind," Maggie said. "And for my brother."

Peter hid down near the lake, behind the faculty's two-car garage. He watched the side door of St. Bartholomew Hall. The rain had let up. Just an occasional big drop from the garage roof gutter splashed him. But Peter didn't move, nor did he take his eyes off that side door.

Between the garage and St. Bart's was the employee lot. Among the few cars parked there today, Duane's black minivan was hard to ignore. Peter had heard that several priests at St. Bart's considered the vehicle an eyesore.

The minivan's side had a rendering of a Viking goddess in a loincloth bikini. She stood on a mountaintop, brandishing a sword. The dozen bumper stickers on the back ranged from HONK IF YOU'RE HORNY, to PARTY NAKED. The vanity plate on the car was 1HUNK4U.

Until this afternoon, Peter had always considered Duane the lounge lizard type, a slick, sexy loser. As Anton had pointed out, now it made sense why Duane had remained on at St. Bartholomew Hall. He really was a loser—what they called a two-time loser. With his criminal past, he'd probably have difficulty finding work, room, and board anywhere else. Peter had heard stories about Duane. Screwing one woman after another, he couldn't have much conscience or sentiment. But was he really a killer?

Peter glanced at his wristwatch. Anton had probably made the anonymous call by now. If everything was going according to plan, and Duane took the bait, he'd be emerging from that side door at any minute. He'd been instructed to meet his caller at the video arcade on the campus side. An ideal spot, it was close enough so Duane wouldn't need to drive; and he had a ten- to fifteen-minute walk each way. That gave Peter ample time to search the minivan.

Anton was contacting Duane from a pay phone in the student union, so the call couldn't be traced back to him. He wouldn't be going anywhere near the video arcade. He would wait by that phone until Peter called with the results of his search.

Peter glanced at his wristwatch. Another big drop of rain splashed his neck, then slithered down the back of his sweatshirt. He barely noticed it. Something was happening. He saw the side door opening.

Peter ducked back behind the garage, then he cautiously peeked around the corner.

Duane stepped outside and kicked at a rock. The lean, crudely handsome janitor ran a hand through his messy brown hair. He looked angry. He had a windbreaker on and patted something in the front pocket. His head down, he stomped toward the forest and Whopper Way.

Even as Duane disappeared down the trail, Peter continued to stare. He couldn't move. Now he knew. Duane was the man who had attacked him, the man who had killed Johnny. He'd taken the bait.

After a minute, Peter glanced around to make sure the coast was clear. He kept scoping the area as he briskly walked across the wet pavement toward Duane's minivan. He got closer and closer to that Viking goddess on the sliding back door. He reached for the door handle.

Locked.

"Shit," he muttered. He yanked at it again—to no avail. He tried the front passenger door: locked as well.

He hurried around the front of the minivan and tugged at the handle on the driver's door. "Goddamn it!" he hissed, pulling at it again and again.

Obviously, Duane had locked up the minivan after Anton's aborted break-in this morning. The big question was, while doing so, had he taken some evidence out of the vehicle?

Peter needed to know if anything was still in there. He thought about taking a rock and just breaking a window. Then he remembered the flexible metal ruler he'd used to spring the lock to Johnny's room a few weeks back. He glanced at his watch, then raced toward the side door to St. Bartholomew Hall.

Sprinting up four flights of stairs, Peter was out of breath and trembling by the time he unlocked his door. His sweatshirt was damp with rain and perspiration. Once inside his room, he headed to the desk. He found the thin metal ruler and a pair of scissors. With shaky hands, he cut a little ridge on the side of the ruler, something to catch the van's door lock. He'd never broken into a locked car before, but he'd seen someone do it in the movies once—with a gizmo that looked something like his modified ruler. He had no idea if it would work or not.

Before heading back out, Peter glanced from his window at Whopper Way. No sign of Duane. He wouldn't be returning for at least another ten minutes.

Still, Peter didn't have much time. He hurried down the stairs and out the side door. Approaching Duane's minivan, he walked slower. He couldn't quite catch his breath.

He checked out the area, then pulled the ruler out from under his sweatshirt. He tried to slide it between the passenger window and door. But the ruler kept bending. "Damn it," he muttered. He tried wiggling the makeshift device, and eventually it slid past the rubber lip at the base of the window. He had no idea what he was doing. He glanced over his shoulder to make sure no one saw him, then he guided the ruler toward the edge of the door by the lock. He kept moving the metal strip up and down in hopes that it would hook onto the latch.

"C'mon, c'mon, c'mon," Peter whispered. "Please, God . . ."

He felt it catch on to something. He kept wiggling, then

pulled up on the ruler. Nothing. He tried again and heard a click. On the other side of the passenger window, the lock button popped up.

"Oh, my God," Peter murmured, stunned. He couldn't believe he'd done it. Anton would be so proud of him.

Peter took one more look behind him, then he opened the door and ducked inside the car. The seats were covered in a fake zebra-skin fabric. A cardboard air freshener with a Playboy bunny logo dangled from the rearview mirror. Still, the minivan smelled of stale cigarette smoke. Peter pulled open the ashtray, and picked out one of the cigarette butts. He read the brand name on it: MARLBORO. He suddenly felt silly for checking. Why would he doubt Anton?

He dropped the butt back in the ashtray, then opened the glove compartment. It was full of packaged condoms, maps, and a bag of what looked like marijuana. He felt around under both front seats. He didn't find anything except a couple of empty beer cans.

In the back, Duane had folded down the seat and laid out a futon, with leopard-pattern sheets. The makeshift bed was messy. Over to the side were some books and a couple of candles.

Reaching behind the seat, Peter unlocked the back door, then he climbed out the front and let himself in back. Crawling on top of the futon, he couldn't find any clothes amid the bedding, so he pried up the corner of the thin mattress. He saw a woman's sleeveless blouse tucked under there. One of Duane's dates must have left in a hurry. He also found a sock and a black T-shirt. Peter moved farther down, peeling back another corner of the futon. He discovered more clothes: a pair of underpants, one black sock, and a red tank top.

He couldn't get a good look at everything underneath the pad if he was still on top of it. So Peter climbed out the van and lifted up one whole side of the futon. About a dozen garments had been flattened beneath the pad. But he noticed only one: a gray T-shirt with a crew neck and long sleeves that were navy blue.

Johnny had a shirt just like it. Of course, the Gap probably sold three million of them a couple of years ago. But Johnny's T-shirt had a picture of Homer Simpson over the left breast.

Still holding up the futon, Peter reached for the T-shirt and shook it out. He saw the cartoon of Homer Simpson.

"Oh, God," he murmured. He felt that old lump in his throat, and tears brimmed in his eyes, another sneak attack of grief. But Peter fought it.

He let the futon drop, and several of the garments scattered as the pad fell back in place. He clutched Johnny's shirt to his chest. He wasn't sure whether or not this had been the shirt Johnny had worn on the night of his death. If so, where had Duane hidden his other clothes?

Part of a bra stuck out from under the futon now. Peter wondered if Johnny had been one of Duane's sexual conquests. Or did all these other garments belong to people Duane had killed?

Peter rolled up Johnny's T-shirt and stuffed it beneath his own sweatshirt. He had to phone Anton and tell him what he'd found. Covering his tracks, he quickly shoved the bra back under the thin mattress. He pulled the leopard-pattern sheets back over the futon, trying to duplicate the way he'd originally found them. He set the lock on the sliding door, and before pulling it shut, he took one last look at Duane's little love nest.

"What the fuck do you think you're doing?"

Peter swiveled around.

Duane glared at him. "You really shouldn't be messing in there, Pete."

Peter held on to Johnny's T-shirt, hidden under his own

sweatshirt. He was so stunned he couldn't say a word. He merely shook his head.

"That's dangerous business, poking around in someone else's private domain," Duane said, with a hint of a smile. "Did you find anything?"

"No," Peter said. "The door was open, and I came by to shut it—"

"What are you hiding under your shirt?"

"Nothing." Peter backed away and bumped into the van.

"A future priest shouldn't be lying." Duane grabbed his arm. "Tell you what, Pete. If you're so anxious to poke around in there, maybe you should climb in and we can go for a ride someplace."

"No!" Peter yelled. "Leave me the fuck alone!"

He wrestled away from Duane and bolted toward the side door to St. Bart's.

"Hey, man, go ahead and run," he heard Duane call after him. "I know where you live, Pete. I know where you live."

"All right, calm down," Anton said over the phone. "Where are you now?"

"I'm on the pay phone on the second floor," Peter whispered, glancing up and down the corridor. He was still shaking. He had Johnny's T-shirt tucked under his arm. "I know Duane's going to be looking for me up on my floor—if he's not already up there, waiting."

"He won't come after you while people are around. Don't worry, Pete." Anton's voice was very calm. "I don't think you're in any danger right now. But you definitely can't stay there tonight."

"Can't we just call the police?"

"No, we don't have enough on him yet, only the shirt. And you aren't even sure it's the one Johnny was wearing that night he was killed."

"Listen, you need to help me get out of here," Peter said anxiously. "I can't keep standing in this hallway, waiting for him to find me. And I can't go back up to my room either."

"You'll have to, Pete," Anton said grimly. "You need to go back for the jacket. He knows we have it. I told him so on the phone. We have to grab that jacket before he breaks into your room and finds it."

"Oh, Jesus," Peter murmured, with another wary glance toward the stairwell.

"To build a case against him, we need the lumber jacket and Johnny's shirt," Anton continued. "Get a buddy on your floor to go to your room with you. Grab the jacket and, while you're there, throw some overnight things in a bag. We'll hide out tonight and plan our next move. I have a place in mind. Duane will never track us down there. You'll be safe, Pete. But I'll need to get a car and make some arrangements first. It'll take a while."

"How long?"

"A couple of hours," Anton said. "Can you lay low for a while, then meet me in the Burger King lot at seven?"

"I think so," Peter murmured, uncertain.

"I'll be looking for you by the crossing," Anton said. "Try to be on time, because if you're not there by seven-fifteen, I'm calling the police."

"I'll be there," Peter said.

Jack stared at the red wine stain on the white altar cloth. No one had seemed to notice when he'd spilled it during the Offertory.

He'd had a hard time keeping his mind on the Mass, and even flubbed a line of the Gospel reading. His homily was a short recycled sermon from months back. All during the service, images kept flashing in his head: Johnny's toes looking as if they'd been gnawed off; Jonie's burned and blistered face slowly turning toward him to reveal the missing teeth; and this afternoon, seeing nearly half of Dorothy McShane's digits picked off those withered gray hands and feet.

Jack had stumbled through Mass like a zombie. Fortunately, there hadn't been many people in attendance. With so many students gone for the three-day weekend, there couldn't have been more than twenty people in the congregation that Sunday afternoon.

Now the chapel was quiet. Jack stood with his back to the empty pews. He gazed at the burgundy stain he'd made on the white altar shroud. It looked like blood.

Jack started folding up the cloth so he could replace it with a clean one from the sacristy. He'd never seen the altar stripped bare before. It was an impressive piece of rose-colored marble. A grapes-on-the-vine motif had been carved along the altar's edge. Set in the middle of the sacrificial table was a small square of blue marble, with an inscription:

ST. GABRIEL LALEMANT
MDCX-MDCIL
DI NVMERARE POSSVM OMNIA OSSA MEA

This was where they'd enshrined a relic from the martyred Jesuit. Jack barely glanced at the epitaph as he gathered up the altar cloth. He should have been able to decipher the Latin, having taken five years of it in the seminary. But he didn't even try.

He took the altar cloth into the sacristy and got a clean one out of the closet. Returning to the altar, he started to spread the new cloth over the marble top. But he stopped and stared at the epitaph for the martyred St. Gabriel again. He realized it was a quote from Psalms 22. Jesus had said it on the cross: "I Can Count All My Bones."

Jack slowly shook his head.

"He's putting their bones in an altar," he whispered out loud. Those fingers, toes, and teeth had become saintly relics. Somewhere, this killer had an altar with the bones of his "martyrs."

"Are you Father Murphy?"

Jack turned around and saw the woman standing in the aisle. He hadn't heard her come into the church. A thin blonde in her late sixties, she wore a smart, pale blue suit. Glaring at him, she stepped up to the altar. "Father Murphy?" she asked again.

This close, he could see the contempt in her eyes. She was trembling.

"Yes, I'm Father Murphy," Jack said.

"My name is Irene McShane," she said steadily. "And this is for my daughter in law. . . ."

She spit in Jack's face.

Startled, he stepped back and bumped into the altar. He wiped away the spittle. "What—"

"You think you've been so clever," Irene snarled. "Did you figure no one could get to you? Dorothy kept a journal. I know she had an affair with you. I know about the abortion. Is that why you killed her?"

"What are you talking about?" Jack asked.

"You thought you'd gotten away with it," she continued, her voice quivering. "You knew Dorothy's reputation would be ruined if the truth got out—"

"Mrs. McShane, wait a minute," Jack said firmly. "I don't have any idea what you're talking about."

"Weren't you at the Enright Funeral Home this afternoon?" she asked, her teary eyes narrowed at him. "They called me, and said a priest from Our Lady of Sorrows had come to bless Dorothy's remains. A Father Murphy, they said. He told them that I'd requested this 'blessing'."

"I didn't mean any disrespect, Mrs. McShane—"

"I went along with your lie," she cut him off. "When they said you were from Our Lady of Sorrows, I knew who you were. I wanted to see you, Father Murphy. I wanted to see the animal who murdered my daughter-in-law."

"I didn't kill her, Mrs. McShane," Jack said. "But I'm trying to find out who did. Whoever it is, he's murdered a number of people—including some seminarians here at the school."

Mrs. McShane was shaking her head.

"Your daughter-in-law's journal could have left some clues—dates they'd gotten together, discussions they'd had. We might be able to put together a profile of this man. Did the journal mention this priest's age or what he looked like?"

"You aren't fooling me, Father Murphy. I don't believe a word you're saying. You're morally bankrupt. You're a murderer—"

Jack grabbed her arm. "Wait. What did you just call me?"

Mrs. McShane suddenly looked so frail and scared. She tried to wrestle free from him, but it was in vain. "I called you 'morally bankrupt'," she whispered defiantly.

"Where did you come up with that term?" he asked.

"It's a phrase Dorothy used. Maybe you've heard it before."

Jack nodded. "Yes, I have."

The 5:30 Sunday Mass at Our Lady of Sorrows Church always seemed like an endurance marathon. It usually lasted an hour and a half. Peter generally avoided it. But not tonight. He needed to lay low until seven o'clock, and he'd found the perfect place to do so, amid the congregation in the big church.

As he walked down the aisle after communion, he subtly checked out the crowd. No sign of Duane. And his duffle was still in the pew, where he'd left it to go receive the Eucharist.

Peter knelt down in his pew and thanked God for the umpteenth time today.

He still couldn't believe he'd made it out of St. Bart's. After hanging up with Anton, he had ventured up to the fourth floor. To his amazement, Duane hadn't been up there, waiting for him. He got a fellow seminarian, Tommy Hoang, to come into his room with him. Tommy left after a few minutes, while Peter packed his duffle.

He didn't make a completely clean getaway. Father Zeigler spotted him with the overnight bag, heading toward the stairwell. Zeigler grabbed him, then pushed him against the wall. "Where do you think you're going, Mr. Tobin? Have you signed out?"

Peter apologized, saying he'd just plain forgotten. Zeigler dragged him down to his room, and made him complete a sign-out/overnight form. Peter wrote that he was spending the night at his parents' house. He also scribbled something else on the form, because he hated Zeigler and he was feeling reckless. He was taking a stupid chance, but he knew Zeigler probably wouldn't notice. The priests never really bothered to look at those things.

He apologized to Zeigler one more time, then left his room and hurried down to the stairwell. He kept expecting to run into Duane. But he didn't see him, not in the lobby, not outside, and nowhere along Whopper Way.

Despite all the people, and the beautiful music inside the glorious church, Peter still didn't feel safe. He knelt and prayed that he'd make it through the night. He knew it was corny, but he prayed to Johnny, and asked his friend to help him.

While the priest recited the blessing, Peter glanced at his watch: ten to seven. He told himself that he'd be okay. Within minutes, he would file out of the church along with everyone else. From there, it would only be a short walk to the Burger King parking lot.

And Anton would be waiting for him.

The lot next to Parker's Pantry was full. Maggie had to park on the street and walk two blocks to the restaurant.

The Sunday-night dinner crowd—along with the usual quota of morbidly curious—had descended on the place all at once. About a dozen people were standing inside the front door, waiting for tables. With silverware clanging, babies crying, laughter, conversation, and the wait staff yelling at each other, the place seemed too noisy for a pleasant meal.

Maggie made her way up to the front counter, where a haggard-looking teenage girl with braces and a touch of acne worked the register. The girl glanced up at her. "Smoking or nonsmoking?"

"Is Doreen working tonight?" Maggie asked loudly over the din. She still had the newspaper article, which included the name of Lucy Ballatore's friend, the last person to see her alive.

Nodding, the girl retreated toward the kitchen. Maggie could hear her yell, *"Doreen!"*

A minute later, the tall, slim, fiftysomething waitress emerged from the kitchen. She had frosted blond hair and sharp features, especially her thin, long nose. Carrying a plate of food to a man at the counter, she glanced at Maggie and seemed to recognize her. She fetched a bottle of ketchup for her customer, then she locked eyes with Maggie again and started toward her. "Hey, hon," she said, wiping her hand on her apron. "I haven't seen you in an age. Where have you been?"

Maggie shrugged. "Every time I've come by, the place has looked too crowded for me."

Bracing one hand on the countertop, Doreen leaned closer

to Maggie. "Tell me about it. Listen, were you the one asking to see me?"

Maggie nodded. "I was hoping you could spare five minutes to answer a few questions. But my timing stinks, doesn't it? Could I come back at your break?"

"No, it's okay. I'm dying for a cigarette anyway." She glanced back over her shoulder at another waitress. "Hey, Ellen, could you cover my tables while I grab a smoke?"

"Now?" the other waitress asked.

"I'm only gonna be five minutes. It's not like I'm asking you to donate a kidney."

"Fine, go ahead," the waitress grumbled.

"Thanks!" Doreen called, then she leaned toward Maggie and whispered, "For nothing. Jesus, this new bunch of people they hired are the worst! I thought Lucy was a screwup, God rest her soul, but oh, these new ones . . ."

She led Maggie out a side screen door for deliveries. They stood under a floodlight, amid piles of empty plastic crates. Doreen pulled a pack of Parliaments from her apron pocket and lit one up. "You said you wanted to ask me some questions, hon?"

Maggie nodded. "About Lucy. I'm sure you must get this all the time. You're probably sick of it."

"Oh, I don't mind talking about Lucy with our old regulars. You were one of the nice customers—and a good tipper. Everyone liked you—including Lucy."

Maggie shrugged. "Well, thanks. You know, I was here on her last night."

"Yeah, I remember." Doreen exhaled a cloud of cigarette smoke. "She screwed up your order or something. You were really nice about it, too. Lucy screwed up a lot. A sweet girl, but not exactly the best waitress in the world."

"Did you notice a Volkswagen parked in the lot when you closed that night with her?"

"No. I think the lot was empty."

"I know this is a weird question," Maggie said. "But did anyone walk into the restaurant that night with a clown mask? Maybe one of the customers playing a joke on a friend or something?"

Doreen frowned and shook her head. "No, I think I'd remember that."

"That night, while I was waiting for my order, I heard you two talking. You were razzing her about a . . . a secret boyfriend."

Doreen took a long drag on her cigarette and nodded. "Yeah, I told the police about him, but I don't think they were ever able to track him down."

"You don't have any clue who he was or what he even looked like?"

Doreen sighed. "Sorry. That's one secret Lucy took to her grave."

Maggie bit her lip. *Just like Jonie,* she thought.

"We get these ghoulish types in here all the time now," Doreen said. "They always want to know about Lucy." She studied Maggie for a moment. "You don't seem like the ghoulish type, hon. What's all this about?"

"That night, you mentioned a priest. You were teasing her about him."

"Oh, yeah, the hunky man of the cloth." She chuckled and tossed away her cigarette. "I was just kidding with Lucy about him. He was this young, cutie-pie of a priest who came into the restaurant one night a while back. Lucy flirted with him a little. But I seriously don't think he was the guy she was seeing."

"Why do you say that?"

"Well, for one, I remember Lucy said he asked about you."

"He asked about me?" Maggie whispered.

Doreen nodded. "Yeah, you were there the same night

as him. You might have seen him. He was kind of brawny—
like a football player. Um, blond hair, I think—''

The side screen door opened, and a young man with an
apron stepped out. ''Hey, Doreen, they're going crazy in
there.'' He retreated back inside, and the door slammed shut.

She gave Maggie a helpless shrug. ''Sorry, hon. I better
scoot.''

''Are you sure this young priest was asking about me?''

Doreen nodded. ''Yeah, Lucy said that he seemed to know
you. He asked how often you came by, something along
those lines. Anyway, I don't think Lucy had much luck
clicking with him.''

''And I was there in the restaurant that night?''

''Yeah, if I remember right, he came in a couple of minutes
after you did.'' She glanced toward the side door. ''Listen,
hon, I really gotta haul ass back to work. Can I put an order
to go for you?''

''Oh, no, thanks,'' Maggie answered numbly. ''You—
you've been a big help. Thank you.''

''Take care,'' Doreen called, then she hurried inside. The
screen door slammed shut behind her.

In a daze, Maggie wandered away from the restaurant's
loading area. As she started down the darkened sidewalk
toward her car, she felt as if someone was watching her.
She kept expecting to see that man in the clown mask again.

The car was still a half block away, and Maggie already
had her keys out. Nervously gazing at the shadowy bushes
along the sidewalk, she picked up her pace. She unlocked
the door and glanced at the backseat to make sure no one
was hiding there. Then she jumped behind the wheel and
locked her door.

Trembling, Maggie tried to catch her breath. This ''priest''
was young, and he'd been asking about her. He'd been
watching her. Was this before or after he'd murdered
Johnny?

Her cellular phone rang, and gave Maggie a start. With a shaky hand, she switched it on. "Um, yes, hello?"

"Sweetheart?"

She sighed. "Oh, hi, Steve."

"I just tried you at home. Where are you?"

"In the car. I was just at Parker's Pantry, talking to a waitress friend of Lucy's. It's the same pattern as some of the other cases I told you about—including Johnny's. Lucy seems to have been secretly involved with a priest. That's our killer."

"I have a funny feeling about this Father Murphy you seem to trust so much—"

"No," Maggie cut in. "Jack's in his forties. So is this other priest, Father Garcia. The waitress tonight told me this priest was young."

"Listen, we should go to the police," Steve said.

"I think we ought to wait—at least until we know if Lucy's corpse was in the same kind of condition as the others. You were going to check it out."

"I've checked it out, Maggie," he said soberly. "A finger and thumb were missing."

"I knew it," she murmured.

Suddenly a shadow passed over the dashboard. Gasping, Maggie turned to see a man coming toward the car. But he kept walking. As he passed by her car, Maggie noticed the man had a Jack Russell terrier on a leash.

"What just happened?" Steve asked.

"Nothing." She sighed. "I'm a bit jumpy, that's all."

"So—how about it? I'm seeing this buddy from the Seattle force in a few minutes. He's the one who found out about Lucy Ballatore for us. Let me tell him what's going on here."

"Not just yet," Maggie said. "Let me call Father Murphy first. He has most of the information. He should be in on this. It's no good coming just from us. Don't say anything to the police yet.''

''Okay, but promise me in return, you'll go right home, lock your doors and windows, and stay put until I get there. Don't leave the house for any reason, understand?''

''All right.''

''Now, I won't make it there for at least a couple of hours. I agreed to help my buddy with an internal affairs thing tonight. But I should be at your place by ten at the latest. Will you be okay?''

''I'll be fine,'' Maggie said. ''Don't worry about me.''

''Well, I am worried. I just looked up something on the Internet a while ago. Remember you told me your real name was Agnes Marie? Well, St. Agnes was killed the same way as St. Lucy. She was stabbed in the throat.''

''If you're trying to scare me, you're doing a bang-up job.'' Maggie let out a skittish laugh. ''But c'mon, I—I can't imagine this guy would know my real name.''

''That's just it, sweetheart,'' Steve replied. ''I'm afraid he knows you better than you think.''

Peter waited alone in the car. Through the newly cleaned windshield, he watched Anton talking on a pay phone. They were parked in a Chevron station and minimart just north of Everett.

They'd been driving for over an hour. As promised, Anton had been waiting in the lot behind the Burger King. Peter was overjoyed to find him there, leaning against a spiffy red Toyota. When Anton gave him a hug, Peter didn't want him to let go. But a car started coming around to the drive-thru, and Anton muttered they should get going before anyone saw them together. He didn't want it getting back to Duane that they were in cahoots. He grabbed Peter's duffle, tossed it in the back, then got behind the wheel. Peter climbed in the passenger side.

They weren't even out of the Burger King lot when Peter started unloading on him about everything that had happened—from breaking into Duane's minivan with the ruler to his taking refuge among the congregation at Our Lady of Sorrows.

"Pete, I'm proud of you," Anton said, watching the road ahead. "I don't know if I could have kept my cool like that."

"Are you kidding?" he replied. "I'm a total wreck. I'm still wired for sound."

"Well, we're going to unwind and relax tonight. This place is very quiet, secluded. No one will know where we are. It'll be like a regular overnight. We'll have fun, Pete, you'll see. Once we've mellowed out, we'll sit down over a couple of beers and figure out our next move."

Peter nodded. Half listening, he had his eyes glued to the side rearview mirror. He couldn't stop checking it. He didn't see a black minivan behind them; no pale blue VW bug either. He kept having to tell himself that he was okay. He took a deep breath, then sat back. "Where are we headed, anyway?"

"You can keep a secret, right?" Anton asked as he pulled onto the expressway ramp. "I mean, you haven't told anyone about us, have you?"

"No, of course not."

"Well, here's another something to keep under your cap. We're spending the night at my house. It's a little hideaway I have. Not too many people know about it." He glanced over his shoulder as he merged onto Interstate 5.

"You own a house? It's yours?" Peter asked.

"All mine. It's nothing spectacular, just a little rambler."

"Still, you must have a lot of money."

"Yeah, well, a trust fund from my dead granny." Anton moved into the left lane and picked up speed. "I don't tell people, because priests aren't supposed to have a lot of earthly possessions. And I'm not sure I want to give up my secret hideaway. For emergencies like tonight, it comes in pretty handy. It's about an hour and fifteen minutes south of here, Pete. So sit back and relax. You can even fall asleep, if you want to."

"I don't think I could," he replied with a skittish laugh. "I'm still pretty jumpy."

"I know just what you need to chill out," Anton said, smiling. He studied the highway in front of him. "A little time in the old hot tub."

"You have a hot tub?" Peter asked.

"No, but my neighbors have one, and they let me use it all the time. In fact, they encourage me to use it."

"Really?"

Anton chuckled. "Yeah, I think they like seeing me naked. I'm pretty sure they're a couple of closet swingers. Whenever I come over for a dip, they always pretend they're going to bed. But they leave the back light on for me. I know they're looking when I'm out there, naked under the stars. I strut my stuff for them. It's kind of a kick."

Peter squirmed a bit. He didn't want to put on a show for anyone. That wasn't going to relax him at all. "Well, I'm not sure I'm up for it," he admitted, shrugging. "I'd feel funny using someone else's hot tub."

"Hey, if you're worried about these people, I'm pretty sure they're headed out of town tonight." Anton glanced at the fuel gauge. "In fact, we have to stop for gas in about forty-five minutes. I'll call them. I hope they're gone. The hot tub would do us both a lot of good. You'll love it, I guarantee."

For the next fifty minutes, they listened to Anton's oldies tape, and every once in a while, Peter checked that rearview mirror. They pulled into the Chevron station along I-5, just north of Everett. After filling up the Toyota's tank, Anton parked by the minimart's rest rooms and phones. ''Be right back,'' he said, jumping out of the car.

He'd been talking on the phone for about five minutes now. Obviously, his neighbors were home. It was just as well. Peter didn't need to add to his nervousness the prospect of getting naked with Anton in a hot tub tonight. Any other evening, he'd have jumped at the chance. But this evening, he just wanted to go to this hideaway house, lock the doors and windows, and stay inside.

As long as Duane was still out there, Peter couldn't really rest. Just sitting in the car in the gas-station lot, he was afraid. Every pair of approaching headlights kept him on his guard. Each time, Peter squinted past their beams to see if it was a black ''Viking'' minivan or a VW.

For all he knew, Johnny's killer might be driving some other vehicle now. Maybe he'd been following them ever since they'd left Leroy.

Peter glanced at Anton by the pay phone. He thought about tapping the car horn to make him hurry.

But Anton finally hung up the receiver. He turned and gave him an okay sign with his finger and thumb. Peter wasn't quite sure what that meant—if they had permission to use the hot tub, or if the neighbors were gone, or what.

Ambling toward the car, he winked at Peter, then opened the driver's door. ''We're on for the hot tub tonight,'' he announced, scooting behind the wheel. ''My neighbors are catching the red-eye to Hawaii in an hour. We'll have the place all to ourselves, Pete.''

''That's cool,'' was all Peter could think of to say.

Anton started up the engine and began to back out of his parking spot. ''My house is on a cul-de-sac. With these neighbors gone, it's like we're alone in the middle of the country.''

Anton shifted gears, then pulled out of the gas station. "Sit back and relax. We'll be there soon. Leave everything to me."

Chapter Twenty

Sitting in the front pew, Irene McShane stared up at the altar. With her nice blue suit, every blond hair in place, and that sad, dazed expression on her face, she looked as if she were daydreaming during Mass.

But she and Jack were alone in the little church. He sat at the end of the pew, some distance from her. She still didn't trust him entirely, and he knew it. He wasn't going to get any closer. It was enough that she'd sat still and listened to him for the past few minutes. He could see the tears in her eyes, and he offered her a handkerchief.

She shook her head, then reached into her purse and pulled out a Kleenex. Irene dabbed her eyes and nose.

"A few weeks ago, I heard one of the seminarians—a senior—call another boy 'morally bankrupt'." Jack sighed. "I'd never heard that expression before. And I haven't heard it since—not until you said it a couple of minutes ago."

"So, you're telling me this 'martyr' killer is one of the seniors here at the school?" she asked.

"It's possible," Jack reasoned. "He picked up an expression of Dorothy's, one she must have coined. Then again, he might have heard the term from Dorothy's killer. Maybe it's one of his teachers, or some other priest. I'll have to look into it."

She glanced down at the balled-up Kleenex in her hand. "What are you going to do when you find this murderer?"

"I'll see that he's put away, of course."

"And what about the families of his victims? Haven't they suffered enough?" Folding her arms in front of her, she glanced down at the kneeler. "Didn't you say that he seduced most of his 'martyrs' before he killed them?"

Jack nodded. "It appears that way, yes."

"How do you think the families are going to feel? Maybe the parents of these murdered boys would rather not hear about their sons' sexual proclivities. Maybe they'd rather not have it become public knowledge. I know how they feel."

"You don't want it getting out that Dorothy had an affair," Jack said.

Irene shrugged. "With a priest—or a seminarian—no less. And she also had an abortion. All that would come out, Father Murphy."

"You want me to let it go?" he asked. "To save Dorothy's reputation?"

"I just don't want to cause my grandchildren any further heartache," Irene said. "I'm thinking of the others, too. Haven't we been through enough? We've all buried our dead. We don't want to go through it again. These 'martyrs' aren't really saints, Father. If this killer is brought to justice, the sins of his victims will be held under public scrutiny."

"What would you have me do?" Jack asked, leaning toward her in the pew. "Mrs. McShane, since he killed your daughter-in-law, this man has 'martyred' at least three more people, including my friend—and those are just the ones we know about. He has to be stopped."

"I know he does," Irene whispered, wiping away another tear. "I only wish it could be done quietly."

Jack shook his head. "I'm sorry, Mrs. McShane. I don't think it will happen that way."

"Check this out," he said, picking at his food with a fork. "I ought to look for a pot of gold at the end of this meat."

Marty Schriver's gristly roast beef had a rainbow gleam. St. Clement Hall's cafeteria fare wasn't any better than the food at St. Bart's.

He shared a table by the entrance with Jack. The cafeteria crowd had thinned out, and the staff was already starting to clean up the place. One of the workers was setting chairs upside down on the tables so they could mop the floor.

Marty was the other resident adviser on Anton Sorenson's floor. Jack figured he knew Anton as well as anyone else. He'd had his doubts about Anton back when they'd first met. It was strange how Anton had offered him an alibi without any solicitation. What had he claimed to be doing the night Johnny drowned? He'd gone to the Cinerama Theater in Seattle to watch *The Great Escape*. So, he had the movie and showtime down; it didn't mean he'd actually gone to Seattle. Some alibi. Jack shouldn't have let it throw him off. He should have sought out a "character witness" like Marty a month ago.

The senior had long, ratty black hair, a stubbly beard, and tired-looking brown eyes. He appeared as if he'd just rolled out of bed, and Jack guessed that he probably always looked that way. He wore a rumpled, untucked oxford shirt.

With the fork, Marty held up the piece of meat. "I know we have several seminarians from foreign countries who might consider this gourmet fare, but we're in the U. S. of A. now. Do you know what I ate here for dinner last night?''

Jack shook his head.

"Same as I'm gonna eat tonight." Marty dropped the fork on his plate, then picked up a slice of bread. "Jell-O and white bread. If not for beer and beef jerky, I'd starve to death in this joint. So . . . Father, tell me more about this Big Brother organization for next year."

"It's still in the development stage," Jack lied. "The guys starting their theologate would spend time with the freshmen at St. Bart's. We're screening some of the applicants. I was wondering if you thought Anton Sorenson would be a good Big Brother. I understand he's . . . a bit eccentric."

Marty chuckled. "That's one way of putting it."

"How well do you know him?" Jack asked,

Marty scooped up some lime Jell-O with a spoon. "We were freshmen together at St. Bart's. I did my best to avoid him."

"Why is that?"

"Anton was always getting into trouble. He's bigger than most of the other guys. Of course, he had a couple of years on everybody."

"He's older?"

"Yeah, I think he's twenty-three. His folks held him back a couple of years in school or something. I don't think they knew what to do with him. He's one of those guys who got shipped off to the seminary because he was a problem kid. I remember his first week at St. Bart's, he grabbed one of the smaller freshmen and held him out the fourth-floor window for several minutes, all part of some joke. Anton was the only one who thought it was funny. The poor kid wet his pants. They almost expelled Anton, but I hear his old man smoothed things over with the big shots in administration. Anton was always pulling stuff like that."

Marty finished up his Jell-O. "Is any of this going to get back to Anton?" he asked warily.

Jack shook his head. "Nope, this is all confidential."

"Well, then here's my own personal Anton story," Marty said, pushing his tray away. "This happened back in St. Bart's. I was in my room, sitting at my desk, minding my own business. It was the middle of the afternoon, and I had my door open a crack. So Anton saunters in with his shirt off. He still does that, patrols the halls practically bare-assed. I guess if I had his body, I'd want to show it off, too. But to a bunch of guys? It's kind of creepy. Anyway, I didn't know him very well at the time, but I have to admit, I was a little scared of him—especially after hearing about how he held that kid out the window."

Jack nodded. "I'd give him some distance, too."

"Yeah, so he walked into my room with his shirt off. And he said—pardon me, Father—he said, 'How would you like to blow me?' Then he unzipped his jeans, pulled out his dick—pardon me, Father—and he started stroking it." Marty shook his head. "I tried to laugh and make like it was this big joke. But he was serious. He even started to get hard. He was coming at me with it, like he expected me to go down on him—whether I wanted to or not. I mean, I really thought he was going to force himself on me. All this time, my door was open. So I finally yelled at the top of my lungs, 'Get the hell out of here, you pervert!' or something along those lines. I could hear someone coming down the hall, and I think that made Anton back off. I don't know what he would have done if I hadn't yelled out."

Jack stared at him. "And they made Anton a resident adviser here? After that incident with the other freshman and what he did to you?"

Marty tossed his napkin on the tray. "Well, I didn't exactly broadcast to anyone what he did to me. Besides, not long after that, Anton suddenly turned superstraight, Mr.

Model Seminarian. But I think he still has a wild streak in him. He did a really weird thing later that year at St. Bart's. I don't know if it's true or not, I just heard it. He asked for a room reassignment. He wanted to move into Room 410. You know, where that murder-suicide happened?''

Jack squinted at him. ''Did he give a reason?''

''Huh, not that I know of.''

''You and Anton were freshmen when Oliver Theron hung himself. Were either of you acquainted with him?''

''I wasn't. I can't speak for Anton. That was a bizarre year. We had a kid who drowned, too.''

''Julian Doyle. Did Anton know him?''

Marty shrugged. ''Beats me. Anton and I didn't exactly travel in the same circles.''

''Did you ever see him with John Costello?''

''You mean the kid who drowned a few weeks ago?'' Marty said. ''I never actually saw him on our floor, so I can't say.'' His eyes narrowed at Jack. ''Do you think Anton had something to do with all these people who died?''

''Oh, no,'' Jack said. ''I just got sidetracked.''

Marty slouched back further in the chair and clasped his hands behind his head. ''Well, to answer your question, I don't think Anton Sorenson would be such a terrific Big Brother for your program. I know he's supposed to be reformed and all that. But I see him wandering the hallways half-dressed, and I can't help thinking maybe he's still doing to some of those guys what he did to me that one afternoon.'' Marty shrugged. ''Except for St. Paul after he fell off his horse, I don't think people can really change that much.''

One of the cleanup staff started to turn off the lights in the cafeteria. Jack glanced around and noticed that he and Marty were the only customers left in the place. ''I think somebody's giving us a hint,'' he said.

When they stepped out to the lobby, Jack shook Marty's

hand. "Listen, thanks for your honesty, Marty. I was going to talk with Anton tonight. I'm glad I spoke with you instead."

"Well, you couldn't have seen Anton anyway," Marty replied. "He checked out this afternoon. Won't be back until tomorrow. That's another reason he'd make a crummy Big Brother. He's never around. He comes and goes at the weirdest hours. Practically every weekend, I have to cover for the SOB."

"Do they keep records for when people sign out?" Jack asked.

"Nothing permanent," Marty said. "They keep a note on file while a resident adviser's away, but when he comes back, they toss out the note."

"I'm just curious," Jack said. "Do you have to say where you're going when you sign out?"

"You can if you want. But it's not mandatory—not like at St. Bart's."

"Do you know where Anton went tonight?"

"Sorry, Father. I have no idea where Anton is most of the time." He gave Jack a crooked smile. "I'm still keeping my distance."

Jack thanked Marty once again, then watched him head toward the stairwell. He stood by St. Clement Hall's front entrance for another minute.

"Hey, Chad, I locked myself out again!"

Jack stepped aside as a student who smelled of beer came in the front door. He ambled up to the front desk. "Chad, I need my key."

The tall, lanky seminarian behind the desk gave the other boy a deadpan stare over the black rims of his glasses. Chad had a brown crewcut. He muttered something to the other young man, but Jack couldn't hear.

He watched as Chad turned and opened a cabinet behind the desk. The cabinet held scores of keys, labeled and hanging on hooks. Chad found the key for his friend. The seminarian teetered toward the stairwell. "I owe you, Chad!" he called over his shoulder.

Jack waited another minute, then limped up to the front desk. He made sure Chad saw his last few faltering steps.

"Evening, Father," he said. "Can I help you?"

"You sure can," Jack said, leaning on the counter. "Somebody called me last night, saying my sweatshirt is down in the laundry room here. I lost it about a week ago, and I'd really like to get it back."

"Oh, well, you can go ahead, Father," Chad said. "The laundry room is down the stairs, then you take a right—"

"Actually," Jack interrupted, "I did a number on my ankle while jogging this morning. I'm trying to stay off it as much as I can. Could you check the laundry room for me? In the meantime, I'll watch the front desk here for you. Okay?"

Chad shrugged. "Sure, I guess it won't be a problem." He stepped out from behind the desk.

Jack took his place, hobbling around the counter. "A gray sweatshirt with *Murphy* on the name tag sewn inside," he said. "Thanks a lot. I owe you."

Chad didn't find a sweatshirt in the laundry room, but Jack found a key in the cabinet behind the front desk.

When Chad returned from the basement empty-handed, Jack thanked him anyway, then limped out from behind the counter. He said something about needing to see a seminarian on the second floor, and he hobbled toward the stairwell.

The third floor seemed deserted. All the doors were closed. Jack didn't hear anything except the muffled noise from a TV in a room down the hall.

He unlocked Anton's door with the stolen key. The dark room smelled of Old Spice. Jack quietly closed the door behind him, then he moved over to the window and shut the drapes. He made his way in the dark to the light switch, then flicked it on.

Anton's room was extremely tidy. The neatly made bed could have passed a military barracks inspection. In the corner of the room were a set of weights and a padded bench. Flemish prints—one of the Last Supper, and another of the Crucifixion—decorated the walls.

Jack peeked inside the closet. The perfectly lined row of conservative shirts and trousers was disrupted by two loud, Hawaiian short-sleeve shirts. There was also a black jacket, along with a clerical shirt and collar on a wooden hanger. The seminarians at Our Lady of Sorrows usually didn't receive their clerical garb until after they'd graduated from the college and started their theologate. Anton shouldn't have had those clerical clothes yet.

Moving to the desk, Jack noted the same kind of thin, metal crucifix that was in every seminarian's room. Aside from the lamp, it was the only decoration on the desktop. Jack started riffling through the drawers. One of the drawers was full of junk: scrap paper, old receipts, rubber bands, paper clips, and matchbooks. Jack checked all the matchbooks, hoping to find one from Parker's Pantry, but he didn't have any luck.

Several of the receipts were from service stations. Anton had been buying gas all up and down western Washington state. Jack wondered whose car he was using—unless he had his own, stashed away some place.

In another drawer, he found an old tabloid, carefully stored in a clear plastic sleeve. It was something called the *True Crimes Gazette,* and the date was December 4, 1949. SCREAMS IN THE NIGHT SHOCK QUIET SEMINARY blazed the headline. Below that was a grainy black-and-white photo of Gerard Lunt's room from the night of the murder-suicide. Jack slipped the newspaper out of the sleeve, and a holy card drifted onto the floor. It showed a forlorn Blessed

Virgin, her heart bleeding. On the reverse side of the yellowing card was the inscription:

In Loving Memory
GERARD STERLING LUNT
1931–1949
Redeem His Soul, Dear Savior

Staring at the holy card, Jack shook his head in disbelief.
He wondered how in the world Anton had gotten his hands
on this memento from a funeral half a century ago.

He gingerly slid the old tabloid and the holy card back
into the protective sleeve, then returned it to its place in
Anton's desk drawer.

Jack found some old letters and bills in the bottom left-
hand drawer. Most were addressed to Anton at St. Clement
Hall. Among them, he discovered a card with TO OUR SON
ON HIS BIRTHDAY scrawled across a misty photo of a young
man running alone on a beach at sunset. The preprinted
sentiment inside was equally misty. Scribbled on the bottom
of the card was a message: *Your Father and I send our
Love & Best Wishes, Mom.* Jack glanced at the envelope
and the return address label for Mrs. Paul Sorenson of
Springfield, Oregon.

Yet several of the other letters and bills for Anton were
addressed to him at 410 Prentiss Drive North in Seattle. It
wasn't merely a summer residence either, because some of
the postmark dates were recent.

Jack took out his pocket notebook and scribbled down
the Prentiss Drive address. That same locale was also on an
old bill receipt from a Texaco station in Leroy: a twenty-
two-dollar monthly parking charge for a 1999 model red
Toyota, license-plate number JOB607.

Indeed, Anton had a car stashed away someplace. Jack

jotted down the automobile description, along with the license-plate number.

He checked out the bathroom. On the bathtub's corner ledge was a bottle of shampoo, Vita Z, the same brand Jonie had squandered on Johnny.

Jack turned and opened the medicine chest. The entire bottom shelf was crammed with Vita Z hair products, gels, conditioners, holding spray, even some temporary hair dyes.

He imagined Jonie indulging Anton with supplies from the salon—right up until the time he killed her.

She snatched up the receiver on the second ring. "Hello?"

Silence.

"Hello? Anyone there?"

Maggie stood in her kitchen. She'd just been turning on some lights when the phone had rung. "Is anyone there?" she repeated, loudly this time.

She heard a click.

Maggie hung up, then quickly dialed *69: *"The number called cannot be reached. . . ."*

"Salesperson," she said out loud, hanging up again. She went to the refrigerator, pulled out a bottle of chardonnay, and poured a glass. Her hands were shaking.

Something moved in the window. Maggie saw it out of the corner of her eye. Swiveling around, she almost dropped the glass. It was just the neighbor's cat, jumping up on the windowsill outside. "Sidney, you scared the crap out of me," Maggie muttered.

The tabby was named Mr. Sidney Jenkins. Maggie's neighbor, a divorcée, would call to him using the full name. It sounded like someone being paged at an airport: *"Mr. Sidney Jenkins! Mr. Sidney Jenkins!"* The cat was always hanging around Maggie's backyard, probably trying to escape his owner. Sidney pawed at the window as if he wanted to get inside.

Maggie sighed and tapped on the glass. She hoped no one else wanted to break into the house tonight.

She'd already checked all the rooms and closets. She'd even braved the basement and garage. She was alone in the house, very much alone. No one could get inside without her hearing.

It was only 8:15, not even completely dark out yet. Still, every tiny sound in the place had Maggie holding her breath—whether it was the refrigerator starting up again, the house settling, or her other neighbor's dog barking.

The phone rang again, giving her a start. Quickly she grabbed the receiver once more. "Yes, hello?" she said, an edginess in her voice.

"Maggie, it's Jack."

"Oh, hi," she said, relieved. She reached for her glass of wine. "Did you just try to call?"

"No. Why? Did you get a hang-up?"

"Yeah. Probably just a salesperson."

"Are you there alone?" Jack asked.

"Yes, but my friend, Steve, is coming over at ten. I'll be all right until then." She leaned against the kitchen counter. "FYI, you can include Lucy Ballatore in the group of 'martyrs.' Steve did some snooping for me. He got it from a police contact; Lucy was missing a finger and thumb."

"I think this guy is saving the bones as relics," Jack said. "Bone chips of martyrs and saints are enshrined in churches all over the world. Almost every altar in every church built before 1950 has a saint's relic in it. I'm pretty sure he takes their clothes for the same reason. The clothes of saints are considered relics, too."

"My God, Jack," she murmured.

"I might know who it is," Jack said. "A senior here named Anton Sorenson. He seems to meet the profile of this killer. Plus he has priest's clothes hanging in his dorm room closet."

"Is that so peculiar—in a seminary?" Maggie asked.

"For a senior in the college, yeah," Jack replied. "He also has a shelf-load of hair products in his medicine chest."

"Hair products?" she said. "You mean, like Jonie gave Johnny?"

"The exact same brand," Jack said.

"You didn't happen to find a clown mask while you were searching through his room, did you?"

"You mean like the one that man was wearing in the parking lot outside Parker's Pantry that night? No. What kind of car was he sitting in? Was it a Toyota?"

"No, a pale-colored Volkswagen beetle."

"Light blue?" Jack asked.

"That's very possible. Why?"

"Jonie drove a light blue VW beetle. Anton could have borrowed her car that night. He's been keeping his own car under wraps. Anton also seems to have his own place in Seattle. That gives him a home base. And with his car, he has the mobility to commit these murders in different locations."

"Where is this Anton right now?"

"I don't know. He checked out of his dorm for the night."

"Oh," she muttered, warily glancing out her kitchen window.

"Listen, isn't there a neighbor or a friend you could call to come over? I'd feel a lot better if you weren't alone."

"My good friend at work, Adele, she's gone for the weekend."

"A neighbor?" Jack pressed.

Maggie thought of Mr. Sidney Jenkins's mommy, and

decided she was better off going it alone. "I'll be fine, Jack," she said, taking another sip of chardonnay. "I've locked the doors and all the windows. Don't worry about me. Steve will be here in less than a couple of hours."

She let that sink in and waited for Jack to say something. But he didn't.

"Anyway, I'll be okay," she went on. "Steve thinks we should go to the police. But I told him we might not have enough to make a case."

"You're right, actually; we don't," Jack said. "We haven't found anything incriminating on Anton yet, just circumstantial stuff. We can't even connect him to any of the victims—except maybe Jonie, and the police here are still calling her death an accident."

"Is there any way to link him with Johnny?" she asked.

"He's the resident adviser over that group of sophomores whom Johnny was seeing. I talked with Anton a while back. He claimed to have seen John hanging around the dorm, on his floor. But he said he didn't know him beyond that."

"Do you think Peter could tell us if Johnny was involved with him?"

"You're reading my mind," Jack said. "I'm just about to head back over to St. Bart's to talk with him. As soon as I get anything, I'll call you."

"Good."

"In the meantime, if you get scared, call me. I'll keep checking my messages."

"For the umpteenth time, I'll be fine, Jack. But thanks."

"All right," he said. "Talk to you in a bit."

After Maggie hung up, she had another sip of wine, hoping it would take the edge off. She went into the living room and peered out the front window. She didn't see anything.

She felt a little silly. After all, she'd spent nearly all her time in this town house by herself, and she'd never really been scared before. But tonight was different. She couldn't shake the sensation that someone was outside the house right now, watching and waiting.

Maggie retreated back to the kitchen and had another sip of wine. She told herself to take it easy with the chardonnay.

She had a long night ahead.

Chapter Twenty-one

Peter sat on the passenger side with his window open. They were driving along a dark, creekside road. The houses on the other side of the street varied from tidy little ramblers to genuine dumps with overgrown lawns. Peter kept checking the side rearview mirror. It didn't look like anyone was following them at all.

He glanced at Anton, his handsome face illuminated by the dashboard light. He was watching the road. He didn't talk much while he drove. At first, Peter was uncomfortable with the silence. But Anton seemed to be listening to his oldies tape.

He wasn't exactly crazy about the hot tub idea. Why couldn't they just stay inside tonight and play it safe? He could tell Anton was trying to make this overnight seem like an adventure. But Peter wondered why they had to be so vulnerable out there. He wasn't going to relax at all.

At the same time, there was some enticement in the danger, and being naked with Anton. It was strange. He felt the tension in the pit of his stomach. There seemed to be a risk involved every time he did something with Anton lately. And on each occasion, Anton kept pushing the envelope. Peter couldn't help thinking about their adventure in the woods, and that "trust test" on the roof.

He glanced out the car window. He had no idea where he was—someplace north of Seattle. "Is it much further?" he asked. "I'm not anxious or anything. I'm just wondering."

"We're almost there," Anton replied, turning right onto Prentiss Street.

The homes along the poorly lit road weren't much of an improvement over the ramblers and shacks across from the old creek. Anton started to slow down for what looked like a gravel driveway on their left, but then the headlights illuminated two street signs at the intersection: PRENTISS DRIVE and NO OUTLET.

Turning onto Anton's street, they passed a couple of mailboxes on a post. The gravel road beneath them had a few potholes, and Peter was jostled inside the car. On his right, he saw a darkened, run-down, two-story stucco, and straight ahead was a long narrow driveway. The other house was hiding behind some bushes and a tall evergreen. Peter caught only a partial glimpse of shingles on the roof. At the end of the drive was a plate with iridescent numbers: 410.

"Is that your house at the end?" Peter asked.

"Indeed it is, sir," Anton replied with mock formality.

Peter nodded toward the dumpy stucco on his right. "Are those the neighbors with the hot tub?"

"Yeah, that's them. Take a look at my address. Does the number look familiar?"

"Four-ten?"

"Yeah. What does that remind you of?"

Anton pulled into the driveway. Peter got a better look at the squat cedar Shaker. The shades were drawn in the

front windows, but the porch light was on. The house—
along with the yard—looked as if it could use some sprucing
up, but the place seemed habitable.

"Don't you know what that number means?" Anton
pressed. He parked the car in front of the garage. "Four-
ten. It's why I bought the place. That's Gerry's room number
at St. Bartholomew Hall."

"You mean, Gerard Lunt?" Peter asked. "You actually
bought this house because the address matched his room
number?"

"Bingo." Anton grinned at him. "I knew you'd catch
on, Pete."

Peter shrugged and managed to smile at him. He wanted
to ask Anton if he was serious, but decided to just go along
with it.

Anton switched off the headlights and cut the ignition.
"C'mon, let's go inside," he said. "Grab your duffle. I'll
take the groceries."

Without the car engine humming and the oldies music,
he could hear the crickets chirping. The sky above was
full of stars. He told himself everything would be all right
tonight.

Once inside the house, Peter was impressed. It amazed
him that a guy like Anton, only a few years older, could
own and maintain a house—like a regular, responsible adult.
All the furniture in the living room seemed beat-up and
secondhand. But the big-screen TV and VCR looked brand-
new.

Peter put down his duffle. He stopped to gaze at a sword
displayed on the wall, behind the ugly brown sofa.

"That's a Japanese saber from World War Two," Anton
said, stepping up beside Peter and nudging him. "It's identi-
cal to the one Gerard Lunt used when he cut off his friend's
head."

Peter shuddered, but tried to laugh. "Geez, Anton, I'll

have to sleep with the goddamn light on tonight. You really creep me out with that kind of talk. Are you serious?''

Frowning, Anton pulled away from him. ''What do you mean?''

Peter uttered another nervous laugh. ''Well, that story about buying the house because the address is the same as Gerard Lunt's room number, and now this business with the sword, it's all kind of morbid. In fact, it's *beyond* morbid.''

With a wounded expression on his handsome face, Anton stared at him. ''I thought you knew me,'' he murmured. ''It's why I took you to Gerry and Mark's secret place in the woods. Now it's our secret place, too. Some people might call that morbid, but you're not just 'people' to me, Pete. I thought we were friends.''

''We are,'' Peter whispered. ''Only I don't get this thing you have for that murder-suicide.''

''Don't you see? I'm the only living person who really understands what happened between Gerry and Mark that night. No one else has been able to figure out why Gerard did what he did. I'm the only one. It's something I want to share with you, my disciple.'' Anton held him by the shoulders. '' *'You are Peter, and upon this rock I will build my church.'* ''

Wide-eyed, Peter stared at him. The only thing he could do was laugh. ''You're screwing with my head. You're putting me on, aren't you?''

Anton glared at him for a moment. Peter saw such contempt in his eyes. Then Anton suddenly broke into a grin, and he started to chuckle, too. ''Hey, I almost had you totally freaked out, didn't I?''

Before Peter could answer, Anton playfully grabbed him in a headlock. ''Just a horny, hungry, beer-drinking college kid, that's all you are. You're like, *'Forget this, let's have dinner, grab a few beers, and get naked in the hot tub!'* Am I right, knucklehead?''

Anton's hold was like a vise. Peter had to follow along as his friend swung him around in a weird sort of dance. Peter tried to laugh.

Anton let go of him. "C'mon, the beer is this way," he said, heading toward the kitchen in the back of the house. "Plus I want to get out of these stinkin' clothes."

Peter started to follow him, but he stopped in the corridor. Besides the kitchen, there were two other rooms off the hallway: a bathroom and a third room, which was closed off. The door was like no other in the house, an old-fashioned, dark-stained wood with an ornate trim design. Peter had seen the same type of doors in St. Bartholomew Hall, from when the dorm was first built. Some of the janitors' closets still had those original doors.

"Is this your bedroom?" Peter asked, trying the doorknob.

Anton paused in the kitchen entry. "That's just a storage closet. It's locked. C'mon in the kitchen. I'm thirsty. Aren't you?"

"Sure," Peter said. He ambled toward the kitchen, but took one more curious glance over his shoulder at that shut-off room. He noticed something else that was strange. Above the doorway hung a plain wooden crucifix, the same type of cross displayed over the door to every bedroom in St. Bartholomew Hall.

Jack glanced up at the wooden crucifix above Peter's door. He knocked again. "Pete?" he called.

He didn't hear any activity inside the room.

Down the hall, one of the seminarians emerged from his quarters. Jack waved at him. "Hey, Ernie, have you seen Pete Tobin around?"

He shook his head. "Not since this morning, Father." He continued down toward the bathroom.

Jack knocked on three more doors before he found someone else who hadn't gone out for the evening. Tommy Hoang was the only Vietnamese student on the floor, and something of a loner. But Peter hung out with the thin, bookish seminarian once in a while.

Jack caught Tommy studying. "Yes, Father?" he asked in his broken English.

"Tommy, have you seen Pete Tobin tonight?"

He pushed back the long black hair that fell over his forehead. "I saw him in the hall earlier, and I came into his room, while he packed a bag. I didn't stay long."

"Did he say where he was going?" Jack asked.

Tommy shrugged. "No."

"What kind of bag did he pack?"

"Oh, you know, small. Overnight."

"When was this?"

"About three hours ago."

"Thanks, Tommy. Sorry to bother you."

As he started down the hall, Jack could hear Tommy behind him, closing his door. If Peter was spending the night someplace, he'd have needed to sign out with one of the advisers on his floor or the front desk.

Jack heard the TV going in Harvey Zeigler's room. It sounded like an action movie. Machine gun fire and death moans were accompanied by a pulsating soundtrack. Jack knocked on Father Zeigler's door. There was no answer, but suddenly, the TV got switched off.

Jack could hear someone moving around in the room. He knocked again. "Harvey, it's me, Jack," he called. "Sorry to bother you. Can I see you for a minute?"

More rustling. "Hold on," Zeigler finally growled. "Be right there."

Jack waited. He was about to knock again, when the door opened. Harvey Zeigler was wearing a T-shirt. His black pants were unzipped at the top. "What do you want, Jack?"

"Sorry, but I'm looking for Peter Tobin. Did he leave for the night?"

Father Zeigler nodded impatiently. "Yeah, he was trying to sneak off. But I made him sign out."

"Did he say where he was going?"

With a heavy sigh, Zeigler retreated to his desk, while Jack remained in the doorway. He noticed the TV was on, but the screen was blue, indicating a videotape in stop mode.

Harvey Zeigler swiped a piece of paper off the desk. He read off the form. "Checked out at five-twenty. Destination, his parents' house in Seattle, where he's spending the night. Phone number's right here." Scowling, he handed the document to him. "Anything else, Jack?"

He glanced at the form. Under PURPOSE OF TRIP, Peter had written: *Visiting my parents in Seattle for many personal reasons, and Zeigler, you suck.* Jack chuckled.

"Anything else?" Zeigler asked again.

"No, thanks, Harv," Jack said, backing away from the door. "Sorry to interrupt your movie."

Once in his own room, Jack picked up the phone and dialed the Tobins' number. Peter's mother answered. "Hello?"

"Mrs. Tobin?"

"Yes, who's calling?"

"This is Father Murphy from Our Lady of Sorrows. I just want to double-check on something. Pete signed out for the evening, and he said on the form that he was spending the night at home."

"Tonight?" she asked. "Well, he isn't here, and we weren't expecting him."

"Well, I'll look into it," Jack said in his best, soothing voice. "He's probably staying at a friend's house. Most likely, he didn't know the phone number, so he just put down home as the destination. That's not unusual. A lot of the boys have done that."

Jack wondered if she believed one word he was saying.

"I don't understand," Mrs. Tobin remarked. "You're saying you don't know where Peter is? How long has he been gone?"

"Just a couple of hours. He signed out around five-thirty tonight. I'm sure he's at a friend's house. I'll track him down and have him call you. I didn't mean to cause you any unnecessary worry, Mrs. Tobin."

She let out an audible sigh. "But *I am worried,* Father, very worried. After what happened to John Costello last month, I can't help being concerned."

"Mrs. Tobin, Peter signed out on his own," Jack said delicately. At any other college, freshmen weren't held on such a tight leash. "He's a very mature, responsible young man," Jack continued. "I'm sure he's okay. Nevertheless, I'll find out where he is, and get back to you. If, in the meantime, you hear from him, could you please have him call me?"

Hanging up with Mrs. Tobin, Jack knew he hadn't quite convinced her that her son was all right.

He needed convincing himself. It was too much of a coincidence that both Peter and Anton had signed out for the evening. As far as Jack knew, the two of them weren't acquainted with each other. But this killer always kept his relationships with his "martyrs" a secret. Peter lying about the visit to his parents seemed like part of the pattern. All of the unwitting victims had concealed their relationships with the killer.

Jack let himself into Peter's room with his pass key. Switching on the light, he started going through the desk. He wasn't sure what he was looking for, but maybe Peter kept an address book or an appointment book. Perhaps he'd jotted down the phone number of where he was going tonight. Jack paged through Peter's spiral notebooks for school. In the back of one of them, after a section of blank pages, there was writing. Peter had made a few drafts of a letter to Maggie. Three different versions had been crossed out, before he'd seemed to settle for one particular draft:

Dear Maggie,

It's been a couple of weeks now, and I still can't believe Johnny is gone. I know you must hurt as much as I do still. So I've been thinking of you. I've met a guy at school here, and he's been helping me a lot. We've been looking into what really happened, and why Johnny died. I hope it doesn't cause you any pain for me to tell you this, but I'm not giving up until I find out what really happened to Johnny.

This friend of mine is very nice. But he's not Johnny. I still get awfully sad and lonesome for my best friend. So I imagine how you must feel. You probably know this already, but Johnny loved you. He really admired you too. He used to talk about how much you gave up so you could keep the family together and take care of him, etc. He was very proud of you, and he said how lucky he was to be your brother. Anyway, I'm sure you know all this. But I thought I'd tell you anyway.

I hope we can still get together now and then. Thank you again for letting me sit with you at the funeral mass. It made me feel better to be with you.

Peter had apparently struggled with the sign-off, crossing out *Sincerely,* and *Yours Truly,* then settling on *Love, Pete.*

Jack closed the spiral notebook. He'd suspected Peter had been meeting someone across the lake. Was this "helpful" friend Anton Sorenson?

Jack went through another drawer, and found a small envelope with MAGGIE COSTELLO and her return address on the preprinted label. He pulled the letter out and glanced at it:

May 18th

Dear Pete,

   Thank you so much for your wonderful letter. You're such a sweetheart to write to me. Your note made me cry, of course. But it was one of those good cries.
   I've always thought Johnny was very lucky to have you as his best friend. Seriously, Pete, you're one of the nicest guys I know. I think Johnny was a better person because of his friendship with you. . . .

Jack didn't read any more. It was none of his business what Maggie had said in a private letter to Peter Tobin. He couldn't help feeling that Peter had done more for Maggie than he had. The only thing he'd given Maggie Costello was heartache and disappointment.

Jack stashed the letter back in Peter's desk drawer, then tried the next drawer down. He didn't find anything except art supplies, old tests and term papers, and various junk. The search was all too reminiscent of his investigation of John's room after he'd drowned.

He couldn't help thinking that Peter might already be dead.

Jack tried the closet shelf, but all he found were neatly folded sweaters. In his frustration, he started pulling them down from the shelf. He thought Peter might have a secret journal hidden underneath one of the sweaters. Didn't Mrs. McShane say that she'd found Dorothy's diaries in a closet?

He cleared off the whole shelf and found himself standing amid a pile of tangled sweaters on the floor. Jack didn't know what he expected to unearth. He just needed the identity of this "helpful" friend of Peter's. Was it Anton?

He started in on Peter's dresser, going through the drawers. The thin, pewter crucifix standing on top of the bureau tipped over when he slammed the second drawer shut. "Goddamn it," he hissed, leaving Peter's clothes in a mess. He continued his search.

In the bottom drawer, all he found were more art supplies and a sketchbook. Frowning, he pulled out the sketch pad. Nothing was hidden underneath it. Jack flipped through the pages. He glanced at Peter's cartoons: MORE AMAZING AMOEBA ADVENTURES! There were several sketches of Johnny. One page just had renderings of eyes—male and female.

Sighing, Jack flipped to the next page in the tablet. "My God," he murmured.

It was a very detailed pencil drawing of a male figure that appeared godlike, with an ideal physique. Peter had drawn him from the torso up, and given his icon the face of Anton Sorenson.

Anton emerged from his bedroom with a towel wrapped around his waist.

Seated at the breakfast table, Peter snacked on a beer and barbecue potato chips. He tried not to gawk at him.

"Just a quick shower," Anton announced, slapping Peter's shoulder as he passed by. "Then I'll get dinner started. Burgers and taters okay?"

"Sounds great," Peter said. He had to hand it to Anton and the way he was treating this like an ordinary sleepover. He hadn't mentioned Duane since they'd gotten here.

Anton backed up and grabbed the beer out of Peter's hand. He took a sip. "Thanks, bud," he said. Turning around, he let the towel slip, allowing Peter a long look at his buttocks.

His mouth open, Peter couldn't help staring as Anton strutted toward the bathroom. It was almost as if he'd dropped the towel on purpose, and wanted him to look.

Anton left the bathroom door open. Peter heard the pipes squeak, then a rush of water from the showerhead. After a minute, steam drifted out to the hallway. Peter glanced out the kitchen window. He didn't see anything. Anton was right. They were all alone out here.

He wandered toward the living room. Passing through the hallway, he ever-so-casually glanced into the bathroom. Beyond all the steam, he glimpsed Anton's naked image on the other side of the opaque shower curtain.

He didn't want to be caught staring, so he ambled into the living room. He looked out the front window. Nothing. He wondered if he could really relax out here.

He sat down at Anton's desk and looked at a framed photo on display. It was a picture of a slightly younger Anton standing in front of the Vatican. Peter wanted to ask him for a photo. The pictures he'd drawn of Anton were all from memory.

Also on the desk was a pewter beer stein full of pens, pencils, and a pair of scissors. Peter recognized one of the pens, and he plucked it out of the flagon: GOWER GRAPHICS: THE FINE POINT FOR FINE ARTISTS.

How had Anton gotten ahold of one of his special drawing pens? Anton had never been in his room at St. Bart's. Peter didn't lend those pens out. In fact, he'd always had a cow whenever Johnny "borrowed" one from his supply. It had only happened a few times, but Peter was bugged to no end whenever he found one of his special pens in someone else's dorm room. It was a definite sign that Johnny had been there and carelessly left the pen behind.

Dazed, Peter sat at Anton's desk and stared at the pen. He could hear the roar from the shower and Anton whistling.

* * *

"It's Sorenson, Anton, 410 Prentiss Drive in Seattle," Jack repeated into the phone, reading the address he'd written down in his pocket notebook.

"I'm sorry, sir. I don't show a listing for that name."

"You mean, it's an unlisted number?" Jack asked. "I don't want to be pushy, but this is an emergency—"

"I don't show a listing, sir," she said emphatically.

He sighed. "All right, thank you anyway."

Jack disconnected. He started to dial 911 but hesitated. He'd be sending a police car over to Anton's address based on—what—a drawing a teenage boy had made? Bottles of hair products in Anton's bathroom? His own intuition? He wasn't even sure Anton was behind all the deaths.

"Damn it," Jack muttered, hanging up the phone. Once again, he glanced at the Prentiss Drive address in his notebook. It would take about ninety minutes to drive to Seattle. Jack flicked off the lights and hurried out of his room.

Down at the front desk, the seminarian on duty handed Jack the keys to the faculty garage.

There was a full moon, and a cool breeze swept off the lake. Cutting across the dark, near-deserted employee lot, Jack headed toward the two-car garage. He unlocked the side door and stepped into the garage. "Oh, shit," he muttered.

Both faculty cars were gone. The sign-out sheets on a clipboard by the door showed the cars had been reserved until 10:30.

Jack slammed the garage door shut and backtracked across the employee lot. He glanced at the four cars parked there. Duane's minivan stood out among them. Jack stopped and stared for a moment at that Viking goddess-warrior painted on the side door.

He really didn't have any other choice.

* * *

Duane's key chain had a silver-plated Playboy bunny emblem on it. "Don't lose these, padre," Duane said, handing the keys to Jack. Wearing cutoffs and a T-shirt, he stood in the doorway to his basement apartment. "They're my only set," he continued. "You'll probably need to fuel it up, too."

"Thanks," Jack said, nodding.

He'd told Duane that a dying man needing last rites in Seattle's Harbor View Hospital had specifically asked for his *old friend, Father Murphy,* to administer those rites. The doctors didn't think the elderly man would make it through the night.

"You don't happen to have a map of Seattle, do you?" Jack asked.

"Yeah, check the glove compartment. And hey, by the way, padre, I've got a beef with one of your guys. I caught Pete Tobin monkeying around in the ol' Viking Van this afternoon."

"Peter? When was this?"

"Around four-thirty. I was coming back from the campus side. Some joker called me, saying my old arrest sheet from twelve years ago—complete with mug shots—was posted in the lobby of St. Matthew Hall. Well, I got over there, and the guy was lying. Some stupid prank. Anyway, I came back, and found Pete Tobin messing around in my van."

"What exactly was he doing?" Jack asked.

"I think he was after something in my glove compartment. I won't say what. But tell Pete that it ain't there anymore. I took it out. And next time he tries breaking into my van, I'm taking him for a ride. Anyway, the vehicle's clean, Jack. It's okay for you to drive it."

Jack wasn't sure what Duane was talking about. It sounded as if Peter had been trying to break into the van for some dope. But Jack couldn't picture Peter Tobin doing that. Then again, Johnny had been full of surprises, too.

"You shouldn't have too tough a time finding that hospital in Seattle," Duane said. "But listen, Jack. Don't get stopped by a cop, because my tabs are expired."

Jack managed a smile. "Well, thanks, Duane. I owe you." He turned and hurried toward the stairs.

"I hope you get to this guy before he dies," Duane called.

Jack glanced over his shoulder and waved to him. "Me, too, Duane. Me, too."

Peter listened to the humming pipes and the shower's steady torrent. Every once in a while, Anton let out a satiated growl.

Peter couldn't put the pen down, nor could he move from the desk. Anton had claimed that he didn't know Johnny. So how did this Gower Graphics pen get here?

He told himself that Johnny could have given the pen to one of those sophomores he was seeing. It easily could have fallen into Anton's hands though one of them. He couldn't label Anton a liar—or a murderer—simply because he'd picked up a pen somewhere.

Still, Peter could almost see Johnny, sitting at this same desk. He couldn't help thinking that he was repeating everything Johnny had done with Anton. Had they had a special "secret friendship," too?

Peter got to his feet. He stared at the open bathroom door. The escaping steam clouded up the little hallway. He wondered about that mysterious "storage room" next door. What was hidden in there?

When Anton had been undressing in his bedroom earlier, Peter had heard him rattle some keys.

He moved through the hallway and kitchen, then into Anton's bedroom. A light from the open closet was all he had to go by, but Peter found a set of keys on top of the dresser. They were beside a folded-up cell phone and Anton's wallet.

He needed to move quickly. Anton had been in the shower for almost five minutes. He could be finishing up any second now.

As Peter crept back to the corridor, the steam from the bathroom enveloped him. He tried one key after another on the "storage room" lock. One finally slipped into the groove, but it wouldn't turn. Peter kept trying, twisting and forcing the key—until it snapped, breaking off in the lock.

"Crap," he muttered. Panicked, he glanced over toward the bathroom, where the shower was still churning.

The key ring in his fist, Peter retreated back to Anton's darkened bedroom. He set the keys on his dresser. Anton was going to notice the broken key in the door—maybe not right away, but eventually.

Peter imagined Anton asking him, *"What were you thinking?"*

And what was he thinking anyway? Was he nuts? Anton was no more a murderer than he was. He'd have to come clean about the keys. He'd just be honest and tell his friend what happened. He was a little paranoid, and hadn't been thinking right for a few minutes. He'd had a pretty crazy day. Maybe they'd even have a good laugh about it.

While they were being so honest, he'd ask Anton about the pen. There was sure to be a logical explanation. He trusted Anton.

But if that were entirely true, why hadn't he really closed his eyes for that "trust test" up on the roof? Why had he checked the ashtray in the minivan to make sure Duane really smoked Marlboros? In truth, he wanted to trust Anton, but he couldn't completely.

At a time when Peter thought he'd lost everything, Anton had come along and rescued him. This sexy, handsome senior wanted to be his friend, and he was helping him track down Johnny's killer. If something didn't feel quite right about Anton and their relationship, Peter didn't want to question it.

He gazed at his shadowy reflection in the mirror above the dresser. In back of him, the closet door was open. The light was on, and he could see the clothes bunched together on hangers. One garment design stood out among the others: a blackwatch pattern.

Turning around, Peter started toward the closet. He pulled the lumber jacket off its hanger.

At first, he thought Anton had unpacked his duffle bag and hung up Duane's jacket. But this mackinaw was different. The label inside was from Eatons department store in Vancouver, British Columbia. This was Anton's jacket.

Peter examined it and wondered why Anton had never mentioned owning a lumber jacket exactly like the one they'd been trying to track down for so many days. While Anton claimed to be going from room to room in an exhaustive search, this jacket had been hanging in his closet all the time.

One of the things about his new best friend that Peter never wanted to question was his amazing timing that afternoon he'd fished him out of Lake Leroy. Anton had arrived upon the scene just moments after the attack—or so he claimed.

Peter stared at the mackinaw in his hands. The other jacket was a phony. This was the genuine article. This was the jacket Anton had been wearing when he'd attacked him on the tributary crossing.

Peter heard the water shut off in the shower, the pipes squeaking again. He dropped the jacket. He hurried to the dresser and grabbed the keys.

"Hey," Anton called. "You getting bored out there?"

Peter stepped into the kitchen in time to see Anton poke his head out the bathroom doorway.

"I'm fine," he said nervously. He clutched the keys in his hand.

Anton leaned farther out the bathroom doorway. He was working a towel over himself, but his chest was still glistening wet. Through the steam, Peter could see the muscular curved line around his abdomen and the top of his thigh. "I'll be just a couple of more minutes," he said.

Peter nodded. "Take your time," he said. "But . . . um, would you mind closing the door? With all the steam, it's like a sauna in this kitchen." He smiled and fanned himself.

Anton gave him a crooked grin, then ducked back into the bathroom and closed the door.

Peter thought he was going to be sick. Taking a deep breath, he shoved Anton's keys in his pocket and started toward the hallway. He crept past the bathroom door to the living room, where he'd left his duffle. He unzipped his bag and pulled out the lumber jacket he'd found in the Dumpster. Was it really Duane's jacket or a fake?

Anton had planted it in his head that they should hunt through all the Dumpsters. He'd even said the old mackinaw was probably purchased at a local thrift store. Was that where Anton had bought it? He'd slipped him a note the day of Johnny's funeral, saying he'd checked the Dumpsters outside several campus buildings. Maybe he'd only been through one—when he'd buried this decoy jacket in the Dumpster behind St. Bartholomew Hall.

Peter reached into the pocket and pulled out the empty Marlboro pack, Duane's brand. He wondered if Anton had even been inside Duane's room. Was the ski mask Anton had shown him really Duane's—or his own? He'd been the one who had presented Duane as their main suspect. He could have picked this empty cigarette pack and those butts out of Duane's van. Peter remembered the bag of marijuana in Duane's glove compartment. Was that where Anton had gotten the stuff they'd smoked on the roof? Had he found Duane's stash while he was planting Johnny's shirt in the minivan?

Peter heard the hair dryer starting up. He stuffed the jacket back in his bag, then hoisted it up. He glanced out the front window at Anton's car in the driveway. If he got out now, Anton might not hear the car over his hair dryer.

Maybe he was being paranoid. But he didn't think Anton could really answer any of his questions. His hero couldn't explain it all away. And if he was right about Anton, this was his last chance to escape.

Peter pulled the keys out of his pocket. With a look over his shoulder at the bathroom, he opened the front door and stepped outside. His heart was racing and he still felt as if he were going to be ill. He heard Anton's hair dryer wheezing. Quietly, he closed the door behind him.

Hurrying toward Anton's Toyota, he fumbled with the keys. For a minute, he couldn't find the right one. Finally, he got the car door unlocked. He opened it, then threw his duffle bag on the front seat. Glancing back at the house, he saw a shadow pass across the living-room window. He dropped the keys. "Shit!" he hissed.

Peter stooped down to snatch them off the ground. Just then, he heard the front door opening. "Pete?"

He straightened up and saw Anton on the front porch, hands on his hips. He'd thrown on a pair of jeans, but was shirtless. "What are you doing out here?" he asked.

Peter's first instinct was to make a run for it. But he froze. Wide-eyed, he stared at Anton. "Um, I noticed you left your headlights on," he heard himself say. "So I—I came out here to turn them off."

Scratching his bare chest, Anton ambled toward him. "Really? I could have sworn I turned them off."

"Nope, they were on," Peter insisted. He stole a glance

at his duffle on the front seat of the Toyota. He shut the car door and the interior light went off. "I didn't want you to have a dead battery," he said.

"Well, thanks, partner," Anton replied. He slung his arm around Peter's shoulder. He smelled of soap and shampoo. "Why don't you come on back in the house? Help me get the burgers on."

Peter glanced down the driveway. It was too late for a mad dash. Anton was squeezing his shoulder. His only chance was to pretend he didn't know anything, then make an escape sometime later when Anton's guard was down.

"Pete? Aren't you coming?"

"Yeah, sure," Peter said, nodding more times than necessary. He let Anton lead him toward the front step.

"Can I have my keys back, please?" Anton asked, holding out his hand.

Managing a smile, Peter surrendered the keys. Then he stepped back into the house.

Anton followed him inside and locked the door.

Chapter Twenty-two

When Jack stepped out of the van to fill up the tank, the clerk came to the door of the gas station's minimart. The guy must have wondered what a priest was doing, driving a minivan with a seminude Viking goddess-warrior painted on the side door.

The skinny, young man with a ponytail and goatee ambled toward the minivan, grinning at Jack. "You really a priest?"

"Yes, I am," Jack said, setting the automatic lock on the gas nozzle. "You don't happen to know where Prentiss Drive is, do you?"

Jack came around the side of the van and opened the glove compartment. He pulled out a Seattle map, and some condom packages fell to the car floor.

"Holy shit," the clerk muttered.

Jack unfolded the map. "Could you please just help me find this place?"

* * *

"According to the guy at the gas station here, I'm about thirty minutes away from Anton's house." Jack stood in a phone booth by the side of the minimart. Moths circled around the light overhead. "Anyway, I'm on my way there. I just wanted to make sure you're okay."

"I'm fine," Maggie said. "Thanks, Jack."

"Have you heard from your friend?"

"Steve? No, but he should be here in about an hour. I'll be okay until then."

"Listen, if I'm not able to find Anton or Peter at this place, would it be all right if I came by?"

"Sure," Maggie said. "Did I give you my home address?"

"Yeah, it's on the back of your business card. Lake City Way exit, right?"

"Right."

"Will I be interrupting anything between you and this— Steve?"

"No, Jack. You wouldn't be interrupting anything."

"Good," he said.

"You sound like you care."

"I do, Maggie," he whispered. "You know I do."

He realized it was wrong to admit that to her—and over a pay phone in a gas station, no less. It was hardly the time or place. He didn't hear anything on the other end of the line. "Maggie? Are you still there?"

"I wouldn't hang up for the world right now."

"We'll have to talk about it later, okay?" he said. "Listen, whether or not I'm able to find Pete at this spot, you and I should get together tonight. It's time to tell the police what we know. We shouldn't wait any longer."

"You're right," Maggie said. "Maybe we can go to this friend of Steve's. It might help to have an 'in' with someone on the force."

"Good idea," he said. "Well, listen, I need to hit the road. I'll call you within the hour."

"Thanks, Jack," she said. "Good luck, and be careful."

"You, too, Maggie," he said. Then he hung up.

The hamburgers sizzled on the griddle. They'd been frozen, and still needed some time to cook. Anton spread some Tater Tots on a cookie sheet and shoved it in the oven. He'd put on a T-shirt and now had a dish towel draped over his shoulder. "Chow should be in about fifteen minutes," he announced. He reached for his beer on the kitchen counter.

Peter sat at the breakfast table. The Miller Lite and the barbecue potato chips were still in front of him, both untouched since he'd come back inside the house. "You sure I can't do anything to help?" he asked, a bit awkwardly. He was trying too hard to act as if nothing was wrong.

"Nope. I've got it under control," Anton said, leaning against the kitchen counter.

Peter managed to smile. He stared at the handsome senior and wondered how he could be so evil and scheming. Was there a chance he was wrong about Anton?

He started toward the table, and Peter flinched. Reaching into the potato chip bag, Anton squinted at him. "Are you okay, Pete? You seem tense."

"I'm fine," he said, with a shrug and a little laugh.

"No, you're not," Anton said, munching on a couple of chips. "I could tell earlier, when I was talking about the saber I have on display in my living room. You think it's weird that I have such a strong connection to the Gerard Lunt case, don't you?"

"I wasn't thinking that," Peter said. "Honest."

Anton wiped his hands on the dish towel. "Remember I told you how I spent hours and hours in room 410 at St. Bart's? I figured out some things while I was in there. I realized why it happened, why Gerard Lunt did what he did.''

''Yeah?'' Peter murmured.

''Have you ever heard of St. Mark and St. Marcellian?''

Peter shook his head again. He took a furtive glance at a knife Anton had left on the counter.

Anton moved to the refrigerator and started to pull out condiments. ''Well, Mark and Marcellian were twins, high-ranking in the Roman army. They came under a lot of pressure to abandon their Christianity. It was a *'do it or die'* thing. Even their wives and families were urging them to renounce their beliefs. But Mark and Marcellian wouldn't compromise their faith, and they were beheaded.''

Staring at him, Peter nodded. ''Huh, interesting,'' was all he could say.

Anton set the ketchup, mustard, and pickles on the countertop. ''That's why Gerard Lunt sliced off his friend Mark's head,'' he explained. ''And Gerry jumped out of that fourth-floor window, because St. Gerard of Csabad was thrown from a great height into the Danube. You know, witnesses who saw Gerry's broken body on the ground that night say it looked as if he was hurling himself toward Lake Leroy. In fact, Gerard Lunt landed only a few hundred yards from the lake's edge.''

Peter squirmed in the kitchen chair. He wondered why Anton was talking this way—as if he were reading from a book or teaching a class.

''Do you understand what Gerry was trying to do?'' he asked.

''I guess,'' Peter replied, giving him a wary look. ''But he was crazy.''

''That's what they said about all the great prophets and leaders,'' Anton retorted. ''The only difference between the so-called 'nuts' and the great men of history is that the great men had people who understood them, people who carried on their work. Gerard left behind those locks of hair for someone to find. They're relics from a pair of martyrs. I was meant to find them. I was meant to carry on Gerard's work.''

''To—make martyrs?'' Peter whispered.

''That's right, Pete.''

''Was there ...'' He hesitated. ''Was there a St. John who drowned?''

Anton smiled and nodded.

Peter didn't move or say a word.

Anton ambled toward the refrigerator. ''You left my coat in a heap on the bedroom floor,'' he said. ''Didn't your mom teach you to pick up after yourself?''

Peter couldn't respond. He glanced at that knife on the counter again.

Anton opened the refrigerator. ''So, do you want cheese on your burger?''

He pulled out a package of hamburger buns, along with some cheese slices. ''I'll put some cheese on there for you.''

Peter took a deep breath. ''That shirt of Johnny's you planted in Duane's van,'' he heard himself say. ''Was Johnny wearing it the night you killed him?''

Anton let out a little laugh. ''No, I'm preserving the shirt he wore that night. It's a holy relic now.'' He set the food on the counter. ''The shirt you found was something he left behind here a few months ago—one night after I fucked him.''

Peter cringed. ''So you had a secret relationship with Johnny, just like we have, right?''

Anton chuckled again. ''Well, not *just like* the one we have. I haven't fucked you yet.''

''Yes, you have,'' Peter whispered. ''You've been fucking with me for a while now.''

''Huh,'' Anton said, grinning. ''I guess I have at that. But you have to admit, I've helped you, too. I was there at a time when you really needed me. It was the same way with Johnny. He didn't want to be a homosexual. Yet he was messing around with all those sophomores on my floor, and I was screwing him. Plus, well, you were his best friend, and he knew you were queer. But he just didn't want to be.''

Anton moved over to the stove and flipped the hamburgers. ''So one day I told him where to get his hair cut, and which girl to ask for. Her name was Jonie. I made sure she took Johnny home and helped him feel more like a real man again. She would have done anything for me. I was screwing them both at the same time, but neither one knew.''

''And she's dead now?''

''St. Joan was burned to death,'' Anton answered.

''Is that how you picked them?'' Peter asked. ''Because of their names?''

He nodded, then opened the oven door. ''Taters are almost done.'' He tossed a couple of hamburger buns on the oven rack. ''It's not just the names, though that's what first attracts me to them. They have to be alone and vulnerable. They have to need rescuing—like you did when I met you. I guess you could say I'm their savior. Yours, too.''

''Why didn't you just drown me after you pushed me off the crossing that afternoon?'' he asked quietly.

''Because it's not how you were meant to die, Pete. If you looked up a list of saints, you'll find a lot of St. Peters. But none of them were drowned.'' He walked over to the broom closet. ''Do you know how St. Peter was martyred?''

Peter watched him pull out something that looked like an ax handle, only there wasn't any blade on it. ''Wasn't he crucified upside down?'' he murmured.

''Yeah, that's St. Peter, the apostle,'' Anton said. He set the long, thick wooden handle on the counter, then checked the oven again. ''A couple of more minutes,'' he announced.

Anton leaned back against the sink. "Do you know the story of St. Peter Chanel?"

Peter shook his head.

"Well, he was the first martyr of the South Seas," Anton said, folding his arms. "He was a young priest with the missionaries in Fortuna in the Pacific. This was the 1800s, and cannibalism had recently been forbidden among the natives. Peter Chanel converted and baptized many natives, including the local ruler's son. Well, this chief, he was very jealous of Peter Chanel, and he felt threatened by him. So one night, when Peter's fellow missionaries were away, he sent his men to club Peter Chanel to death."

Paralyzed with fear, Peter watched him reach for the ax handle. "Don't," he whispered.

"Pete, I want you to know," he said. "I'm not jealous of you."

The last thing Peter saw was Anton bringing the makeshift club down toward his head.

Maggie was in her bedroom, changing out of her old jeans and an R.E.M. T-shirt. She couldn't stop thinking about Pete Tobin. She carried around this feeling of dread like a knot in the pit of her stomach. She remembered Pete writing her a couple of weeks back, and he'd mentioned a new friend who was helping him get by. Was it this Anton character?

She put on a pair of black jeans and a rust-colored pullover. She was fixing her hair back with a barrette when she heard the noise, a loud crash in her kitchen.

Maggie froze. Someone else was in the house. She stood paralyzed for another minute, waiting for the sound of footsteps downstairs. But she didn't hear anything.

She crept to the phone at her bedside. Lifting the receiver from the cradle, she listened to the dial tone. At least they hadn't cut the line yet. She wanted to call the police, but couldn't be sure someone had really broken into the house. Except for the crash, she hadn't heard any more noise down there.

Maggie gently hung up the phone, then she tiptoed across the hall to Johnny's room. After grabbing his old baseball bat from the back of his closet, she went to the top of the stairs. Clutching the bat, Maggie started down the stairway, aware of every creak. She didn't see anyone in the living room, nothing unusual; nothing had been disturbed. She cautiously inched toward the kitchen.

The neighbor's cat darted in front of her. For a moment, Maggie thought her heart had stopped. "Goddamn it, Sid," she muttered.

She saw the broken cereal bowl on the floor, beside a saucepan and ladle. On the kitchen counter, the drain rack was askew. The stupid cat had knocked into it.

Maggie glanced over at the kitchen door and the windows—all closed. She wondered how the cat could have gotten into the house. Had it followed someone else inside?

Maggie still had the bat poised as she stepped around to the pantry. The basement door was open. She'd given the cellar a once-over earlier—to make sure no one was hiding down there. But she hadn't checked the windows. She'd never opened the cellar windows. It was a one-room basement, with a furnace and washer and dryer. She'd stored some boxes down there from the move, mostly old clothes, and some Christmas decorations.

Maggie switched on the light and descended the basement stairs. From the distance, she couldn't see anything behind the furnace, just shadows. She tightened her grip on the bat. The two windows were small and close to the ceiling, but a good-sized man could have easily crawled through one and hoisted himself down.

Kicking aside an empty laundry basket, Maggie reached up for the first window. It was locked. She couldn't get past the sensation that someone was watching her from behind. She glanced over her shoulder toward that dark area behind the furnace. Nothing. Maggie moved to the second window and gave it a tug. The window swung open easily. The lock was broken. She noticed paw prints on top of a Bekins Storage box under the window ledge.

Maggie wasn't sure how long the window latch had been broken. Had it happened earlier today? Sighing, she backed away from the window. She couldn't fix the latch, not right now.

Carrying Johnny's bat, she turned and retreated up the basement stairs. At least there was a lock on the basement door—one of those flimsy button-on-the-knob devices, but it beat nothing. She pushed in the lock.

Maggie took another look around the kitchen and living room. She even checked the front hall closet. Returning to the kitchen, she found Mr. Sidney Jenkins on the counter. She had to put down the baseball bat for a minute so she could scoop up the cat. She opened the back door. "Okay, Sid," she muttered. "O-U-T." She set Mr. Sidney Jenkins on the stoop and gave him a gentle push.

The phone rang. Maggie stepped back into the kitchen and grabbed it on the second ring. "Hello?"

"Sweetheart?"

"Oh, hi, Steve," she said. She closed the kitchen door and double-locked it. "I left you a message a few minutes ago, but you probably haven't gotten it. Where are you?"

"On my way. I should be there in twenty or twenty-five minutes. Are you all right?"

"Fine. The neighbor's stupid cat just gave me a heart attack, that's all." She took another glance out the window. "Listen, Father Murphy is coming over later. He thinks it would be a good idea if we went to the police after all. He has a lead on this guy. He thinks it's a senior from the seminary, a guy named Anton."

"Really?" Steve said. "Well, wait just a sec."

Maggie heard him muttering to someone.

Then he got back on the line. "Sweetheart? Sorry, I was talking to Neil, my buddy on the force here." His voice dropped to a whisper. "I haven't said anything to him yet. Want him to come over with me? Might help if we talked to someone I know. How about it?"

"Yeah, thanks, that's a good idea," Maggie said.

"Maybe we'll send over a patrol car, someone to keep you company until we get there. I'd sure feel better. What do you think?"

"Well, why don't we wait until Jack—Father Murphy is here before we tell your friend about this? He has all the information the police will need on this Anton character. Let's just wait for Father Murphy."

"You sure?" Steve asked.

"Yes, Steve. I'm sure. I'll see you soon."

"Maggie, I think you're making a big mistake. Why do we have to wait for this priest? Why won't you let *me* make sure you're safe?"

"I'd rather just wait for Father Murphy, that's all," she said stiffly.

He let out a long sigh. "Fine. Be stubborn. You'll wait for the priest, all alone there. I don't like it. I don't it at all. I'm leaving now, Maggie."

"I'll be okay, Steve."

"I hope you're right, sweetheart. I hope I'm not the one who has to call a priest when I get there."

Chapter Twenty-three

Jack almost missed Prentiss Street. He'd been speeding along the poorly lit, creekside road for nearly ten minutes now. On the passenger seat beside him, the map was folded over and marked. It fluttered from the wind sweeping through the open window. Jack couldn't read it anyway with just the dashboard light. He was beginning to think he was lost until he spotted the turnoff.

He veered left onto Prentiss Street at such a speed, he thought the Viking van might tip over. His stomach seemed to drop for a moment. But Jack straightened out the wheels, then followed the road until he saw the sign for Prentiss Drive. He slowed down and steered onto the thin, gravel drive. He switched off the headlights. The van rocked and pivoted on the rough pathway. In the moonlight he could see the dilapidated two-story stucco on his right. Straight ahead, the road became even thinner. Over to the side, in front of some overgrown bushes, a little plaque was spiked into the ground. The numbers were iridescent: 410.

Jack crawled to a stop. He cut the engine, then opened his door and stepped outside. Staying close to the shadowy bushes, Jack scurried up the driveway. He noticed a couple of lights on inside Anton's rambler, but it didn't appear as if anyone was home. There was no car in the driveway. The place seemed so deathly still.

He snuck around back. The kitchen light was on. Skulking up to the door, he peeked through the windowpane. He could see one of the chairs from the dinette set tipped over on the floor.

Jack tried the door. Locked. He stepped back and checked the windows. They were all closed. Snaking through the bushes against the house, he struggled with a couple of them, but they wouldn't budge. He peered into the window of a darkened bedroom. Only the closet light was on.

Jack gave the window a tug and it moved. Then it seemed to catch on something. He forced it, and the wood creaked as it pinched against the guides. If Anton was home, he could certainly hear the noise. Jack kept pushing at the window, then he hoisted himself up and crawled through the opening.

Once inside, he brushed himself off and glanced around the bedroom. On the wall across from the bed was a framed series of sixteenth-century art prints: three panels showing the death of St. John the Baptist—in grisly detail. There was John kneeling before his executioner; a gory rendering of his decapitation; and finally, Salome being presented with the severed head on a platter. Jack winced as he studied the reproductions. He wondered why anyone would want this kind of artwork in their home, not to mention their bedroom.

As he moved on toward the kitchen, he smelled something burning on the stove. A couple of hamburger patties, charred and shriveled up, were sitting on the griddle. The stove and oven had been turned off.

A steady drip emitted from the faucet. In the sink, someone

had dumped a cookie sheet full of burnt-up nuggets that must have been Tater Tots.

Mystified, Jack glanced at the tipped-over chair by the breakfast table. A beer can had been spilled too. It made a puddle on the floor.

He crept through a hallway that led to the living room. Stopping by the bathroom, he noted a couple of Vita Z hair products on the corner of the tub.

There was another door in the hallway. Jack tried the knob, but it didn't budge. Part of a key had broken off inside the lock. The door wasn't like any other in the place; it must have come from another house or an antique store.

He gave the doorknob one final, futile tug, then headed into the living room. He didn't see anything unusual: a few votive candles here and there, and a couple of antique mounted holders on the wall. Something had been on display over the brown sofa. But it was gone now.

To the right of the front entrance was a set of doors. Jack opened the first one, a closet. Among the jackets and coats, he found another priest's outfit, a full cassock. He also noticed something beneath a sweatshirt hanging from one of the coat hooks. Moving the sweatshirt aside, Jack fingered the semitranslucent clown mask. It hung from the hook by an elastic band in the back.

Jack tried the next door. Locked. He pulled out his wallet. He didn't have any credit cards, so he tried to trip the lock with his laminated driver's license. The license kept bending as he wedged it into the door crack.

Exasperated, Jack retreated to the kitchen and searched through the drawers until he found a knife. On his way back toward the living room, he stopped at the other locked door, the one with the crucifix over it. Using the knife, he tinkered with the lock. He kept jiggling the knob. Nothing seemed to be happening. "Oh, for God's sakes," Jack muttered. He kept thinking about Pete and Mrs. Tobin. He thought of

Maggie, alone in her house, waiting. He grew impatient with every wasted minute.

"Fuck it," he whispered under his breath. Jack tossed the knife on the ground, took a step back, and kicked in the door.

The old door split as it slammed open. Splinters flew in the air. If Anton was anywhere in the house, he certainly heard the noise.

Jack found the light switch on the wall. It was the old-fashioned type of switch plate with a button that popped out below the one he pressed. He hadn't seen a light switch like that since the sixties.

In fact, the entire room was caught in a time warp from before the sixties, duplicating a dorm room from St. Bartholomew Hall. Jack guessed that the era captured here was the forties. The battered desk had an old-fashioned study lamp, a couple of fountain pens in a shaving mug, bottles of ink, and a writing tablet. Over the desk, a stack of vintage schoolbooks lined the shelf, along with a standing crucifix. One of the books that caught Jack's eye was titled *The Register of Christian Saints*. A doily covered the top of the tall dresser, where a pocket watch had been placed—along with a bulky set of nail clippers, and a razor-and-brush shaving kit.

Jack gazed at the single bed, with its off-white coverlet that had rows of tiny raised fabric knobs. There was another crucifix on the wall above the bed's headboard, but it was slightly off-centered.

Jack recognized the room. He'd seen a picture of it in that police gazette newspaper from Anton's desk.

Anton had painstakingly recreated the room where Gerard Lunt had killed his friend and then himself. Every detail was there, from the button-type light switch plates to the off-center crucifix. Anton had seen to everything.

There was one significant difference. A high wooden table

stood in the center of the room by the window. An altar apron had been draped over it.

As Jack approached the table, he saw a photo album, surrounded by small, polished wooden boxes that looked like jewelry cases. He counted nine of them, and noticed a different name wood-burnt onto every one of the lids. A cross had been etched above each of the martyrs' names. They were all there: *Oliver, Julian, Dorothy, Joan, John, Lucy.*

He didn't know about two others, *Stephen* and *Agnes*. But *Peter* was also among the names.

Jack swallowed hard, then picked up the box labeled JOAN. He pried off the lid and stared at three cleaned, polished human teeth on a patch of black silk. Tears filled his eyes as he put the box back on the table. He reached for the case with John's name on it. He gazed at the small bones that had been extracted from Johnny's toes. Jack had to swallow his anger and pain.

He didn't want to look inside the container with Peter's name burned on the lid. But he needed to know if Pete was dead. He held his breath for a moment, then opened the box. Empty.

There was a good chance that Peter could be alive. Anton's altar of relics was not yet complete.

Jack opened the photo album to one of the pages near the middle.

Pressed under the clear, protective plastic was a patch of rose-colored silk fabric. A little piece of paper had been slipped between the plastic sheet and the material. It was a typewritten label: RELIC OF ST. DOROTHY — FEB. 8TH.

Jack paged through the album. There was a piece of Oliver Theron's blue jeans, and under the label ST. LUCY — MAY 6TH, Anton had pressed part of the white collar and brown polyester fabric that must have been a section of her waitress uniform.

Jack found a patch of maroon fabric for ST. JOAN — MAY 25TH. He could still see Jonie wearing that maroon pullover when she'd talked to him outside the chapel's confessionals, just hours before she was "martyred."

He heard a noise, a banging that came from some other part of the house.

Jack put down the album, then hurried out of the room. He listened for the noise again. In the duration of silence, he glanced down at the floor and picked up the knife he'd discarded earlier. He didn't move for another few moments.

Then he heard it again, a strange thud, almost like something pounding against a wall. It seemed to come from below.

Jack moved over to that other locked door. Was it access to a basement? He tried to trip the lock with the knife, but it looked like a dead bolt. There was no tinkering with it.

Biting his lip, Jack worked on the lock. He heard the rapping sound again. It was definitely coming from the other side of this door.

Jack put the knife down on the floor. He backed up, then kicked at the door, right by the lock. He heard something splinter, and for a moment, he wasn't quite sure if it was the door frame or his foot. He felt a shooting pain as he stepped back again to give the door another try. He decided to use his shoulder this time.

Jack slammed against the door, and it gave a little. He heard a crack again. He tried one more time. As the door flew open, a huge chunk of the door frame broke off—along with the metal lock receptacle.

Jack got his breath back. He picked up the knife and stepped over the large splinters of wood on the landing to the basement stairs. His foot hurt like hell every time he put weight on it. He found the light switch and hobbled down the stairs to the dank, dim cellar. It smelled like chemicals. He saw a long, battered freezer at the foot of the stairs. A chain lock was wrapped around the handles.

There was a worktable in the center of the room, with a fluorescent light above it. Jack pulled the light string. His eyes narrowed at the collection of surgical cutting tools and small saws. There were empty soaking pans, a measuring cup, bottles of hydrochloric acid, and thick rubber gloves. Rolled up on the corner of the worktable was a denim shirt. Jack unfolded it. He saw a name tag sewn inside the collar: PETER TOBIN. Bloodstains ran down the left side of the shirt.

Suddenly, the pounding started again. It was so close now. Jack glanced back at the oblong freezer, and his heart sank. Was Peter locked in there?

"Oh, Jesus," he murmured. Jack put down the knife and moved toward the freezer. He stared at that chain lock wound around the handles. "Pete?" he called.

More banging. Jack stopped dead. The noise was coming from behind a door to the left of the freezer, by the foot of the stairs. Jack saw the door move; the bolt across the top was visibly straining.

Quickly, he unfastened the latch and opened the door. Peter Tobin fell onto him. He had a deep cut on his head. The blood trailed down the side of his face and neck to his undershirt. Heavy gray tape covered his mouth. His hands had been tied behind him, and his feet were bound together with the same thick tape. Peter's body was soaked with sweat. His eyes rolled back as he trembled in Jack's arms.

Jack pulled him to the stairs and set him down. He peeled the tape off his mouth. Dazed, Peter gasped for air.

Jack retrieved the knife and cut away at the tape around Peter's ankles and wrists.

"It's Anton," Peter cried, panic-stricken. "Anton—he killed Johnny."

"I know," Jack said, examining the cut on Peter's head. "I've got to get you to a doctor."

"Where is he? Where's Anton?"

"He's not here," Jack said, pulling Peter up to his feet. "C'mon, let me help you upstairs."

With his sore foot, Jack grimaced in pain at every step. But he managed to steer Peter up the stairs. "Can you see okay, Pete?" he asked.

"Everything's a little blurry," he said weakly.

Jack guided him toward the sofa. "Don't close your eyes," he said. "You might have a concussion. Don't fall asleep on me, Pete, whatever you do."

Jack sat him down on the arm of the sofa, then glanced around for a phone.

"It's gone," Peter muttered.

Jack turned to him. "What?"

Peter was squinting at the mounted antique holders on the wall. "He took it down," Peter said. "Anton took the sword."

Sitting in a hard-back chair near the front window, Maggie waited for Steve and his friend to show up. The baseball bat leaned against the chair leg. Maggie kept the lights low in the living room so she'd have a clearer look outside. The desk lamp was on—shining down on the picture of Johnny and her. The flickering television made part of the room swim in an eerie colored light.

Pretty Woman was on. Maggie had hoped it would distract her, and pass the time. The sound was off. She'd kept turning down the volume every time she heard a noise in the house. Maggie had finally decided to leave it on mute. Right now, Julia Roberts was trying on clothes.

As Maggie gazed out the window, she secretly hoped Jack would come by first. The fact that he hadn't called yet meant something was probably holding him up at Anton's place. She wasn't sure whether or not that was a good sign.

Maybe he'd found Pete. She hoped Johnny's friend was okay. Pete had been such a comfort to her, sitting by her side at the funeral Mass. A part of Johnny was still alive in him. She prayed he wasn't hurt.

Maggie sighed and glanced at her watch.

She heard a noise. It seemed to come from the bushes in back of the house. She told herself it was the stupid cat again, or maybe just a raccoon.

Maggie stood up and grabbed the bat. She started for the kitchen, then stopped dead. Someone darted past the window.

Maggie gasped. For a few seconds, she couldn't even move. She hadn't seen his face. He was just a blur, a man in a dark jacket and jeans.

She couldn't call the police. The phone was in the kitchen. He'd see her through the window.

A tapping started. He was gently knocking on the kitchen door.

Uncertain, Maggie tightened her grip on the baseball bat. The rapping became louder.

She inched toward the kitchen until she could see the back-door window. She heard him whispering urgently, "Maggie? Maggie, let me in!"

Stepping closer to the door, Maggie saw his face in the window. For a moment, she didn't recognize him, then she let out a sigh. "Steve? Oh, my God . . ."

She unlocked the door and flung it open. "You scared the hell out of me!" she cried. "Where's the car? Why did you sneak up on me like that?"

He shushed her, then came inside and quietly closed the door. "If this Anton character is watching the house, I don't want him to know I'm here. I parked a block away and snuck through the back bushes."

Maggie still clutched the bat. Her other hand was over her heart. "Where's your policeman friend?" she asked.

"He should be here in about fifteen minutes." Steve stood close to her. He smiled. "God, you look good. I'm so glad you're okay."

He kissed her on the lips, then started to embrace her. But Maggie gently pulled back.

"Everything's okay, sweetheart," he said, stroking her arm. "I'm here now. What's with the baseball bat?"

"It's been keeping me company for the last hour," she said. "You want something to drink?"

He nodded. "A beer, if you got it." He peeled off his jacket and sat down at the kitchen table. "I'm sweating up a storm. I drove like a maniac on the way here. And I ran all the way from the car."

Maggie set a beer on the table in front of him. She stopped and stared at him. She'd thought there was something different about him, and now she put her finger on it. He was blond. "Your hair," she murmured.

He smiled and ran a hand over his scalp. "I got a lot of sun in the last couple of days," he said. "I'm usually a towhead all summer long. It's been that way since I was a kid. Magic hair." He sipped his beer. "So, have you heard from this Father Murphy?"

She sank down in the chair next to him. "No, not since you and I talked."

"Well, is he on his way here?"

"He's coming by after he makes a stop at this suspect's house."

"Anton?" Steve said.

Maggie nodded. "We think a friend of my brother's might be staying the night at this hideaway Anton has in North Seattle. I'm really worried. I mean, this is my brother's best friend."

Frowning, Steve shook his head. "Jesus, you guys were crazy not to have gone to the police sooner. How much do you and Father Murphy know about this guy?"

Maggie shrugged. "Well, that's just it. Father Murphy has a lot of circumstantial evidence on Anton, but nothing really incriminating, nothing we can bring to the police. We're hoping to find something substantial in Anton's house."

"Do you have a pen and paper handy?" Steve asked. "We should write some of this stuff down before Neil gets here."

Maggie retrieved a notepad and pen from the junk drawer. She set them on the table, then glanced at her watch. She was wondering about Jack.

"How many people do you think this Anton character has killed?" Steve asked.

Maggie sat down again. "Well, there's Johnny, and the waitress I told you about, Lucy . . ." She watched him jot down the names. "Um, this girl who Johnny was seeing. Her name was Jonie. There were a couple of seminarians from three years ago, Julian Something and Oliver Something. Oh, and Jack thinks he's responsible for that judge who was missing for so long, Dorothy McShane."

"That's six people," Steve said, looking at his list. "Have you or Father Murphy—or *Jack,* I guess you call him— have either of you talked with anyone else about this guy?"

"Who, Anton?" Maggie shook her head. "No." She shifted a bit in the chair. She decided to let the "Jack" remark pass.

"Are you absolutely sure no one else knows about Anton?" Steve pressed.

"Pretty sure. Why is that so important?"

Steve put a finger to his lips. "Wait a sec," he whispered. "I heard something out front." He got to his feet and switched off the kitchen light.

Maggie stood up. "It's probably Father Murphy," she said. "Or maybe it's your buddy on the force."

"He's not coming for another ten minutes," Steve said,

backing toward the pantry. "Go to the front window. I'll be back here. If it's this Anton guy, he should think you're alone."

Maggie hesitated, then walked into the living room. With the desk lamp and the television's flickering light, she figured she could be seen from the street. She stepped up to the window and peered outside.

Maggie put her hand up to her mouth to conceal the fact that she was talking. "I don't see anyone," she said.

"He could be hiding," she heard Steve reply. "Look for something shiny."

"Something shiny?" she repeated, a hand still in front of her mouth. She stared out at the front yard and the shadowy bushes that bordered the neighbor's lot. "What would he have that's shiny?"

"Remember how your saint was martyred? St. Agnes?" Steve whispered. "He probably has a sword with him."

Maggie stared out at the darkness. "I wish you hadn't said that," she murmured behind her hand.

Chapter Twenty-four

"Pete, are you okay out there?" Jack called as he searched around Anton's bedroom. He'd turned on the lights, but still couldn't find a telephone. "Pete?" he called again. "What's going on?"

No response. Jack hurried out of the bedroom and through the kitchen. With every step, pain shot up from his foot. He stopped in the hallway.

Peter had wandered into Anton's secret shrine. He stood in front of the makeshift altar. Jack had loaded some ice cubes into a Baggie for him, and Peter now held it to his forehead while he inspected the relic boxes.

"I can't find a phone anywhere," Jack said, pausing in the doorway. "Let's just go. First gas station we see, we'll call the police."

"Are these all the people he killed?" Peter asked numbly.

Jack nodded. "I think so."

"What are these, bones?"

"Yeah, I'm afraid so," Jack said. "He took bone chips

or teeth from his victims. That's how I figured you were
still alive. Your box is empty. I'm not familiar with a couple
of the names, Agnes and Stephen.''

Peter opened up the box labeled AGNES.

''C'mon, Pete, we need to get you to a hospital,'' Jack
said.

''The box for Agnes is empty, too,'' Peter remarked.
''How did St. Agnes die?''

Jack started to shake his head. ''Pete, we need to go—''

''How did she die? It's important.''

Jack shrugged. He didn't recall how she was killed. Then
he remembered *The Register of Christian Saints* on the
bookshelf above the desk. Grabbing the book, Jack quickly
flipped through the pages. He found her listing and impatiently skimmed over the background on her. She'd died
around 304 A.D., barely in her teens.

Lowering the Baggie of ice from his head, Peter came up
beside him. He weaved a little as he walked. He kept a hand
on the desk to balance himself.

Jack found what he was after: ''It says, '*St. Agnes died
protecting her chastity, and was executed with a sword-
thrust to her throat.*' '' Jack put the book down. ''Just like
Lucy,'' he whispered.

''Father, Anton took a sword from the wall,'' Peter said,
tugging at his arm. ''Johnny's sister, her real name is Agnes
Marie. I know, because Johnny used to tease her about it.''

''My God,'' Jack whispered. ''We've got to get to a
phone.''

''Did he take his cell phone?'' Peter asked. ''It was on
his dresser earlier—in the bedroom.''

Jack wanted to ask why the hell he hadn't said anything
earlier, but he realized that Peter was a bit disoriented. He
ran into the bedroom, and found the portable phone on
Anton's dresser top. Grabbing the phone, Jack pressed a

button to activate it. A MESSAGE note blinked on the little window above the touch pad, but he didn't get a dial tone.

Jack hurried out of the bedroom, and found Peter in the kitchen. He seemed to be holding himself up by bracing one hand on the kitchen counter.

"Pete, how the hell do you work this?" Jack asked anxiously. "All I'm getting is a stupid message signal."

"Lemme see." He put down the bag of ice, then held out his hand.

Jack gave him the phone. Peter squinted at it and pressed a couple of buttons. Jack studied him with concern. The bleeding on the side of his forehead seemed under control, but he was pale. He seemed to have a hard time focusing on the key pad. Yet he managed to push several numbers before handing the phone to Jack.

"You'll get the recording," he said. "You'll have to punch in the code after the beep, but I don't know the code."

"What are you talking about?" Jack asked.

"To get his message, you need to punch in his three-digit code," Peter said impatiently.

"Pete, I don't want to hear the message. I need to talk with 911—or Maggie Costello."

He heard Anton's voice on the recording: *"Hello, I can't come to the phone right now. . . ."*

"Maybe the code is his birthday," Peter said. "No, God, wait a minute. I know what he'd use—"

"Pete, it doesn't matter—"

"Dial four-ten," Peter said. "Four-one-oh, that's the code he'd use. It's Gerard Lunt's room number, and the address here."

Appeasing him, Jack quickly punched in the three digits. He was surprised when he heard the recorded voice: *"You have one message. Press star-one to play messages."*

Jack pushed *1. Peter leaned on the counter, staring at

him hopefully. *"Message one,"* the recording announced. Then another voice came on the line:

"Hi, Steve, it's Maggie. I'm not sure if you'll get this message before you come over, but what the heck. I talked with Father Murphy. He's coming over later, too. We're going to the police with this. Maybe we can talk to your friend. Anyway, call me back if you get this message. I'll see you soon."

From the living-room window, Maggie couldn't see anyone in the front yard. "Steve, I think it's a false alarm," she said, glancing over her shoulder.

The kitchen was too dark. She couldn't see him. "Steve?"

Maggie stepped back into the kitchen and switched on the light.

He stood near the back door, which was open a crack. He had a strange look about him. Or maybe Maggie just wasn't used to his blond hair. "What are you doing?" she asked.

"Just checking to see if anyone's in the backyard," he said. "Sorry for the false alarm. I didn't mean to scare you, talking about the sword. But we have to pay attention to the way these people died." He sat down and tapped his finger on the notes he'd started. "It seems to be this Anton character's modus operandi."

Maggie sat next to him. She glanced at the list of "martyrs" he'd written down:

> *John Costello*
> *Lucy B.*
> *Jonie*
> *Julian*
> *Oliver*
> *Dorothy McShane*

"Anyway, I didn't mean to frighten you, sweetheart," she heard him say.

Maggie kept staring at the list. There was something wrong with it—or rather, something alarmingly correct about it. Unless he'd been acquainted with her, how in the world did he know Jonie spelled her name that special way?

"What's the matter?" he asked.

"Nothing," she murmured. She looked at him and tried to smile. The sun hadn't changed his hair. His blond color looked natural. Was the previous auburn-brown shade something from a bottle? Had Jonie showered a collection of hair products on him that included temporary dyes?

"Let's see who we have written down here," she said, pretending to study his list. All the while, her mind was reeling. Now it made sense why he was so anxious to find out if anyone else knew about "Anton." If he killed her and Jack, he'd be free to go on "martyring" people. Then again, he must have wanted to add her to his list all along. Suddenly she realized why Steve had come into her life when he had.

She'd always thought he was too good to be true.

Maggie peered up from the list and watched him reach for his beer. "Anton?" she whispered.

He stopped and locked eyes with her.

"Anton—he has a pattern of getting to know his victims," Maggie said, trying not to miss a beat. "He—um, was seeing both Lucy and Jonie, we know that much. . . ."

He seemed to be listening intently. He nodded along with everything she said. But a smirk slowly crept over his face.

"He apparently has a strange power over his victims. He seduced them first," Maggie continued. She casually glanced around, looking for the baseball bat. "I have a feeling that Johnny fell under his spell—"

The phone rang. Maggie got to her feet.

"Don't answer that, Agnes Marie." he whispered.

Maggie stood paralyzed for only a moment. Then she made a grab for the phone. All at once, he lunged at her. Maggie's chair tipped over. She felt herself falling back through the doorway to the living room. She tried to fight him off, but he was too big.

Anton slammed her into the desk. Everything from the desktop came crashing to the floor. Maggie clawed at him, even hit him in the face. Still, he overpowered her, easily grabbing her wrists.

Maggie tried to knee him in the groin, but missed. He started to laugh. In response, she stomped her foot down hard on top of his. He let out a howl. "Fucking bitch!"

She didn't see the punch coming. A sudden blow against the side of her face knocked her to the floor. Dazed, she lay there amid the broken artifacts from her desktop. Trying to push herself up, she felt shards of glass digging into her hand. They came from the shattered lamp—or perhaps from the frame that held the photo of her and Johnny, she didn't know. But her hand was bleeding.

Through a fog, Maggie could hear Jack speaking into her answering machine, warning her that Anton was on his way, and "Steve" wasn't who he appeared to be. All the while, Anton snickered. He was on top of her now, holding her arms down.

"Maggie, if you can come to the phone, please, pick up!" Jack was saying. "I'm at Anton's place in North Seattle. I found Peter. He's hurt, but I think he's going to be okay. . . ."

Anton stopped laughing.

"I'm getting him to a hospital. But first, I'm calling the police and sending them to your place. If you're in trouble, Maggie, hang in there. I love you, okay?"

Maggie heard him click off. She had to keep fighting. Jack's message filled her with determination. Though it seemed in vain, she struggled under Anton's weight. "It's over!'' she cried angrily. ''He's phoning the police right now. You won't get away with it. . . .''

She tried to wiggle out from beneath him. But Anton's grip on her wrists only became tighter. Then, one after the other, he pulled her arms under his knees so they were pinned to the floor. He took a piece of rope out of his jacket pocket.

''You're a fighter, Agnes Marie,'' he grunted. ''Just like your kid brother when I was holding his head under the water.''

Enraged, she flailed at him with a new fervor. He tried to tie her hands with the rope, but she resisted. ''You can't kill me,'' she said. ''You don't have a sword. You can't make it count unless you use a sword. . . .''

''It's right outside the kitchen door, Agnes,'' he said, wrapping the cord around one wrist.

Maggie jerked up her knee, then slammed it into his spine.

''Goddamn!'' Anton winced in pain, then buckled forward.

Twisting around, Maggie managed to free one hand. She blindly grabbed the first thing within her reach. The thin, pewter crucifix had fallen out of its stand. Clutching the top of it, she swiftly plunged the long bottom stem into his back, near his shoulder blade.

Anton recoiled and gasped loudly.

The crucifix snapped off at the base, just below the feet to the figure of Jesus. The rest of the pewter cross—at least a couple of inches—was stuck in the hard muscle of Anton's back.

''Fuck!'' he bellowed, frantically reaching behind him to pull out the piece of metal. But he couldn't get at it.

Maggie rolled out from under him and crawled toward the front door. She could hear a police siren in the distance.

Anton was on his knees. His handsome face turned crimson. He kept twisting and straining to grasp that section of the crucifix imbedded near his shoulder blade. Blood seeped down the back of his T-shirt.

Maggie managed to get to her feet. As she reached for the door, she glanced over at him.

He was standing now. He glared at her. His hands were clenched and covered with blood. One hand opened up and the piece of metal rolled out of his glistening palm.

The wail of the siren seemed to become louder.

"They're coming!" Maggie said. "You're too late. . . ."

Frantically, she pulled at the door, then realized she'd triple-locked it. Maggie tugged at the dead bolt and fumbled with the chain.

She felt his wet, bloody fingertips brush the back of her neck.

At last, she threw open the door and ran outside, almost tripping on the front stoop. Breathless, she gazed up the street and saw the red strobe lights. The siren seemed blessedly deafening.

Then she saw the firetruck, and it passed by her block.

Maggie suddenly realized she was alone out there. As the siren's blare slowly died, she turned and gazed at the house. She didn't see him. She wasn't sure if he'd fled, or he'd merely stepped out the back doorway to retrieve his sword.

She glanced to her left and right. Both neighbors' houses were dark. Their cars weren't in the driveways.

Maggie heard the phone ring inside. With uncertainty, she took a couple of steps toward the open front door. The answering machine picked up the call. After a moment, she recognized Jack's voice speaking into the recorder. She couldn't quite make out what he was saying. At the same time, she didn't dare go back inside the house.

Biting her lip, she took another step closer to the open door.

"Maggie? Are you there?" he was saying. *"Can you come to the phone? Maggie?"*

* * *

Maggie didn't pick up.

Jack clicked off the cell phone. He stood at Anton's living room window, and tried not to put any weight on his injured foot. He glanced at his watch. He'd called the police at least ten minutes ago, and still no sign of them yet.

He turned toward Peter, who sat on the edge of the sofa. His face had drained of color. Dried blood covered the front of his T-shirt. "How are you doing, Pete? Or shouldn't I ask?"

Peter let out a weak chuckle. "Not so hot. I feel a little like I'm gonna toss my cookies."

"Try to hold on," Jack said. "The ambulance should be here any minute." He glanced out the window again and realized that Duane's Viking van was blocking the driveway.

"I better move the van. The ambulance won't be able to pull in. Pete, will you be okay for a couple of minutes?"

"Sure," he nodded sluggishly.

"Promise you won't lie down," Jack said.

"I promise," he muttered.

Jack hurried out the front door. Holding on to the cell phone, he hobbled down Anton's driveway, past the minivan, and onto the end of the cul-de-sac. Catching his breath, he stood by the signposts at the turnoff. He glanced up and down Prentiss Road: no police cars, no flashing red lights. He didn't even hear any sirens, just crickets. The night was perfectly still.

"Damn it," he muttered to himself. "Where the hell are they?"

Limping back up the cul-de-sac, he clicked on the cellular and punched in 911 again. The operator answered after one ring: "Police emergency."

"Yes, hi, I called about ten or fifteen minutes ago," Jack

said, a bit short of breath. "I have someone with a head injury here at 410 Prentiss Drive. We need an ambulance."

"There's one on the way right now, sir."

"I also asked you to check on another address, where I believe a woman could be at risk—"

"Yes, sir," the operator said calmly. "A patrol car has been dispatched to that address."

"Well, I just tried calling there," Jack said, reaching the minivan. He pulled Duane's keys out of his pocket. "I didn't get an answer. Can you tell me if the police have arrived there yet?"

"I'm sorry, sir. We don't have any confirmation at this time. I show you're calling from 555-1123, is that correct?"

"That's right." Jack opened the door and got into the front seat.

"If you remain by the phone there at 410 Prentiss Drive, we'll have an ambulance there for you shortly."

"Thanks very much," Jack said. He started up the engine, then pulled forward, parking in front of Anton's garage. As he climbed out of the car, Jack thought he heard a siren in the distance.

He tried Maggie on the cell phone again. "C'mon, pick up, Maggie," he whispered. Hobbling toward the house, he held the cellular to his ear and counted the ring tones.

Her answering machine came on: *"Hi, this is Maggie, thanks very much for calling—"*

Jack was so damn sick of hearing it that he hung up. He heard the siren's distant cry. It didn't seem to be coming any closer.

Frustrated, he retreated back into the house. He saw Peter, and his heart sank. For a moment, Jack thought he was dead. Peter slumped against the sofa arm with his eyes closed. He'd smeared some of the blood on his face and hands. The Baggie of ice lay in a puddle by his feet. "Pete? Oh, my God . . ."

He stirred on the couch. "I'm awake," he muttered. "I didn't go to sleep. . . ."

Sighing, Jack sat down next to him and put his arm around Peter's shoulder. "C'mon, try to sit up. Okay?"

This close, he could see the gash on Peter's forehead seeping some blood. "Do you still feel like you're going to throw up?" he asked.

"Little bit, yeah," he murmured.

The cellular phone rang. Jack clicked it on. "Yes?"

"This is the 911 operator. Am I talking to Father Murphy?"

"Yes," Jack said anxiously. "Have you heard anything about Maggie Costello? I just phoned there again—"

"No, sir. I'm calling to let you know that an ambulance is on its way to you at 410 Prentiss, but there may be a delay. The main access to Prentiss Road is blocked due to an accident about a mile from where you are."

"Oh, no," Jack muttered.

"I've rerouted another ambulance to you. It may take ten or fifteen more minutes."

"Would I be better off driving to this accident site?" Jack asked. "Do they have an ambulance there?"

"I advise you to stay where you are. Keep your friend comfortable, but don't let him doze off. If there's any change in his condition, such as convulsions or vomiting, call us back. We can patch you through to a doctor on call at Harbor View Hospital. Once again, the ambulance should be there in a little over ten minutes."

Jack gave Peter's shoulder a squeeze. "I'm sorry, kiddo," he whispered. "You'll have to hold on a little longer."

"I ain't going anywhere," Peter muttered.

"Listen, thank you," Jack said into the phone. "Could you do me another favor, and call me once you find out anything on Maggie Costello? I'm really worried."

"Yes, Father. Just stay where you are and keep the line open, okay?"

"Will do. Thanks again." Jack clicked off.

"Is Maggie okay?" Peter asked quietly.

"They'll call as soon as they find out anything," Jack said, patting his shoulder. He got to his feet and scooped the wet Baggie off the floor. "I'll fetch you some more ice. Don't nod off, okay? Keep talking to me."

"About what?" Peter mumbled.

Jack hobbled toward the kitchen. "Are you coming back to Our Lady of Sorrows next year? Talk loud so I can hear you."

"I'm not sure," Peter called in a lethargic tone. "I don't really want to be a priest. And with Johnny gone, there doesn't seem to be much reason to stay...."

At the refrigerator-freezer, Jack loaded some ice into a fresh Baggie. "Yeah, you might be better off at a school with a good art program," he replied, a bit distracted. He tied up the top of the plastic bag. "You're a talented artist, Pete. You might want to go someplace where you can make the most of that."

Jack dried off his hands, then reached for the cell phone on the counter. He started to dial Maggie's number again, but stopped.

He heard a noise from the side of the house. It sounded like a door opening. He didn't move for a moment. He just listened.

"Father?" Peter called.

Jack switched off the phone. He left the bag of ice on the counter, then made his way to the living room. "Pete, is there an outside door to the basement?" he whispered.

Peter shrugged. "I don't know. Why?"

"I think someone's downstairs," he said in a low voice.

He put a finger to his own lips, then crept toward the broken basement door. He peeked down the stairs. The light was on down there—as he'd left it. He couldn't see anything amid the shadows, but he heard a rustling noise.

Jack stepped back from the basement door, then dialed 911 again. "Police emergency," the operator said.

"Yes, this is Father Murphy calling from 410 Prentiss Drive," he whispered. "I talked to another operator there earlier."

"Yes, let me put you through to Matt."

After a moment, the other operator got on the line. "Father Murphy, I have confirmation. The police have arrived at that other address you gave us. But I don't have any word yet as to the condition of Ms. Costello. I'll keep trying—"

"Thanks," Jack whispered hurriedly. "That accident a mile from here, could you tell me if a red Toyota was involved?"

"Yes, a red Toyota was speeding and collided with an RV."

"Did the driver of the Toyota get away?"

"Why, yes, I understand he walked away from the scene. Actually, he ran away. I don't think he'll get far. I heard he's in pretty bad shape—"

"He's here—in the basement," Jack interrupted, hobbling toward Peter. "Tell your people to hurry. Please."

Jack clicked off, then reached for Peter. "I'm getting you out of here," he whispered. "C'mon, let me help you up."

Confused, Peter managed to stand, but he teetered. Jack held him by the arm and led him toward the front door.

Suddenly all the lights went out. "Oh, shit," Peter muttered, flinching.

Jack grabbed for the doorknob, but he couldn't find it. He blindly grasped at air until his hand hit the knob. All the while, the sounds in the cellar became louder. There was a crash of something being knocked over, then footsteps.

As he guided Peter out the front door, Jack glanced over his shoulder at the basement doorway. He could see an eerie glow coming from down there.

Digging the keys out of his pocket, Jack hurried Peter along to the minivan. He opened the driver's door for him. "Climb in," he said.

"What? You want me to drive?" Peter protested weakly. "I don't think I'm in any condition—"

"Hurry," Jack commanded.

He scooted behind the wheel. "Are we getting out of here?"

"Not yet," Jack said, watching the house. He could see Anton in the darkness of the living room. He was carrying a single candle. He used it to light three other candles in the room. His movements seemed unsteady and sluggish, almost like a drunk man. In the flickering light, Jack thought he saw blood on Anton's face. He watched him stagger back toward the basement.

"Pete, I want you to stay here in the van with the doors locked." Jack handed him the cell phone and Duane's keys. "The 911 operator I've been talking with is named Matt. If you get drowsy, call and ask for him. Bug him about Maggie. We still don't know if she's okay."

Jack glanced back at the house again. Anton was lugging an old canister of gasoline through the living room, toward the back of the house. He faltered and stumbled, but kept moving. He looked as if he was dying.

Jack closed the driver's door. Peter quickly rolled down the window. "What are you going to do?" he whispered.

"If I'm not out of the house in five minutes, you'll have to drive away without me," Jack said. "Should Anton come out, take off, don't even look back—"

"What, are you crazy?"

"You'll probably see some emergency lights down that road by the creek," Jack continued. "It's only a mile, Pete. Police and response vehicles ought to be there. You'll get help."

In his panic, Peter suddenly seemed very alert. He was shaking his head. "You can't go back into that house—"

Jack shrugged. "I have to go, Pete. He's dying, and he's all alone. He needs a priest."

With his faltering walk, Jack headed for the front door. He hadn't brought anything along to fight off Anton or overpower him. But he wasn't going into the house for that.

Pausing in the doorway, Jack gazed into the living room. "Anton, it's Father Murphy," he called.

Beyond the living room, the hallway radiated a flickering amber light. Shadows danced along the corridor's walls. The light seemed to be coming from Anton's secret room.

As Jack approached the corridor, he heard a strange, hollow gurgling sound, then something splashing. He could smell gasoline. Anton let out a grunt, and a stream of liquid splattered across the threshold—just missing Jack's feet.

Jack came to the door of Anton's "shrine." About a dozen candles were placed around the room—several on the makeshift altar, others on the desk and dresser. The gasoline fumes were overpowering. Hoisting the old gas can, Anton doused the bed. He looked badly beaten up. He had several cuts and one long, severe laceration down the side of his handsome face. Blood, sweat, and soot drenched his scorched T-shirt. As if delirious, he kept splashing gasoline around the little room.

"Anton, let me take you out of here," Jack said.

"This is my church!" he yelled, brandishing the gas can.

"It's all over," Jack said. "Come on with me. You'll die in here"

"I'm dead already," he replied, laughing. He hurled the canister at Jack.

He dodged it, but gasoline splashed him. The can made a hollow, tin sound as it hit the floor. The gas soaked the front of Jack's trousers.

Anton grinned. "Now you're a dead man, too—if you stay." He reached for a candle.

"Anton, do you want to make a confession?" Jack asked urgently. "Are you sorry for your sins?"

"I'm Anthony Daniel!" he proclaimed.

He threw the candle on the bed, and it exploded in flames. A trail of fire sped across the floor to Anton's feet. All at once, the blaze engulfed him.

Jack recoiled. He quickly made a sign of the cross. "I absolve you in the name of the Father, Son, and Holy Spirit," he called out over the crackling blaze. The smoke and fire flared up around him. He staggered back toward the living room.

Already the flames were licking the hallway wall. A black cloud and choking fumes billowed out of the room, pouring through the little house. Jack could barely see the front door. The blast of heat seemed to roll over him, and he couldn't breathe.

At last, he found the front door and ran outside. Coughing and rubbing his eyes, he hobbled toward the driveway. He spit black soot out of his mouth.

Over the roaring fire, he heard Peter call to him. "Father Murphy, are you okay?"

Jack couldn't speak for a moment. He was still trying to get a breath. He nodded and waved at Peter, then made his way to the minivan. The front yard was illuminated by the inferno consuming Anton's secret hideaway.

In the distance, Jack heard the police siren. It seemed to grow louder. He felt Peter grab his arm. The two of them were so exhausted and battered that they had to hold each other up. "I talked to that guy on 911," Peter said. "He has a message for you, Father."

Jack gasped for air. "Yeah?"

Peter smiled. "He said that Maggie wants you to call her."